LOST SOUL

DIRTY SOULS MC - BOOK 1

EMMA CREED

Lost Soul - Dirty Souls MC Book 1

Copyright 2021 by Emma Creed

All Rights Reserved

First Edition

No part of this book may be reproduced or transmitted in any form or by any means, electronic or mechanical, including photocopying, recording, or by any information storage and retrieval system without written permission of the author, except for the use of brief quotations in a book review.

This is a work of fiction. Names, characters, businesses, places, events, and incidents are either the product of the author's imagination or used in a fictitious manner. Any resemblance to actual persons, living or dead, actual events, or locales is entirely coincidental. The use of any real company and/or product names is for literary effect only. All other trademarks and copyrights are the property of their respective owners.

Cover design: Rebel Ink co
Interior design: Rebel Ink Co
Model: Sander The Netherlands
Photographer: Paul van der Linde
Editing: Sassi's Editing Services
Proofreading: Sharon Powell

Dedication

For Sharon, who chose to come on the ride with me…

Author Notes

Warning

Lost Soul and all future books in the Dirty Soul's Mc series are all a work of fiction. Due to the nature of the series you should expect to come across subject matter that some readers may find disturbing.

Lost Soul is intended for readers 18+

'Bound not by blood but loyalty.
We live, we ride, and we die
by our own laws'

10 YEARS OLD

I know there was a time before he came into my life, but I don't remember a single moment of it.

For me, the day my life began was the day my daddy brought him home to me.

I was only ten years old, but even back then I knew I would love Jessie Donavon's beautiful lost soul until my final breath left my body.

I could sense that he knew he didn't belong in our home, his eyes gave him away. I also knew that Jessie being here would have something to do with the club, with Daddy, everything had something to do with the club.

Everyone in Manitou Springs knew that my daddy was different to regular daddies. He didn't dress in a suit and work a nine to five. He didn't pick Mama flowers up on the way home from work on a Friday, or watch football at weekends. No, Jimmer Carson rode a Harley, he smelt of leather and cigarettes, and his home wasn't here with Mama and me, it was at his club with the members of the Dirty Souls MC.

Daddy lived at the club compound, an old holiday resort that was tucked up in the mountains on the border of our town. It was a place I hardly ever visited, which suited me just fine because I hated it there. I hated the people who lived there too. They had all of Daddy's attention, he spent all his time with them, when he should have been here with me.

Mama was always telling me how much he loved us, just that he *showed it in his own way*. But the way I saw it, there would always be *us* and *them*. His club *brothers*... his real family. And today, looking at Daddy's face, and how it was all twisted up somewhere between sad and angry, I could tell that something terrible had happened to one of them.

"The kid's daddy died for the club, baby." Daddy spoke to me as if the boy stood behind him wasn't even there. "He's one of us, and he's gonna stay here with you and Mama for a while." I watched his eyes narrow warningly as they shifted over my shoulder to where Mama stood, they softened before fixing back on me though.

"I'm counting on you being a good girl. Make him feel welcome, and be sure he knows the rules. Keep him in line, princess." Daddy winked, attempting to ruffle my hair as he stood up. It didn't budge though, it was too strong. I got my hair from Mama, long, jet black, and poker straight. Daddy always told me I got my stubbornness from her too, but I knew better than that.

I nodded my head back at him like an excited puppy, thinking how cool it would be having another kid around. I never really got to play with kids my own age, the kids from school's parents never let them come over. I guessed that was because of Daddy. He seemed to scare everyone, everyone except me that is.

Looking at the boy, I wondered if he'd be as cruel as the other club kids I'd encountered at the compound. Daddy tried hard to keep me away from the place he loved so much, so I rarely had to hang out with the kids that lived there. They were mean anyway, especially the boys. When they thought no one important was listening, they'd call me spoilt and tease me 'coz me and Mama lived differently to them. I understood why.

Daddy never failed to give me what I wanted. He never came calling without a gift for me, and I always got my way with him. All I had to do was make my green eyes a little wider, and give him a pleading smile.

Still, none of the gifts he'd brought me in the past compared with the beautiful broken boy stood in front of me that day.

Jessie was silent, it could have been his grief, but it seemed more like he was too grown up for his age and didn't want to be treated like a kid.

When Daddy left the house to get back to the club, I showed Jessie around the house. He didn't speak the entire time, just let his eyes roam as I led him from room to room. Daddy hadn't instructed me on where the boy was supposed to sleep. I made that decision for myself, showing him into the bedroom directly opposite mine.

I wanted him close. Something about him intrigued me, and even the cold vibe he gave off didn't stop me from feeling drawn to him. Though, I didn't doubt that had a lot to do with the way he looked.

Jessie was tall, much taller than the other 7th graders at my school. His eyes were such a crystal blue they didn't seem real, they even sparkled when the light caught them right. A few freckles sprinkled over the bridge of his nose, slightly softening the hard expression his face seemed determined to keep in place. But before I left him alone in his new room, I'd already decided my favourite feature of his were his lips. Rigid and straight, they were much more peachy than pink. When I left him alone closing his door behind me, I squeezed my eyes shut, balled up my fists, and wished really hard that one day I'd get to see what they'd look like smiling. Something sad told me it would take a really long time, but it would be worth the wait.

That night, just before I fell asleep, I wrote Jessie a letter. Using the pretty stationery set Daddy had brought me from the run he went on last month and my mama's fountain pen. I took my time, making sure all my letters were even in size and sat perfectly on the lines. My words were promises to Jessie, vows that I would take care of him and teach him that he could still love and be loved back, despite all he'd lost.

I sealed the envelope and wrote his name neatly on the front.
Jessie.
I liked his name. It suited him.

Tiptoeing my bare feet across the hall, I stood for a while and stared at his door. Wondered what he was doing on the other side. Silently I prayed that he wasn't feeling lonely, or worse... crying. His eyes had looked a lot like they wanted to cry earlier, and I wanted so badly to take away the pain he'd tried so hard to hide.

Bringing the letter to my mouth, I pressed a kiss on to the pastel-colored flowers printed on the border of the envelope. Then just before I slipped it beneath the crack of his door, something made me pause. All my confidence suddenly vanished and I felt like a silly little girl.

The boy was one of *them*, and Dirty Souls don't want to be loved, they don't need silly promises like the ones I'd made him in my letter. Straightening myself up slowly, I backed myself away from his door and crept back into my room.

I hid my letter to Jessie in a shoebox that I kept under my bed. It was my safe place where I kept all my precious things, like the Russian banknote Daddy had given me, the dolphin keyring I'd convinced Mama to buy me from SeaWorld—despite her argument that I didn't own a set of keys—and a really pretty stone I'd found in the backyard. They were my treasures. No one else knew where I kept them because they were special to me, just like the promises I'd made to Jessie in my letter.

Over the next few months, I tried so hard to make the boy feel like he belonged with us. I wanted to heal him of his sadness, so he could be a child and have fun. But despite my hopes and efforts it soon became clear that the boy I wanted so desperately to fix, just saw me as an irritation.

Jessie spent most of the time in his room, alone, and when he did venture out, he ignored me. Mama saw how it made me sad.

"He's sad baby, he lost his mama a few years ago, and now he's lost his daddy too. Just give him some time." She'd tell me. I tried to understand, but it was difficult. Sure, I didn't see my daddy as often as I'd have liked to, but he was alive, and Mama always made sure she was there for me.

My parents may have shown their love for me in different ways, but I knew it was there. To lose even one of them would be unimaginable. And that was the blissful oblivion that I lived in for the next four years. Something that I took for granted right up till the day the unimaginable happened.

CHAPTER 2 — HAYLEY

AGED 14

The way Jessie changed around me hadn't gone unnoticed. My fourteenth birthday had just past, and with Jessie turning seventeen only a few months before there was a new awkwardness between us now. For so long it had seemed like he couldn't stand to look at me, yet lately I felt him watching me more often.

I like the way his attention feels, I crave more of it. So much so that I'd started carelessly leaving the bathroom door unlocked when I was taking a shower in the hope he might walk in accidently. I made sure my newly developed curves were shown to their full potential by wearing revealing tops, the kind my daddy would strike a match to if he ever saw me in them.

I wasn't the only one who had grown up over the past few years, Jessie was even taller now and he'd filled out perfectly. He wasn't too big like some of the other guys at the club were, but every inch of him was solid. His hair was longer than most boys his age, hanging just above his shoulder when he wore it down, and he'd grown an impressive covering of sandy colored facial hair that I really liked too.

It hadn't come as a surprise when Daddy made him a prospect on his fifteenth birthday. Jessie hung out at the club every chance he got, and the club owed it to Jessie's daddy to take care of him, and they always took care of their own, it was their way.

Since Jessie had become a prospect, the brothers Chop and Skid had given Jessie a part-time job at the club garage. It sucked because he spent all his time there these days. I hardly ever saw him, which meant I really had to make the times we were together count.

Today he must have come home after school instead of heading straight to the club like he usually does. I was making my way across the hall from the bathroom to my bedroom with the smallest towel in the house wrapped around my chest. It only just covered my ass cheeks, and it wasn't even intentional on this occasion, because seeing him caught me completely by surprise.

The timing is perfect, I couldn't have got it better if I tried, and when he steps onto the landing from his room the shock on my face is genuine and I almost drop the towel completely.

My stomach somersaults as his eyes search me over, and I can't help but smile when his lips lift into a smirk. I love Jessie's smirk. I've seen it so many times before when he's offered it to the older girls at school, but here, today, that smirk was all for me.

"I didn't think you'd be home," I say, trying to sound annoyed, but at the same time savoring every moment of his eyes being on me.

"I'm just headin' to the club now." Jessie moves towards the stairs, and just as I'm about to open the door to my room his low voice stops me.

"You shouldn't have ridden back from school with those boys today, your daddy wouldn't like it."

I roll my eyes at the door before glancing at him over my shoulder, as if he is lecturing *me* about who I hang out with. The boys he's referring to aren't half as bad as the company he keeps at the club.

"Well maybe if you offered me a ride home I wouldn't have had to," I add, feeling proud for airing that one out with him. Me and Jessie had been walking to and from school together since the day I started high school. Granted, Jessie had always been a good few strides ahead of me, but the fact that he never left without me was what meant so much. Since he'd gotten his bike, he hasn't offered me a lift once, which in my opinion is rude.

I make sure I give him a wet flick of my hair before storming into my bedroom. A few seconds later I hear the front door slam, followed by the loud rumble of a bike engine that fades as Jessie rides further away.

Mama got home around seven. She hangs out at the club for most of the day. It's the only way she gets to spend time with Dad. Even now that I'm older I still get kept away from the club. There are times when it's been unavoidable, during lockdowns, and the family BBQ's that even Mama insists I attend. Then there are the school holidays when I never get to go to summer camp like the other kids at school do. Instead I have to endure the club's makeshift version, which consists of all the club kids, of all ages, in one of the cabins being overlooked by a few of the old ladies.

I hate it, and even more so since Jessie has become a prospect. The boys never used to tease me when Jessie had been around.

Mama and I eat dinner together. She watches some crap on TV while I finish off some homework, and after a few hours spent mostly in silence, she kisses my forehead and stumbles on to her feet.

Mama seemed to be drinking a lot in the evenings lately, or perhaps she'd always drank and I just hadn't noticed. I put it down to her worrying about what Daddy gets up to at the club when she isn't around. Since I've been born, she's stopped going there at night. Choosing to spend her evenings with me instead.

It was one of the reasons I felt better than the kids who lived at the club.

Their mamas never choose them.

Around eleven I decide to head upstairs myself. Jessie still isn't home, but that's nothing to worry about, some nights he doesn't even bother to come home at all anymore.

Climbing the stairs, I try not think about him being near the women at the club. Especially the ones who linger around anything in a leather cut like flies attach themselves to shit.

I check in on Mama as I pass her room. She's still clothed, sprawled out on the bed like she was trying to make a snow angel in her duvet. I manage to shift her body enough to pull the covers from under her and tuck her in.

Mama is beautiful, I really hope I age the way she has. Despite being forty-three, there isn't a trace of grey in her thick mass of black hair. Nor a single crease on her olive skin. Often I find myself wondering if she deserves better than the life Daddy gives her. Maybe he even knows it himself and it's the reason he doesn't want us living at the compound like the other families do.

Mama stirs, uttering sentences I can't quite understand, but I do manage to decipher a, "Love you Hayley," somewhere among them.

"I Love you too, Mama," I whisper back, placing a kiss on her cheek and creeping back out of her room. I close the door quietly and take the few paces to my own room.

Snuggling myself into bed, I roll onto my side and wait for tiredness to kick in. It's no surprise that Jessie is my last thought before I drift off. It's been that way since the first day he came to me.

BANG!!

My body jolts awake, and my ears ring painfully. Whatever I'd been dreaming about had felt so real the boom rattled my chest. It startled me, but I manage to shake it off, curling back beneath the covers ready to try and get back to sleep. Seconds later, there's a second loud BANG, and I realize I'm not dreaming.

The noise sounded like it came from a gun, and was loud enough for me to know that it's close. Fear pins me to my mattress like a bug trapped in a web, my limbs paralyzed, while my head screams at my rigid, tight body to run for safety. Instead, I duck beneath my covers and clutch my knees to my chest. Praying that this is a just a terrible nightmare and I'll wake up real soon.

Silently, I curse myself for never locking my bedroom door. Especially when I hear the handle rattle, followed by the sound of the door opening and then quickly shutting again. The lock clicks, trapping me inside with whoever the footsteps trudging towards my bed belong too.

My breaths come out too loud, and the sound of my heart as it slams against my ribs makes me sure whoever is in here will hear how petrified I am. I'm trapped, helpless, and even if I want to scream out to Mama, I doubt my voice could pull together enough strength to make a sound.

My eyes squeeze shut when the covers are ripped away from me. The giant hand slamming over my mouth causes pure terror to creep up from my throat. The sound it makes on the way out muffles into the hand that suffocates me, and I fight hard. I lash out as I'm dragged backwards and forced tight against a solid chest that seems to beat almost as rapidly as my own.

"Shhhh. I'ma get you out of here. Okay?" The breathy voice that speaks in my ear instantly floods my body with relief.

Jessie. The voice belongs to Jessie.

I don't have time to think about what's happening, Jessie takes my hand and drags me towards the window. Then making sure we keep our backs against the wall by pressing his arm across my chest, he pulls back my curtain to check outside.

"Come on," he whispers, forcing my window to slide up and

then gestures his head out towards the thick tree branch. I look back at him, reluctant to do what he's asking.

"Now don't be pretendin' this is the first time you've climbed out this window." He cocks an eyebrow at me. How he even knows that, can't be my concern right now. I have to focus. We're in danger.

"It's not that. Jessie." I shake my head. "We can't leave, what about Mama?" I ask, watching his face change, his jaw tensing the way it does when he gets mad about something.

"You're gonna need to be brave darlin'," he tells me, trying his best to make his voice sound calm.

Darlin'? This is new. He's never called me that before—irritating little brat, sure, but never darlin'. It warms me all the way up because I've heard the other guys call their old ladies it sometimes.

"Ya hearing me, Hay?" Jessie interrupts my dreamy thoughts. This time his tone is firmer and snaps me back to reality.

"It's too late. They got her, come on we got to move." His words abolish any warm feelings. Replacing them with a heavy dread that sinks to the pit of my stomach.

"Hay... come the fuck on. We haven't got time for this, I'm gonna take you to Prez! You hearing me? I need to get you safe." Jessie's shouting now. Calling over another loud strike, that's followed by the sound of a bullet pinging the lock off my door. It's enough to get me climbing on to the branch of the tree, survival mode kicking in and overriding my shock and panic.

Jessie is close behind me when I jump from the branch, my feet landing on the ground with a thud that makes my ankles feel as though they've snapped. He snatches up my top, hoisting me up from the ground and pushes me forward.

"Fuckin' run," he calls out as another blast sounds from my bedroom window. I hear a low growl that sounds a lot like it comes from him, but I'm too scared to look back. Having no idea where exactly I'm running to, I aim for straight ahead, braving a look behind me to check that Jessie is still there, and relieved to see that he is.

He's clutching at his shoulder like it's injured as he runs to catch up with me, and when he's made up space between us he wraps his arm around my waist, opens up the door to his truck and pushes me inside.

"Keep ya head down," he orders, as I shuffle along the seat and make space for him in the driver's seat beside me. The engine starts, and my body slides across the bench seat as he swings the truck into reverse. We take off with an ear-splitting shriek of tires, and the sound of bullets ricocheting off the truck bed.

It isn't until I look back in the rear window and our house is no longer in sight that I finally take a breath, which allows a new wave of panic to suddenly hit me. 'It's too late. They got her.' I'm sure that's what I'd heard Jessie say back in my room.

Mama?

Who had her?

"Jessie, where's Mama?" I ask, despite being petrified of the answer.

"I'm so sorry, Hay, I wasn't quick enough. I had to choose." His eyes are soft when they glance across at me but they turn cold when he focuses back on the road, his fist clutching hard at the steering wheel. I notice his T-shirt, becoming darker and darker as it absorbs more blood from his wound.

"Fuck! Jessie you're bleeding," I scream, suddenly terrified for him, but Jessie doesn't seem much bothered.

"I got shot..." he tells me casually, pulling out his cell and wedging it between his uninjured shoulder and his ear.

"Skid, it's Jessie. Is Prez there...?" He speaks into the phone. "...Well drag him off her, this is fucking big..." Jessie turns his head away from me and lowers his voice. "...like his old lady's just been shot fuckin' dead kinda big, Skid, put him on."

I'm surprised at the tone Jessie takes with Skid, the guy's a tower block of a man and nobody disrespects him, especially not a prospect.

Daddy must come to the phone after what seems like a life-long wait.

"Prez. Yeah, she's with me." Jessie takes his eyes off the road to scan me over for injury.

"Fine but shook up to hell… No there were two of them, I only managed to take one out. Sorry, Prez, I couldn't get to them both… Yeah, shit reeks of Bastard… about ten minutes away, I'ma need the doc for myself, but she's okay I swear." When he's finished, he lets the phone drop to the footwell then tells me to steady the wheel while he uses his good arm to drag his T-shirt up over his head.

"Here." He takes the wheel back and tosses the shirt at me. I can't help but look at his body, at the muscles that tighten around his rib cage and ripple over his stomach. "Hold it over the wound, press as hard as you can to stop the bleeding."

I automatically do as he asks, my hands shaking uncontrollably as I hear the same words over and over.

Shot fuckin' dead… Mama… *shot fuckin' dead.*

Neither of us talk for the rest of the journey, and Jessie makes it in just over five minutes instead of ten. When we pull up at the club, Daddy and his brothers are already waiting for us in the yard. My door rips open the moment Jessie stops the truck, and Daddy pulls me out erratically checking me over before hugging me so tight I swear his strong arms will crush me to death.

"Princess, let Carly take care of you. I got to deal with business." He holds me out from his chest and grips the top of my arms. "You're safe now, 'kay?" he assures me, pulling me back into him for one last hug before he lets Carly take over. I don't want him to let me go. After everything that's just happened to me, I want to be the fuckin' business he has to deal with. When his firm grip around me is replaced with a much softer touch, I feel my heart break all over again. It's not that I don't like Carly,

Skid's old lady seems friendly enough. But just this once, I thought Daddy might make me his priority.

Carly offers me a sad smile as she leads me towards one of the parked cars and I look back helplessly over my shoulder, watching Daddy walk towards his men.

"Church," he bellows at his brothers.

"You too, son." His glare lands on Jessie as he marches through everyone. I never had the guys at the club down as religious men, but they seem to spend a lot of time in the old chapel on the compound, and I guess now is as good a time as any to pray.

Carly drives me up the compound's dirt track, all the way up to the big lodge on top of the hill where Daddy lives. Once inside, she guides me through the kitchen and into his living room, where we sit, and she hugs me while I cry.

She stays silent the entire time, what can she possibly say to make me feel better? Words aren't gonna bring my mama back, and there is no comfort to the emptiness that seems to be growing hollower inside me. Tears soak my cheeks until my eyes dry out and my heavy lids finally close. I drift off with my head propped on Carly's lap, her hand stroking through my hair.

I don't know how long I've been out for when I feel her shift from beneath me. Her legs being replaced with someone else's, and a much heavier hand taking over her long, lazy strokes.

There's a glorious few seconds right before my brain reminds itself of what's happened, and when I open my eyes to face reality, it's Jessie who's looking down at me. His bright, blue eyes brimming with unshed tears of his own. Seeing him like this gives me enough strength to sit up and comfort him. My hand automatically lifts to touch his cheek, and my thumb strokes the bristles on his spikey jaw.

"I'm so sorry, Hay." His face leans into my hand, welcoming my comfort, and I pull him closer. His arms wrap around me, clinging to me as if I'm the anchor that's keeping him grounded.

"I couldn't save you both. There were two of them. One outside each of your doors."

"It's not your fault," I whisper. "There was no way you could have got to us both." My words do little to soothe him, his nostrils flaring out, and the softness in his eyes turning to stone.

"They'll pay for this. You know that, right? The Bastards will pay," he snarls through his teeth. I nod because I know that they will and I want them to, even though I know that means in death. I want it more than I want my next breath.

"I'll never let anything happen to you. You know that don't you, Hay? I will always protect you." Jessie's hands grip the hair on either side of my face, his eyes holding mine and making sure I heard him.

I nod before wiping my tears away with my palm and bury myself into his chest. My heart feels broken beyond any repair, but just Jessie being here, holding me like I'm all he has now, is enough to let me know that everything will be okay.

CHAPTER 3
JESSIE

AGED 17

I have a lot to thank Jimmer Carson for. When my pa died, he could easily have let me go into the system, but the man took me in as one of his own.

He moved me in with his own family, he loved me like the son he never had. All surprising actions from a man who was supposed to be soulless, a man that even his own club members feared. Still, you don't become president of the biggest MC in the state by being any other way.

I've seen a side of the man that many others never would. I watched him cry when he said goodbye to my pa in the mortuary, heard the promise he made to his lifeless best friend to love me like a son. And that was the moment I decided I wanted to be just like him. I wanted a brotherhood bond that couldn't be broken, not even by death.

I wanted to be a Dirty Soul, and I wouldn't rest until I wore the same cut that my father had died for.

I spent the next four years living in Prez's family home, but most of my time hanging around at the club. I watched how the other brothers worked, knew far too much for a kid my age. But in the end I'd always go home to them, to Hayley and Mary-Ann. My family.

I always wondered if Prez had put me with them to offer me a choice. He could easily have kept me at the club, paid a club whore pittance to make sure I ate and slept. Instead, he gave me that glimpse of normality. He gave me Hayley.

Hayley is everything a little sister should be, irritating, nosey, and a complete brat. Still, I've always felt an overwhelming urge to protect her. It isn't something Prez ever asked of me. No, back then it was instinct, and one I felt the need to keep to myself. I sure as fuck didn't want anyone thinking I was adapting to the civilian life Prez had placed me in. My blood runs blue, I was born to be a Dirty Soul.

My pa, just like Prez, had been one of the original Dirty Dozen, a founder of the club. One of Twelve kids, who twenty-five years ago sat down together to write their own rules. Forming a club that years later would be twelve Charters big, with hell knows how many members.

I wanted to make my pa proud, to follow in his footsteps, and as soon as I was old enough, Prez gave me the chance. At first, he offered for me to prospect at my dad's old Charter in Utah, but it didn't feel right. I'd been hanging out with the guys here since I was twelve years old. I belonged with them, and the way Prez's mouth hitched up when I told him that, showed he was happy with my decision to prospect here with him in Colorado.

Over the years I balanced my life between the club and home, never really letting Hayley or Mary-Anne get too close, yet appreciating having them around.

It had been late when I got back from the club tonight. I couldn't get to sleep, Hayley is growing up, boys were starting to notice her, and she doesn't help herself. I've seen the tiny tops and the extra swing she puts in her hips nowadays, and it only spells trouble. I'm starting to wonder what shot at a normal life Hayley is gonna get with her dad being who he is. Hell, it wasn't as if she could bring some nice kid home from school and introduce him to the folks. If Prez caught a kid looking at Hayley in the wrong way I'd put money on his parents receiving their son's eyeballs, along with his dick via courier the next day.

I thought I heard footsteps coming up the stairs and slowly clicked my door open, just enough to see through the crack. That's when I saw them, two dark figures creeping down the corridor of the home that had become mine, guns in their hands that were threating the lives of my family. The family that I tried so hard not to care about, but couldn't help but love.

I watched the figures separate, each of them taking position outside the bedroom doors, and I knew then I was gonna have to make a choice.

I'm tall for my age, I use the gym at the club every day. The other prospect, Troj, has taught me enough about fighting for me to be confident that I can take at least one of them out. But both men are armed, as soon as I took one out, I'd be shot by the other, leaving both Mary-Ann and Hayley definitely dead.

The thought of losing either of them twisted my guts, and the fact I had a choice seemed to make everything worse.

In the end, impulse took over. I've lost a parent before, two in fact. I'd dealt with it. But I didn't know how I'd deal with losing Hayley. I reached to the nightstand for my knife, then quietly crept up behind the guy who was about to open Hayley's door. His gun fired, the bullet bouncing off one of the pictures on top of the stairs. And I didn't have the time to register the lack of remorse I felt as I sliced my blade swiftly across his throat. The gurgling sound his body made soothed my anger, blood gushing thick and warm from his neck, coating my hand and spilling on to Mary-Ann's perfect cream carpet. She'd fucking freak when she saw it.

The body made a thud as it hit the floor, and I looked up when the sound of another gunshot alerted me that the second guy had got to Mary-Ann. All I could do for her now was to get Hayley the fuck out of there…

I took my first bullet tonight, and I'd have taken a thousand more if it meant I could have saved Mary-Ann too. Never have I been more scared than I was when I pulled on to the compound. Prez had every right to blame me. Maybe there was some way I could have saved them both, but being a rookie kid, I'd panicked and cost him the life of his old lady.

I watch Prez pull Hayley out of my truck, hugging her tight before he calls Skid's old lady over. Half the club are out in the yard, and suddenly I wish I was somewhere else.

Carly takes off with Hayley, and Prez thunders back towards the club, his small army of brothers parting to make a path as he marches through them and heads directly for me.

"Church," he roars, and as he gets closer, I see the look in his eyes that I've only ever seen once before, the same look he'd been wearing when he looked down at my Pa's stone-dead body. Only this time there isn't any room for tears in them, the anger crowds them far too much.

"You too, son." He nods, grabbing my shoulder and squeezing it in his bear-like hand as he passes. I swallow the lump that sticks to the back of my throat, and wipe palms drenched with blood on my leg. I can't feel the pain in my shoulder anymore, and the fact I should probably see the doc as soon as possible goes on hold. I'm about to go to church, a place prospects never get to see. This is the day I've waited for since I was five years old and had to wait out in the hall for my pa, while he and the brothers in Utah discussed business. I'm finally about to enter church for myself, and all I'm wearing is fuckin' sweatpants.

I try not to let being in the room effect my recollection of what the fuck has just gone down. I know how vital the finer details can be, and I tell the brothers as much as I can remember. When Prez hears what's happened, he shouts his orders to the others. Grimm and a clean-up team are sent to the house to get rid of the Bastard's body, and Skid goes to fetch the doc. One by one the brothers clear out the room, all knowing there'll be no sleeping or fucking tonight. I'm about to follow the last of them out, but get halted by Prez's voice.

"Not you, son, you stay. Me and you gotta talk."

I watch him stand up from his seat at the head of the table, walk over to the cabinet, and pull out a bottle of single malt with two glasses. He places them on the table and half-fills them.

"Your daddy brought me this bottle the day Hayley was born...." he starts. "Knowing ya pa he would've had ten cases of the stuff stolen from an Irish import, but it was the thought that counted." I snort a laugh that matches his, anxiously taking the glass he offers from his hand.

"You know me and your old man were best friends. Two of the original Dirty Dozen. He sat beside me in that chair right there for ten years before he left to set up his own Charter," Prez lifts his glass up towards the VP spot that Chop now occupies.

"We rode together, fucked whores together. Ain't nothing in this world I wouldn't have done for that son of a bitch. Hell, I even raised his boy." He slams his now empty glass down, topping it back up, reminding me that I haven't touched mine. Consciously I bring the tumbler to my mouth and take a swig of the thick, amber liquid. The burn numbs my insides as it slides down my throat and settles in my stomach.

"I'm grateful for that, sir," I take the opportunity to tell him, knowing that I don't say it often enough.

"You know Mary-Ann never wanted this." His heavy fist lands heavy on the table. "Nights like tonight remind me why," he laughs. The guy's old lady is turning stiff as we speak and he's fucking laughing.

"I saw it in your eyes," he changes the subject. "The day your pa left this world, I saw the determination, the hunger. You wanted in. You wanted retaliation for it. Am I right?" The humor dropped right out of his voice.

"Yes, sir," I agree, it's been my focus since I got here. I just hope that I haven't fucked it for myself.

"Well, tonight you proved yourself. You saved my girl, took a fuckin' bullet…" His lips pick up into a smile. "So you're in."

"What?" I check I'm hearing him right.

"You made the cut kid…" Prez moves to the cupboard at the back of the room.

"We already voted last week, I wanted to save this for when you turned eighteen, but tonight I couldn't be any fuckin' prouder." My eyes fall to the cut he's holding, the same one my Pa wore. The one I've been waiting to wear since as long as I can remember.

"I don't know what to say, Prez," I manage, still trying to catch up with tonight's shit show and how it's turned out like this.

"I do need you to answer me a question though." Prez sounds serious as he holds out my new cut for me.

"Sure," I shrug, taking the cut and sliding it on my shoulders.

"Why Hayley? I get that you could only save one of 'em, but Mary-Ann was like a mother to you." Prez looks puzzled.

"I dunno, instinct I guess," I answer. Prez nods, seeming to accept my answer, but I'm not finished, I'm curious myself.

"Honestly. I always wondered if you sent me to live with them as some kinda test. Like you wanted to see which life I really wanted. I'd choose this club over anything. I was born to wear this cut..." I grip the lapels of it tight, remind myself that I'm actually wearing it. "But you gave me a mother and a sister at the same time, and I won't pretend that I don't care about them, because I do. I chose Hayley because I've lost a mother, I lived through it. But I ain't ever lost a sister before. Didn't quite know how I'd handle that…" There it is again, that horrible feeling in my chest brought on by thoughts of any harm coming to her.

"I cared for them, but I'm no civilian, Prez. I belong here," I assure him in case there's any doubt.

"You're right there." Prez grips the back of my head. "And

you're fuckin' smart boy, your dad would be proud."

"I like to think so." I knock back what's left in my glass.

"And Hayley, you really see her as a sister?" he asks, a small hint of threat in his tone.

"Yes, sir. I love her like she's my own flesh and blood." I see his satisfaction, and it makes me relax a little.

"Jess, I don't know why the Bastards went after my family tonight," he admits, taking his seat again. "But until I find out, I'm gonna need someone looking out for my girl, someone she trusts. Last thing I want is to scare her with Squealer or Screwy, you think you're up to it?"

"Yes, sir," I nod, there ain't no one better for the fucking job.

"Boy, you stop with that sir shit, I'm your Prez now."

"Sure. Sorry, Prez"

"And for the record, I was never testing you. I saw something in you that reminded me of your father, I trusted it. Kinda hoped you'd naturally take on the brother role with Hayley. Never expected you to be smart enough to hide it from me though. You must have got that smart shit from your momma." He sniggers.

I smile because he's probably right, I never knew her, she died when I was two, but Pa was always telling me how smart she was.

"So, you'll look out for Hayley for me?" he asks

"No need to ask, she's family," is my response.

"Yeah... Well, you proved that tonight. She can never know about this. I don't want her thinking she's in any more danger. But you gotta stay close, and I want her shielded as much as possible from the shit that goes on around here. She may have to be around the club from now on for protection, but it doesn't mean she needs to know what we're about."

"Sure thing, Prez," I nod in agreement.

"Me and the brothers already talked about you moving up here after you patched. You can lodge up with Troj. We had to give Grimm his own place. He didn't take to sharing his space too well."

"Sounds good," I agree, trying to imagine anyone sharing a cabin with Grimm, he's always struck me as a little tapped. Troj would be the perfect roommate though. We were both prospects, and around the same age. Without competition, he's the prettiest person with facial hair I've ever seen. His impressive height teamed up with long, brown hair has bitches dropping their pussies at his size elevens. But being deceived by his charming looks is a costly mistake to make, the kid is fucking lethal. He grew up on the streets, and he fought on them too before the club found him. Troj was discovered when he knocked Squealer clean out during a bar brawl. Squealer was, and still is, almost double his size. Pure man muscle, like his twin Screwy. So a kid taking him off his feet got Prez's attention. They ended up bringing him back to Manitou Springs with them. It wasn't like Troj had fuck all to stay in Denver for. I've always been convinced that he'd get his patch before me, guess I'd been wrong.

Living with Troj would be a blast, but my excitement didn't stop me worrying about Hayley. She knows nothing about the club, been kept away from it her whole life, and now for her protection, she's gonna be forced to live in the center of the chaos.

"You've had a long night, go get ya head down," Prez's voice interrupts my thinking.

"Prez?" I ask thoughtfully, he tips his chin at me.

"Can I go to her? I mean she's probably gonna wanna see a familiar face and you're gonna be busy tonight."

"I think that would be a good idea, Jessie, I'll send the doc up to the lodge." His head gestures to the door permitting me to leave. And despite the horrors of the past few hours, I step out of church feeling ten-feet tall. If I'm nothing to anyone else, I'm everything I've ever wanted to be.

I'm a Dirty Soul.

AGED 16

Something shifted between us the night Mama died. Jessie changed, he suddenly became my rock.

I moved into Daddy's lodge at the compound straight away, and hated it from the moment I got there. I was no longer an ordinary girl, sheltered from club life. I was a part of it, and despite knowing jack shit about *club business*, I wasn't stupid. I was aware of the other shit that went on around here that Daddy and Jessie tried to hide from me.

Jessie held me the whole way through Mama's funeral, and it made me happy and sad at the same time seeing him wearing his daddy's cut. I know how much becoming a Dirty Soul meant to him, but I couldn't help feeling sad for my own selfish reasons. I may not know much about the club, but I know the club rules, and the biggest one of them is that Prez's daughter is off limits.

The whole club showed up for Mama. Charters from miles away all riding in to show their respects. For me, only one person's presence really mattered, and it was *his* hand I squeezed for strength as I watched Mama get lowered deeper into the damp, worm-riddled earth.

"She's not there you know," Jessie whispered to me under his breath, as if he could read what I was thinking. I looked up at him, my vision blurry through tears.

"She's in here." He moved his finger up and tapped it gently against my temple. "Always here," he spoke so softly, smiling at me through his own pain.

I didn't care who saw when I slipped my hands under his cut, wrapping my arms around his waist, burying myself into him. I comforted him just as much as he did me. I'd known since I was ten that I loved Jessie Donavon, what I'd learn over the next few years was how much I'd needed him.

Two years passed, and living at the club dragged from one long day to the next. There was always a drama, and soon Mama's death just became one of them.

For everyone else, but not for me.

In between working for Chop and Skid at the garage, as well as dealing with club stuff, Jessie hung out with me as much as he could. He'd tease me, I'd irritate him, and I loved every moment we spent together.

He dropped out of high school the day he patched in, and didn't give college a second thought. Meaning that I had to share rides to school with Tommy and Maddox. They were both obviously jealous of Jessie's club status. Though, I doubted either one of these jack asses would ever make it to prospect, let alone the full cut.

The club became quieter after Mama died, most of the families who lived here chose to transfer to other Charters. Guess they figured if the Prez's old lady couldn't be protected, they were safer elsewhere. Only Tommy, Chop's son, and Maddox, whose Mama worked down the club at night, were any traces left of what had once been a family-based club.

I've suffered a long day. Tommy and Maddox have been

chatting their usual, delusional shit the whole journey home. So when Tommy pulls in to the yard, I get out of the car and head straight up the track towards Daddy's lodge.

"Hey baby girl, you wanna study?" Tommy yells after me, leaning over the roof of his car

"I'm good thanks." I look back over my shoulder. The pair of them make my skin crawl, all they ever talk about is how they want to study their smart ass's out of the club life. I'll admit to being the teeniest bit jealous. School's never been something I've excelled at. A part of me can't wait until I get to drop out like Jessie did. The other part wants to cling on to normal, to do college and live the dream that Tommy and Maddox talk about, not that I'll ever admit that to them.

I often wondered what Daddy wants for me. He made it clear from the day I was born he didn't want me involved in his club. Situations forced his hand. I'm here because there was nowhere else for me to go. I don't belong here, but it's the only way he can keep me safe. Though he's never taken the time to speak to me about it, I know me being here is an inconvenience.

"Figured... Prez's daughter's too good to hang out with the likes of us," Tommy taunts, interrupting my thought train. Maddox mumbles something under his breath that seems to amuse them both. I don't care, my eyes have already fallen behind them, where Jessie is walking towards me.

No, not me. Them. And something is up. I can tell by the pace of his strides and how his arms swing at his sides. Furious eyes focus on Maddox, and the angriest scowl I've ever seen on his face tells me Jessie is really pissed about something.

There's no hesitation as he reaches out and grabs Maddox by the back of his head, smashing him face first into the hood of Tommy's car. When he drags his face back up, I see blood seeping from his nostrils. Jessie's fist grips tightly at Maddox's hair, tugging his head back so far that I see the boy's Adam's apple bulging from his throat. I watch it quake as Jessie mouths something that looks a lot like a warning tightly into his ear, something that has Maddox bobbing his head in agreement, like a good little bitch.

If I wasn't so shocked—and incredibly turned on—I'd laugh.

"Chill man," Tommy sniggers, holding up his arms, but Jessie ignores him, dropping Maddox in a heap to the floor. He leaves the two of them behind and chooses to walk towards me, dusting his hands together while that cocky grin spreads across his lips.

"Hey pretty girl," his chin lifts up at me.

Christ, he is perfection. His hands still dirty from working on engines and his overalls stripped down to his waist. He's wearing his cut over his bare chest and his white T-shirt hanging out his back pocket. I never imagined I'd find a cut and a violent streak attractive in a guy, but Jessie pulls them both off.

He walks me over to his truck and gives me a ride up to Daddy's lodge. I've lived there since the night Mama died. That's another reason I hate living on the compound, Jessie doesn't live with me anymore. He lives in one of the cabins down by the lake, with the one they all call Troj.

It's not all bad, Jessie does spend a lot of time at our place. Daddy's never home, too busy running the club. So, most of my company comes from him. Of course, I always feel a surge of jealousy when he leaves in the evenings, I hate thinking about him down at the club, acting like the other brothers do. The thought of the women down there throwing themselves at him, grates against all my nerves.

"Don't listen to those asswipes, Hay," Jessie tells me. As we walk into the kitchen, he pulls a chair out from under the table and twists it round so he can straddle it. I open the fridge and I'm instantly depressed at how empty I find it. A trip to the grocery store is well overdue.

Pouring us both the last of the juice, I take the seat opposite his.

"Guys like them don't know how to act around the chicks they like, so they become jerks." He downs his juice in one swallow, then takes a pack of smokes from his cut, lighting one up and tosses his zippo on the table once he's used it.

"Those guys don't like me. They hate me," I correct him, sliding an ashtray across the table, reminding him to use it.

"That's what you think, pretty girl." His eyebrows wiggle, and I throw him a glare back that's stern enough to make him change the subject.

"So, what we got for dinner? I'm starving," he asks, blowing a steady stream of smoke from between his lips.

"Sorry, fridge is empty, I gotta go shopping." I roll my eyes, I'm the only one that ever worries about things like groceries around here.

"I'll take ya," he offers. "And we can stop at Bernie's on the way back, grab a burger and a shake."

I beam back at him because nothing beats a Bernie Burger. Quickly finishing up my juice, I rush to my room to change, making sure to pick out something that will show off my curves. I have to be more careful now that I'm around Daddy more often, but the tight vest and skinny jeans I choose seem to flaunt my assets without it being too obvious.

"So, what did Maddox say that got you all riled up?" I question Jessie ten minutes later as I climb into his truck, Jessie never takes the bike when I'm with him. And yes, of course I've asked him to.

He pretends he hasn't heard me, his fingers tapping the steering wheel to the music that comes from the stereo.

"Come on I'm curious," I reach out to tickle his ribs knowing that it's his sensitive spot, but he manages to shoo me away. "What warrants getting your face dented into the hood of a car around here?" The sickly-sweet voice I put on is rewarded with a smile from him but he soon turns serious again.

"You don't need to know." He shakes his head.

"Yeah, I do, Jessie. Don't do that," I warn, my own smile fading as I straighten myself up in the bench seat.

"Do what?" He pretends like he has no idea what I'm talking about.

"What you always do, trying to shield me from the truth, it pisses me off," I sulk.

"You gonna make me wash your mouth out with soap now?" he asks, looking at me with his forearm resting over the wheel, taking another shot at skirting around the truth.

"Jessie…" I warn him again.

"You really wanna know?" he sighs, his voice almost begging not to make him tell me.

"I really wanna know," I assure him.

"Okay fine," he shrugs. "Tommy said some shit 'bout Prez's daughter being too good to hang out with him, and then that Maddox fucker…" He takes a long inhale through his nostrils, looking as if he might back out of telling me.

"Jessie. I can handle it."

"Fine. He said that you weren't too good to be choking your throat around a DSD like a club whore." Jessie's eyes drop to the wheel, and for the first time in a long time he looks embarrassed.

"DSD?" I screw up my face. Jessie lets out another long breath before explaining.

"Dirty Soul Dick."

I press my lips together tight to stop myself laughing.

"That's ridiculous." I let a little giggle escape, and it seems to ease him up slightly.

"I know right? Especially since his mama's sure had her fill of it over the years," Jessie sniggers, making me instantly wonder if Maddox's mom has had her fill of him.

"Idiots don't know shit. I wouldn't choke." I wink cheekily, waiting for his reaction.

"Girl… You're barely sixteen years old." Jessie takes his eyes off the road to eyeball me like I've gone crazy. "And I don't wanna hear that shit coming from you again... you're set for better things than this place. It ain't what your mama wanted for ya," he reminds me, his tone turning serious.

"Says the guy who has wanted to wear the cut since he sprouted his first pubic hair," I tease. I know this because I used to sneak into his room when he was out, he'd draw the club's patch on just about everything.

"You eat, sleep, and shit this club, Jessie," I point out.

"Yeah. I do, but we're talking about you now."

"Well then, don't I get a say in what I want?" I cross my arms over my chest.

"Sure. So tell me, pretty girl. What. Do. You. Want?" he asks with a curious smile that reaches all the way to his blue eyes, and for the briefest of moments, I feel brave enough to tell him. My heart pumping full of adrenaline as the words near my tongue.

You Jessie. I want you.

I hear the words in my head, and just like when I was ten years old, with a letter written on pretty pink stationary. I hide them away again.

"What I really want is a burger and a shake from Bernie's." I smile a fake smile, and when he snuffles a laugh back at me, I feel myself fall that little bit harder for him.

CHAPTER 5
JESSIE

PRESENT DAY

There's tension in the room. The sort that has every fucker sat around the table on edge. We're here, in church, to discuss the latest in a long piss stream of fuck-ups, and there's no surprise that it involves the Bastards. It always involves the fucking Bastards.

Our rival club is situated about twenty miles south of town, and despite being taught the consequences enough times, they're increasingly bringing their shit to Manitou Springs. These days the fuckers weren't even showing us enough respect to be sly about it.

Over the years the Dirty Souls have built stable relations with the local PD. A relationship that up to now has worked perfectly. We uphold our side of the deal and keep the town clean, and as a thank you they keep the fuck out of our business.

Recent Bastard behavior is jeopardizing our agreement and making our job increasingly difficult. There's been a sudden influx of local kids using, and despite what the people in town are thinking, we ain't the ones supplying.

We ain't stupid enough to shit on our own doorstep.

As if all that isn't enough to deal with, The Bastard scum seemed to be getting the upper hand on all our deals just lately.

They somehow know all that's coming in and what's going out. And they're undercutting us on all the big deals.

They're always one move ahead of us, and every brother sat around this table knows we can't let that shit lie for much longer.

The room's clouded with smoke, the sun pouring through the glass windows reflecting their colors on the huge wooden table that centers the old chapel.

Ten years ago, when the club took over this run-down holiday resort, the irony that it had its own chapel wasn't lost on Prez. The pews where past vacationers would sit to pray on Sundays were ripped out and replaced with the club table and a gavel. These days, it ain't songs of praise that echo these walls. Plans are made for gun and drug runs, and the names of the damned are whispered when anyone tries fucking up our shit.

"They have to be getting their intel from somewhere." Skid's fist lands heavy on the table, the guy isn't known to fling his kibby very often. In fact, he's the calmest out of the lot of us. Skid always keeps his shit together. It's what makes him the perfect road captain. He thinks about everything strategically, never acts on impulse. So to see him so wound up makes all this a shit load more serious.

"What you saying, Skid? You think someone's ratting?" Prez's VP, Chop, folds up his arms and leans back in his chair, making sure his wide chest puffs out.

"Is that what I fuckin' said?" Skid throws himself up from his seat, looking set to launch at his brother across the table. "Don't spit words into my mouth," he warns, pointing his finger at Chop. I look across the table at Troj, both of us thinking the same thing. That if these two were gonna start, it's gonna take a hella lot to stop them.

"Hey, guys, chill the fuck down." Troj's arm slams across Skid's chest, thankfully it's enough to ease him back down into his seat, though his dark eyes still burn like lasers at Chop.

"We all know there ain't no one around this table who would

rat. There's got to be something else." Troj seems satisfied that he's calmed Skid, and sits himself back down. He got his patch a few months after me and took over Skid's role as Sergeant at arms when he became road captain last year.

Troj may be young, but like me, he's earnt his place around this table.

"Way I see it, they can't go on undercutting us for much longer, we were dragging our balls through a grinder to make some of them deals pay, right Thorne?" Troj looks down the table to our club secretary, and Thorne nods back, running his fingers through his short, slightly greying hair.

"I can't figure how they're making it pay. No one's paying more than four hundred for an AK nowadays. It was barely worth the run for us with the price we offered. I can't see how they could come in any higher… Unless it ain't money that's the issue." Thorne's judgmental eyes set on Squealer, who immediately holds up his hands in defense.

"Nah-ah, don't try dumping that shit at my feet." His head shakes.

"Well, the Russians were happy to throw business our way before it happened," Thorne makes a valid point.

"How was I supposed to know she was a fucking relation? She was at the party. She was free game." Squealer shrugs looking to his twin brother Screwy sat on his right side, and then to Grimm on his left like they should agree with him.

"So, the fucking accent never gave her away," Chop laughs, earning him another scowl across the table from his brother Skid.

"If you're implying that me burying the bone into Fedulov's sister is the reason the Russians are looking at other buyers, then you're wrong. The fuckers should be giving us the guns for free after the shift I put in to that one."

"It wasn't his sister, Squeal, it was his daughter," Tac corrects, trying to curb his amused grin.

"Yeah… well there may be a tiny chance that it was both."

Squealer pulls an awkward face, then uses his tongue to flip the wooden pick that sits between his perfectly straight teeth.

Most people believe it's his twin Screwy who's the unhinged one. And sure, that guy's head is fucked beyond any fixing. I've never heard him talk in all the years I've known him. But you have to question who the real psycho of the family is. The sixteen-year-old kid who one day, flipped and killed his father with his bare fists. Or the twin brother who banged his head against a solid brick wall until he was guaranteed a stint in the loony trap right alongside him.

"None of that shit fucking matters," Prez shouts across the table. "We can't blame Squealer and his dick for the deal with the Mexicans falling through last month."

"Nope, ain't had Mexican pussy for months..." Squealer nods proudly. Making a pretend gun out of his fingers, he cocks it with his other hand, then points it towards Thorne before he fires.

"Speaking of Mexican, that shit's getting far too fuckin' regular downtown, it's startin' to become a problem. We need to get a message out to the Bastards. They wanna deal, they do it on their own territory. Got any ideas, Jess?" Prez looks to me now.

After just a year of being patched, I got a role of my own too; Club Enforcer. I learned from one of the best, Vex, and took over from him when he retired. Prez didn't have to ask which way I wanted to deal with this shit. He knows I'll want to handle it the same way we had four years ago when the Bastards screwed us...

Brutally.

But this time we have to be smart, think about what's best for the club and the town we're protecting. Right now, all we need is to ruffle enough feathers for them to know that dealing in Manitou Springs won't be tolerated.

"Figure the Bastards have trappers running their shit around town," I start. "Ain't no way they'll have enough balls to show up around here themselves. We could start by finding out who their guys are. I could play around with the fuckers for a few hours, test their loyalties before we send them back to Clunk and his boys with a message." I spin the handle of my knife in my hand. It's surprising how inventive I can get with a blade and flesh when I put my mind to it.

"We could keep any product for ourselves, enjoy a night sampling what we missed out on," Tac suggests.

"Fuckin' party ehhhhh kid." Squealer grabs Grimm by his shoulders, shaking him roughly, trying to evoke even the slightest reaction from him. But the cold expression doesn't leave Grimm's face, only his eyes flick sideways to eyeball Squealer before he rolls them away again.

Grimm is only a year older than me, but he looks so much younger. His frosty-blue eyes contain a good helping of psycho, he chooses to stay pretty much silent, but unlike Screwy, Grimm will speak up when it's necessary. I guess he just never has all that much to say.

Conveniently, Grimm has a condition called OCD, obsessive-compulsive disorder. It works to our advantage and has earnt him the role as leader, master, and fucking king of the clean-up crew. The kid is insane good at cleaning up the nasty shit that club business sometimes leaves behind, and guaranteed, there isn't anything Grimm wouldn't have thought of and erased all traces of before he leaves a scene.

"That will be a start," Prez nods his head at me. "Skid, get Rogue to do some listening around town, see if she can find out some names of dealers. If she insists on hanging around here like fuck warts on a whore, she might as well make herself useful."

"I'll talk to her boss," Skid tips his chin. Rogue means a lot to Skid, none of us know much about her other than the fact she's a hard bitch who can fix an engine better than most the men in this room. She's been helping out Skid and Chop at the garage since she was a kid.

"Tommy could ask around too," Chop adds.

Yeah, you heard that right, Tommy *too good to be a fucking Dirty Soul* himself became a prospect last month.

Tommy is Chop's son, and Chop is one of the oldest members of this Charter, he's a no shit kinda guy and despite coming off as an ass most of the time, is respected by everyone. That went a long way in making the decision to take Tommy on as our newest prospect, not what he could actually bring to the club.

It's obvious to most of us that Tommy doesn't have an ounce of Dirt in him. I reckon we'd have come off better offering Rogue the prospect Jacket, and if she'd been born with a dick we would of.

We already have Nyx, he's been prospecting over a year now and would be getting his patch before long. We needed someone to take his place, and as Tommy was already trusted by the club, it had seemed a better option than letting in an outsider.

"I'll get Nyx to speak with some of the fresher's when they come in the shop," Tac goads Chop.

Tac is Nyx's sponsor. It means he's responsible for him. He'd brought Nyx to us after he'd taken him on as an apprentice at the tattoo studio. Despite the chip Nyx has fixed on his shoulder he's a good kid. He gets shit done, which is more than could be said for fucking Tommy, who in my opinion might as well have a pair of tits.

"Nyx. Really? Kid ain't got no friends, no fucking respect either if you ask me," Chop sniggers back at Tac, and the look on Tac's face says just about what everyone around the table beside Chop is thinking. Sure, Nyx is another quiet one, no one can ever entirely be sure what's spiraling around in his head. He's a little reckless, and doesn't let anyone talk down to him. But no one doubts his reliability. He's proven his worth to this club on more than a few occasions.

"They can all put the feelers out, ain't gonna hurt. See which of them comes through for us," Skid says aiming a smug look right at Chop. He's laying down a challenge, and my bucks are on his little protégé being the one that pulls through. That bitch is savage. Skid's eyes are set like concrete, and I swear I hear Chop hiss under his breath.

I have no fucking idea what's going on with the two of them, but it's taking sibling rivalry to a new extreme.

"Settled." Prez slams down the gavel, and one by one the brothers make their way out of the large oak door and into the daylight.

Church finishes up, just in time for me to get in my truck and drive to pick Hayley up from college. With her dad being president of the club, money is never set to be a problem for her, but she still insists on getting herself a good education.

I always pick her up on a Friday and we grab something to eat at Bernie's. It's our thing. Not something Prez has ever asked me to do, but something I do because I want to.

Hayley's turned in to a sassy thing since moving to the club, and although she still pisses me off like a bratty little sister, I'd be lying if I said I didn't enjoy hanging out with her.

Prez never spoke about anyone else taking over the job of looking out for her. Neither of us had to say it out loud, we both knew it would always be me. Way I see it she's as much my responsibility as she was the Prez's and as annoying as she can be, I love her for it.

I wait in the truck, outside Pine Peaks College, watching her skip excitedly down the steps when she sees me. She swings open the door and hops inside, leaning over to peck me on the cheek before I pull off.

"You're in a good mood, pretty girl." I smile, Hayley always cheers me up when shit gets too much, so she is just what I need after the intensity of church today.

"I got invited to a party tomorrow night," she tells me, clapping her hands together like a performing chimp.

"And… you know your daddy ain't never gonna let you go to

it," I remind her, feeling bad for having to burst her ecstatic little bubble. Though her smile doesn't drop like I expect it to.

"Well, I did worry about that, but then I had an idea…"

"Shit that sounds dangerous." I side glance her and wait for one of her snappy responses.

"Oi." She punches my arm. Hard. It makes me proud, I obviously taught her well.

"Come on then out with it, what's the plan?" I give in and ask.

"I was thinking that he might let me go if someone he trusted agreed to come with me." The way she looks up at me, doing that cute as a fuckin' kitten thing she does with her eyes pre warns me for what's coming next.

"Ohhhhh no. Not a fuckin' chance, Hay," I laugh, parking the truck outside Bernie's. I'm still laughing to myself as we walk across the lot towards the door.

"You know if I ask Daddy…" she starts, still trying to be cute as she jogs to catch up with me, I did wonder how long it would take for the brat I know and love to show up. She will try to pull the princess card, and she should know by now it won't work on me. So, I play back the only way I know.

"Yeah, he'd make me go babysit you. And Hayley, I would babysit you… Club style," I warn, opening the door and stepping aside for her to enter the diner. She rolls her eyes at me because she knows I've won and the girl hates being defeated. We walk straight to our usual booth, and I wait for her next brainwave to hit.

The place is crammed on a Friday, but our booth was always left empty. Our waitress, Debbie, makes us priority and our regular order is placed in front of us within ten minutes of us sitting down. I'm just about to sink my teeth into the best burger in the state when the bell above the door makes me look up, and I see my other Friday afternoon treat step inside.

I know jack shit about the girl, just that there's something that makes her real fuckin' special, and that I fail to be capable of concentrating on a damn thing whenever I see her. She never notices me, in fact, I sometimes wonder if she notices anything at all. Whoever she is, she seems completely detached from her surroundings, and oblivious to the damage she could do to a guy, especially one like me.

She's nothing like the girls who hang out at the club. The ones pushing their lips and tits together, begging to be noticed. She moves as though she doesn't want to be seen, like she's content to fade into the background. But she fails to with me. There ain't words to describe her, not ones that I know how to put into a sentence anyway. Just that she's fucking beautiful, so beautiful that every time I see her I wonder if I made her up.

Today, like all the times I've seen her, her long blonde hair is pulled up off her face, tied up in a neat bun on top of her head. She's got that real English-rose complexion, light, milky skin that my fingers twitch to reach out and touch, to test if it feels as soft as it looks. Her iris's illuminate her eyes, making them pop from beneath the black-rimmed glasses that sit over the bridge of her delicate little nose.

I can't help picturing her pink, naturally full lips wrapped around my cock whenever I look at them. And it ain't helped at all by the fact that every time I see her, she's chewing down on the bottom one.

Today is no different from the other Fridays. She glides into Bernie's completely unnoticed by everyone except me. I don't understand how it's possible, but I don't take it for granted. I'd hate anyone else looking at her the way I do, maybe even enough to kill whoever tried. The girl is my undiscovered treasure, and that's exactly how I want her to stay.

I watch her settle into a booth, pulling out her laptop from her shoulder bag followed by a textbook that she opens up, and sets to work.

"Um... earth to Jessie." Hayley's voice becomes clearer

when she clicks her fingers in front of my face, breaking my focus from the girl. "Have you even been listening to me?"

"Sorry. What were you saying?" I shake myself back to reality.

"I said... please... Jessie. Like I'm actually prepared to beg you. Everyone at the club gets to have fun, when do I ever get mine?" she points out, again, trying the 'poor princess' look through batting eyelashes.

"Hay, do you know who that girl is? The one in the booth over to the right, blonde, glasses, wearing the red hoodie." I don't actually mean to ignore Hayley's question this time, and I'm not sure why now, after months of seeing the girl, I decide to share her with Hayley. My mouth just blurted out the question before my head caught up enough to stop it.

"Who, her?" Hayley cocks her head towards the girl looking gob smacked.

"Yeah, her," I whisper, trying to hush down her voice, I don't want the girl to hear us. When I glance over to check that she hasn't, and I find her with her lips wrapped around her straw sucking her milkshake through her cheeks, my cock goes into fucking spasm.

"I don't know her name, she takes an English class with me though. No one really speaks to her, she's weird. I mean she doesn't even wear makeup, and don't even get me started on her dress sense, it's tragic." Hayley picks up a fry and dunks it deep into her strawberry shake, it always makes me cringe when she does that.

"Find out more about her for me?" I lean forward, whispering because I suddenly feel embarrassed.

"You're kidding, right?" Hayley's eyes peek up at me through her bangs, a mocking grin on her lips.

"No, I ain't fucking kidding, I wanna know about her," I hiss.

"But why?" Hayley shakes her head in confusion. "Unless... wait this isn't club shit, is it? 'Coz you know my daddy wouldn't want me involved." She holds up both her hands and despite trying hard not to let it show, I can see the thought excites her.

"No... it's not club shit. This is personal," I tell her seriously. "Just find out what you can for me. Yeah? And Hay... don't tell anyone, this has gotta stay between us, okay?"

"I thought you and your 'brothers' shared everything," she points out sarcastically.

"I mean it, Hay, not even your dad," I warn.

"And what's it worth?" she teases, leaning forward on the table, and resting her chin on her knuckles.

"It's worth me not telling your daddy that you asked Nyx to hook you up with a fake ID the other week." I grin back. Hayley looks unimpressed by my offer, but also a little shocked that I knew about it. Of course, I fucking know, it's my business to fucking know.

"I never had you down as a rat, Jessie," she says, her head tipping to the side and one of her eyebrows rising higher than the other.

"Okay, okay. So how about..." I can't believe what I'm about to suggest, "...You get the info on the girl and as a thank you, I'll work on getting you to that party tomorrow night." I take my own turn at swallowing defeat, and watch Hayley's eyes light up like fireworks.

"You will?" she checks, excitement raising her tone by a few decimals.

"Yeah, well, I'll agree to wait outside for you, I ain't goin' into no lame ass party. And you will give me no reason to have to." I throw her a stern look.

"You're the best," she squeals leaning over the table and wrapping her arms around my neck. Hayley's high-pitched squeal attracts the girl's attention and for the briefest, sweetest of moments, our eyes connect, but I lose them before I have the chance to figure what to do about it.

I keep my eye on the girl while we eat. It seems what Hayley told me is accurate, she is a loner. This place is loaded with kids, all from the same college she goes to, not one of them speak to her or even bothers to look at her. It puzzles me, because I struggle to keep my eyes off her.

Her long fingers type away at her laptop, eyes occasionally looking up over the screen catching me watching her. I figure I could sit and stare at her all day, but it isn't doing me any good. So, I get up and pay the check, before me and Hayley make our way back to the compound.

The club is only a fifteen-minute drive from town. The Blue Spruce Resort had been popular back in the early nineties, but business had died out during the turn of the century. The owner of the resort ran up a debt with Prez, and the club had taken over the land and buildings as payment. It's been home to the Dirty Souls ever since. The place is perfect for club needs, with twenty vacation cabins, all surrounding the large lake that centers the resort. Then another fifteen staff cabins that edge the woodland, us members call it *Sluts sanctuary* because it's where the club whores reside. At the very top of the resort are two much bigger lodges, where Prez and Chop live, and the main building that years ago would have hosted entertainment evenings for families taking their annual vacation in the peaceful Colorado Mountains became our clubhouse. The club only made a few alterations to it, it still has a decent size bar and a stage.

We also have two smaller bar rooms on either side of the foyer that are a lot less rowdy and have a strict member's only policy. On the second floor, is an industrial kitchen, that despite being a little dated still works, and a dining hall that's perfect for lockdowns and special occasions—though it's never used much anymore. The club lost the family vibe it used to have after Mary-Ann died, a lot of the brothers with families had chosen to change Charters. So upstairs doesn't get used all that often, except for the old offices that have now been pretty much converted into rutting rooms.

I pull into the compound driving up the long dirt track, passing the clubhouse and the garage opposite that Chop and Skid run. I take a left where the track splits for the quickest route up to Prez's lodge.

"You know a girl like that would never go for a guy like you?" Hayley breaks our comfortable silence by bringing up the girl from Bernie's again. The sarcastic smirk on her face pissing me off, mainly because she's right, and I hate how much it stings.

"She'd take one look at that cut and run a mile," she continues.

"Hey, chicks dig the fuckin' cut." I nudge her playfully trying to distract myself.

"Yeah, the ones you hang around with, not girls like her. You want in her panties, you're gonna have to lose it," Hayley taunts.

"Well, there's shit all chance of that happening. You won't catch me taking this cut off for no pussy," I tell her firmly, pulling to a stop outside the lodge.

Hayley opens the door and slides out of the truck. "And you promise you'll take me tomorrow night?" she checks, narrowing her eyes at me, daring me to go back on my word.

"Do your homework on the girl, and yeah. I'm sure I can talk Prez round." Hayley takes me off guard when she jumps back inside, wrapping her arms around my neck, and then smiling before she shuts the door behind her. I watch her inside before I move on, following the track down to my own cabin.

Hanging out with Hayley always loosens me up a little, she doesn't look at me with the same fear that she does the other guys. Sometimes I wonder if she forgets that I'm one of them, if she blanks out all the things I do that make me equally as sick, if not worse.

Of course, there was every chance she doesn't know. No one

discusses club business outside of church. So, the fact that I'm one of the most fucked up people who attends probably gets overlooked by anyone who doesn't know better.

My blonde hair, blue eyes, and the all-American look hold a deception. Not many would believe that I'm the one Prez sends in when rules have been broken. If we needed someone to talk, I'm the guy who will willingly reach my fist down the throat of a man and tear out all his secrets.

I'd been taught by the master, Vex, an original like my pa and Prez, there ain't nothing worth hearing that he hadn't managed to pry out of a man's soul.

As soon as I patched in, I began my own fucked up apprenticeship with him as my mentor. Vex got too old to ride, and stepped down a year ago. I'd been honored when he'd suggested to Prez that I step up and take over his role. The old man lives somewhere off the grid now, enjoying his retirement. The stubborn old fucker was far too proud to let any of us take care of him.

He always told me that I had something in me that couldn't be taught.

No conscience.

No remorse.

I could sleep like a baby after putting an end to a waste of a life, and I held no empathy when torturing the truth out of someone. Ninety-nine percent of the time if the guy got to me, his fate had been decided anyway.

I've never killed a man who didn't deserve to die, in my opinion the actions I perform lay on everyone's conscience. We make all our decisions as a club. I'm just the guy that sees them through.

I enjoy the rush of keeping someone dangling on the edge between life and death. Take pleasure from the power of a sorry assed fucker's next breath, depending on my patience. And I revel in watching the final seconds of life, the moments just after the panic calms and the realization settles in that no matter how hard you fight, it's over. It leaves only the hope that death will come quickly. And there's something real fascinating in the relief that washes over the eyes when life slips out of them.

Where nothing quite beats watching the life drain from another man's eyes, spending time with Hayley comes a very close second. She doesn't see the monster in me. To her, I'll always be the guy who saved her life, the older brother she looks up to. The good guy who she shares her happy times with.

I like being that guy for her, and sometimes I like being that guy a little for me too.

Still, I don't doubt that Hayley knows more than what we tell her, she's a savvy girl and must have guessed my hands aren't clean of violence. So I conclude that just like me, she's happy to pretend that side of me doesn't exist.

I pull into the yard in front of the long stretch of cabins that are built in a huge half circle arched around the lake. When I park up outside mine, there's no sign of Troj being home. No doubt he'll be at the outbuilding that's been converted into a gym. He's got an upcoming fight, and has been hitting it hard lately.

I head straight for the bathroom and grab myself a quick shower, some nomads are riding in tonight, and it'd be rude not to show them a good time on their first night at the club. I try, but fail to stop my mind from wandering back to the girl at Bernie's, and the fact that Hayley's right.

She's far too innocent for me. I'll bet that I'm exactly the kind of guy her mama and papa warn her to stay away from, and I don't doubt that she's the good girl type who listens to them. Abiding by all the rules they set for her.

Still doesn't stop me thinking about how good her open thighs would feel pressed against my legs if she rode the back of my bike. Her dainty arms gripping tightly around my waist as I throttle the fuck out of the engine, making sure she feels its vibration all the way through her pussy. Thoughts of making those big, round, innocent eyes of hers glint with wickedness makes me steel fucking hard—fuck, I ain't never thought about putting a girl on the back of my bike before.

I shake the thoughts out of my head as I leave my cabin, jumping on to my bike and making the short ride down to the club. First thing I'm gonna need is a drink, the second is for Mel to ride this persistent boner right fucking out of me. And I already know exactly whose pretty little face I'll be thinking of while she does it.

CHAPTER 6
HAYLEY

It doesn't take long for me to learn her name; what people ever did before Facebook doesn't bare thinking about. *Maddy Summers.* Even her name is a sparkling rainbow of unicorn vomit. I try to look for more information, but her profile is tight. So, my finger 'accidentally' slips and I send her a friend request—better the devil you know than the devil you don't, right?

Leaving my phone on the bed I draw myself a hot bath, trying my best to keep Maddy-perfect-fucking-Summers off my mind while I soak. Besides, tomorrow night I will be at the party, Jessie will be taking me, and everyone from college will see us together.

I've already decided to wear the dress I'd picked up at the mall last week. The one that's far too short and looks like it's been sprayed onto my skin. Jessie likes it when girls dress like that for him, which is why this whole Maddy Summers nonsense makes no sense.

I finish up in the bathroom, and when I check my phone I notice she's already accepted my request.

Phase one complete. Now I just have to do what Jessie asks of me and get some information, before I scare little miss sunshine away for good. I start by sending her a friendly message, the icebreaker.

The, *hi, don't we share an English class together?* kinda crap that gets people talking.

I get a reply almost immediately and feel a smile like the Grinch that stole Christmas raise the corners of my mouth. This is gonna be too easy.

After a few messages, I bore of her small talk. Tonight has been a success, and I intend to celebrate it.

Instead of pulling on some sweats and settling to watch the usual reality crap on TV, I squeeze into my tight skinny jeans, and put on the black top that hangs just a little off my shoulders. I even brave open-toe heels knowing the walk down to the club could be quite a trek. But it'll be worth it.

Putting my phone inside my clutch, I snap it shut and leave for the club.

Daddy will be mad at me. I know the rules about going down to the club after dark. But I have to risk it to see the look on Jessie's face when I tell him what I've done. I can't wait to see his proud smile when he finds out how far I'm prepared to go for him. He doesn't have to know that there's an ulterior motive behind my plan.

I make it down to the club after an unsteady walk and head straight through the club doors before nerves get the better of me. The lobby is a huge open space. I imagine how it would have been years ago, bustling with excited vacationers ready to check in for their annual break. The wide, stretched reception desk is all that's left of those times now. The Dirty Souls hooded devil and the club motto, *Bound not by blood but loyalty. We live, we ride, and we die by our own laws*, carved into its polished wood.

The carpet beneath my feet is frayed and stained with alcohol, the elaborate wallpaper starting to peel from the walls. Seriously, you'd think these guys would take care of their sacred club a little better.

I avoid the smaller bar to my left, knowing that's where

Daddy usually hangs out, and I follow the loud music through to the large room behind the double doors. Making one final check over my shoulder, I push them open and step inside.

Stale beer, nicotine, and marijuana all assault my lungs at the same time, and smoke stings at my eyes as I scan the room trying to locate Jessie. The place is packed full of people, and I pray that Daddy won't be the first person I run into as I try blending into the crowd, also avoiding anyone wearing a cut.

The one they called Squealer is using the pool table, but not for its purpose. He has a woman laid out butt naked on the green felt, a neat line of white powder trailing from her belly button and blending into a thin strip of pubic hair. She giggles, and he licks his lips as one of his humungous forearms crushes over her ribs to keep her still. With the wickedest of smiles he looks up at her, leaning forward and inhaling the long line from her skin through his nostrils. Collecting up any residue his nose left behind with his finger before he buries it deep inside her widespread pussy. I rip my eyes away, starting to understand why Daddy doesn't let me down here at night.

I notice a few of the 'brothers' sat at the long bar on the other side of the room knocking back shots, none of them Jessie. So, I make my way towards the group of black leather sofas that are pushed up against the back wall.

That's where I find him, slouched back, with a cigarette dangling from his lips. His legs wide, and one of the club whores straddling his lap. Her skirt has risen over her hips, and Jessie's fingers are squeezing into the cheeks of her ass. I watch how he tilts his head back over the back of the couch, his eyes closing tight, while the skank whore's hand works his cock from the inside of his jeans.

I take a few steps closer... too close. Running a massive risk of being seen. I'm fully aware that I'm staring, but I'm unable pull my eyes away from what I'm seeing. That smirk I love still hangs on his lips despite his mouth being slightly open. The girl who wears nothing on the top half of her body, sliding him through her fist. I'm mesmerized at how gorgeous he looks.

His eyes are open now, and full of pleasure as he nods his approval to her while she works him. His open-mouthed smile is just waiting to be kissed, and that bitch must read my mind coz she leans in ready to help herself to it.

Thankfully he stops her just before she reaches his lips. His arm reaching around the back of her head and gripping a fistful of her shitty weave. I'm surprised it doesn't fall out in his hands when he uses it to wrench her away from his face.

"Only one place that mouth should be heading t'wards darlin'," I hear him tell her, and the bitch takes rejection like a pro, smoothly sliding down his body to rest on her knees. My eyes widen when she takes him out of his jeans and holds him upright in her palm. I've wondered for a while now what his cock might look like, and it doesn't disappoint. In fact, I'm curious to see how the girl is gonna attempt to fit it inside her mouth.

She starts at the base, dragging her tongue along the under length of his shaft before she slowly rolls it around his tip.

My mouth waters to taste him in the same way, and I watch in envy as she licks over every solid inch of his thick cock.

"Hayley!" I hear my name come from his mouth with a startled shriek, and my attention immediately moves from his dick up to his eyes. Jessie looks furious as he stands up on his feet and sends the girl tumbling backwards, her ass hitting the floor with a thump.

"Hayley, what the fuck you doin' down here?" he shouts, tucking himself back into his jeans as he thunders towards me. He doesn't give me time to answer his question, his hand rapidly wrapping around the top of my arm and pushing me back out the way I came.

I'm forced outside, the cool evening air slapping harshly against my burning cheeks.

"What the fuck, Hay? If your dad catches you here he'll bust a nut," he barks at me.

"Looks like you were about to bust one yourself," I tease hoping he'll lighten up a little.

He doesn't.

"I came to find you," I answer him, liking that his attention is on me instead of the whore now, even if he is raging mad.

"Why, what's up? Ya hurt?" Concern quickly overrides his anger, and it takes all my will not to smile.

"I did what you asked," I state proudly. "The girl's name is Maddy Summers."

"That's great, Hay, awesome, but did you have to come down here to tell me that, couldn't it wait until tomorrow?" His eyes dart around the yard cautiously.

"I did something else too," I add, twisting on my heels, ready for my big reveal.

"What, Hay?" His eyes aren't focused on me anymore, they're too preoccupied looking for Daddy I suspect.

"What did you do?" He sounds irritated, and it puts a tiny lump in my throat. Even though I know he won't be mad for much longer.

"I invited her to that party tomorrow night, and she's coming." My voice is full of excitement, yet Jessie responds with silence. Not what I'd been expecting, but he doesn't know the whole plan yet.

"I'm gonna make friends with her, Jessie," I explain, already seeing his face crease with curiosity.

"I'm gonna make her trust me enough to tell me all her secrets, and then I'm gonna share them all with you." I smile, because hearing it out loud, my plan sounds even more genius than it did in my head. And the way Jessie is struggling to form any words tells me I have his full attention back. His ocean-blue eyes sparkle with interest, and yet he still isn't smiling.

"I'm not sure that's a good idea, like you said a girl like her would see the patch and run a fuckin' mile." His reaction surprises me. I honestly expected him to be lifting me off the ground and spinning me by now.

"Which is exactly why my plan is foolproof. You can use what I tell you to get her to trust you," I explain. "Jessie, you seem mad at me?" I point out, unimpressed by his lack of enthusiasm at my efforts.

"I ain't mad at ya. Just surprised that's all, you were the one who said she was a bad idea."

"Well I've kept my end of the bargain, so it's time for you to deliver yours. Now run along, find Daddy and tell him you're taking me to the party tomorrow night." I know I'm being a brat, especially when I cross my arms and tap my fingers impatiently. But I just love getting under his skin.

"Hayley, no one tells your daddy anything," he reminds me, before whistling loudly over to one of the prospects. Nyx, lifts his head up from the conversation he's having with Thorne and Tac, then strides over from the other side of the firepit looking like a cat just crapped on his Cocoa Krispies.

"Nyx, take Hayley home before Prez sees her," Jessie orders him, and Nyx nods before heading off to get one of the trucks. Jessie looks back at me, letting out a long sigh of defeat.

"Fine, I'll make sure you get to your party. But I don't want you saying anything about me to the girl… Maddy. Okay?"

"Of course, I'm on your side remember." I roll my eyes, another habit of mine that he likes to pretend pisses him off.

"Yeah, thank fuck. Now get on home before your daddy sees you and your ass gets grounded. There'll be no parties then." He gestures his head past my shoulder, where Nyx has already pulled up. I smile triumphantly, jumping into the passenger seat without protest, and there's silence as Nyx drives me back to my prison on the top of the hill.

Ok, so Jessie's reaction wasn't quite what I'd expected, but the plan doesn't end there, not for me anyway. Maddy Summers will get to see the real him, and I can guarantee that when she does, she'll run scared. At the same time, Jessie will learn that he has someone he can always depend on. Someone, who loves him regardless of what he is.

He might actually see me.

After Nyx drops me home, I get changed into something more comfortable and do a little more Facebook research before bed. The girl appears to have a dull life, rarely goes out by the looks of things. The number of followers she has is embarrassing, and she doesn't even have an Instagram account.

She's no threat, just a useful stepping stone to getting me what I've always wanted. There is something that confuses me though. The way Jessie looked at her earlier, as if he'd discovered some unknown species. Jessie obviously sees something in her everyday looks and the lack of effort she puts into her appearance. Yet, the woman he was with at the club tonight couldn't have been further away. There was nothing understated about her. Sure, she'd been attractive, but everything about her was unnatural. From her draggy hair extensions, right down to her knockoff Louboutin heels. Her face was so plastered with makeup I'll bet she'll look like a kindergartener's drawing by the end of the night.

After finding out all I can from Maddy's social media. I tire of looking at Maddy Summers innocent fucking face. Slamming my laptop closed, I decide that an early night is what I need.

I'm gonna require all my patience and willpower tomorrow, because tomorrow I'm going to become the best fucking friend Maddy Summers ever had.

CHAPTER 7

JESSIE

That was way too fucking close, if Prez had caught Hayley down here shit could have gone badly. Luckily, he'd been buried balls deep in Haven upstairs in one of the private rooms. I'm about to go back inside when I feel a hand slither under my shirt.

"Come back inside, baby," Mel whispers in my ear. "There's a job I need to finish." Her hand drops under the waist of my jeans.

"I'm good. Go see if Chop needs you for anything," I tell her, untangling her arms from around me before I head back into the club.

"Chop... really?" she calls out from behind me.

"You all of a sudden getting fuckin' picky?" I spin around and snap at her.

"I just thought, well you've only been using me lately, so I figured that maybe..." She twists one of her synthetic hair strands around her finger in a failing attempt to be seductive.

"You figured what?" I choke out a laugh. "That this was some kinda exclusive arrangement, that I'd wanna make an old lady out of ya?" Mel pouts her botched, collagen-filled lips together

"Go find Chop," I tell her again, shaking my head.

I walk across to Grimm who's sat at the firepit, at least I can guarantee he won't try and talk to me. Sitting beside him, I take the half empty bottle of Jack he offers and knock back a good mouthful.

Maddy Summers, I shouldn't be surprised that her name is every bit as pretty as she is.

Hayley's plan is impressive. I'll give her that much. Maybe she did have some of her father's traits after all. Before, I'd been pissed at myself for wanting to know everything about the girl, there was fuck all I could do with the information anyway. Hayley's plan gave me options.

So why ain't I keen on letting her go through with this whole fake friendship thing? I push away the thought that when it comes to her, the timid little creature may have rooted something inside me that resembled a conscience. I take another mouthful of Jack before handing the bottle back to Grimm. Standing up I pull my sorry ass together, leaving to find Prez and hoping Haven has done a decent job of putting him in a good fucking mood. Because I needed to convince him to let Hayley go to that god damned party.

CHAPTER 8
HAYLEY

Hearing Jessie pull up, I rush out the door, smiling wide when I see him sat waiting for me in his truck. His head shakes with disapproval as I walk towards him, but he's still grinning, so I take it as a good sign.

I've spent the whole afternoon getting ready, balancing myself somewhere in the middle of Maddy sickly sweet, and the club slut look, and I wonder if Jessie will notice.

The purple, halter-neck dress I wear is short, so short that it sits just under my ass cheeks, but my hair is loose over my shoulders, and my makeup understated so I have that whole Maddy-au-natural vibe about me.

"Your daddy see you leave lookin' like that?" Jessie scrolls his eyes over me, half smirking.

"Sure," I lie. As if there was any chance of me leaving the lodge if Daddy had seen me.

"And he's cool about you heading out dressed like it?" His head cocks to the side doubtfully.

"Says I'm in safe hands." I shrug hopping in and buckling up before he can argue. I try hard not to focus on how gorgeous he looks with his shoulder-length hair pulled back into a ponytail and his facial hair a little longer than usual. Rough, just how I like him. He wears his cut over a plain white T-shirt and those jeans that I love that hang slightly too low off his waist.

"So are we picking up your 'friend'?" he asks sarcastically as he pulls off.

"No, she's gonna meet us there."

"Correction, she's meeting you there, I will be parked outside," he reminds me of his terms and conditions. Killjoy.

"You could just come in you know. Enjoy the party. Who knows we may be able to find you your very own club slut replica," I tease, with just a hint of malice.

"Hayley, you shouldn't have come down to the club the other night, Prez made it clear it ain't the place for you to be hanging around." His tone is serious now, and he must pick up on the awkward atmosphere it creates because he quickly picks the mood back up.

"Besides I hardly think I'd fit in with your preppy friends." He smiles, his eyes falling to the leather cut that fits against his body.

"Nothing's stopping you leaving that in the truck. Tonight you could just be Jessie Donavon. Regular twenty-two-year-old guy who attends regular parties." I may sound like I'm joking, but I'm really not. Nothing would make me happier than him losing his cut and forgetting about club rules, even if it was just for one night. To pretend along with me that the chance of *us* was even remotely possible, that we could go to a party, drink, and dance, maybe even make out like normal kids our age.

"Darlin', you know you'd only get this cut off my back if you pried it from my cold, hell-bound body. Ain't gonna be taking it off for no one. I am who I am, and those who don't like that ain't worth my fucks." Jessie shrugs his shoulders and winks irresistibly before turning his attention back to the road that leads into town.

The closer we get, the more nervous I feel. I have no reason to be, I'm a popular student, most probably because everyone knows who my daddy is. They all assume I live a super cool life at the club, when in reality they couldn't be more wrong. The whole party and drinking thing's new to me.

Jessie pulls up outside the house, and the music from the party thumps out onto the street. The lawn is already scattered with kids drinking from red plastic cups. There are a lot more people here than I expected to see. Taking a deep breath, I try to hide my unease from Jessie.

"Guess I'll be seeing you later, come find me if you change your mind." I fake confidence as I slide out of the truck and start to cross the street to join the party.

"Oi," Jessie calls after me. I turn, and he strikes me senseless, his elbow resting on the window and a cocky grin seated on his handsome face.

"Don't get into any trouble, 'kay, pretty girl," he warns, still smiling. I roll my eyes before carrying on, sashaying through the people on the lawn towards the house. I wonder if Maddy will already be here, I doubt she'd have thought to show up fashionably late. The girl has already text me twice. Once asking what to wear and then again asking what time I would be getting here.

Jesus she's needy.

It makes me laugh to think of her and Jessie together, ain't no way she could ever handle a guy like him.

I've been pretending since as far back as I can remember that I don't know what Jessie is capable of. Mainly for his sake.

He never talks about the club around me, it's another one of the 'club rules'. But that doesn't stop me hearing things.

I listen to the guys working at the garage while I study on the benches in the yard. Hear them say how Jessie gets a kick out of what he does.

The women whisper that he fucks relentlessly after he's finished an interrogation. I've listened for four years. Taken in all the little things that no one would deem relevant and pieced them all together. I know Jessie better than I know myself and I know that just like everyone else, he has a vice. His is infliction.

It didn't come as a shock, especially as I'd seen it for myself when I was just eleven.

It had only been a week since I started high school and Jessie had been waiting for me by the gate ready to walk me home. I was proudly walking towards him, hoping that everyone would see me leaving with him. That's when Stevie Fisher purposely stuck his leg out to trip me as I walked past the bench he sat on. I'd ended up in a heap on the floor in front of him. Of course, Stevie and his friends had found it hilarious, laughing at me while I gathered up the things that had fallen out of my hands. I'd ignored the soreness of my grazed knees and struggled holding in tears. I remember how Stevie and his friend's faces froze mid-laugh, how their skin turned white. It caused me to look in the same direction they were. At Jessie, coming towards them, eyes focused on Stevie, his nostrils flaring.

He'd grabbed hold of Stevie by the front of his checked shirt and used it to pull him to his feet. Taking one of his arms, he twisted it behind his back at what looked like a very painful angle, forcing it up so high that we all heard the pop and crack it made when it dislocated from the socket.

Jessie didn't show an ounce of empathy for the kid who laid screaming in agony on the floor. He just bent down and helped me collect my stuff, walking me out of the gates and back home without saying a single word about what had happened.

Watching him hurt Stevie had made my skin shiver. It wasn't even what he'd done, which judging on the accuracy of his pressure and timing I could safely assume wasn't his first dislocation. But, the fact that during his assault I'd seen him smile for the first time since he'd come to live with Mama and me.

I'd never seen him look happy before that day. I'd been imagining it for so long, and it looked so good on him that I didn't care what had caused it. I wanted to see it again and again, even if that meant getting tripped by Stevie Fisher again tomorrow, and every day for the rest of my life after.

I'd known then that Jessie was different from other kids his age, and never doubted for a second that he would wear the same patch as my daddy someday. He was a natural Dirty Soul.

I scan my surroundings, and when I see no sign of Maddy hanging around outside I head in the house. A group of girls I take a business class with are hanging in the kitchen. They're nice enough, friendly and bitchy at the same time. But just because I hang out with them at college, doesn't necessarily make them my friends. They don't know me, I don't share any of my secrets with them, and I've never told them about Jessie. But I do enjoy laughing at their jokes and listening to their gossip. I also figure that gossiping alongside them stops them talking about me.

Maddy eventually rocks up about a half an hour later looking sickeningly stunning. All the boys ogling her like they're seeing her for the first time. I have to give her credit, she certainly looks different. She's decided to ditch the glasses and wears her hair wavy, flowing down her back. Even her outfit choice isn't terrible.

"Hey," she says nervously, as she approaches us. And I fix on a fake smile to greet her.

"Maddy, you made it... Wow, girl, you look awesome." I pathetically clap my hands together, causing her to smile back shyly. Then I waste no time taking her to get a drink. Time for the real party to begin...

Five drinks later and I'm starting to think the whole getting Maddy drunk plan could have gone better. For starters, I probably should have remembered to stay sober myself. I've enjoyed having fun far too much. Now, the music beating in my head doesn't match the rhythm of the moves my body makes, and I'm a sticky, sweaty mess. I need fresh air, so I grab Maddy off the coffee table that she's using as a stage and drag her out the house on to the porch.

The fresh outdoor breeze hits me with a rush that makes me even giddier than I'd been inside.

Both of us stumble, bouncing off each other's shoulders as we head for the porch swing and sit down beside each other. We're still giggling over Rachel Kelly's attempt to slut drop backfiring massively, resulting with her on her ass, legs in the air —bad night to forget your panties Rachey.

It hurts to admit, but after a few drinks Maddy is kinda fun, not at all what I'd been expecting, but I'm happy to roll with it. At least it will make the whole fake friend's fiasco a damn sight easier. I notice two guys who were checking us out earlier conveniently make their way out after us and when one of them nods over, I see an opportunity and decide to grab it by the balls.

Without looking I know Jessie will be watching from his truck, he promised Daddy he'd keep his eye on me. There would have been a list of rules, and keeping drunk, touchy-feely boys away from me would be right on the top of it. Jessie isn't known for his tact when getting a message across.

I throw the blonde one a friendly smile, and it doesn't take long for him and his mate to make their way over. Time for Maddy to meet Prince Charming.

Or not.

I talk to blondie, ask him how college football is going, then act as if I'm fuckin' interested when he tells me. He talks crap, and I pretend to listen, waiting for Jessie to strike. His friend sits next to Maddy and doesn't waste any time making a move on her. She gets up from the swing and moves towards one of the porch columns, I'm guessing in an attempt to get away from him, and I can't blame her if he's anywhere as dull as his friend is.

He follows her, leaving a space beside me for blondie to sit down, which he immediately takes advantage off. I look down at his hand when it squeezes my knee, and it makes me smile. It won't be long now.

Blondie must have mistaken my smile for encouragement because his hand starts to travel a little higher.

"You got a beautiful smile ya know," he whispers in my ear, and my body jolts when I hear metal slam on metal. Looking up, I'm not surprised that it's come from Jessie's truck door and all the smugness fades from my smile when I see how angry he looks. Suddenly I panic that I may have gone too far as Jessie paces across the lawn, his jaw tensed tightly, his mouth scrunched into a snarl that would rival a wild animal's.

My heart sinks to the pit of my stomach when he gets closer. Not just because the murderous look in his eyes isn't on blondie next to me, or the fact that he's marching straight towards the guy who now has Maddy pinned against the column. It sinks because of what I don't see, the part of him that's now missing. Jessie Donavon has taken off his cut… and he's done it for her.

CHAPTER 9

JESSIE

I watch Maddy arrive from the truck, she's alone and totally overdone, but at least her dress has more fabric to it than Hayley's does. Her hair is loose and reaches all the way down to her waist. It's the first time I've seen it that way and I like it a whole fucking lot. She looks real nervous walking along the sidewalk, stopping hesitantly as she approaches the party. At one point I think she might back out, but she manages it all the way to the front door, stopping when she gets there to chew her thumbnail before knocking. I can't believe what I'm seeing, the door is already wide open, the party has spilled out on to the front yard, and yet there she is knocking at the fucking door, bitch is somethin' else.

I shake my head, and laugh at how cock twitchingly cute she is.

Some girl drags her inside the house, and I sit back and fight all my urges to take Hayley up on her offer and go in after her.

I distract myself by trying to get my head around the latest shit we have with the Bastards. We still have no idea how they are managing to undercut our deals, and it's becoming a real pain in our asses. Things have only just started to cool down between our clubs, since we'd got our retaliation for what happened to Mary-Ann. Unlike them, we didn't kill women and children, so it was six of their soldiers that had to pay the price, and with almost half their Charter taken out, they'd been no real threat to us for some time now.

Recently, things were heating up again. They're starting to rebuild in numbers, and I have no doubt in my mind that there's a lot more than luck behind their sudden run of good fortune. They are managing to outbid us on deals with the Russians, deals we were already scrimping our asses on just to stay in the game. So how they were coming in with higher bids and still making money doesn't add up in my head. Something is coming, something big. I can feel it brewing like a midsummer storm, and I don't like it one bit.

It's been a few hours since I've seen or heard from Hayley. The party doesn't look like it's out of hand, but I'm starting to have enough of playing childminder. I'm fed up of watching lame ass teenagers who can't hold their liquor spew into bushes, I should be with my brothers, drinking and dipping into pussy.

I take out my cell ready to text Hayley and tell her it's time to leave. Then notice them both stagger out the house, two drunk messes using each other as a prop before they slump on a porch swing, giggling like pair five-year-old girls.

It feels good seeing Hayley connect with someone other than me, she's always so quiet around other people, but then I only ever see her at home, where she's kinda sanctioned away from everyone else.

I can't decide if she's generally having a good time with the girl or if this is all a part of her devious plan. If she's acting, she's scary good. I watch the girls for a little longer, both of them contrasts of each other. One blonde the other brunette, Maddy shy even in her drunken state. While Hayley seems to ooze confidence.

Some guys headed over to them and start trying to hit them up. I look on as Hayley chats to one of them, clearly enjoying the blonde guy's attention. I remind myself that she's a teenage girl and this is the sort of shit she should be doing. Not spending her evenings alone in her daddy's lodge. Maybe I could talk to Prez, see if he can loosen her reigns a little. She's eighteen now, how long does he expect us to shelter her for?

The taller one of the guys tries sliding his arms behind Maddy, and she shrugs him off politely. Clearly, she's not interested, even I can see that and from all the way over here. Which makes me wonder why the fucker still ain't getting the hint himself and continues to get in her personal space. She stands up and stumbles clumsily to the other side of the porch. Resting against one of the wooden posts that are keeping the porch roof up she fumbles through her bag, eventually taking out her phone.

She's tipsy, I can tell from the way her eyes are squinting to focus on the screen.

Mister can't-take-a-fucking-hint struts over to her, stretching out his arms to lean on the pillar she's using as a prop and caging her body between them. She looks uncomfortable, especially when the guy's hand moves up and begins playing with the loose strands of hair that falls around her face.

I want to kill him for it.

Slowly, and with something blunt.

She closes her eyes, and for a moment I wonder if she's gonna let him kiss her. It sets all my rage bubbling to the surface, and it only shimmers slightly when she pushes his hand away and makes it even clearer that she isn't interested.

The stupid fucker seals his fate when he decides to take her wrists, pinning them to the pillar behind her, then forces his lips hard on to hers. I see the way her tiny body struggles against him, her free hand pushing at his chest, and I'm done watching.

Shrugging out of my cut, I quickly tuck it under my seat. Hayley's right, the girl would run for days and not look back if she knew what I am, now isn't the time for that. She's been scared enough by the jack ass who's currently trying to force his tongue into the back of her throat.

I jump out of the truck and march across the street, on to the lawn, and right up to the son of a bitch. I vaguely hear Hayley scream my name, but it's drowned out by the blood pumping red-hot through my ears.

I pull back my elbow, ready to pound my fist into the asshole's face, who by now has at least had the sense to pull far away enough from Maddy to see me coming. Before I set hell free, I make the mistake of looking at her, and something makes me pause.

I've never been this close to her before, and her big, bright eyes are all the more fascinating up close. Clenching my fists tightly at my side, I attempt to cool myself the fuck down, I don't want her to see me like this. A merciless monster who feeds on pain and is starved of a fight.

I planned on having the guy eat the top step of the porch, my boot seated firmly into the back of his head, but the innocence in her pretty little eyes seem to plead with me not to hurt him.

"I think the girl made it clear that she ain't interested." I struggle hard against the instinct to hurt, and manage to get the words out through my teeth. The fucker shows his gratitude by folding his arms and shooting me a 'whatever' face that tests every single one of my restraints.

"Seriously you should just go," Hayley tells him, her voice coming with a warning from behind me, that, and the glare I'm giving him should tell him that listening to her would be a really fucking smart idea. The pussy backs the fuck off, grabbing his beer from the porch and gesturing with his head for his mate to follow him into the house.

I stare him all the way back into the party, the guy's pride will be a little dented, but he's come out lucky. I look back at Maddy, her eyes dancing over me in shock, I feel them prickle my skin. She opens her mouth, like she's about to say something but suddenly stops, the color fades from her face and her eyes expand in horror.

"Oh god, I think I'm gonna throw up," she manages to stutter, slamming her hand over her mouth and quickly spinning around just in time to aim over the porch and into the flower bed. I throw a look at Hayley who's already snorting with laughter, but abruptly stops when she stumbles herself. She's in just as bad a state as Maddy, but at least she's managing to keep it down.

"Come on, I'll get you girls home," I say, pulling Hayley by the wrist and scooping Maddy's tiny waist up in my arm, her limp body tucks perfectly into mine as I try to keep both girls moving towards the truck. In her drunken state, I don't think she realizes that she's leaning against me, and my fingers twitch against the fabric of her dress, so close to feeling how smooth her skin is beneath it.

I manage to get them to the truck and hate having to let her go so I can open the door. Still, I can't risk letting go of Hayley, who is most definitely a flight risk. She's been protesting and trying to pull her wrist from my grip since I dragged her off the porch, I've just been too distracted by touching Maddy to really notice. I guide Maddy, on to the back seat of the truck, and her body launches itself forward across the seat, unintentionally pushing that peach perfect ass right up in front of me. I moan out loud and hope the pair of them are too drunk to notice.

"Ouch you're squeezing me too tight," Hayley complains. Trying to wriggle her wrist free. I ignore her, pushing Maddy further into the truck and managing one handed to get her in an upright position, so I can buckle her in.

Slamming the door, I take a deep breath before attempting to get Hayley into the passenger seat. She pulls stubbornly out of my grasp and tries to straighten herself out, brushing me off and insisting on getting in the truck by herself. So I let her, immediately having to catch her again when she slips on her heel and starts to fall backwards. She giggles, and I roll my eyes before helping her into the truck, this time she doesn't protest.

When I eventually get behind the wheel myself, I realize I

have no idea where Maddy lives, and I doubt Hayley's in any fit state to ask her.

"Hey darlin', where we headin'?" I turn around to ask, Maddy's head is rested back against the seat and her eyes are already closed.

"Granderville Street, 279," she manages in a sleepy whisper.

"Pssst. Nice area," Hayley says with a laugh that spills straight out of her nose. Granderville Street is in the roughest part of town, and I'm a little shocked myself, I didn't think anyone from around there would have the funds to send their kids to the college Hayley goes to. Fees are high, unless she'd gotten herself a scholarship, which would mean she's super smart. Looking at Hayley I shake my head sharply, there's no need for her to say out loud what we both were thinking, even if Maddy has already fallen asleep in the back.

"Lost your cut, rider?" Hayley asks, her eyebrows raise and a sarcastic grin spreads right across her drunken face. Shaking my head, I avoid the question by starting the engine. I don't have the tolerance to deal with her shit right now, and I'm still debating whether or not to go back and teach the guy who put his hands and mouth on Maddy the lesson he deserves.

"So much for prying it from your cold, hell-ridden body." She laughs, and although I try to ignore them, her words hurt. I've never been ashamed of who I am or my club before. I've worn my cut with pride since the day I got it. My eyes lift from the road up to the rear-view mirror. Maddy is sleeping peacefully, her forehead pressed against the window.

I'd already come to terms with the fact I'm bad news for a girl like Maddy Summers, but tonight's proved something I hadn't expected. Turns out, Maddy Summers is real fuckin' bad for me too.

CHAPTER 10
HAYLEY

I wake up to no less than five messages of apology from Maddy. Apparently, she also feels like she's died, and since I'm playing host to a banging headache myself I struggle to find sympathy for her.

I still play nice though, and when she asks if I want to meet her in town for lunch later, of course, I take her up on her offer. She's my new best friend after all.

When I finally manage to haul my ass out of bed and into the kitchen, I'm greeted with the smell of bacon and Jessie's handsome smug face waiting at the breakfast table.

"Mornin'..." His eyes give me a once over. "...Pretty girl." his cocky smirk alerts me to the fact that I probably look like I've just been resurrected. I realize that the annoying black thingy catching the corner of my eye is one of the fake eyelashes I must have been halfway through peeling off when I collapsed on to my bed last night. Tugging it off, I toss it into the trash before attempting to flatten down my unruly bed hair.

"Made you breakfast." His eyes move to the plate of bacon and eggs laid at my place at the table.

"Thought you might wanna line your stomach," he says, shoveling a fork full off his own plate and into his mouth.

"I don't know why you're looking so smug, I didn't do anything last night that you and your friends don't do every night in that filthy clubhouse of yours," I remind him, picking up my fork. Christ, the smell of the food alone was making me wanna vom.

"Difference darlin', is that I can handle it." He laughs as he gets up from the table, putting his plate in the sink then moving towards the door.

"Wait where are you going? I was gonna ask if you would take me into town, I'm meeting Maddy..." He stops at the mere mention of her name, then turns around slowly.

"Sorry. No can do, Prez called church. Last night while I was playing babysitter some shit went down with—" Realizing he's about to divulge too much he stops himself mid-sentence.

"Well I've made plans." I cross my arms over my chest. I'm doing this for him, the least he could do was help me out.

"Then I'll get Nyx to take you." He smiles cleverly.

"If Daddy let me have a car I could take myself. I have a license, remember."

"You're lucky your daddy lets you take a poopy by yourself, princess." He laughs again. As he turns to leave I pick up an apple from the fruit bowl and launch it, aiming for his head. He snatches it from the air like he's something from the matrix, rubbing it against the leather of his cut before crunching his teeth through it on his way out the door.

I wait to hear his bike pull off before I scrape my breakfast into the bin. I didn't want to be ungrateful, but there's no chance I could stomach it. What I need is a shower and a magical cure for a hangover, because this afternoon I'm gonna need to be on my game.

Nyx picks me up an hour later. I have no problem with him, other than the fact he isn't Jessie. He's around the same age as me, maybe a little older, and undoubtedly handsome with muscles in all the right places and beautifully chiseled features.

Nyx has an edge about him, a darkness that keeps him inside his own head that I imagine would be violent if unleashed.

Our car journey is silent, apart from the mumble he gives me when I get out to say he'll pick me up at 2pm. That gives me three hours with Maddy. Three hours which hopefully I can use wisely.

I meet her in a cute little coffee shop in town. The exact sort of place you'd expect to find someone with a name like Maddy Summers. It's bright, clean, and decorated with pastel colors. I order myself a black coffee because I heard that's what people drink when they're hungover.

It tastes like piss. Bitter and lukewarm. Not that I've ever tasted piss before, but if I ever do I imagine it will taste just like this coffee.

Maddy sits opposite me, her hair loosely tied on top of her head, wearing not a scratch of makeup. She's clearly put no effort into her appearance, and it annoys me that she can still look so flawless. Just another reason for me to hate her.

She stirs her hot chocolate slowly, watching the creamy froth spin around the giant mug.

"So, on a scale from one to ten, how big a fool did I make out of myself last night?" She looks up and cringes.

"Well, you were sick in Mitchel Renton's Mom's shrubbery if that gives you a basic idea." I fake a giggle that seems to relax her a little.

"I feel like such an idiot. I've never drank before, now I know why. I feel like I have a brass band playing in my head. Thanks for getting me home safe. It was a good job your boyfriend showed up when he did." She smiles perfectly over the rim of her cup before she takes a sip.

"Jessie isn't my boyfriend," I correct her, feeling a little stabby when her eyebrows raise enough to suggest that she's pleased at that information.

"Sorry I just assumed." She places her cup back on the table gracefully. My god, conversation is dry with this one. It's time for me to liven things up a little.

"So, that guy last night. The one who jammed his tongue down your throat. He was hot, right?"

"I don't really do the whole boy thing…" she tells me timidly. I feel my smile widen all the way to my ears. Who would have thought, Maddy Summers into girls? "I mean what with school and everything I haven't really got time," she adds, shrugging her shoulders and pissing all over my excitement.

"So were your parents mad at you for being late? We tried to be quiet when we dropped you off. Didn't want to wake them," I casually delve for some information on the folks.

"My mom was at work, she's cool about stuff like that though. What about your parents? They cool too?" I'm surprised she even asked, everyone in town knows who my dad is and what happened to my mom.

"It's just my dad and me," I answer. "And yeah he's cool, just a little… overprotective."

Understatement of the century.

"I never knew my dad. He took off when I was a baby, so it's always just been Mom and me," Maddy admits, sounding a little sad.

"Well, that's one thing we have in common then," I say, taking her hand in mine. "Both of us have single parents." I take the opportunity to act up on this whole friendship thing, impressed at how naturally it comes.

"Yeah, it can be tough sometimes, my mom works a lot. She's not around very often, and I don't know if you've noticed, but I'm not exactly popular at college." Her finger traces around the rim of her mug as she speaks. "Why did you invite me to that party?" she asks me bluntly, like she's been trying to find the courage for some time. "You have a ton of friends, you didn't need me to go with you."

Shit, I hadn't prepared for this…

"None of those people are my real friends. Sure, they talk to me, and they hang out with me around campus, but none of them really know anything about me. I guess I just thought you and I could get to know each other a little better. You seemed lonely, and I guess deep down I am too." I'm shocked at the relief saying the words out loud brings me, especially when I realize just how accurate they actually are... I am lonely. I don't have anyone who I can call my real friend, apart from Jessie.

"Well, there's another thing we have in common." Maddy smiles warmly. "You wanna come back to mine? We can listen to some music, and you can teach me how to do that thing you did with your eye makeup last night. It looked hot."

"Yeah sure. Sounds good." I finish up my mug of lukewarm piss, and we leave the coffee shop together. Me, and my new best 'friend'.

We spend the afternoon hanging out at Maddy's, the place is small and very minimal. But it's neat and cozy. Her mom isn't there, and I wonder if she's gone back out to work again already. Figure she must work hard, being a single mom and putting Maddy through college.

Maddy's room is spotless, everything has its place, unlike my room which looks like it's been raided by Vikings. We listen to her music, and I take a look through her makeup bag, it's sparse to say the least, but I work with what's there. Maddy is one of those lucky girls that doesn't need makeup but damn, when she wears it, she pulls it off. When I tell her that, it makes her blush.

I find comfort in her modesty. Like if I wanted to, I could be myself around her. We chat about school and some of the other girls. She asks me again who Jessie is to me and I brush it off, not ready to tackle that one just yet.

She invites me back to hers after school on Monday, and by the time Nyx picks me up I'm battling to convince myself that I haven't actually just enjoyed myself.

Nyx's music blasts out from the speakers. Which I suppose is an improvement to the complete silence we had on the way here.

When we drive past the clubhouse, I notice that Jessie's bike is parked outside.

"You can just drop me here," I tell him, and he grunts pulling the truck to a halt for me to climb out. I thank him for the ride and don't get a response, but then I wasn't really expecting one either.

He at least waits for me to shut the door just before he takes off with a skid of dust that catches at the back of my throat and clouds my eyes. I head straight for the club doors. It's the middle of the day so Daddy's rules don't apply, and I want to give Jessie an update on how things with Maddy are going.

I'm distracted, brushing the dust off my jeans and not really paying attention to what's in front of me until my path is obstructed by something solid. I follow the tall structure all the way up, stretching my neck to see Troj towering over me.

He's tall and toned so tightly that you can't help but stare and appreciate. His long, brown hair hanging wet over his thick-set shoulders, and he's wearing nothing beneath his cut that's open at the front enough for me to appreciate all those perfectly defined chest and stomach muscles.

"Where ya headin', princess?" he asks me, his eyebrows raising. God, he's beautiful. That golden tanned skin and well-kept beard team up perfectly with his warm chocolate brown eyes.

Still not a scratch on Jessie though.

"I'm just looking for Jessie," I tell him, attempting a side step around him he immediately blocks me again.

"Now's not a good time," he tells me, any trace of a smile gone, his brows hooding his eyes.

"I'm heading on home, I can get someone to give you a lift. I look down at his hands, noticing the blood-stained T-shirt he has wrapped up in one fist and how the knuckles of the other are battered raw.

"Or you could give me a lift up?" I suggest, flicking my eyes over to his bike then back to him. I already know the answer, but it might distract him long enough for me to get inside.

"Nice try darlin', but I haven't got a death wish. I'll get Tommy to give you a ride."

"What happened to your hand?" I ask looking closer at his knuckles.

"Oh this," he looked down at them casually. "Just a scuffle, nothin' for you to worry about."

"Is Jessie okay?" I check because I get the feeling that shit has gone down and if I'm right, I can guarantee he'd have been right in the middle of it.

"Oh yeah, Jessie's just fine," Troj nods his head, the grin on his lips suggesting there's a lot more in his answer.

CHAPTER 11

JESSIE

I may come across as cool on the outside, but inside my blood is lava. Adrenaline is thumping too fast through my veins, like they might erupt under pressure.

Sat in the chair in front of me, arms tied behind his back, is the latest cunt stupid enough to fuck with our club. The guy may have a couple inches height on me, but that wasn't about to make shit all difference, not down here.

The basements that run beneath the club are soundproofed for good reason, reasons this fuckwit was about to find out for himself. We never ask Grimm to clean up down here. A prospect and a hosepipe do a decent enough job. I think it's a nice touch for our guests to see what's on the itinerary for their visit. Gives them something to think about while they wait for me to decide how I'm gonna fuck 'em up.

This guy is a stranger to us. None of us recall seeing him around before, but he wears a patch that we know well. Whether he's a new member or from one of their other Charters he's still one of them, and he'd been one of the three who tried breaking into our warehouse last night. That makes him our enemy. And down here enemies don't do so well.

The Bastards must have thought they got away with it, right up until a group of us stormed into one of their hangouts along route 24.

We could have taken any one of them, there were four of them sitting at the bar, but this asshole in front of me is the fucker who had shot at Thorne.

Thorne turned up to check on the warehouse last night when our watchman hadn't checked in. He caught the Bastards clearing us out and got shot by this piece of shit in the process. So this was the Bastard that we all decided was gonna turn rat, and I'm the one who gets to make him squeak.

"You wanna tell me your name?" I ask him, staying calm. He shakes his head, and that's fine by me, I don't need to know. He'll have a new name by the time I'm done with him. One that he definitely won't want anyone to know.

"Last night, you and your brothers decided you'd clean out our warehouse," I remind him, and the cocky shit smiles back at me like we're about to sit down to a fuckin' pot roast together.

If he thinks that kinda shit is gonna get to me, he's wrong.

Sitting down in the chair opposite him, I lean forward and rest my elbows on my knees.

"What I need to know, is how you knew where to find it?" I ask him, watching his lips pick up and spread into a laugh. His mouth is still full of blood, a few teeth short due to his introduction to Troj back at the bar.

We could have let him finish the job there and then, but we need information, and the way Troj takes care of shit leaves no time for talking.

Me? I have all the time and patience in the world. So, this fucker can laugh back at me all he wants.

I grin back at him, his optimism is as endearing as it is amusing. It even gives me an idea to use later. We'll see who's laughing after our first session.

Turns out one session was all I needed to make the rat squeak. Twenty minutes of waterboarding is all the fucking pussy could handle before he talked, and although what he had to say wasn't exactly useful in solving the bigger problem, I now know where our stash is being kept.

He splutters and chokes as I pour water over the soaked cloth, and I watch the fabric suck between his mouth and nostrils, finding amusement in his desperate gasps for air. It isn't quite as satisfying as slicing open his stomach and letting his intestines hang loose would be, but I always like to start off slow. It makes the build-up to the more extensive treatments more intense. And I admit to being a little gutted that he's given up so quickly.

Turns out the Bastards sent him and two others to get the last of our gun supplies, they somehow knew we were low and that we hadn't made any deals lately. He swore he had no clue how they knew, and I believed him. I've always been able to tell a lie from the truth. Another quality that makes me good at this shit. I do, however, find out where they are keeping the guns they got away with, and I have a hunch that if we move fast enough, we'll get them back. Maybe even score some of the Bastards' supplies in the process.

"You know I've tortured weedy little addicts who lasted longer than you." I laugh at him before slamming my elbow into his face.

"I've told you all I know. Now fuckin' let me go," he chokes, drawing the last of his strength.

"I'll be back." I crouch over him. "We still gotta talk about what you did to my friend."

Walking out the door I slam it behind me, pull my cut back on to my shoulders, and make my way upstairs to the club. It doesn't take me long to find Prez, he's drinking in the lounge bar with Chop and Skid.

"Fast work, blowtorch?" Prez asks clearly impressed at my timing.

"Nah he was much more of a water sports guy." I pull out a stool and look up for Tommy to pour me a shot of something strong.

"So, what's he saying?" Chop asks, tossing me a cigarette. I catch it, grab a lighter from my back pocket and light it up, taking a long drag before I answer.

"They know a lot of shit. Knew those guns were the last of our supply, and obviously knew where to find them. They're stashing them in a storage container at the scrap yard not far from their compound."

"He say where they're getting their info?" Prez stands up and leans on the bar beside me, tapping his glass on the bar for bitch boy to fill.

"He didn't know, and I believe him. How's Thorne?"

"Upstairs. Doc fixed him up, nothing major," Skid informs me as he slaps me on the back. "Good work kid."

"I'ma go check in with him." I down my shot of Jack in one swallow, slamming the glass back on the bar because I know how much it pisses Tommy off when we do that.

"Church in one hour, spread the word," Prez grunts, sending me off with a smack on my shoulder.

I climb the stairs to one of the rutting rooms on the second floor. The rooms are sparsely decorated, kitted out more for fucking in than to be used as an infirmary, but they do the job.

Thorne calls me in when he hears me knock.

"How ya doin?" I ask, taking a seat on the chair beside the bed.

"Been better. Doc stitched me up, said it ain't nothin' too serious. How about you, you get the Bastard talking?" I throw him an arrogant look back.

"Course ya did." Thorne winces when he starts to laugh.

"You still got the slug?" I ask.

"Yeah, Doc took it out. I think it's over in that bowl." His head gestures to the silver bowl on the bedside table, and sure enough laying amongst the gauze and bloodstained bandages is a small silver bullet. I pick it out and roll it between my fingers, before flipping it in the air and catching it again.

"What you want with that?" Thorne asks looking confused.

"Just making sure I return it to its rightful owner for ya brother." I wink, leaving him to get some rest.

When I open the cell door. The Bastard looks up hopefully.

"I've spoken to Prez, and he's satisfied with what you've told us, we're gonna let you go home," I inform him, watching hope glint in the eye he's capable of opening. The fucker's covered in his own vomit, his face cracked and bruised, and he still manages a smile. I love an optimist

"Almost forgot. Thorne asked me to return this." I pull the bullet from my back pocket and hold it up between my finger and my thumb so he can see it, and I watch all that hope drain right off his face. I take a step closer, and he shakes his head in a silent, pitiful plea.

"Wwwwatcha gonna do with that?" he asks, a tremble in his voice. I don't reply, just smile back at him as I take a tuft of his hair and wrench back his head. I force my fingers into the back of his throat, and naturally the fucker tries to bite me. This isn't my first rodeo, so I pull his head back further, and push the hand I already have inside his mouth lower to stretch his jaw wider. After shoving the bullet as far down his throat as I can get it, I force his mouth closed, cupping my hand over his lips and pinching his nose shut at the same time, leaving him no choice but to swallow.

He wretches and struggles against his roped restraints, but

eventually he gives in and swallows down the bullet he used to shoot Thorne.

"Prez wants you to get a message back to your brothers. You fuck with Dirty Souls, we hit back twice as hard."

"I will, I'll tell them I promise, just let me go," he pleads, and I smile taking the knife out of my boot and pressing the tip of the blade against his skin. I make a neat little dimple in the side of his cheek, and watch beads of sweat roll from his forehead and drop onto my blade. Edging the tip a little deeper into his flesh I let it pierce the skin, sticky blood trickling onto the knife and merging with his sweat.

I take my time, slowly moving the smooth edge of the knife down and resting it between the corners of his lips, giving the fucker a taste of his own blood.

"You like to smile, right?" I check, and when fear prevents him from giving me an answer. I answer for him, slicing the blade from the crease of his mouth and tearing it up through the flesh of his cheek all the way up to his ear.

He cries out in agony, and I give him the same treatment on the opposite side of his face, gifting him with a smile he can take all the way to hell with him.

His eyes bulge, and tears stream out, dripping into his open wounds and stinging him with more torture. He chokes, blood spraying all over my shirt. But I'm not done. Not yet.

I continue to use my master craftsmanship to engrave his forehead with his new name, RAT.

He tries to speak. Maybe to beg? Who the fuck knows? The wide gashes on his face prevent him from forming any words, leaving him with just pitiful sounds.

Lucky for this one, I don't have a lot of time, church is in less than an hour. So he'll be blessed with a quick death. I contemplate how to do it, I could slit the fucker's throat, end his life in the same way I took my first, the night I'd saved Hayley's life. But that shit makes a lot of mess.

So taking his chin in one hand and the back of his neck with the other, I twist my shoulders, forcing it all the way around until I hear a snap and feel his head fall limp in my hands. Then I let him go, his lifeless head slumping forward. Using the Bastard's shoulder to wipe my blade clean I step over to the far side of the basement and scratch another tally line into the wall. With the knife tucked back into my boot I sit on to the floor, forgetting about the blood soaking my fingers as I run them through my hair. My breathing begins to regulate again, my heart starting to calm and beat to a normal rhythm. I stare right through the body of the man whose life I've just taken, and for a few seconds I see him again…

His face is covered with what looks like a ski mask, and he stands tall and big over my pa's body. It's hard to make much out through the thin wooden slats of the wardrobe door, but I see how he kicks my pa to check that he's dead. I wonder why he bothers, even back then at that young age I knew that a bullet to the brain was foolproof. My pa isn't gonna be jumping up and fighting back anytime soon.

The man left as quickly as he came but I still can't move from my spot in the wardrobe. Probably through fear, maybe shock, or the fact that my PJ bottoms were stuck to my legs from where I've pissed myself. I stay put, staring on at my pa's body and watching it grow colder. His lips turning the same shade as the cheap motel carpet. The only person I had left was gone, forever. Night turned to day. Sunlight eventually creeping through the curtains and lighting up the dingy room again.

Yet I still sat and waited, I wasn't quite sure what for, or even if I really wanted whatever it was to come. I was lost. And in those lonely hours, I didn't think I wanted to be found again.

A loud bang on the cell door shakes me from my dark memory. I stand up and manage to gather my shit together just before Skid walks in. He takes one look at the slumped body that's still tied to the chair in the center of the room. "Hell's fucked, take it you're finished?" He laughs getting a closer look at what I've done to the Bastard. I nod, walking over to the rusty basin to wash my hands.

"Didn't wanna keep ya waiting, so I made it quick," I tell him, lifting the cigarette packet from my inside pocket, sliding one between my lips then offering one out to Skid.

"Nah. I'm good." He shakes his head

"You quit?" I ask, surprised, Skid is never without a smoke.

"Me and Carly are… trying." He smiles awkwardly. "Apparently smoking slows down your swimmers."

I don't mean to laugh, but that shit sounds too funny coming from him. Still, I'm not surprised. Skid looks like a mean assed fucker, tall and broad, with a black beard as solid as his loyalty, but he's softer than any of us. He's never hidden the fact that his old lady means everything to him. And since Prez lost Mary-Ann, and half the club moved to safer Charters, he's been the only one of us around here who fucking had one.

"That's awesome." I slap him on the back. Skid would make a great Pa, when I first started hanging out at the club, he taught me everything I needed to know about bikes at the garage. Now he has Rogue under his wing, she's been hanging out at the garage since she was eight years old and has grown into a proper firecracker. No one really knows what her deal is, but it's obvious that Skid takes care of her, loves her like a little sister, perhaps even a daughter.

"Jess, do me a favor, don't mention it to the others."

"Sure thing, bro," I nod, taking another drag at my smoke. "Let's head for the table, I got plans for this piece of shit." I tip my head at the ever-smiling Bastard before we head out of the basement and up to where the air doesn't smell of blood and fear.

I don't have time to change before church, so I go as I am, ain't like any of the fuckers who sit around that table are squeamish and If we want to get our guns back, we're gonna have to act fast.

CHAPTER 12
HAYLEY

Neither Daddy nor Jessie come back to the lodge that night, but Jessie is waiting for me in the kitchen when I get up the next morning. Drinking a coffee and despite looking tired, he's still smokin' hot.

"For what do I owe this pleasure?" I ask sarcastically, grabbing the box of cereals and pouring them into a clean bowl. Jessie passes me the milk, and I soak the flakes before grabbing a spoon and digging in.

"C'mon I've been busy, with—"

"Club shit," I interrupt harshly before he has the chance finish.

"Yeah, Hay, with club shit. It's always gonna be my priority you know that," he says unapologetically.

"Story of my fucking life," I shrug. This club has been priority to everyone in my life, I'm used to coming second to it. Doesn't make me feel any better about it though.

Jessie must sense I'm upset because his voice turns softer.

"Look, your dad loves you. I know he can be a little overprotective, but after what happened to…" His jaw clenches, we never talk about Mama or what happened that night. "…Well you can't exactly blame him, especially since we nearly lost you too." A tense silence settles between us and I smile when I realize he'd used the word we. Jessie has missed my point entirely though. Yeah, the fact my daddy never lets me do standard teenage stuff bugs me, but not as much as the fact that he never spends any time with me.

"Come on, eat up and I'll give you a ride to school," Jessie breaks the silence first, finishing up his coffee while I quickly eat the rest of my breakfast.

We head down the hill and past the club, continuing down the dirt track that leads to the main road, and I notice a cop car pull off the road heading towards us. Jessie shifts the truck over to let it pass then rolls down his window and tips his head.

"Beautiful day ain't it, chief?" He smiles at the officer. "What brings you out here?"

"Mornin' Jessie, heard there was some trouble over in a bar near Pueblo yesterday, wondered if any of you knew about it?" he asks, his eyebrows raised suspiciously. Jessie smirks, his head shaking slowly.

"You're gonna have to speak to Prez about that." Jessie winks. "Head on up, he fell asleep in one of the rooms upstairs last night, you'll find him at the clubhouse. Maybe Jill might cook you something up for breakfast." The officer rubs his lips together greedily, then with a small salute of his fingers pulls off and continues on the track up towards the club.

I recognize him, he's the only law person that's ever brave enough to come on the compound, and he seems friendly with the guys too. If I've managed to figure out that what goes on around here is far from legal, I'm sure he has too.

"Was that trouble something to do with you?" I ask Jessie.

"What do you think, darlin'?" He glances at me out the corner of his eye.

"I saw Troj yesterday afternoon. I was trying to find you when I got back from Maddy's, he looked like he'd been in trouble."

"You don't need to worry, pretty girl." Jessie's face turns a little more serious as he shakes me off.

"Yeah but that cop must know stuff, he's always sniffing around the club." I'm not gonna give up that easy. Jessie should know that by now.

"Roswell's kinda on our side." Jessie shocks me almost silent.

"What?" my voice comes out a squeal, and he laughs at my reaction.

"Your dad's a clever man, Hay. We've always kept our trouble out of town, and if we hear about anyone else bringing any in, we eliminate the problem. And more effectively than the local PD would be able to."

"So, you guys kind of run town?" I've always known that people fear the club, I never realized how much power they actually had.

"Sure do, pretty girl." Jessie treats me to that boyish smile that never fails to make me melt, and he lets me take control of the music while he drives me to college. Now feels like a good time to bring up Maddy.

"You can tell Daddy I won't need a ride home until later tonight, I'm going to Maddy's after school."

"You sure that's a good idea?" he questions, stopping at the lights.

"Yeah, how else am I meant to find out about her for you?" I ask, watching his eyes roll.

"So what you got so far?" he gives in to curiosity.

"Okay." I twist my body to face his, wanting to see his reactions "So, her mom's single, no Dad in the picture. Mom clearly works hard, I'm guessing to pay Maddy's college fees. No siblings. Maddy is totally single and apparently doesn't do the whole boy thing. Oh, and she has shit taste in music," I reel off all I know just as he parks up on the curb outside campus.

"I'll get someone to pick you up from hers at seven."

"I'll call you when I'm ready," I tell him, and wait for the irritated smirk to make its way on to his face.

"Do you always have to be so damn awkward?" He lets out a long breath.

"Would you love me if I wasn't?" I tease, stepping out of the truck on to the sidewalk.

"Probably not."

I slam the door and rush off to join the group of girls that hover at the entrance. They all stare at Jessie as if he's some kind of god before he pulls away, and where I can't exactly blame them for looking, it still pisses me off.

Classes seem to go so slowly, and I have to admit to being ever so slightly looking forward to hanging out with Maddy. We arranged to meet outside the entrance, and I get there before her. To pass some waiting time, I take out my phone and do my usual scroll through social media. I don't take much notice of what's going on around me, but I do catch a glimpse of the guy who'd hit on Maddy Saturday night when he passes with some of the football team. I try not to stare too hard, but when I see the state of his face, my jaw goes slack.

One of his eyes is forced shut due to swelling, his bottom lip split, and his right arm is cradled by a sling. Whoever got to him had done a good job, and I don't have to think too hard or for too long about who it might have been. Blondie who had talked to me at the party notices me looking over, and when my eyes meet his, he quickly avoids them.

"Hey," I hear Maddy's voice call from behind me, and I turn to see her prancing down the steps. Her ponytail bobbing on top of her head and eyes full of enthusiasm to see me.

"God, today has dragged... Come on let's get out of here," she says, wrapping her arm into mine and leading us off campus. And I pretend to myself that I didn't notice not having to fake the smile I give her back.

We walk the short distance to her house, talking about mindless stuff, the sort of shit that isn't gonna help my plan but will build the pretense of friendship. She asks me about the club and for some reason I don't lie to her like I do to everyone else. I tell her how I get left out of everything and how I don't get to go down to the club unless there's a *family event*, which was rare. She still seems impressed.

"So what are they like? The bikers, are they really as bad as everyone says?" she asks as we get closer to her house

"Honestly? They're probably the most dangerous, vile men you'd ever have the displeasure of meeting, but to me, they're just my daddy's friends." I shrug. It's boring, but it was the truth. I've spent the last four years living among them, but I still don't know anything about them. Other than Jessie, Skid is about the only one that speaks to me, and that's only because Carly invites me over to their cabin for dinner sometimes.

I hear music as we step onto Maddy's street, and I'm surprised when I realize the music is coming from her place. We follow the noise through the front door and into the kitchen where we're greeted by a tall, thin woman, who pulls a large pot out of the oven. Her red curly hair is piled high on top of her head, and I'm taken back by how she's dressed. The skirt she wears is far too short, her huge tits are crammed so tight into her vest top that they spill over, and she wears so many bangles on her wrist that she jangles when she moves.

"Oh hey, girls." She smiles wide. "I gotta go to work. Made you a little something for dinner later... You must be Hayley." She looks me over as she places the pot on the counter, then pulling off her oven mitts, grabs me for an unexpected hug.

"I'm Marilyn, Maddy's mom. I've heard so much about you." I glance over her shoulder to Maddy, whose face is glowing redder by the second.

"Pleased to meet you too, Mrs. Summers," I manage, her hug crushing me so tight I can hardly breathe.

"Oh, Marilyn, please. Mrs. Summers makes me sound old." She stretches out her arms, holding me in place so she can examine me. "You're beautiful…" she declares before letting me go again.

Grabbing her bag, she roots around inside it, eventually pulling out a pocket mirror and a lipstick. "Look I really have to go." She quickly draws the lipstick across her lips then snaps the mirror shut. "You girls help yourself, and be good," she warns, popping her lips together before slinging the bag over her shoulder and bursting out of the door like a mini tornado.

I look from the door and then back to Maddy, who is awkwardly chewing her thumbnail.

"Your mom's really cool," I tell her, unable to disguise the shock in my voice. Maddy turns down the sound system before responding with a half-smile and a shrug.

"Yeah, she's fun I guess."

"Where does she work?" I ask Maddy as she leads us up the stairs to her room.

"She's in sales." Her voice is almost snappy, and the uncharacteristic sharpness tells me that she's keeping something from me. Something that I know I'll get out of her eventually, just like I would everything else.

We spend the rest of the afternoon gossiping and listening to more of Maddy's shitty music. When I finally manage to get us onto the subject of boys, the atmosphere shifts to borderline uncomfortable, but I push past it.

"So what's the furthest you've ever got?" I flop front first on to her bed and grab one of her fluffy pink cushions.

She's sat across from me with her legs crossed looking embarrassed.

"I haven't," she answers, looking down to where her fingers twiddle the laces of her converse.

"What not even a kiss?" I ask, surprised. Sure, Maddy isn't exactly popular, but as much as it kills me to say, she is gorgeous. Even I know that it's criminal for her to have never been kissed. I decide not to share that the furthest I've ever got myself is watching Jessie get his cock noshed by one of the club sluts. Maddy will assume, like everyone else, that I am beyond experienced in that department and I, of course, will let her.

"Not even a kiss," she confirms. "I always figured it would happen when the right guy came along, and that hasn't happened yet. I want it to be special... No offense," she quickly adds. Assuming.

"None taken," I shrug it off. "Is that why you didn't kiss the guy at the party?"

"I didn't kiss the guy at the party because he was a jerk..." she tells me flatly, and we both giggle.

"I guess I don't see the point in kissing someone just for the sake of it. I want it to be with the right guy. Everyone remembers their first kiss, right?" She moves off the bed changing the subject before I can press for more.

"So, what should I wear to Katie's party Saturday? Figured now that I'm hanging out with you I'm sure to get an invite." Her eyes roll, and I laugh again, but only half-heartedly. Her words from before are still stinging. The only guy I've ever imagined kissing is Jessie. He's the only guy I've ever wanted to. It's looking more and more unlikely that I ever will. I try to shake off the constricting feeling crushing at my chest, brought on by the thought of only ever watching. It might never be me.

I smile at Maddy, containing the tears that threaten my eyes as I watch the girl in front of me. Wiggling her ass to crappy music, comfortable, carefree, and completely unaware that she holds the potential to have everything I ever wanted. Then I piss myself off by thinking that the more time I'm spending with her, the harder it's becoming to hate her for it.

CHAPTER 13
JESSIE

Everything went to plan last night when we raided the Bastards' storage container. We cleared the lot, taking back what was ours, and a whole lot that wasn't.

We did leave them with something though. The mangled body of their rat, propped against the wall of the now empty storage container. It was a clear enough message that trying to fuck us over was a real bad idea.

Despite the success of our evening, I can't shake off the feeling that something isn't right. They still have a source of information, and I know this is far from over.

Roswell is still at the compound when I get back from dropping off Hayley. We all know how important keeping him onside is, not having the law constantly on our backs is critical to keeping things running smoothly around here. It helps keep ATF off our backs too. Now that the Bastards' shit is popping up in Manitou Springs, Roswell is getting curious about what we plan to do about it.

"We're workin' on it," Prez tells him, sipping at his expresso and rubbing his temples. We all celebrated a little too hard last night when we got back to the compound, turns out what the Mexicans supply to the Bastards was pretty good.

"We just had a few problems of our own to take care of."

"I get that Jimmer, but I have people to answer to, and those people are starting to climb down my neck. Manitou Springs has always managed to keep drugs out of town, and all of a sudden we're getting more and more reports. Teresa Monroe's boy had to have his stomach pumped two nights ago. So now she's on a one-woman mission to resolve the drug problem in town herself. You guys don't need me to spell it out to you where everyone's gonna assume that shit's coming from."

"I hear ya, and be assured my boys are onto it." Prez reaches behind the bar and slams down one of the blocks we took from the Bastards' lock up last night.

"As you can see, we've already worked on shortening the supply."

Roswell smirks. "You know I should really take that in for evidence."

"Nah-ah," Prez shakes his head. "Finders keepers." He returns the block to where it came from, and Roswell shrugs his shoulders.

He gives us some details of the incidents that have been reported, and we promise to take care of it. When he stands up to leave, I walk with him to the door. I like Roswell, despite the fact he's a cop. When the last chief retired five years ago, the club worried we'd lose our relationship. But Roswell proved he was a sensible guy and decided to follow in his, very successful, predecessor's footsteps. It made his job a hella lot easier to work with us, rather than against us.

I see him out to his patroller and watch him pull off just as Screwy and Squealer cross the yard from the garage. Squealer raises his arm to Roswell and Screwy tips his head in a recognition that could easily be missed.

"What he want?" Squealer follows him out the yard with his eyes, chewing on the toothpick between his teeth. Squealer holds suspicions of anyone with a badge, even the ones on our side.

"Just came to see what we're doing 'bout the drug situ in town," I assure him. "Surprised to see you boys up so early, especially after last night." When I'd left last night, they'd both still been balls deep. Screwy was hanging out the back of the slut with all the tattoos, while his twin tested out one of the new hangouts.

"We're heading in to see Tac at the studio," Squealer speaks for them both.

"You got any more fuckin' space?" I look them both over, the pair of them are covered with ink. It's the only way to tell them apart.

"I reckon I got a good eleven inches," Squealer grabs his crotch and winks, I choke a laugh back at him. Screw's face doesn't change, but then I don't expect it to.

The twins get on their bikes, and I head over in the direction they came from. I stop by the garage and check in with Chop. He looks busy, and just as I'm about to offer to get greasy, Skid pulls up with Carly on the back of his bike. She gets off and he tugs at her tiny waist then kisses her with a whole lotta feeling, same way he always does. She waves over to me and Chop, before heading into the clubhouse.

Anyone can see that Skid's crazy about her, she's the only bitch, aside from Hayley, who gets any respect around here. Skid would fuck up anyone who didn't show it.

After bringing the boys up to date with Roswell's visit, I carry on up the dirt track and stop off at the gym. By gym, I mean the large outhouse that's filled with weights and equipped with a full-sized fighting ring. It's nothing fancy, but it has everything we need.

"Been a while since your ugly face showed up in here," Troj shouts across at me. We're alone, except for Tommy, who's in the far corner, watching himself in the mirror, struggling to bicep curl a fuckin' 20.

"Prospect, go down the club, the sofas need a wipe down," I call over at him, I drop my voice to Troj, but make sure Tommy can still hear me. "Squealer went hard at it last night, slut splodge everywhere."

Tommy eyeballs me through the mirror. I'd be lying if I said I don't get enjoyment out of degrading the nasty little shit. Here, we're all assholes in our own right, but at least we're upfront about it. Tommy's slippery as snake shit, and I don't trust him one bit. "Do I look like a fuckin' cleaner?"

"You look like a fuckin' twonk wearing a prospect cut who needs to learn some fuckin' respect." I cold stare him, until he slams the dumbbell back on to the bench, and storms out of the gym.

"So seriously, what's got you here?" Troj asks, already starting to glove up.

"Figured you might want to get your ass kicked." I gesture my head towards the ring and watch Troj beam.

"Jesus loves a trier Jess, why the fuck not?" Lifting up the top rope he ducks under. I can tell by the way he's sweating that he's already done a full workout this morning. If he's tired, maybe I stand a chance.

I'm hoping that Troj might knock some sense into me. I know that while I'm fighting my mind won't be on Maddy, and my head really needs a break from her.

Who am I kidding?

Twenty minutes later, and we're both fucked. Of course, Troj gets the better of me, he gets the best of everyone. He's too fuckin' quick not too. I do manage to sneak a few good ones in, but it's been a pointless exercise, not even getting my skull pounded by Troj's thunder fists gets Maddy Summers out of my mind. I have to face facts, I'm jealous.

Hayley is spending time with her, and all I get is to hear about it. Even that fucking asshole at the party got more action than me. He touched her with his lips.

The fucker was lucky Maddy's pretty eyes had convinced me to let him walk away, but she wasn't there to save him after I dropped them both home and went back to the party. I wanted to drag him down to my cell in the basement, but instead, I gave him a warning. A broken arm, cracked rib, and smashed up face kinda warning.

Now isn't the time to be lettin' a bitch get under my skin, the club needs me thinking straight. Everyone has to be on their game, but there seems to be shit all I can do about it. With her, nothing seems like enough. I'll always want more.

I spend the rest of the day sleeping in my cabin, last night was a long one, and with all the shit going on I haven't been sleeping well. When I eventually wake up it's way past six, so I grab a shower, jump on my bike, and ride down to the club. I left my truck down at the club earlier, knowing Nyx would need it to fetch Hayley from Maddy's place later. And at seven-thirty when I get the call from Hayley to say she's ready, there's no sign of him anywhere.

I get in the truck and go for her myself. I'll be picking her up outside, doubt I'll even see Maddy, but I take my cut off anyway. I'm not on club business, so there's no need to wear it, or at least that's what I tell myself.

The whole way there I remind myself what a lousy idea this is… I should be trying to forget her. I could have sent Tommy or worked harder to find Nyx, and yet I continue to drive towards Maddy's house and when I get there, they're both sat waiting on her porch steps.

I almost choke on my own fuckin' breath at the sight of her. The simple white vest and short denim cut offs make her look incredible without even trying. Both girls stand up when they see me pull up, and I can't help staring as Maddy lightly dusts off her hands on her back pockets and follows Hayley over.

"Jessie!" Hayley looks surprised to see me.

"I thought Nyx was picking me up. I told Mads that he would give her a ride to church. Hope that's okay?" The fake smile she gives me is taunting as she leans through the open window.

Church, is she freakin' kidding me, and what was with the 'Mads' all of a sudden?

"Sure thing, *Mads*, jump on in." I place my arm over the wheel and lean forward, looking around Hayley to where Maddy's biting the nail of her index finger nervously. The girl's sweeter than honey, and it almost makes me feel bad for the things I imagine doing to her.

Almost.

She climbs into the back of my truck, and I twist to watch her buckle up. "So, church?" I let my eyes absorb her up, everything, from her soft golden hair to her perfect round tits, and I can tell she notices me looking by the rush of pink that flushes to her cheeks.

"Yeah, Monday nights they do this study group for the local kids. I help out," she explains, in a voice that's smooth and as pretty as she is. I wonder if it would still sound as sweet screaming my name while I slammed inside her.

Fuck.

I focus forward again, ignoring my cock when it grows uncomfortable against my jeans.

"Been up to much today?" Hayley asks, a sarcastic bite in her tone when she notices the absence of my cut again.

"Nothing special," I answer her with an equally fake smile, but eyes that warn her not to push. And for once in her stubborn little life, she does as she's told.

It's a short journey, that Maddy could easily have walked, but I'm pleased Hayley offered her a lift. I enjoy admiring her in the rear-view mirror. She's twitchy and fidgety and I all I can think about is sucking the color out of the bottom lip that she keeps grazing through her teeth.

"Thanks for the ride." She smiles up at me when I stop the truck.

"Welcome, darlin'," I tell her before she opens the door and steps out.

"See you at school tomorrow," Hayley sounds convincingly excited as she leans over me to say goodbye to her friend.

"Bye Hayley... Jessie." Maddy ever so slightly drops her head when she says my name, and I have to grip the steering wheel. Hayley at least waits until I've turned the truck before she reaches under her seat, pulls out my cut, and slams it hard into my chest.

"Safe to put this back on now." Her eyes roll.

"What? It's a hot day." Even I laugh at my pathetic excuse.

"You realize it's never gonna happen right? You just dropped the girl off at fucking church for Christ's sake."

"I go to church," I say through a smirk.

"I don't think you sing from quite the same hymn sheet." Hayley's arms cross over her chest. "Besides we spoke today about... you know."

"You've been friends less than a week, and you're already talking to her about sex? I thought nice girls were shy about that kinda shit."

"Well I'm not shy, and unlucky for you she is. She's a nice girl. So nice she hasn't even gone to first base." Hayley kicks her feet up on the dash. "Saving it all for that someone special apparently. Delusional is what I call it."

"That's sweet I guess." I lift my shoulders, conflicted. The thought of Maddy never even being kissed—not willingly anyway—makes me happy, but knowing that I ain't the kinda guy to ever be anyone's 'someone special' tears me up a little at the same time.

"Sucks for you though. I don't think this 'special guy'..."—Hayley's fingers make air quote's—"she's waiting on rides a Harley, drinks Jack like a whale takes on water, and sticks his dick into just about anything it'll fit in." She smiles, and I spend the entire way home pretending her words don't wound me.

Hayley seems disappointed when I drop her back at the lodge

and don't go in. Tonight I need to be at the club, the guys will still be celebrating last night's bust, and I need to forget.

Forget Maddy Summers. Forget that I'll never know what it feels like to be up inside her tight virgin pussy, or see how her cheeks flush pink when she comes on my cock. But most of all, I want to forget that with her, even that would never be enough.

CHAPTER 14

HAYLEY

Saturday night comes around quickly, I've hardly seen Jessie over the past few days and get the impression he's avoiding me. Nyx has been running me around, and well… he's just no fun at all.

I knew something was up when Jessie hadn't picked me up yesterday. Friday at Bernie's has been our thing ever since Mama died. I also know there's no chance of Jessie taking me to Katie's party, so I had to come up with a plan of my own.

I wait for the clubhouse to be in full Saturday night swing, then walk through the woods that line the compound. I find the hole in the fence that's just big enough for me to squeeze through, and meet Cobie and Dan on the main road. Cobie was happy to give me a ride, he's had a crush on me since middle school. So I flirted with him for a few days leading up to the party. He even agreed to pick up Maddy too.

No one from the club ever checks in on me at night, everyone's far too busy having fun, and Daddy rarely comes home to the lodge. It will be just as easy for me to sneak back in after the party.

I'm eighteen years old, no other girls my age have to have a chaperone, and life is too short to be stuck in by yourself on a Saturday night.

Everything has gone to plan, and we make it to the party without being caught. It feels good to be free. We drink and we dance, I'm nowhere near as drunk as I'd been last weekend, but I'm steadily getting there. Maddy looks stunning as ever and is clueless to the fact that she has the attention of every guy here. Tonight, she's being sensible and has decided to stay sober.

She disappears to use the bathroom and I carry on dancing by myself. When I feel hands rest on my hips, I let them touch me, and sway along with the rhythm of the music.

"You having a good time?" a voice whispers into my ear. I look over my shoulder at Cobie and nod, continuing to dance along with him.

"You want an even better time?" he adds, spinning me around to face him. His eyes stay on mine as he takes a small plastic baggy from his pocket and squeezes it open. I watch him take out a small round tablet and place it on his tongue, he pokes it out to show me before flicking his tongue back into his mouth and swallowing it down.

His eyes dare me to do the same, and without a second thought I opened my mouth and stuck out my tongue out for him. Cobie smiles a wicked smile, taking another pill out from the bag, and placing it on my tongue.

It tastes vile, so I swallow it fast, reaching out for a drink to wash away the bitter taste that clings to the back of my throat. Cobie chuckles as he passes me his beer, and I knock it back and then… wait.

At first, I wonder what the fuck Cobie has been talking about, I feel no different, he could have given me aspirin for all the good it's done, but after a few more songs I start to feel different, better, lighter. Fucking amazing.

The music gets louder, beating through my chest and synchronizing with my heartbeat. When Maddy returns she watches me suspiciously, but I carry on letting the beat of the music control my movements. I'm dancing on clouds, my body weightless. For once, I'm the one having fun, and any care that I ever had, seems to have been swallowed away with the magic pill Cobie has given me.

I feel her hand when she grips my wrist and laugh at her fierce yank when she drags me through the house to the bathroom.

"Wow, Hay, chill the fuck down you're sweating," Maddy says throwing me a towel. I pat it against my forehead and check my make up in the mirror, struggling to focus properly.

"Are you okay?" Maddy asks, concern all over her pretty perfect face.

"I'm fine. Why?"

"You just look kinda spaced that's all."

Her head falls to one side, and she studies me curiously.

I laugh at her again.

"I'm good," I assure her—not good, fucking amazing. I manage not to add that though. Not that I care what she thinks, tonight Hayley Carson answers to no one.

"Okay... So, I need to ask you something?" she starts nervously, resting her ass on the edge of the bath.

"Shoot," I try my best to sound serious, lifting my hair up from my sticky neck, it's so hot in here and the music is so loud that the walls are vibrating in unison with the bass.

"That guy, Jessie. Who is he?" she asks awkwardly.

"Jessie's... he's just Jessie," I shrug casually, missing out the part that Jessie is fuckin' everything, including the reason that my heart beats.

"He's kinda hot," she admits, biting her lip nervously while she waits for my reaction. "And... he seems really nice," she adds when I say nothing.

"Hmmm nice." I throw my head back and laugh like a Disney villain, and Maddy looks back at me confused.

"Jessie isn't who you think he is," I tell her. A sudden surge of jealousy starts to kill my buzz. I need to get the fuck out of this tiny room before the walls that are moving inwards close in on me completely.

I open the door and rush past the people in the hall, looking for Cobie. I don't care whether Maddy follows me or not. I can't listen to her gush about Jessie, not when I can't tell her how I feel about him myself.

Cobie's face lights up when he sees me walking towards him and when he places his hand on my waist and pulls me against his body, I let him.

"You feelin' good, baby?" he whispers inside my ear.

"I think, maybe you could make me feel better." I smile, sliding my hand into his pocket. And he nods when I pull out his little baggy. He takes another one of his pills out, popping it on to my tongue. This time I don't worry about how it tastes, my whole body hums with the bitterness. I let the music take over again, not caring about what happens around me.

Slowly, I start to care less and less about Maddy or Jessie. The music is my only focus, the only thing that matters is the next beat. Everything else I shut out. Maddy is trying to talk to me, yelling over the music, but I blank her out too. I can't remember how long it takes my brain to start fighting to escape my skull, but Maddy is still pulling at me trying to get me to go with her. I push her away, turn my back on her, and continue dancing with Cobie.

The room spins so fast I want to get off, and I tip my head back to look up at the ceiling. Something catches me, and the humidity of the room vanishes, replaced with a cool breeze that dances over my skin. I hear slamming, panicked voices, and the word 'hospital'. Voices in my head argue, and a girl cries, I wonder if it's me.

The ground stops moving under me, and I feel the breeze

again. Somehow my body moves without any work from my feet, and I fall on to something soft. I try to focus on something, anything other than the pounding in my head, but I can't. I want to leave, to escape the sinking feeling but I'm trapped. I can't get out of my body.

CHAPTER 15

JESSIE

The clubhouse is packed tonight, and everyone seems to be in a good place. I swear I even saw Grimm crack a creepy smile when I looked over at him earlier.

I'm still sober. Sober enough to grab Mel before Squealer gets to her. Fuck being the second man in after him. Bitch'll be lucky if she sits down after a week.

Mel is riding me like she's about to win the Kentucky fuckin' derby, but my head is in another place. Too busy wondering what Maddy is doing with her Saturday night.

Mel catches me off guard, moving in for my lips. I quickly lower my head, scraping my teeth against the tight skin at her neck until she cries out, and her pussy clenches my cock tighter.

"Jesus, Jessie," she moans, slapping her ass even harder against my thighs. My phone rings in my jean's pocket, and I stand up, managing to keep Mel still attached to the end of my cock. I slam her ass on to the basin unit, and take control of the thrusts as I pull my cell from my pocket. When I see it's Hayley calling, I crush my hand over Mel's mouth to stifle the whimpers she's making.

"Now's not a good time, pretty girl," I answer, trying to ignore Mel who's already started gnawing at my fingers like a rabid dog.

"Jessie, is that you?" The voice on the other end throws me

off, but I recognize it straight away, I may have only heard it a few times but was I fuck about to forget who it belongs to.

Words fail me as I thrust deeper and deeper into the drenched pussy sucking hungrily at my cock.

"Jessie, are you there? It's me… Maddy." My mouth dries up, and then in one single sentence, she finishes me.

"Jessie, please I need you."

Her voice is panicked and needy, and it sends me right over the edge. My cock juts and I offload. Mouth open, I only just manage to hold in the long moan as I empty out.

There isn't time for easing down, not when her voice blurts so desperately at me down the phone.

"Jessie… Please."

"I'm here," I say, pulling out of Mel and ripping the rubber off my still solid dick.

"Thank god. Jessie, I need you to come to my house. Right now." There's a shiver in her voice that has the hairs on the back of my neck standing to attention. "It's Hayley. I don't know for sure, but I think she may have taken something."

None of what she's saying makes any sense. But I don't question her, rushing out of the room and down the stairs. I keep the phone pressed to my ear hearing Maddy's panicked little breaths.

"I'm on my way, okay?" I hang up when I get to my bike, I hear a voice calling out from behind me, someone asking where I'm going but I ignore it. I don't have time for explanations, especially when I don't know what the fuck's happening myself.

I speed out of the compound as fast as I can. Not sure if I'm feeling more angry or worried as I make the journey to Maddy's house in record timing. Parking my bike on her drive, I storm straight inside without knocking.

"Hayley," I call through the house.

"We're up here," Maddy's shaky voice guides me upstairs, and I take them two at a time.

As soon as I see Hayley, I know she's taken something. Her eyes are practically rolling in her head, and the dopey smile on her lips is completely vacant.

"Fuck, what's she taken?" I barge past Maddy and scoop Hayley into my arms, her body a dead weight slouching against mine.

"Hayley, it's me, Jessie." I tap her cheek gently. "Hayley, what you take?" I shout, my taps becoming harsher when she doesn't answer me.

"How long's she been like this?" I look up to Maddy who's hand covers her mouth, terror sketched on her pretty little face. "Maddy, you need to tell me what she's taken." I don't mean to shout at her, but the girl is losing it.

"I… I don't know," she cries, her head shaking from side to side.

"Fuck's sake."

I take Hayley's limp body and throw her over my shoulder. "Where's the bathroom?" I ask, already moving towards her bedroom door.

"Next left," Maddy answers, following me out into the hall.

"I've tried getting her to drink water," she tells me.

I rest Hayley's back against the bath panel. Her head rolls, and she smiles as she tried to focus on me.

"Jessie," she says playfully reaching her fingers out to my hair. "Whatcha doin' here… wait, where is here?" She absently looks around the room.

"I'm real sorry, darlin'," I say.

"Sorry? What you sorry fo—" I don't give her chance to finish her sentence, ramming two of my fingers towards the back of her throat, pushing far enough for her to retch, then managing to pull her across to the toilet just in time for her to chuck her guts up.

"For that," I tell her, holding her hair off her sweat-soaked face while she flushes whatever crap she's taken out of her body.

I wait until she's thrown up just about everything other than her internal organs, and she snuggles into my chest before I carry her back into Maddy's room. When Hayley's big eyes find mine, and when she sighs with relief, I finally convince myself that she's gonna be okay.

"You came," she whispers.

"Course I fuckin' came," I tell her, lying her down in Maddy's bed and tucking her underneath the covers. I stroke her face and wait for her eyes to close and her breathing to slow before I turn around to Maddy.

"You take anything?" I look her up and down. My voice comes out sterner than intended, but I have to know that she's okay too. Maddy shakes her head, her eyes full of tears and her face still wide with shock. And despite everything that's just happened, I can't help think she's never looked more fuckin' beautiful.

"You sure about that?" I question again, and she nods back at me slowly.

"I wouldn't lie to you," she whispers. I believe her.

"Who gave her the shit?" I ask, plucking up enough courage to look her in her eyes. When she doesn't reply, I start to walk towards her and she backs up against the wall cowering like a scared puppy.

"Who?" I ask her one more time, watching her long neck as it swallows nervously. I want to punish myself for the way it turns me on.

"Kid called Cobie, I think. I asked him to take us to hospital but he wouldn't. So he brought us back here instead, bailed as soon as we got inside." Her lips quiver as she speaks, and I imagine stilling them by closing my mouth over them.

"Cobie who?" I get even closer, taking in her sweet scent, and watching her eyes flick from side to side as she searches her brain for an answer. I try not to be distracted by her frantic beating chest. So close now, that if I move even a fraction, I'll feel it against mine.

"Cobie... um..." She squeezes her eyes shut tight as if scanning her brain. "Turner. Cobie Turner."

I nod at her, backing away just enough to take out my phone.

Troj answers on the second ring, and I keep my eyes on Maddy while I speak to him.

"I need you to pick someone up for me."

"Who's the lucky fucker?" Troj asks.

"Cobie Turner. Some kid from town. Bring him in, I'll meet him downstairs tomorrow morning."

"It's done, brother," Troj assures me before I hang up.

When I slip my phone back in my pocket I see the fear in Maddy's eyes, fear that I've put there, and it makes my heart feel heavy.

"I'm sorry," I breathe, the disappointment in myself making me sound like a bird with a broken wing.

"Its fine." She fakes a smile as she pushes herself off the wall.

"Where are your parents?" I ask looking over at Hayley, who is now snoring comfortably.

"Just my mom, and she's at work, won't be home till later tomorrow."

"You should get some sleep. I'll watch her." I sit down in the chair at the corner of the room.

"You're staying?" she asks, sounding shocked, and maybe a little relieved at the same time.

"Ain't going anywhere," I tell her, eyes still fixed on hers.

"Okay," she nods back. "I'll sleep in Mom's bed." She's halfway out of the room before she stops, and when she turns to look back at me, she's already chewing that bottom lip.

"Night, Jessie, and... thank you." She looks as though she's about to cry again, and I don't want that to happen.

"Hey..." I stand up, walk towards her, and she doesn't back

away from me this time. I'm not even thinking when I take her head in my hands, her soft blonde hair slipping between my fingers, as I tilt it back enough for her eyes to reach up to mine.

"You did the right thing, Maddy. She's gonna be okay," I tell her as softly as my voice will allow me to.

"I was so scared." She tries hard to hold back her sobs, but they blurt out anyway.

"Everything's gonna be fine. I promise."

Her head moves in my hands as she stares back at me through her thick, black lashes and nods. Her pupils magnified by the tears just waiting to release. She has me fixed, her eyes somehow managing to pierce through my thick surface and claw all the way into my fucking soul. I shouldn't let them, but I can't pull away from her. Her front teeth hold her bottom lip, and I torture myself imagining how it would taste trapped between mine.

I wonder if she's thinking the same thing as me, how it would be easier than breathing to lean in and take those lips. Make them mine here and fuckin' now. But it doesn't matter what my head is telling me, I know what she wants. She wants special, she deserves special, and there ain't nothing special about the man standing in front of her.

"You should go to bed. I got this," I force my eyes away from her and gesture them to Hayley.

"Yeah, you're right." She smiles and carefully pulls her head away from my hands. "Goodnight Jessie," she whispers as she backs away and leaves the room.

I slump back into the seat, taking in her room for the first time. Just when I think Maddy Summers couldn't get any cuter, I find myself in her fuckin' room. Baby pink walls and bedding with frills, the fuckin' works.

While Hayley sleeps, I wonder what possessed her to sneak out and do something so stupid. Prez is gonna spit flames when he finds out, and that little bit of freedom she's tasted would be gone.

The call came in from Troj around 4am, he and Grimm have picked up Cobie, and he's in the basement awaiting my arrival. I look forward to meeting him.

I stay awake watching Hayley breathing until the sun fills the room. Needing to stretch, I get out of the chair and make my way across the hall, unable to help a peek inside the room where Maddy sleeps. She's laid on top of the covers, her long, blonde hair fanned out in all directions, some strands covering over her face.

I creep closer.

So close that I feel her breath on my face.

Too close.

My fingers tremble as they reach out and slide across her skin, brushing the hair from her face and causing her to stir a little. She makes the most perfect humming sound, and I let my hand rest on her cheek. Feeling her sinless skin inside my tarnished palm fills something inside me that until now, I hadn't noticed was hollow. My thumb trails her bottom lip, like sandpaper rubbing over silk. The blessed touched by the dammed, and I promise myself that I'll never cast the shadow of my darkness over her perfect glow.

I'll protect her from my dirty soul,

It'll be the only good thing I could ever do by her.

Already, I know it's gonna hurt me like hell, but it's better than the alternative. For me to hurt her.

I pull my hand away and move out of the room, but her faint, groggy voice has me turning back around before I make it to the door.

"Jessie." Maddy's already sitting up, arms stretched over her head and mouth open mid-yawn. "Is she okay?" she asks lazily.

"Yeah still sleepin'. She'll be fine."

"You're one of them, aren't you?" Her eyes fall to my cut.

I'd been too preoccupied with worry for Hayley to even think to take it off.

"Yeah darlin', I'm one of them," I tell her, knowing I've set her free the moment the words leave my mouth. I nod my head at her before I leave the room. Ashamed at myself that for the first time in my life, I'm sad to admit being part of the club I'd die for.

I've made my decision, I have no reason to hide who I am from her anymore.

When I cross the hall back to Hayley, I'm relieved to find her sat up, legs dangled over the edge of the bed.

"Why does it feel like I've swallowed an exhaust pipe?" she lifts her head up to ask.

"That will be because during my attempts to save your life, I had to ram my fingers down the back of your throat." I cross my arms over my chest.

"Well next time do me a favor and let me die. Hell knows where those fingers have been," she says, leaning forward and cradling her head in her hands.

"What the fuck, Hay? I always knew you were a little stupid but that shit you pulled last night..." I shake my head. "... Fuckin' suicidal. If Prez finds—"

"Prez won't know though, will he, Jessie?" she interrupts. "Because right now, he's probably still at his club, with some whore spread out on top of him, not giving two shits about me."

"Hay, that's bullshit. Your dad just wants you safe. He loves you."

"If you love someone, you wanna spend time with them," she bites back, and I hate that I fail to come up with an explanation for my Prez. Jimmer doesn't show affection all that well, but no one doubts how much he loves his daughter.

"You could have died. Not that it matters now, your dad's gonna kill us both when he finds out about this anyway," I remind her.

"I just wanted to have a little fun," she shrugs, her voice weakening.

I let out a defeated sigh and sit beside her on the bed, wrapping my arm around her shoulders. All my anger seems to vanish when I see the sadness laying behind her eyes. She's right. What sort of life does she have all alone at the lodge every night? How can I blame her for acting out?

"Look I'll speak to your dad, see if we can sort something, I ain't promising shit, but I'll try," I tell her calmly as I can. Her mouth lifts into a smile that tells me we're okay.

"You scared me kiddo," I admit.

"I scared myself. I'm so sorry, Jessie. It won't happen again," she promises. "Besides I feel like utter shit." She closes her eyes.

"You deserve to feel like shit." I nudge her with my shoulder then take her hand and pull her up from the bed. "Come on, let's get you home."

She follows me out to the hall where we meet Maddy coming out of the bathroom.

"Thank god you're okay," Maddy sighs, launching herself forward and throwing her arms around Hayley. "I didn't know what to do. I had to call him." Hayley looks guilty for what has to be the first time ever.

"I'm so sorry, your mom... what must she think?" Hayley's hands cover her face shamefully.

"Relax, she hasn't come home yet," Maddy stops her fretting.

"I'm gonna get her home. You good?" I ask Maddy, and it doesn't matter how hard I try not to make eye contact, those eyes pulled me in like iron to a magnet.

"I'm good," she tells me. I lift my head as a goodbye before I brush past her and bolt down the stairs to my bike.

From now on I need to keep myself as far away from Maddy Summers as possible.

No one cages a wolf with a deer and expects it not to devour.

I wait on my bike for Hayley to come out, kicking it to start and revving up the engine hoping it might hurry her up. When she comes outside her eyes open up wide, and her mouth hangs open.

"Problem, darlin'?" I call over the loud rumbling.

"You want me to ride the back of your bike?" she asks, managing a massive smile despite how shitty she must feel.

"Well, I don't want you riding on front of it," I tease.

"It's just I've never…" She looks at me still in shock. She's right, I can't remember Hayley ever riding on a bike, which was unthinkable considering who her dad is.

"First time for everything, pretty girl. Hop on we gotta get you home before Daddy wakes up and realizes Rapunzel let down her fuckin' hair."

Hayley nods, taking a deep breath before she climbs on behind me. Her arms wrapping around my waist and squeezing tight. I check over my shoulder that she's ready before I take off real steady. On the ride home she rests her head on my back, but her body is tense enough to let me know she's still awake, I still worry about her falling asleep the whole way back.

There's no sign of life when we get to the club, the firepit is still smoking and empty bottles scatter the dusty yard. I ride right on past, straight to the lodge. Hayley's legs are a little wobbly from her first ride when she gets off and hugs me tightly.

"Thanks, Jessie… You should go get yourself some sleep," she whispers. I nod back at her, then watch her inside. I should listen to her advice, head back to my cabin for some sleep but I'm wound up too tight. Pissed at myself for taking my eyes off her long enough to let her get into danger, I'd let myself get distracted by something I can't even fucking have.

What I need is a release, one that not even a club slut with a diploma in riding dick could satisfy. It's time for Cobie Turner to learn from both the very fatal mistakes he made last night.

Number one: You don't supply drugs in Manitou Springs.

Number two: You don't go giving those drugs to the most powerful man in town's daughter.

The scrawny figure sits tied to a chair in the middle of the room when I get down to the basement, and I resist the urge to smile. He's pretty busted up already but it doesn't surprise me, Troj wouldn't have left all the fun for me. What does have me smirking, is the fact he looks almost relieved to see me.

"Please," his weak little voice speaks out. "Whatever it is, I'm sorry. Just let me go, man... Please... My dad's got money." The closer I get, the more the stench of his piss offends me.

"See you met my friend," I say, taking a look over Troj's handy work.

"Not him again... please," the boy weeps.

"You reckon the worst I could do to you is have Troj come back down here?" I throw a laugh at the kid. He looks up at me, eyes bulging from their sockets, tears streaking down his face and merging with the blood-tinged snot leaking from his nose.

He's a mess.

"My friend was just the fuckin' warm-up act," I warn, crossing over to the table where all Cobie's belongings are laid out neatly. I don't have to guess who handled this aspect of the kidnap, Grimm, is a perfectionist. The wallet, cell phone, and a baggy of what looks like MDMA are all lined up in size order. I take the cell phone and tap at the home button with my thumb. It's locked, of course, so I ask Cobie for the passcode, and he doesn't hesitate in giving it to me.

"thr... three... f... four... five... se... seven," he stutters

I scroll to the camera app and flip it on to video mode.

"Right, Cobe. There are two ways this could go, how it does... kinda depends on you. I need you to answer me a few questions. Nothing too personal, and if you answer them without giving me any trouble, you get to receive your punishment and still be home in time for dinner." Cobie nods his head enthusiastically.

"You decide you wanna make me work for those answers, then I'm gonna get all mad 'n' shit, and that's when I get careless… Things go wrong. I ain't gonna lie to you, buddy, there have been some people sat in that chair who haven't made it home."

"I'll tell you everything. I swear, just let me go. Please." The boy breaks down again, his pathetic pleading voice already irritating the fuck out of me and I haven't even started.

"Cobes, I can see you're a smart kid." I smile at him. "I'ma do something for you that I don't usually do… Here," I hold the phone up in front of him.

"I'll give you the chance to record a message to the person you love the most in this whole world, and if…" I shrug, "I do 'accidentally' end up losing my shit. I promise I'll personally deliver it to them for you." I smile again.

The boy lets out a weak moan, but he doesn't have time to panic.

"Aaaannd action." I hit record and do fuck all to stop my cocky smirk as he records a wailing message to his parents. He apologizes for everything he's ever done to let them down and tells them how much he loves them. When he's done, I take the phone and place it back on the table. Grabbing the bag of pills, I drop my friendly act, and push his stash into his face.

"Where you get the shit?" I ask him, my calm tone flipping to rage when I remember Hayley's eyes rolling back in her head.

"Some guy called Sp..Sp..Spider," he stammers. "Wears a cut like yours, only his has a smiling devil on."

Fucking Bastards, I saw this one coming.

"Do you know who we are?" I ask him, and he nods his feeble little head up and down slowly.

"Dddddirty Souls," he squeaks through tears.

"And you know that the girl you gave these to last night is our president's daughter, right?" The kid closes his eyes and nods again.

"If you didn't stink of your own piss I'd be asking if you're brave or just fucking stupid." I stare down to his urine-soaked pants.

"She just wanted to have a good time," he cries like a kid fallen off his bike.

"You could have fucking killed her," I yell out. Blood flying from his mouth as my knuckles impact with his jaw.

"I'm so sorry. I didn't know she wouldn't be able to handle it, thought she'd be used to shit like that," he manages eventually.

I nod as if I understand the sorry piece of shit's excuse, when what I'm really thinking about is the best way to fuck him up. It doesn't take me long to come up with something.

"You like getting high?" I ask, my voice finding a steady calm again. The wet fucker doesn't know how he should answer me. "Come on man, answer the question. You like to get high, right? Who don't?"

The kid nods cautiously, unsure if he's giving me the answer I want.

"Tell you what. I'll get you some proper shit, shit that will make this..."—I shake his little stash in front of his pathetic face—"seem like swallowing fuckin' skittles." I go to walk out.

"No! I'm cool... Thank you. I ju...ju... just wanna go home," he mumbles nervously.

"Come on Cobe we're havin' fun. You just chill out there. I'll be back. Promise." I wink and slap his shoulder, before I head up to the club to get Cobie a buzz he won't forget.

I return not too long later with a syringe in my hand and place it on the table beside him. His eyes move nervously between me and the needle, and I swear he's either gonna crap his pants or have a panic-induced heart attack that will ruin all my fun.

"What's that?" he asks me, his voice shaking almost as fiercely as his body.

"That..." I look at the syringe. "That there, my friend, is a fuckin' buzz. Pure heroine. None of the shit you get on the streets around here, best shit you will get for fuckin' miles," I assure him.

"Probably enough in that hit to take down a fuckin' rhino. But you can handle it, right?" I grab his shoulders and shake them with fake enthusiasm.

"I've never. I mean... that's probably too mu... much for me. I've never had a... a hit before," he tries to form words, struggling desperately against his restraints and I watch with great fulfilment as he becomes consumed in fear and panic.

"Come on man." I crouch in front of him, slowly undoing one of the laces from his trainers, then pulling it out completely I tie it tight around his bicep, causing the veins in his arm to pop up like little tunnels. I tap on the inside of his elbow with two fingers and give him a sarcastic smile.

"Please don't," he begs so sincerely that my grin almost hurts my mouth. Then with one final wink I grab hold of the needle and stab it deep into his vein, the liquid releases from the syringe and trickles into his bloodstream. Cobie screams and thrusts against the chair, but he's tied down too tight—Grimm's expertise again no doubt.

He stares at his arm watching in helpless horror as the substance disappears on a one-way trip. Then he cries, pleading for me to stop, and I wait until the syringe is empty before tossing it to the floor. Levelling my eyes to his, I drain one last look of fear out of them before I tap his cheek.

"Enjoy the buzz asshole," I whisper into his ear, leaving him alone in the room with just the echo of his screams to keep him company. I slam the door behind me, making my way upstairs where the atmosphere has become a little livelier. Squealer's now awake, and the whore whose head was wedged between his legs when I'd come up earlier has vanished. Screwy sits on a chair staring across the room at absolutely fuck all. And then in the corner of the room, I spot the guy I'm looking for.

"Tac," I call over. He lifts his head from the table rubbing his smooth head in his hands.

"What?" he rasps back.

"The kid still need skin for practice?" I ask, and he half nods back at me, still not fully functional.

"Been practicing on pig skin, done a few things on the brothers. He's good."

"Tell him to bring his kit here, I got him a volunteer."

"You want more ink?" Tac asks knowing I'm not as inclined to tattoos as most of the others are, the only ink I've got is club related.

"Not me." I pull the bottle of Jack out of an unconscious Troj's hand and knock back a large mouthful.

It doesn't take long for Nyx to show up, with a holdall slung over his shoulder. I've never seen him look so eager, and there's almost a hint of excitement in his expression.

"Follow me." I lead him to the foyer and then down to the basement. When we walk into the room, it's silent, Cobie is out, just like the doc assured me he would be. Nyx turns his head to me, confused.

"Blank canvas for ya kiddo, he should be out for at least eight hours." I pull up a chair next to the limp body and gesture for Nyx to sit down.

"What's the deal?" he asks, and because I got respect for the kid, I tell him.

"Just been taught a lesson about what happens to dealers in Manitou Springs. Fucker went out thinking I'd jacked him up with enough heroine to take out a fuckin' rhino." I pull at a tuft of Cobie's fringe and roll his head back.

"Just something I got from the doc to send him under for a while is all." I wink, and Nyx looks impressed.

"So I get to do whatever I want?" he checks.

"Anything, cover him from head to fucking foot for all I care."

"What shall I do if he wakes up?" he asks, a snigger appearing on his face that reveal dimples I never knew he had.

"Keep goin' if you haven't finished, he's tied down pretty tight. I'll be in my cabin. Come get me when you're done." I leave the kid to work, more than ready to get some sleep now.

"Hey Jessie," Nyx calls after me once I'm back in the corridor, and I back up shooting my head back around the door. "You really are as fucked up as they say you are, ain't ya?" He smiles.

I shrug a little cockily before I head up the stairs and get straight on my bike. I'm so tired now, I could fall asleep standing up, but I still drop by the lodge and check in on Hayley. She's sleeping in her room, no sign of the Prez. I decide not to tell him about what had happened last night, not the Hayley part anyway. All he needed to know is that I'd caught one of the Bastards' errand boys and shat them up enough not to deal ever again.

I get home and go straight for my bed. My head hits the pillow, and when I finally shut my eyes, Maddy's beautiful face is emblazed on to the back of my eyelids, and her sweet strawberry smell fills my nostrils. Somewhere in my head I hear her soft voice whisper,

"Jessie, I need you."

And with the texture of her silky skin still lingering at my fingertips. I give up trying to blank her out, only then do I drift off into a deep, much-needed sleep.

CHAPTER 16
HAYLEY

Jessie let me ride home on the back of his bike. Me... I've never seen anyone ride with him before, not even the skank who he let suck him off. It's every bit as good as I imagined it would be, my arms around him, breathing in his leather while my cheek rested against his cut.

Again, Jessie had been there when I needed him, and not even the world's worst ever hangover ruins that moment for me.

Two weeks later, I'm sat on one of the benches outside the club, still daydreaming about it. The growl of engines, along with the dust cloud that travels up the track from the main road signals they've returned from their latest run, and my stomach flips with excitement. Jessie may have only been gone for three days, but I've missed him terribly. The yard fills up quickly, club sluts appearing out of nowhere and lining themselves up by the club doors, ready to be dragged away and used. Chaos has returned, and I have to admit it feels kinda nice.

Loud whoops and jeers call over the yard when the guys park their bikes and head inside. Some of them pick themselves up an eagerly waiting play thing on the way in.

I want to follow them inside too, especially when Jessie winks at me before he follows Chop through the doors. I have a feeling I wouldn't be welcomed though, even if it is daytime.

I'm about to get up and make my way back up to the lodge

when I feel a hand rest on my shoulder, and when I turn around, it's Carly's warm smile that beams back at me. It's easy to see why Skid adores her so much. Not only is she beautiful, but she has a big heart too.

"You coming inside for a drink?" she asks.

"I don't think my daddy would like that," I tell her.

"I don't think your daddy would know about it." She has a twinkle in her eyes as she gestures her head over at the parked bikes. I didn't notice it before, but Daddy's isn't here.

"Skid called from Nebraska, said Prez is hanging back for a few nights to discuss business. Come on, I'll look out for you." Carly takes my hand, leaving me with little choice but to follow her.

She walks me inside, straight through to the main bar at the back. Club whores are already behind the bar serving up drinks as if their needy little pussys depended on it. Carly heads straight for Skid, who smiles as soon as he sees her. She flings her arms around his neck, and he tips her back and kisses her, ignoring cheers and whistles from all the brothers.

Chop climbs up on to the bar, bringing his fingers to his mouth and whistling so loud that it hurts my ears.

"It's been a long ride brothers. Eat, shower, sleep, and fuck in whatever order you need to, but tonight, we fuckin' party," he announces. Everyone cheers, holding up their drinks, and Chop jumps off the bar and snatches a glass from Tommy's hand.

"Hey, pretty girl," Jessie's voice comes from behind me, and I quickly spin around. My arms instinctively move around his waist, and he pulls me in tight.

"Hey yourself." I smile, so pleased to see him. I hate it when he goes away. It always feels like a part of me is missing, now he's back I hope he has some time to hang out with me.

"Prez had some loose ends to tie up, Troj stayed behind with him. So I thought maybe you could celebrate with us tonight?" he says barely able to hide is grin.

My head is nodding before he's even finished the sentence, and Jessie laughs that playful laugh that always makes me giddy happy.

"Okay then, pretty girl, go get yourself ready, and I'll see you down here a little later on." When he leans in closer to my face, his breath tickles my ear as he speaks again, "Best behavior, 'kay?"

I don't stick around to wait for a lift from Nyx or Tommy. I'm happy to take a walk up to the lodge. On the way up, I pull out my cell and surprise myself when I automatically scroll to Maddy's name. Over the past few weeks, she's become my go-to person. I'm always calling or texting her if I feel lonely or have gossip.

I've pretty much gotten everything out of her that would be interesting to Jessie. But he doesn't seem to care anymore. Before he left for the run, he'd told me that the whole plan was a stupid idea and that I should forget it. As predicted, it hadn't taken him very long to figure out that I'd been right. Maddy Summers was not cut out to be with a guy like Jessie. Deep down he's hurting about it, but he's never gonna admit that to me, and I can happily live with that.

Tonight, is the perfect opportunity for me to show Jessie the difference between her and me. Prove that he doesn't need Maddy and she would never fit in here. Then he can move on and stop pining over her.

When Maddy answers the phone, one of her upbeat Fleetwood Mac tunes is playing in the background, and I picture her, sat on her bed, studying hard for the calculus test we have on Monday.

"You are gonna toss your tits when you hear this," I squeal. I'd somehow managed to keep a lid on my excitement back at the club, but now there was no one for me to embarrass myself in front of I'm unable to contain it.

"What now?" she asks, and I can almost hear the smile in her voice.

"Jessie said I'm allowed to go down the club tonight, they're having some party because they just got back off a run."

"No way! Wait... what's a run?"

"I don't really know, it's where they all ride off together for a few days, they always seem happy when they get back. Anyway, that's not what's important. Did you hear me? I AM SPENDING THE NIGHT AT THE CLUB."

"That's awesome, Hay." Maddy sounds genuinely excited for me.

"I know, right? I think it's gonna be low key, Carly's going, and she doesn't usually go to the club at night, perhaps that's why I'm allowed... I don't even care. I'm just so glad to be included."

"You're so lucky. I can't wait for you to tell me all about it on Monday."

"I won't have to, because you're coming too," I tell her.

"You're inviting me to a biker party?" she giggles infectiously.

"Sure the fuck am," I laugh back at her, picking up on the excitement.

"I'm there. Just as long as I can get there."

"I'll call Nyx and tell him to pick you up when he's finished in the studio if you want?"

"You sure he won't mind? He's always running us about lately, I get the feeling he doesn't exactly enjoy it."

"You're like five minutes out of his way, and that's just the way his face is, guy's got a permanent scowl. Besides, there's got to be some perks of my daddy being in charge. I think he finishes up about 6ish, be ready. Any problems I'll call you, and we'll come up with a plan B."

"Sounds good, I can't wait," she says, before I hang up and quickly text Nyx instructing him to pick her up after his shift. He won't be happy, but he can't exactly say no to the Prez's daughter. Daddy had been the one to give me his number in case I needed him, and in my opinion, this qualifies.

I'm a little conflicted about my reasons for wanting Maddy to come tonight. I really do need to hammer the final nail in so Jessie can bury the idea of him and her. He may have realized, that for too many reasons to count, it would never work. But she still asks about him every time I see her. It pisses me off.

Seeing him and the world he comes from, would surely be enough to put her off for good.

But another part of me, the part that's actually starting to like the girl, actually wants to hang out with her.

I've obviously been hanging around with her too much and I'm turning soft. But after tonight, everything will be how it should be. Maddy will want to be as far away from Jessie as possible when she sees who he really is. And I won't have to be her friend anymore. No more pretending I care about her, no more listening to her crappy music and hanging out in that frilly bedroom. Everything can go back to how it was before Jessie noticed her.

I should be relieved. So why does the thought of not hanging out with her anymore make me feel so sad?

CHAPTER 17

JESSIE

Our run couldn't have gone better. The guns we'd stolen from the Bastards' lockup are now safely stored under the protection of one of our other Charters.

Prez and Troj, his Sergent at arms, stayed behind to see a deal through and if it comes off they'll be coming home tomorrow with a good cut for us all.

Of course, I asked Prez if Hayley could come tonight before I'd invited her. He wasn't happy about the idea, but I reminded him that there's always a real good vibe after a run, how it used to be when kids and old ladies joined in.

Now it's friends of the club or whoever the guys are fuckin' that we party with. Club sluts hate nights like these, they see the women that get invited as a threat to them, but everyone always behaves themselves. It's a family thing after all.

Hayley deserves to be a part of that, and Carly made a promise to Skid that she'd keep an eye on her, so what can go wrong?

I take a quick shower and manage a few hours' sleep before I get dressed.

We've all earned a good night. It's been a while since the club had anything to celebrate. But the Bastards seem to have got the message about fucking with us, and our latest deal has gone without a hitch, so things are looking up.

I ride down to the club, where the firepit has already been lit, and the smell of BBQ smokes filling the air… among other things.

My eyes skim the yard for Hayley, but there's no sign of her yet. No doubt she's still flapping over what to wear. Grimm hands me a beer as I pass him, tipping his chin at me.

"Cheers," I nod, managing to finish off the bottle in three mouthfuls.

"Squealer and a few others are doin' flake in the members lounge," he mumbles at me, before walking over to the firepit and taking a seat by himself on one of the logs. Then he tilts his head sideways and watches the flames dance in front of him.

It doesn't take a professional to see that Grimm has issues, but then there aren't many of us around here who don't. If he wanted to tell us what his deal was, he would. All we need to know is that he's loyal to the Souls. And he's proved that more times than I can mention.

I play pool with Screwy while I wait for Hayley to show. It ain't like I can get smashed with everyone else, not when I've promised Prez I'll watch over her. I can't take my eye off the ball like I had a few weeks ago.

Mel tries her hardest to catch my attention from the bar, but I'm not interested tonight, in fact, my dick has been pretty much redundant ever since I've been trying not to think about Maddy. Mel shamelessly pressing her tits together while she shakes her ass all over my brother's laps isn't doing fuck all to stir it back to life either.

As hard as I try, Maddy won't stop invading my head. Images of my fists spilling full of blonde, wavy hair, while my cock buries deep inside her innocent little pussy, still taunt me despite all my attempts to block them out.

I needed some fucking air. Nodding at Screwy that we're done, I put down my cue and push past anyone in my way to get outside.

Hayley should have turned up by now, she'd been so excited when I told her she could come. I can't imagine her wanting to miss anything and I need her to distract my thoughts away from Maddy.

Squealer stops me just as I'm about to step outside, he's got one of those devilish glints in his eye that always comes out when pussy's around.

"Fuck, man, you really going out there?" he asks, looking disappointed, I nod back wondering what his problem is.

"Shit… Well, I'm calling dibs before you get your pretty boy ass out there. Blonde bitch out by the firepit." He looks back over his shoulder.

"Pretty little thang, actually got me fucking grafting. So, you and that all-American charm thing you do can go get fucked. I'm going to get her a drink." He winks at me and rubs his hands together. Then he relieves a twitch in his nostril by pressing it with his thumb and taking a deep sniff. Clearly, he's already buzzed, and I pity whatever bitch he's set his mark on.

The guy's fucking relentless without a high. I've seen it with my own eyes.

I head over to the firepit keeping my eyes open for Hayley. My head must really be fucked because instead of seeing the blonde chick who's got Squealer's cage all rattled, I swear I see Maddy sat on the other side of the flames. Her long, blonde hair, and perfect, wide eyes taunting me as she looks up from the fire across to me. The girl needs to get the fuck out of my head.

Moving closer, I curse myself for being pathetic, if I'm gonna start transforming every blonde bitch I see into her I'm gonna be in real trouble.

The smoke is thick and clouds most of my vision, but I still see no sign of Hayley. And when I step out of the smoke and everything becomes clearer, my frustration quickly switches up to full on fuckin' rage. What I'm seeing ain't no fucking illusion, it is Maddy.

My fucking Maddy.

I hold back the urge to find Squealer, rip his dick off, and feed it to his twin fucking brother while I double check, but I know it's her alright. That weary look as she takes in her surroundings, how her teeth sink so deep into her bottom lip I'm sure they'll leave a mark. She's unmistakable.

I stand and watch her for a while, noting how she wraps her arms around her shoulders, clearly insecure about the situation she's in. Who can blame her when Tac is screwing the womb out of some bitch up against the hood of his jeep just ten-feet away from her? Grimm is sat on the log beside her, staring into the flames like fuckin' hell boy. And to top all of that, she's just had to tolerate whatever Squealer's idea of grafting is.

Hayley appears out of thin fuckin' air, bouncing on her feet like she doesn't have a single care in the world. Anger keeps the blood pumping around my body in place of a heartbeat. Maddy shouldn't be here, she doesn't belong here. I told Hayley to back off and leave her be. She had no business bringing her here tonight.

Hayley sees me coming and straight away looks guilty. She knows what she's done.

I'm about to speak… no, I'm about to fucking rage, but then I make that same mistake of looking at Maddy first. Seeing her bottom lip release from her teeth and raise into a smile, those eyes lighting up her face as well as my fucking soul. And she steals all the words from my mouth.

"Hey," Hayley sounds chirpy, she can tell she's pissed me off, so she's either nervous or being sarcastic. When I scowl at her, she immediately looks hurt.

"You girls got everything you need?" I ask, trying to keep my shit together for Maddy's sake. But I can't help eyeballing Hayley over her shoulder so she knows I'm beyond pissed at her. Maddy answers me, her voice, soft and timid. A voice that don't fuckin' sound right in these surroundings.

"We're good thanks, umm…"

"Squealer," I hear Squealer say his own name from behind me, and the prick's lucky I don't spin around and punch him right in his ink covered throat.

"Squealer," she repeats his name, and just hearing it come off her tongue makes my fists clench into cannonballs of fire. He nods and gives her a huge grin, then leans over me to pass her a beer.

"Thanks," she laughs, taking the bottle from his hand.

"Somethin' got ya tickled, darlin'?" he asks her, licking his lips and looking at her like she's a snack.

"Squealer's just a funny nickname is all." Her eyes assess his tall, well-stacked body. "Guess you just don't seem much like the squealing type," she tells him with a giggle. I watch the fucker lean into her real close… too fuckin' close.

"I ain't the one who does the squealing, darlin'," he whispers, just loud enough for me to hear. Then turning his attention to me, he wrinkles up his nose and sticks out his long tongue.

"Then who does?" Maddy asks, innocence radiating from her like a fucking halo. Someone calls out to Squealer from the other side of the fire, he doesn't know it, but whoever it is just saved him.

"Stick around you might be lucky enough to find out." He winks at Maddy before heading off in the direction of the voice that called him.

"Hayley. A word." I glare at her and notice her cocky mouth has nothing to say as she follows me out of Maddy's earshot.

"What the fuck is she doin' here?" I ask, trying real hard not to yell.

"She's my friend…" she starts to explain.

"We both know that's fuckin' bullshit, so what's the crack, Hay?" She looks back at me unapologetically, crossing her arms over her chest before she speaks.

"Okay, you want me to tell you the real reason she's here?" she asks, I nod and wait for her explanation.

"Fine, I thought she should see what she'd be letting herself in for. You said it yourself that you and this club come as a package, you don't get one without the other, right?" Hayley raises her shoulder as if she's done nothing wrong, and it makes me twice as mad at her.

"Why would you do that? You know I didn't want her brought into all this. I was stepping away from her because I didn't want her inflicted with all the shit, Hayley." I gesture around me to where Tac is still going hard at it with the bitch on his hood.

"Stepping away?" she snorts. "As if you had a fuckin' chance anyway."

That cuts me deep, but I ain't gonna give her the satisfaction of knowing it.

"Probably not, guess we'll never know. But this stunt, Hayley…" I point my finger at her. "…Way too fucking far." I move to walk away from her.

"Like it would matter, look at her. She's clearly not cut out for club life," Hayley calls out after me, and it makes me freeze.

Yeah, Maddy is out of place, that, we can at least agree on. With no one beside her now, she looks uncomfortable. Exactly as you'd expect someone dragged into mayhem just to prove a fuckin' point would look. Hayley hasn't given two fucks about how it might make her feel bringing her here, and I turn around and march back at Hayley with venom lacing my tongue.

"Yeah, and what the fuck would you know about club life, little girl? Your daddy's kept you out of it your entire life." The tone of my words come out harsh, but I'm so pissed at her for what she's done. Hayley doesn't speak for the longest time, at first appearing shocked. But then a sudden flare of anger appears in her eyes, and she looks like she might swing for me.

"Enough to know that you have a darkness inside you that

you think you have to protect her from," she snaps. "I know that you're petrified that one day you might drop your act when you're around her and she'll get a glimpse of who you really are and see all the fucked up things you're capable of. And I'll tell you something else I know Jessie…" Tears drown out her anger now, and I wonder if she'll be able to finish what she wants to say.

"…I know that it burns you from the inside out that she's right here. Close enough to smell, and close enough to touch. But, you can't have her because you think she deserves better. That it fucking breaks your heart that you'll never be what she wants. There ain't enough people in the world for you to hurt that'll help you get over that."

I lose control, closing the gap between us, so my nose touches against hers. I hate her for calling me out, hate that she's right. But most of all I hate that I've made her pretty green eyes fill with tears.

"You don't know shit," I growl at her through my teeth, before backing away from her and getting as far away from the whole mess as possible.

I storm inside the club and head straight for Mel, grabbing her by the wrist and ripping her up off Nyx's lap.

"You shouldn't have brought the girl here." I point my finger in his face, and he immediately stands up. He's half a foot taller than me, but I ain't backing down.

"Just following orders." He stares back at me without a shred of fear.

"Well next time, check. You're on Hayley watch from now on."

I don't give him chance to argue, turning my back on him, keeping Mel in my hand and dragging her with me as I leave. I pass Hayley and Maddy at the firepit on my way to my bike, and gesture for Melissa to get on the back. Staring over at Hayley. I rev my engine and pull away. I don't know who I'm trying to convince more that she's wrong, her or myself. All I do know is that I need to get the fuck away from Maddy before I break all my own rules.

Troj is still in Nebraska with Prez, so I know our cabin will be empty. I don't bother turning on the lights when I pull Mel inside. It's the first time I've ever brought a girl back here. Me and Troj stick to the same rules when it came to bitches.

No kissing, that shit is way too personal.

No fucking in the cabin, club whores stay at the club or in Sluts sanctuary. I don't want them in my space, and I sure as hell don't want them to still be there the next morning.

And the most important rule, always rubber up.

Mel smiles as I show her into the kitchen, her long fake nails dragging all the way across the wooden table before she hitches her ass up on it.

I go to her, even though I doubt it's a good idea with my blood still simmering. Grabbing my face, she tries pulling me towards her lips, but I grip her hips and lift her off the table before they can touch. I flip her on to her front and pin her to the table in front of me.

I force her tiny skirt up over her cherry shaped ass and slap her bare skin, hard enough to feel the burn on my palm. She lets out a shriek of pleasure and wiggles her ass for more. I rip her panties down to her ankles, the bitch looks over her shoulder and shoots me a satisfied smile.

Taking a rubber from my pocket, I rip it open with my teeth.

"You don't have to wear that, baby." Mel's hands fumble behind her back to loosen my jeans. I know her game, she ain't trappin' me into making her an old lady. I push her hand away and take out my cock, rolling the rubber down my shaft and making sure it's firmly in place. I don't give her any warning, slamming my cock inside her soaked, ready pussy and not stopping until she's accepted every single inch.

Mel groans, her hands gripping tight to the edge of the table as I fuck her pussy over and over. But it's not enough, I'm still thinking of Maddy.

Squeezing Mel's shoulders in my hands, I control her body, pushing her on to my hard thrusts. The noises she makes and the way her neck twists around to watch me irritates me. So I close my eyes and imagine it's Maddy bent in front of me, her hot ass rubbing itself into my hips. It's her needy little snatch that's crushing my cock as I steal all the pleasure from it.

When I open my eyes again, Mel is staring back at me, smiling like a cat getting the fucking cream, and ruining all the illusions my mind has just built. I take my hand and push it on to the back of her head. Pressing one of her cheeks into the table. Then I fuck her like a savage for taking the vision of Maddy away from me.

I close my eyes, and she quickly comes back to me, this time down by the firepit, how she'd smiled at me like I was someone special when she'd seen me. I wasn't making that up.

Was she really that innocent, or is she teasing and taunting me? Making me believe that all I have to do is reach out and take her.

Fuck, I don't even deserve to have her in my head.

Bringing my hand down hard on Mel's ass again, I remind myself that I'm an evil bastard, one who gets his kicks out of inflicting pain. She screams, flooding my cock as she comes and scratches her claws into my table. I curl my hand around her face and crush it into her mouth, so I don't have to hear her. There's only one voice I want in my head…

"Jessie, please. I need you," Maddy's voice sings to me like an angel summoning the devil.

I want to open my eyes so I can escape hers and the way they seem to glisten brighter whenever they meet with mine. But she holds me like a prisoner, refusing to let me fuckin' go.

I'm close, and with one final slam into the body laid in front of me. I turn rigid, gripping Mel's hips, as my cock pumps its release into the rubber I'm wearing.

As soon as I open my eyes, I know there'll be no talking myself out of doing what I'm about to do. I pull out of Mel and snap the rubber off my cock. Tossing it into the bin as I fix my jeans.

"You need to be gone by the time I get back," I tell her, not looking back as I snatch my truck keys from the table. I drive back down to the club, hoping that I'm not too late.

It doesn't matter to me anymore that I'm wrong for her, Maddy Summers being here tonight, and the reaction it's risen out of me has made one thing very fucking clear. She's all fucking mine.

I'm not shocked when I get back down to the firepit and find Squealer sitting between Maddy and Hayley, the smug bastard even cocks his head and smirks at me as I march towards them.

"You wanna go twos, Jess?" he asks, I somehow manage to ignore him. All my focus being on Maddy.

"You," I point at her first. "You're coming with me." The tone of my voice is harsh, and the way she jumps to my command makes me fucking hard.

"The fuck?" Squealer wines like a bitch, looking confused as shit.

"Not now, I'll deal with you later."

"You can tell me now, what's your fuckin' problem?" He stands up from the log, as if he's gonna do something about it.

"Right now, Squeal, you're my fuckin' problem. Don't push me," I warn.

"Cool it, brother," he backs down, holding out his hands in front of him. "Ain't no chick worth getting your hair in a curl over. Bro's over hoes remember."

I nod letting him know he's made the right decision, then taking Maddy's elbow in my hand I steer her towards my truck.

"Keep an eye on her," I tell Squealer, pointing my eyes at a stunned and silent Hayley. "I'll be back soon."

"Take your time, brother," he shouts after me then laughs, I lift up my arm and flip him off behind my back while I lead Maddy to the truck.

Maddy doesn't say a word as I drive down the track and out on to the main road, she sits perfectly straight, arms crossed on her lap, and keeps on nipping at that bottom lip.

"Hay shouldn't have brought you here." I make her jump when my palm slams hard against the steering wheel in frustration.

"Don't be mad at her, she was just trying to include me." The sound of her sweet voice soothes me slightly, but I can't bring myself to speak to her for fear of what might come out. The journey is silent and awkward, and when I pull up outside her house, I notice there are no lights on.

"Thanks for the ride." She smiles before she opens the door.

"Your mom not at home?" I ask, not liking the thought of her being in an empty house.

"Not tonight." There's something sad behind her words, and she tries hiding it with another smile before she hops out of my truck. She shuts the door carefully and then starts making her way up the path to her door.

"Maddy," I hear my voice call out through the open window, and I have no idea why. When she turns her head, the words that follow after shock the fuck out of me. "Would you wanna take a ride with me sometime? Get out of town for a few hours."

"Yes," she answers fast, like she's scared I might retract the offer, then she blushes when she realizes her haste. "I mean... that would be really nice." Her smile isn't fake this time, it's a genuine, happy beam that spreads warmth through my whole body.

"Okay then." I nod, totally aware of the smug grin that's fixed itself on to my face. She backs up along the path to her house. Her lips still spread with that smile that punches me in the feels so hard I feel it bruising. When she turns away from me a few strides before she reaches her porch, I instantly miss her face.

"You watching me inside?" she calls over her shoulder, with a little sass that I've never heard from her before. I lean forward and rest my arms on the steering wheel, getting a better view of the perfectly sculpted ass she has tucked in her jeans.

"What sort of guy would I be if I didn't?" I call back at her. When she turns back around, the automatic light kicks in and lights her up like some kind of fucking angel.

"One of the bad guys I guess," she shrugs sounding playful.

"You better fuckin' believe it," I confirm with a wink. I watch her open the door and step inside the house. The girl has no clue that my black, damaged heart sits right in the palm of her hand, what she decides to do with it now is her choice, just so long as she never gives it me back.

CHAPTER 18
HAYLEY

So, my plan backfired, massively.

Over the years I've seen many sides of Jessie, but not once in all that time has his anger ever been directed at me. Watching him disappear with that whore sat proudly on the back of his bike had just about torn everything out of me, and I only had myself to blame for pushing him.

He avoids me for the next couple of days. I tell myself it's because Daddy has come back and there's been loads of 'club stuff' to deal with, but deep down I know it's because he's still mad at me.

On Monday, Maddy tells me that he asked if he could take her on a 'ride'. Of course, she'd accepted, and I want to hate her for it.

I want to hate the bitch so damn much that I offer to be on standby to do her makeup when Jessie finally grows the balls to take her.

Thankfully, that day is still yet to come, and I can see Maddy growing more and more anxious. It almost disturbs me that I take no pleasure in seeing her suffer.

I'm relieved when instead of Nyx or Tommy, Jessie picks me up from college on Friday, and like always he takes me to Bernie's. It feels good to slip into our usual routine again.

There's no sign of Maddy either, and I'm thankful for that. Her being here would have caused an unintentional awkwardness. After we finish up our burgers, we drive home, and Jessie follows me inside to the kitchen. I can tell he's holding something back from me, he's being distant, and whatever it is I wish he would just hurry up and say it.

"You know I asked Mads out, right?" he blurts out when I start clearing up the dishes that are left out from breakfast.

"Yeah, she mentioned something about it." I pass him the fruit bowl to hold while I clean the crumbs from the table with a cloth, and when I'm done he places it back in the center.

"So?" I throw the cloth into the basin with perfect aim, and then give him all of my attention.

"It doesn't matter," he shakes his head, yet still wears the wounded puppy look all over his handsome face.

"C'mon out with it." I take a seat and look up at him expectantly, it isn't like there's much left he can say to hurt me.

"I guess it's just… well…" The words don't seem to want to come out of his mouth. Being awkward, as cute as it is, doesn't suit him.

"For fuck's sake, will you just spit it out," I say, frustrated at him tiptoeing around the point.

"I don't know how to be with her," he says quickly. It's hard for him to admit, I can tell by the shameful look on his face. "She's just so different Hay. She's… special and I don't know how to—"

"I'm sure you're more experienced than I am," I interrupt sarcastically.

"I've never kissed anyone before." He looks down at his feet avoiding eye contact.

"What?" I laugh because there is no reaction for the level of shock I'm currently feeling. "You're kidding me, right?"

"Does this look like the face of a fuckin' kidder, Hay?" He looks up at me seriously. "I don't get… close to girls."

"Oh I've seen you get pretty close," I remind him, but his face remains straight.

"You know what I mean. I've never wanted to kiss a girl before, not until her." He sits in the chair opposite me. "C'mon, Hay, help me out."

I roll my eyes, mainly at myself for being pathetic enough to feel sorry for him.

"Jess I bet you've run out of fingers and toes to count the number of women you've been with, all of them no doubt experienced. Maddy's a virgin for Christ's sake, you could be awful, and she'll never know."

"That's not the bit I'm worried about… well not as much." He starts turning all weird again. "Look, girls like Maddy, I assume have, like base rules and all that kinda shit."

I give him a look that tells him he's gonna have to be a lot more specific. "Dirty Souls school of fuckery, kinda skipped past the whole first base unit," he tells me scratching the back of his neck internally cringing, and I want to laugh and cry at the same time. I do a good job of holding off both.

"You know what, this was a real bad idea. I'm gonna get going. I'll figure it out." He turns ready to leave.

"No, wait." I stop him standing up by tugging at his arm. "Of course I'll try to help you. I'm just a little shocked that's all, you're telling me you've never kissed anyone?" He's silent for a while and eventually lets out a long breath before he answers.

"I've only been with women from here," he admits.

"You mean club sluts like Mel, right?" As much as I hate him suffering, I can't resist a sly dig, purely for my benefit.

"Right." He nods. "And those kinda girls get shared around, not that that shit bothers me. I always glove up. But when it comes to kissing, I can't think of anyone who would willingly put their mouth near anywhere Squealer's put his dick. You get what I'm sayin'?" He looks at me, and we both pull the same face at the thought. "Well, not without some kinda tongue condom on or some shit," Jessie adds, and we both laugh before things turn serious again.

"Anyway, kissing's kind of personal, you've seen how Skid kisses Carly, there's more to it than just sticking your tongue down a bitches throat. It ain't ramming your dick in someone to get yourself off. You need real feelings to kiss someone."

"And that's what you want with Maddy? What Skid and Carly have?" I ask the question, dreading the answer because I know it's gonna shatter me to pieces.

"I don't know what the fuck I want with that girl." He slumps back and draws his fingers through his hair. "I know this whole thing is a bad idea, but I can't stop it, Hayley, I've tried. I've tried staying away from her but I can't. It's selfish, but the thought of her being with anyone else stops me breathing. You understand, right?"

"Yeah, I understand," I assure him, trying to catch a breath of my own while holding tears in at the same time. I take his hand in mine. Despite every single one of his words stinging me raw, I see real pain behind his eyes.

"You got nothing to worry about," I tell him softly. "When the time comes, just tell her everything you just told me, only do it without words." He looks at me a little confused and when the penny drops, he half smiles back at me.

"You think I'm doing the wrong thing?" he asks me softly, as if my opinion matters to him and all I can do was shake my head.

"I'm bad for her, Hay. I don't wanna hurt her."

"You won't," I assure him, my eyes swelling with tears.

"How can you be so sure?"

I pull my hand from his, and tuck it inside his cut, pressing it against his firm chest.

"Because, Jessie Donavon, buried deep down beneath all the fucked up shit, and those impeccable pecs, you've got a heart. One that beats solely for the people that you care about. If

Maddy Summers is one of those people, she's gonna be just fine." I can feel tears starting to slip free from the corners of my eyes, so I stand up, I'm about to walk away when his hand wraps around my wrist and drags my hand back to his chest.

"You'll always be one of those people, you know that, right?" he frowns. I nod back at him with a smile that takes every strength inside me to pull together.

"I got loads of school work to do. I should get on." I slide my hand away from his chest and grab my bag from the table.

"Yeah I promised to help Skid shift some stuff out of his cabin, it's being decorated," he says, leaping up from the table and placing a kiss on my forehead. "Good talk," he speaks against my skin.

"Yeah, good talk," I whisper, watching him stroll out of the door.

I go to my room and shut the door behind me, then back up against it and slide down into a ball on the floor. Tears stream down my cheeks, like the dam that's held them for so long has finally been broken. I don't know how long I sit there, but it's long enough for my eyes to ache as much as my heart.

Wiping my eyes on the back of my hand I scramble forward to the bedside table, open up the top drawer, and take out a pen and paper. I bleed all my pain on to the paper, then seal it into an envelope and write his name on the front.

I don't even pretend to myself that I'm going to give it to him. I stopped doing that years ago.

Another tear rolls off my cheek and splashes on to the fresh ink, blotching one of the s's in his name. I hold the letter in my hand and watch as one tiny teardrop spreads among the letters, blurring them and making an inky mess on the envelope. Then like always, I blot the envelope to my lips, reach under my bed and pull out the shoe box.

Opening the lid I place it on top of all the others, I'd tossed the other items to make space years ago, keyrings and stones no longer mattered to me, but my letters held their value. Letters Jessie would never read, feelings Jessie would never discover, and words that will forever remain hidden in a shoe box.

CHAPTER 19
JESSIE

"We got company," Nyx calls out, banging on the door while church is still in session. It has to be something important for anyone to have the balls to interrupt us.

"Check it out," Prez instructs Troj, who leaves the table to step outside. He returns moments later with a panicked expression that has me up on my feet.

"Fuckin' Feds," he says. "CCTV's picking them up turning off the bottom road, we haven't got long."

"Clear the vestry," Prez calls across the table. Sending Squealer and Screwy straight to work, they head straight for the back room where we keep some of our gun supply. Thorne leaves to grab the cage, while me and Troj follow the temper twins into the vestry.

They already have the back doors open, and Thorne quickly backs up the transit so we can start loading. We work as fast as we can, hoping that Prez can stall the feds long enough for Thorne to get to the track we keep clear in the woods. The track that leads off our border and on to the Indian reservation the other side. They've made it clear they don't want us on their territory, but in cases of emergency like this one, they'll have to fuckin' deal.

For once I'm thankful that our supplies are low, seems like we did our deal out in Nebraska at just the right time.

I slam the van door shut when we we're cleared out and bang hard on the back, signaling for Thorne to get the fuck out of here, and we all breathe a sigh of relief when he disappears into the tree line.

We take a second to catch our breath before we walk out of church and cross the yard as coolly as we can manage.

I light up a cigarette and watch the fed van along with two cars skid to a stop outside the club entrance where Prez waits, standing on the threshold with his arms crossed.

The back of the van bursts open, four armored officers spill out, and chaos fills the yard.

"Arms up. On the ground," one of them calls out, and knowing they don't have shit on us so long as Thorne is still moving we all lower on to our knees, Prez included.

The cigarette still hangs from my mouth as I drop to my chest on to the rough, dusty ground and wait to find out what all this is about.

"We're looking for Tobias Saunders," one of them says, his polished boot kicking dust into our faces as he walks a line in front of us. Who in the ever-loving fuck is Tobias Saunders?

"That'll be me," Skid says, keeping his hands behind his head as he kneels up. An officer immediately steps behind him and cuffs his hands behind his back while he reads him his rights. It confuses the fuck out of me because I know Skid's real name, and it sure as hell ain't Tobias fuckin' Saunders.

We all watch with the same confusion as he's loaded into the back of the van and the doors slide shut behind him, and just as quickly as they arrived, the feds leave.

"Your brother's just brought you about an hour's head start," Prez turns to Chop as he speaks, and then everyone else's eyes do the same. "Soon as they run Skid's prints they're gonna know he ain't who he's saying he is."

Chop nods in agreement.

"You're Tobias?" Troj asks Chop.

"I thought all that shit got buried fucking years ago," Chop replies, brushing his hand through his beard. If it weren't for the fact his younger brother had an equally impressive amount of facial hair, they would never have just pulled that off. There's a decent age gap between them, the fact Chop keeps himself in shape and Skid looks older than his age sometimes makes us forget that. I just hope it will fool the feds long enough for Chop to get clear.

"It wasn't legitimate, we got someone on the inside to fiddle the warrant," Prez says, clearly thinking hard about what to do next.

"Hey, you know I'd have stepped up if I'd had a clue what the fuck was goin' on," Troj tells him.

"Sure kid, means a lot, but it wouldn't have been no good, the crime was committed before you were an itch in your papa's nut sack. They'd have guessed you were lying." Chop squeezes his shoulder. "I'll take a car from the garage and get out of town. Soon as I can, I'll get a pre-pay and make contact from there. When you see Skid, you tell him I fuckin' owe him."

Prez nods, and we all watch, still in shock, as Chop races over to the garage, speeding out moments later in a silver Mercedes that belongs to the club.

"Tac, get hold of Thorne to tell him the coast is clear before the Cheyanne start shooting arrows at him. Nyx go tell Carly what's gone down, tell her I'm getting hold of Monica the lawyer and that Skid will be back soon," Prez orders, and Nyx jogs over to his bike and gets right on it, while Tac pulls out his cell.

"Squealer I'll reach out to our Denver Charter, You, Screw, and Thorne get that stash out of town, I'll call you with an address in the next couple hours," he commands, and then he looks to me and Troj. "You two head up to Chop's lodge. As soon as they realize they got the wrong guy those feds will be back, so make sure there's nothing for them to add to the heap of shit he's already in. And if anyone sees 's Tommy tell him what's happened and to come to find me." We both nod, wasting no time, and jumping on our bikes to head up to Chop's lodge.

We let ourselves into Chop's place. Like everyone else around here, he doesn't lock his doors, this club is built on trust.

"Would you really have done that, stepped up and been prepared to take the shit for another brother when you didn't even know what it was about?" I ask Troj as we head into Chop's bedroom.

"For sure. I'd fuckin' take a bullet for any one of your asses," he tells me, shifting through Chop's wardrobe and pulling out an AK, followed by a machete. "You?"

"You know I'd die for this club." I crouch down and stretch out my arm to feel around under the bed, locating a handgun between the slats and mattress.

"You ain't got no outstanding warrants or fake names, do ya?" Troj checks as we move through to check the bathroom.

"Nah man you're good." I come back out, winking as I throw him the block of coke I've retrieved from the cistern.

"Good, 'coz I'm too young to die, and this face is far too pretty for prison." Troj hardly has to stretch to check the top of the wardrobe, he pulls down an old trunk and places it on the bed. When we open it it's full of sentimental stuff, old photos and documents, the kinda shit I'm surprised a guy like Chop keeps.

"We'll drop this off at Carly and Skid's, best let them keep it till he comes back, there might be something in here that will help." I grab the trunk, and we both make one final sweep before we leave. I managed to balance it on my fuel tank while we ride down to Skid's cabin, and Nyx is still there when we arrive. He's sat looking awkward as fuck drinking lemonade at the kitchen table. Nyx wasn't the best choice of person to break the news that your husband has just been shipped off by the feds, the kid has the social skills of a mosquito.

"You can head off now, we got this," I tell him, moving

straight to Carly and wrapping my arm around her shoulder. Nyx doesn't have to be told twice. With a tip of his head to Carly, he shoots out of the house before either of us change our minds.

"Why would he do it, Jessie?" Carly asks looking up at me, I'd rather take a punch to the face than have a woman cry around me. I hate it, I never know what to do.

"Hey, it's Skid, you know what he's like, he'll do anything to help someone out. Soon as they realize he ain't Chop, Monica will swoop in and they'll let him go. It won't be long. Promise." I shrug out of my cut and hang it on the back of the chair. "In the meantime, you can make us some lunch and me and Troj will set to work on finishing that decorating Skid's been bitchin about having to get done." I look over at the covered furniture and half painted living area.

"We will?" Troj looks up at me from his phone puzzled, and I give him a look that has him shifting up on his feet and taking his cut off too. He gathers up his long hair and ties it on the top of his head. "Come on then, let's get at it." He kisses Carly on her cheek. "The things some guys will do to get out of a little decorating, huh?" He picks up the roller that's been left on the table and manages to get a little chuckle out of Carly.

"I guess I better grab some beers and start frying up some chicken," she sniffs.

CHAPTER 20
HAYLEY

It's been almost a week since Chop left the compound, being a man down means the club is busy, and that means I hardly see anything of Jessie.

Tommy does nothing to hide his frustration from me when he becomes my new chauffeur. Runaway Daddy issues aside, his bad temper is becoming unbearable. So, I decide to talk to Daddy about it.

I begged him to come home for dinner tonight, even went to the effort to cook his favourite. I invited Jessie too, in the hope I could count on him for support.

I hadn't expected for Skid to be joining us though. Apparently, Carly is out of town visiting her family, so Daddy invited him to join us.

I like Skid, he seems the most reasonable out of all of Daddy and Jessie's friends. Maybe he could help me talk some sense into Daddy too.

I wait till Daddy has a mouthful of spaghetti before I bring it up, at least that way he can't cut me off.

"Daddy. I don't want Tommy taking me to school anymore," I blurt out, feeling a little awkward when I remember that Tommy is Skid's nephew. "I mean, he's clearly cut up about his Dad. I thought it might be better for Jessie to start dropping me at college again," I recover myself, smiling at Skid apologetically. Daddy chews his mouthful, deep in thought, and I swear I can hear the clock on the wall tick while I wait for his response.

"Jessie's too busy with club stuff, baby," he says eventually, taking a napkin and wiping his mouth. I'm about to interrupt him, not too ashamed to beg. The thought of seeing Tommy's nasty scowl on Monday morning is already irritating me.

"But I have been thinking," Daddy continues, "Skid…" His eyes look across to Skid who sucks up the long piece of spaghetti that hung from his mouth before he looks up from his plate.

"Hook my princess up with a car, I want something sturdy and reliable."

"Got just the thing boss," Skid nods, slying me a wink when Daddy tucks back into his meal like what he just said isn't a major deal. I'm getting a car!

CHAPTER 21 - JESSIE

Me and Skid look at Prez with the same shock on our faces when Hayley skips out the room. He crams another meatball in his already full mouth, his table manners apparently up and left along with his daughter.

"Have Tommy follow her on his bike, tell him to hang back enough that she doesn't notice," he muffles in between chomps. Me and Skid smirk at each other when we hear just the sort of shit we were expecting.

"What?" Prez asks when he notices our reactions.

"For a moment then you had us worried, thought you were actually gonna let Daddy's princess out in the big wide world," I laugh.

"Now come on you both know me better than that." He twists his spaghetti around his fork. And he's right, we both do know him better.

CHAPTER 22

HAYLEY

Saturday comes and I'm up at the ass-crack of dawn waiting outside the garage for Skid to arrive.

"Keen much?" Skid laughs at me as he uses his huge arm to lift the shutter door and reveals a shiny red jeep. I watch hopefully as he heads straight for it, opening the driver door to pull the keys out of the ignition.

"Mine?" I ask, catching them when he tosses them to me.

"Serviced it myself yesterday, she's all yours kid."

"Stolen?" I check.

Skid smiles back at me and I'm far too excited to feel bad.

"I can't wait to show Jessie," I screech, hopping up into the driver's seat.

"You want me to take you for a spin, get ya used to her?" Skid offers.

"No need, I'll go pick up Jessie. We'll probably take a trip out to Bernie's for lunch. You want us to grab you something while we're out?" When I stop my eyes from wondering over my new ride and look at Skid, his smile has faded.

"You love him don't ya?" He crosses his arms and leans through the open window beside me.

"Course I do, he's like my brot—"

"Don't try pullin' that shit with me," he interrupts before I can finish. "I see the way you look at him. How you beat them pretty green eyes for him. Come on, talk to uncle Skid. "

"I have no idea what you're talking about." I try to keep my face convincing.

"I want to believe that's true, coz if you did... Love him. I'd have to give you the warning 'bout how dangerous it is." He taps the door with his palm and backs away.

"What could be dangerous about love?" I laugh. Nervously.

"When you're the president's daughter, just about everything for the guy who you catch feelings for. 'Specially if he's a member of this club."

He picks up one of his tools, a spanner I think, and twists it around in his hand before he continues. "You don't fall for her back, that means you've broken her heart, and Daddy wants you dead.

You do fall for her, and decide to make her yours the way the men around here own their women. Daddy makes you suffer before you're dead.

So if you did have feelings, either way, you'd be signing Jessie's death certificate." Skid strokes his hand through his beard as he takes a seat on the stool by the workstation. "Prez loves that boy like a son, but club rules are club rules, and I don't think either of us want that for Jessie."

I nod my head, taking everything he says in like I'm hearing something I don't already know.

"So it's a good thing I don't have feelings for him then, huh?" I try my best to sound upbeat, despite my heart feeling like it's been shredded.

Skid can see how his words have affected me, I'm not that good an actress.

Jessie spends that afternoon, and then most of Sunday driving around with me so I can get used to being behind the wheel again. It feels good to spend time with him, but I can't stop what Skid had said replaying over and over in my head. And of course, he's right. Skid's always right.

Coming to terms with it isn't really the issue, deep down I suppose I've always known I couldn't have Jessie. I'd just chosen to ignore that fact rather than move on from it.

I can't imagine another guy caring about me the way Jessie does. I've never wanted anyone else, I wouldn't know how to. Jessie has been my future since I was ten years old.

Determined not to let Skid's warning knock me down, I drive out of the compound on Monday all by myself, the tunes I've chosen blasting out of my stereo as I drive myself to school. Maddy is waiting for me in the carpark and looks like she's about to burst with excitement when I park up.

"Wow, this is awesome. Looks even better than the picture you sent. I'm so jealous." She checks out my new ride.

"You wanna take a ride when we've finished class?" I ask, grabbing my bag off the passenger seat and hopping out to join her.

"Course I do," Maddy answers without hesitation.

"Cool, meet me here after." I click the automatic lock, and we walk into school together.

School drags like a bitch, probably because I'm excited about going for a drive with Maddy. Being away from the club makes it so much easier to forget the whole Jessie dilemma, and hopefully, Maddy will be too distracted to mention him. I text Daddy and Jessie, tell them where I'm going, and promise to pick up Pizza on my way back through town. When I finally finish my last lecture of the day Maddy is already waiting for me at the jeep.

"Ice Cream over at Pikes Peak," I suggest.

"That's a great shout," she giggles, throwing her bag into the back before jumping into the passenger seat. The ice cream parlor up at the peak do the best cookie dough ice cream in the entire world, Mom used to take me there when I was little.

We head out of the parking lot up towards Pikes Peak. We've only got a few miles out of town when I notice the sign for a gas station, and a quick glance at the dash tells me I'm low. I forgot about all the responsibilities that come with driving.

I pull in and grab my purse before starting to fill up, I'm concentrating on the pump, and don't really pay much attention to the black van that pulls up beside us, not until I hear Maddy scream.

It all happens so fast after that, the side door sliding open, the huge guy wearing black dragging her out from my passenger seat. Maddy struggles but it's hopeless, she's like a fish caught in a net as he roughly throws her inside the back of the van.

I drop the pump to the floor and race towards her. Fully prepared to take out whoever it is that's trying to take her, whoever they are will soon regret it. They've picked the wrong girls to mess with today.

But I'm halted by a strong arm, one that wraps itself around my neck and crushes all the air from my windpipe.

Strong hips force me to move forward, closer to the open van door. Then I'm taken off my feet and tossed inside.

I just manage to catch a glimpse of the terror in Maddy's eyes before the door rolls shut, and traps us both in darkness.

The tires screech, and our bodies lunge forward as the van speeds away, both of us tumbling around the empty space. We scream as loud as we can through our tears, banging and kicking against the solid panels. Our bodies knocking against each other's as we frantically search in the darkness for a latch to open one of the doors.

In the end, we only find each other, and we cling to each other tightly, throats sore from screaming, and heartbeats pumping like they could burn out any second. We sit together in the silence, both too petrified to speak, and we wait for the journey to hell knows where to end.

After what feels like ages, the van noticeably slows down.

Rough bumps beneath the tires throw us around, but we hold on to each other best we can.

The van comes to an abrupt halt, and daylight bursts through the back doors seconds later when it's swung open. I hold my hand in front of my eyes while they adjust to the brightness, but soon a much larger shadow blocks out the light. Two gigantic men stand side by side between the doors, each of them holding a gun that's pointed directly at us. A third man appears, pushing between them, a huge, dirty grin on his face as he looks in on us.

"Ladies." His arm stretches out in an overly sarcastic welcome. I've never seen the man before, but I'm already praying to god that I'll get the chance to watch my daddy and his brothers rip the ugly head off his shitty tattooed neck.

Me and Maddy scramble onto our feet and step out of the van. I try to take in our surroundings, figure out where we are. Derelict buildings stand tall around us. Massive warehouses with missing roofs, smashed windows, and unsteady brickwork.

The armed men make sure the barrel of their guns dig hard into our backs as they urge us to move forward and follow the guy who seems to be in charge. Neither me nor Maddy argue, but I'm Jimmer Carson's daughter… I will not let them see my fear. Unlike Maddy who's a whimpering wreck.

We're led into one of the warehouses, the echo of flapping wings makes me jump when we disturb the nestling birds from the rafters.

I look up and count at least four half ripped out floors, between the ground and the roof. Old, rusty machinery suggests this place must have been some kind of factory when it was functioning. Now, it's just a barren building in the middle of nowhere, the perfect place to take two girls who have been kidnapped.

Daddy and Jessie will find us though. I know they will, I just have to buy us the time we needed until they do.

There's a single chair already waiting in the middle of the

room, and the guy with the gun against Maddy's back gestures for her to sit down. Tears stream her cheeks as the one with the awful tattoos uses rope to strap her arms around the back of the chair. Then he steps off and picks up a plastic chair from the floor and places it beside her.

"Sorry, sweetheart, we were only expecting one visitor." He grabs at my arm, his fingers bruising my bicep before he throws me at the chair.

He ties me to it the same way he has Maddy, and I snarl at him when he purposely brushes his dirty hand over my chest.

"Boss is here," a voice calls out from the door we entered through, it seems so far away. Even if I could get us out of the ropes, it's a long run to the exit and a bullet travels fast. My eyes begin to scan for another way out.

The sound of bike engines gives me hope, and for a wonderful moment, I think that Daddy and Jessie have already found us. That hope is shattered into teeny tiny pieces when a few minutes later another man walks in. This one is older, like Daddy, he wears a cut like him too, except his doesn't bear the Dirty Soul's hooded skull. He has a smiling devil stitched into his leather.

A Bastard.

He's followed inside by several other men, all of them nasty looking fuckers who wear the same cut. They are the men responsible for killing my mama. The Dirty Souls' enemies, which means me and Maddy are in deeper shit than I thought.

"What the fuck is this?" the older guy speaks first, close enough now for me to read his 'president' badge. He stands a little taller than Daddy, and is much rounder. His salt and pepper colored hair is similar too, but his light covering of stubble is nothing compared to Daddy's beard.

He carries the same presence though, and where Daddy has never scared me, this man most certainly does.

"You told us to get the girl, Prez," the guy who tied us says.

"Yeah. A fucking girl. You wanna tell me why the fuck I'm seeing two of 'em?"

"They were together, Prez, we didn't want to leave a witness behind," he explains, transforming rapidly from cocky, arrogant asshole, to brown-nosing weasel.

"Maddy." The president smiles at the quivering mess beside me. "Always good to see you…"

My heart slows, as my brain tries to absorb what my ears have just heard. He knows her name? *Always good to see you,* what would she have ever had to do with these people? I don't have time to think on that anymore, not when his attention turns to me, his forehead creased, as he leans closer and studies my face harder. His wrinkles iron out and his mouth upturns into the grimmest of smiles.

"Well, will you look at what we have here," he chuckles.

"Boss?" the weasel asks, clearly stumped by his Prez's change in reaction.

"Looks like our witness belongs to someone we know boys." His eyes don't move from mine, and I refuse to show weakness by looking away from his first. "This pretty little thing here is Jimmer Carson's daughter." He grips my chin in his hand.

"Jimmer Carson, as in…" one of the men holding a gun starts to speak.

"Yes, Spider. Jimmer Carson, President of the Dirty Souls." The old man's finger flicks the end of my nose. "Well ain't this lookin' to be a beautiful day." The laughter behind his voice is faint, but it still shakes through my bones, while fear screeches inside my head.

I say a silent prayer that Daddy and his brothers will find us before it's too late.

CHAPTER 23
JESSIE

We're just about done loading the cage with AK's ready for our run tomorrow. Squealer and Screwy have collected them from our safe place in Denver, me and Grimm have checked and repacked them ready for transportation over to the Utah Charter.

It was gonna be good to ride out, I was looking forward to hitting the road and catching up with some familiar faces at my pa's old Charter. Maybe when I come back, I might even grow the balls to take Maddy out for that ride.

It's been over two weeks since I asked her. She probably thinks I've changed my mind. The girl couldn't have been more wrong. She's on my mind every minute of every god given day.

The cage Nyx will drive and we will protect all the way to Cannonville, is good to go, and the two of us are ready for a drink. We're making our way towards the clubhouse but are stopped in our tracks when Prez comes storming out. He has a look in his eyes that I haven't seen for years, and it puts me straight on edge.

"Church," he yells, barging past Troj and knocking the beer clean out his hand. Shit's gone down, that much is obvious, and I already feel the trickle of adrenaline in my blood, readying me for whatever that shit might be.

We follow him into church, joined moments later by the rest

of the gang. Prez is stood at the head of the table, while all our eyes glance at each other nervously. Prez standing ain't a good sign, not at all.

"Someone's got Hayley," he speaks calmly, and controlled, though his eyes are wild. I'm on my feet before he's even finished his sentence.

"Who?" I shout.

"Tommy just called, blacked-out van took her and the bitch from school she's been hanging out with lately."

My heart stops, and my skin chills when I hear they got Maddy too.

"He kept back, followed them to some abandoned factory just outside of Pueblo," Prez continues.

"Bastards." The bones in my neck crack when I stretch it from one side to the other. My mind focusing on only one thing, Bastard blood wetting my knife.

If one hair has been touched on either those girl's heads, I'll slice open every one of them and spit on the hell seeking souls that crawl from their bodies.

"What we fuckin' waitin' for, Christmas? Let's go." Troj is up now too, practically bouncing on his feet. He can smell the fuckin' fight, and he craves it as much as I do.

"Tommy's got eyes on the place now. Arm up and let's ride out," Prez tells us.

"Ye hah! It's kill time, Screwy," Squealer shakes his brother's shoulders, and Screwy's eyes light up like it actually is fucking Christmas.

Everyone rushes out, the thunder of bikes starting to fill the yard. Prez pulls me back before I saddle mine, smacking something inside my palm.

"You take care of that till Chop comes back, son." I wait for him to walk away before I looked down into my hand, and I almost choke on the lump in my throat when I see the VP badge staring back up at me. It's worn and faded, the same one my pa had stitched to his cut when he was VP of this Charter. And although I'm only stepping in while Chop's away, I know this is Prez showing me that I have the potential to be his second man someday.

I have little time for emotions now though, and I quickly seat up. Skid nods his approval at me when I take my new position on the left side of Prez. We wait for Prez's right hand, and when it lifts in the air and points forward, we follow our leader out on to the road. It's time to rain a whole ton of shit on the Bastards for thinking they can fuck with our family.

CHAPTER 24
HAYLEY

The men eventually clear out the room leaving just the weasel guarding us. His phone rings not long after and he turns his back on us to walk out of earshot, I see it as my chance.

"Maddy," I whisper.

She looks up at me, her eyes red and raw from crying. "Listen. I think I can untie myself," I tell her.

"So what if you can? They'll kill us if we run." Her voice doesn't hold a thread of hope, and it makes me furious.

"Maddy Summers!" I overexaggerate my voice. "Miss enthusiastic, glass half full, life's one long ride on a fuckin' fun cloud herself giving up… Nah ah. I don't fucking think so."

I stretch out my bound hands, crossing my fingers to make them as narrow as possible, then hook the thumb of my other hand between the ropes. I twist the opposite wrist, working against the rope to loosen it. It's tight but not too taut for me to eventually make a gap that's big enough for my thumb to fit through.

Gradually I start to pull the rope apart, my wrists on fire from the friction of the coarse rope rubbing against my skin. But feeling the knots loosen slightly on the other hand make it all worth it.

"Maddy, do you know who these men are?" I whisper, trying to distract myself from the pain.

"The older guy yeah, but I had no idea he was like your daddy and his guys." She shakes her head.

"He's not," I keep my voice low. "He's the guy who had my mom killed, he tried to get me killed too. He hates my father and the club. How do you know him?" I ask, and Maddy's face drops.

"My mom got herself into some trouble with him." She lets out a long breathe, and the shame on her face tells me not to push any further. Not now anyway. She's clearly riddled with guilt for being the reason we're in this situation, and I need her strong now, we can talk when we're out of this mess.

"Do you think they'll find us?" she asks through trembling lips. And as my hand becomes looser, my heart beats faster, I haven't come up with a plan for what I'm gonna do next. Whatever it is though involves taking the weasel out, and he has a gun now.

"My daddy will find us, and when he does every single man who was a part of this will die," I assure her. Faith is already slipping away from her, and if we stand any chance of getting out of here alive, I'm gonna need her to have some fight.

"And then after the massacre, you and Jessie can go on that ride he promised to take you on," I add, then watch a flicker of a smile battle through her sadness.

"You really like him, don't you?" I smile back at her.

"I know your gonna tell me he's bad for me and I'm not gonna tell you that you're wrong. But I see through all that. To me he's a sweet guy, with beautiful eyes, and a smile you would throw yourself off a cliff for.

I saw the way he took care of you when you were in trouble and the way he looks out for you. Sure, he's a little rough around the edges, but I've seen that he's capable of some real good too." Maddy's really smiling now, and it doesn't sting my chest as hard as I thought it would.

"Yeah I really like him," she admits in her own totally goofy style. Tears well in my eyes, forcing me to work harder at freeing my hands so I can wipe them away before she sees.

My emotions aren't at all what I'd expected. There's no anger, no jealousy, just relief. Relief that someone else has seen who Jessie is beneath the leather cut he wears, if Maddy sees past the blood that stains his hands. Jessie might just get that happily ever after I've always wanted for him.

Deep down I've always known it wouldn't be with me, I just hadn't been ready to let myself believe it. It's going to kill me to watch, but just like Maddy said, a girl would toss herself off a cliff to see that smile on his face.

I hear more bikes arrive outside, and the sound of a scuffle and gunshots causes the man watching over us to tuck his phone back inside his pocket and make his way back over.

"Either one of you bitches make a sound, I swear I will shoot you both in the face," he warns, pointing his gun right at us. My hands are loose now, and I grip at the rope to stop it from falling to the floor. I know that the commotion outside is the Dirty Souls, and I try so hard not to let the relief show on my face. The door at the back of the room smashes open, and Jessie storms through it like a bull released from the chute, he's followed closely by Squealer, Screwy, and Troj.

The man's face drops when he realizes there's no sign of his brothers, he's outnumbered and for a dreadful moment, I think he will turn and fire at them. But unless he's a cracking shot, the building is too big, and they are too far away for him to make a target.

He has nowhere to run, which I guess is why he turns back around to face us, his gun now pointing directly at Maddy's head. She's defenseless still tied to her chair. I hear the feral roar that comes out of Jessie. It bellows right from his soul and saws through the center of my heart like a serrated knife.

I look between him and Maddy, their eyes fused together. Reflecting each other's fear, and I can't let myself even imagine what losing her would do to him. He'll blame himself somehow.

I don't see a man anymore, I see that twelve-year boy that Daddy brought home, a lost soul about to lose another person he loves.

Maddy could bring so much to his life, things I never could. Love, happiness, and all without consequences. He needs her as much as he needs the cut on his back, and with her he could have both.

There's no way I'm gonna let this son of a bitch pointing a gun at her take that away from him. When I hear the gun click and watch his finger pull back on the trigger. There is no choice to make, no decision for me to contemplate. I love Jessie.

I launch off my chair and jump in front of Maddy's body, attempting to shield her from the bullet that painfully rings through my ears as it leaves the barrel.

Concern that I've left it too late to save her vanishes when I feel a sharp burn scorch through my skin from the bullet. I hit the concrete floor with a thud, and despite my whole body throbbing with pain, I still have to touch the wound on the right side of my chest to check that it's real. My hand turns sticky, and I panic when I struggle to catch my next breath. More guns let off, bullets ricocheting from the steel beams, and I pray that Maddy is safe from them.

"Someone call a fucking ambulance," I hear Jessie, his loud footsteps thundering towards me, and he falls on to his knees, crouching over my body, replacing my blood-drenched hands with his own. The pressure he puts against my wound hurts like hell, but I don't make a sound. Just watch as he pulls them away again, and holds them up in front of his face. They're shaking, and his eyes widen as he stares at his blood-soaked palms.

His beautiful blue eyes are frosted with panic, and his chest heaves. He looks at me helplessly, but only for a few seconds before he pulls himself together.

Swallowing down the lump in his throat, he shrugs out of his cut and tosses it. Then pulling off his T-shirt he scrunches it into a ball, pressing it tightly against my wound. He pulls me up into his solid chest, and there I feel safe.

His white T-shirt turns red as my blood-soaks its way through the cotton. I try to speak, but the coppery taste of blood in the back of my throat chokes me, stopping any words from forming.

"Don't try and speak, Hay, it's gonna be okay. Help's coming. Just hang with me a minute." He seems to be getting further and further away, yet I still feel his firm grip, and his heart erratically thump against my body.

"No... No don't you fucking leave me. Not you too. You hear me, Hay. HAY. Don't leave me." His voice is distant, but I hear how desperate it is, and it makes me choke all the more. He's crying, and I want to comfort him, to hug him back and tell him that everything is gonna be okay. Exactly like I'd wanted to when I was ten years old and Daddy first brought him home to me. But I can't speak. In fact, I wonder if I'm even breathing.

I find some strength in determination. I can't give up, because he has to know it's gonna be okay, I'm not a little girl anymore, this time I will tell him.

"It's okay," I manage to force out, my voice unrecognizable. Jessie's rough palm strokes the hair away from my face, probably smearing it with blood, but I doubt that's gonna matter for much longer.

"Sssshhh don't speak." His chin rests on the top of my head and he rocks me in his arms like a baby.

"Don't worry. I got you, you're gonna be fine," he assures me. I'm not sure if he's trying to convince himself or me, but it isn't working much on either of us. I shake my head, but don't think it actually moves.

"It would always have been you," I whisper, words starting to come a little easier, my hand reaches up to cup his face. I'm not sure how I manage it, but I'm grateful to feel the prickles on his jaw.

"I would never have wanted anyone else," I let him know.

"Hay. Will you do as you're told for once in your fucking life? Stop trying to talk."

I let myself look up into his eyes again, they're full of tears, no more anger. Just raw pain, masked by a beautiful, brave face that's put on for my benefit.

"Love Jessie..." I swallow the thick blood clogging in the back of my throat. "I need you to do that for me, okay? I need you to let yourself… love."

"Hay. Help's coming." His voice sounds weak, and the fight's beginning to drain out of his eyes. Then my heart breaks when he loses it all together. My pain is starting to ease, and I guess, in my case that isn't a good thing.

"Promise me!" I battle against the urge to shut my eyes, knowing they won't open again if I let them close. They're so heavy, I won't be able to fight against them for much longer.

"Sure thing, pretty girl," he whispers, nodding his head and treating me one last time to the smile that I'd move hell and earth to see. One of his tears spills on to my cheek, I feel it roll along my skin and I smile too, because for that short moment he's mine. I just wish I could keep him.

I don't fight against my eyes anymore, I let them fall. His face is the only vision I want to remember. I don't worry about what will happen next, or where I'm going. I just pray that wherever it is, I get to keep that with me. I cling on to it so tight, focusing on his blue eyes and handsome smile instead of the fact that my agony has vanished completely. And as the painful cries that scream out my name fade further and further away. I don't fight to go back to him. I leave him behind. Letting myself slip away, because death has to be easier than letting him go again.

CHAPTER 25

MADDY

I've always thought it was a cliché when people tell you everything moves in slow motion during a tragedy. And yet here, watching everything play out in front of me, that's exactly what happens. The armed men bursting in the room, Jessie's terror-filled eyes locking on mine.

All of it happened so slowly that my head will never let me forget a single detail of my own horror movie, the low, dull thumping of my heart playing as its soundtrack. I'll see Hayley every time I close my eyes from now on, jumping in front of me and falling to the ground.

My ears still ring from the sound of the bullets when I realize what she's done, and everything around me becomes a silent panic. Jessie looks wild as he runs forward and falls in front of her, grabbing her up and pulling her on to him. I look up at the other men in the room, and they all seem a lot less scary with devastation hanging on their hard faces. It shows that they're human. They watch with me as Jessie rocks Hayley's body, willing for her to stay with him. I can't hear what he's saying, the shrill, high pitched sound of bullets are still hurting my head.

The sound leaves as quickly as it came, and his cries are the first thing I hear, calling her name, begging her to come back.

Even before her hand falls from his face, everyone in the room including me knows that it's too late for an ambulance. But

Jessie refuses to give up, dragging her limp hand back up and holding it to his face.

"No, Hay, don't you leave me." His eyes drown in tears when her hand lifelessly slides away again. "Hayley. Please don't," he pleads, sounding like a scared child.

He keeps rocking her, pressing his lips tight against the parting on the top of her head. Speaking in soft whispers, and begging for her to wake up. And I watch his pain through my own tears.

Suddenly everyone parts out of the way, an older man with white hair makes his way through them. Stopping still when his eyes fall on Jessie and Hayley like he's just grown roots. His forehead furrows deeper, and his eyes turn glassy. I realize I'm looking at Hayley's Dad.

It seems like hours before anyone moves and it's the tall, long-haired one who steps up first. He walks slowly towards Jessie, and crouches beside him. His hand reaches out to squeeze his bare shoulder and his voice crackles through the unbearable silence…

"Jess. Come on man, you gotta let her go." Jessie doesn't respond, he just keeps rocking. Eyes tranced and focused forward. "Jessie," the man speaks again.

"I... I can't." Jessie shakes his head, his voice broken, and his lips refusing to move from Hayley's hair. The torture in his eyes tears a hole through my chest.

"Come on. We got to move man," the guy tries again, but Jessie doesn't budge. I want to reach out to him, but I'm still tied up and all I can do is sit and watch him fall apart right in front of me.

He kisses her temple and closes his eyes. Inhaling deep like he's absorbing her into his memories.

"I'm so sorry… so fuckin' sorry, Hay," he says through his tears, rolling her away from his body and placing her gently on to the ground.

"Sorry."

The tall guy tries to help him up but Jessie pushes him away. I can't look when Jessie lifts up on to his knees, throws back his head, and a painful noise rips right from the bottom of his throat. Not a cry nor a scream, but something in-between. Like the howl of a wounded wolf.

He slumps back down, his arms hanging over his propped-up knees, and his head dropping between them. Breathless and destroyed.

Nobody seems to be moving, everyone still struck with shock. Seconds pass into minutes and Jessie pushes his trembling fingers through his hair, leaving a blood-stained trail in his sandy-blonde strands.

I fight against my restraints, desperate to get to him. Wanting to wrap him up in my arms and show him some comfort, but the ropes that hold me won't budge. I look up from him and notice the president badge Hayley's Dad is wearing on his jacket as he moves closer, His eyes not moving from Hayley's body and the lifeless look in her eyes matches his own.

Jessie crawls back to her and hangs over her body.

"Wake up," his gravelly voice begs. He grabs at her shoulders and shakes her hard, his voice turning angry. "Wake the fuck up, Hay… Wake up, right now," he demands, wiping his tears away with the back of his hand. "Please…" he eventually whispers, sounding defeated.

"She's gone, son." The older man leans down, tapping Jessie on his back, his eyes still not moving from Hayley.

"No." Jessie shakes his head then looks over to the dead man who killed her.

Like someone just flicked a switch inside his head, he's on his feet, all the hurt in his tear-drenched eyes flipping into rage. With nostrils flared, and his jaw clenched tight. Jessie's lips scowl fury as he charges over to the body of our capturer. His boot smashing into the dead man's face, and then his stomach.

"Fuckin. Piece. Of Bastard. Scum," Jessie growls through his teeth, continuing to kick the ever-living shit into the lifeless body of the man who's just taken Hayley's life right in front of us.

One of the bigger guys try to take hold of him, but Jessie shoves him away, telling him to get the fuck off. The guy backs down immediately, holding out the palms of his hands, and Jessie moves his attention to the nearest wall. I flinch when I hear his fists crunch against the solid brick, and cry when he doesn't stop, not even with blood dripping from his knuckles.

No one tries to stop him, all of them letting him go on hurting himself.

"Why fuckin' her? Huh? Fuckin' Bastards," he screams at the ceiling, kicking his boot against the wall now instead of his fists. Long-haired guy steps up to him again, this time wrapping his arms around Jessie's shoulders and pulling him back. Jessie fights it at first, but eventually, he gives in. His body sagging with defeat against the man holding him.

"I swear I'ma kill every fuckin' one of them," he cries out through his tears. "I will. Hayley, they all fucking pay for this," he calls out to her as the guy backs him out of the building, and most of the other men follow behind them.

Hayley's Dad still stands over her, haunted as he stares down, and I suddenly wish it was me lying in her place.

"Um Prez?" a voice speaks up, I've been so focused on him that I haven't noticed anyone left in the room with us. This guy has a thick beard and kind eyes, and is crouched beside the body of the man who killed Hayley. He looks up with a confused look on his face and holds something out in his hands. Hayley's dad snatches it, then studies it hard, and when his stone hard face slowly twists and meets with mine, I know I'm in trouble.

"She comes with us," he orders, his eyes fixed on me as he speaks. I glance at Hayley, and my chest tightens. That bullet was meant for me. I'd known her little over a month, and she'd taken that bullet for me.

Why?

A face I do recognize, Nyx, comes from behind me and unties the rope releasing my hands from behind my back. Then taking a firm grip of my arm, he drags me on to my feet and forces me across the room.

I turn my head and take one last look at my friend. My only friend. And the sole reason I'm alive... at least for now.

Nyx pulls me out the door, but I just managed to catch the older man drop to his knees and scoop Hayley into his arms. Her dad's whole body shakes when he thinks he's alone, and finally, he lets the tears he's held back escape from his tortured eyes.

"You might wanna close your eyes," Nyx whispers, with a tiny hint of sympathy in his tone. But I don't take his advice. What could be worse than what I've just seen? He keeps us walking towards a black transporter van, and I soon regret ignoring his advice when I see the bodies scattered, their blood staining the ground, seeping through the cracks in the earth and pooling into thick red puddles. Limbs are distorted, throats slit open, and bullets wedged between skulls.

The smell of blood causes my stomach to rise to my throat, it makes me retch, and my vomit spills on to the floor in front of me. Nyx waits until I'm finished before pushing me towards the van. I don't struggle or fight. I have nothing left. Most of the men are sat waiting on their bikes, and I can hear Jessie's angry voice

"Back the fuck off Troj, I told you I'm fine... I can ride." I look back over to where he's shrugging off the long-haired guy.

"It's okay let him be," the man with the thick beard nods, and Troj releases Jessie tapping his back. Jessie throws his leg over his bike and fires it up, revving the throttle and skidding off. Leaving a cloud of dust around everyone behind him. I scramble into the back of the boarded-out van and back up against the wall. Nyx slams the door shut and I'm left all alone, just me, the blackness, and a heart that still beats, even if it is completely weighed down by guilt.

I'll never see Hayley again, after this I probably won't ever see my mom again either. I cry for Hayley, for all the things she will never have the chance to do. I cry for Jessie because his heart is broken and there is nothing I can do to bring her back for him. Then selfishly I cry for myself, for the friend I've lost and the impossible choices I'm now going to have to make.

It seems like a long journey, and I'm almost thankful when the van stops and the doors open.

"Please, Nyx, tell me what's going on?" I ask him when he grabs my wrists and pulls me out, we're back at the Dirty Souls compound, and he leads me inside the clubhouse. I'm not surprised that he doesn't respond, and I don't bother to fight as he leads me through the foyer and into a small bar room.

Hayley's Dad is already there waiting for me, eyes so full of hate that I swear he could use them alone to kill me. Nyx puts enough pressure on my shoulders for my ass hit the chair that's placed in front of him.

"What did they want with you?" The president wastes no time getting to the point, and before I answer him, I close my eyes, scroll back in my memory to the outside of the warehouse. All those bodies, and none of them were his. Subconsciously, I'd searched for it, prayed it would be amongst the dead, but it wasn't.

It means he's still out there. That he could hurt my mom, for all I know he could be hurting her right now. So I keep my lips tightly together and hope Jessie shows up real soon to help me out of this mess.

"My daughter just took a bullet that had your name on it," he tells me, shoving a photo in my face. It's one of me, taken a few weeks ago, leaving school. I remember the day well, it had been the day Hayley had met my mom.

"They had this photo of you. You were the target, not my

girl." His voice trembles a little before anger takes it over again. He takes a fist full of my hair and I scream when he yanks my head back.

"You better start talking, missy, or you'll force me to take drastic measures, and you really don't want that to happen."

I shut my eyes and keep my mouth shut. I have to hold out for as long as possible for Mom's sake. Jessie must know I would never do anything to intentionally put Hayley in danger, he will come and explain. Everything will be okay.

"Come on, Prez, you been through enough. Let's leave this shit to Jessie. Nyx get him a drink," the guy with the beard and kind eyes speaks up. And the grip in my hair loosens so quickly that I fall off the chair and hit the ground with a hard thud.

"Take her downstairs. She can wait for Jessie down there," Hayley's Dad orders, marching out of the room and leaving the man with the beard to help me to my feet.

He stays silent as he walks me back through the foyer and then opens a door that leads to steep, downward stairs. I don't want to go down there. It looks dark and damp, and I have an unnerving feeling that I might not come back up from there alive. The man gestures with his head for me to go down first, and the sheer size of him tells me no amount of struggling would get me away from him. So, taking hold of the wooden banister, I step down the narrow staircase into darkness.

There are a few doors, the open ones leading into rooms that look like cells. And he leads me through the last door on the left, into a square room with just a chair placed in the middle and a table set to the side.

I watch him pull some rope from a draw in the table before he sits me on the chair.

"Sorry 'bout this, darlin'," he says, tying my arms behind my back.

"Name's Skid, Hayley may have mentioned my old lady, Carly, to ya." He talks to me like he's making polite conversation in a grocery store queue, not tying me to a chair in some creepy basement.

"Yes," I nod. I do remember Hayley mentioning Carly. She seemed to really like her. If this guy's married to her, he can't be all bad. Can he?

"I wish I could tell ya not to be scared, but right now you need to really think about what you do next," he starts. "Hayley must have liked you, hell she wouldn't have taken that bullet for you if she didn't. We already know the Bastards wanted you for something, you may be thinking they're the bad guys. But we're the ones who got you now, and up till now as a friend of Hayley's you've only ever had reason to see our good side."

I wouldn't exactly call the bodies I'd seen piled up at the warehouse an example of a good side, but I refrain from telling him that.

"When Jessie comes back from wherever he is, he's gonna come down here, and he's gonna be wanting some answers. And if you have any idea what's good for you, you will give him them." His tone is soft, through a coarse voice, and I try so hard to be brave. "I'll have Carly bring you down something to eat," he tells me before he walks out the room, closing the door behind him. I look around, there are dark stains on the concrete that I try convincing myself isn't blood, and I can't even let myself think about what happened to the last person who'd sat in this chair.

There's no sense of how much time passes, not when all I see is Hayley. I wonder where she is now. They couldn't have left her alone in that warehouse, it's getting dark. She'd be so cold and lonely.

I jump when the door clunks open, and my heart lifts from my stomach when Jessie steps inside. It quickly sinks back to where it came from when I sense the burning rage radiating off him. He's still topless and covered in blood, his eyes so furious I can't bring myself to look into them.

He unties me without saying a word, throwing something soft on to my lap when he's done. Looking down I see a black T-shirt, the logo on the front is the same as the one on the back of his cut. The Dirty Souls MC badge.

"Get out those clothes and put this on," he gestures to the shirt with his head, turning his back to give me some privacy. The shirt is baggy, and it smells like him. If I wasn't so petrified, I would probably take comfort in easing it over my skin.

"I'm done," I say feebly when I'm decent, and he turns back around. His eyes roll over my body before he speaks, the T-shirt I'm wearing may as well be non-existent because it feels like he can see right through it.

"You need to tell me right the fuck now what those men wanted with you?" his voice is a warning, and scary. I've seen him mad before, that night when Josh Tilsey tried to kiss me, and when Hayley had taken drugs, but never has his anger been directed at me before.

I chew on my bottom lip the way I always do when I'm nervous and shake my head slowly. I wish I could tell him, but I can't do that to Mom. I have to go with the small glimmer of hope that she's still alive and do all I can to keep her safe. I flinch when Jessie throws the table at the side of the room against the wall and feel my pulse beat wild when he marches towards me, forcing me to back away from him until my back meets with the wall.

"Arms up," he orders, keeping his fury flared eyes locked on mine, without even thinking I do as I'm told, raising my arms above my head. He takes the rope he's just untied me from and binds my hands to the thick solid pipe above me.

"Jessie, please…" I beg, but he ignores me. His face angry beyond any recognition, he snarls as his forehead presses tight into mine, and the focus in his eyes petrifies me.

"I'm gonna go shower the blood of the girl I loved like a sister off me. The same person who just gave up her life to save yours. When I come back down here, you better have some answers for me or you ain't gonna like the guy you see."

I turn my head to the side, unable to stand the hate he's penetrating a moment longer, and my whole body stiffens when his hand lifts between us, sliding up through my chest and wrapping around my throat. He clamps just tight enough for me to start to panic. "Don't force me to become that person with you, Maddy," he whispers inside my ear. And then he leaves me, his words of warning ringing terror throughout my entire body.

CHAPTER 26

JESSIE

I head back up to the club, and instead of the usual chaos I'm met by a somber silence.

Prez sits at the bar with his head in his hands, he looks broken. Squealer doesn't have anything clever to say, guess there's a first time for everything, and Skid is busy consoling Carly in the corner.

"She talk?" Skid pulls his attention from his old lady, looking up at me hopeful, and I shake my head. That's when Prez gets up, charging at me like a bull, his phlegm flying at my face as he growls,

"Then you get the fuck down there and rip her open until she fucking does." And for the first time in my life the thought of causing such pain makes my bones shudder.

"I mean it, Jessie, what the fuck you still doin' stood in front of me?" he shouts into the side of my face, and I focus forward, accepting the harsh way he's speaking to me because I know he's hurting.

I know because I'm hurting too.

"I'm gonna go take a shower. Then I'll go straight back down to her," I tell him, moving my eyes sideways on to his.

"You sure you got this man? It's been a rough day. She's only a little one, sure I could find a way to break her," Squealer offers, and the cocky smirk on his mouth has me barging my own Prez out the way so I can get to him.

"Back the fuck off Squeal," I warn him with a hard slam to his chest.

"'Kay man, I'm just trying to help a brother out," he says showing me his palms.

"I'll get out of her what we need to know. I always fuckin' do," I promise everyone in the room bitterly.

"Where is she?" my voice softens when I turn back to Skid. The thought of Hayley still laid amongst all that Bastard scum makes the blood itch inside my veins.

"Too much mess spread out at the factory for Grimm to clean up, so we've brought her home," Skid informs me sadly. I nod back because there's nowhere else I'd rather her be, except for right here beside me doing my fuckin' head in and talking about mindless shit.

I look over to Prez, he's calmed down enough to grip at my shoulder, telling me without words that we're good. With a nod back at him, I head out of the club and to my bike. I take the longer track up to my cabin so I don't have to pass the lodge with the thought in my head that she would never be there waiting for me again.

I open the door to my cabin and toss my keys on the table, making straight for the shower. I discard my clothes to a heap on the floor, turn on the shower and stare into the mirror. It's the first time I've seen myself, and I look like shit. My eyes are red and swollen from crying, there's blood smudged into my skin and caked thick in my hair. I look down at my hands and wonder how I'm gonna find the strength to get underneath the stream of water and wash the final traces of her away. Crimson stains are all I have left of her now, she's gone, and she hadn't even got to live yet.

I force myself to step inside the shower, letting myself cry when the water invades my skin, turning the water red as it pools at my feet then drains away. Taking her from me forever.

I scrub my body clean and shut my eyes tight as the water rinses through my hair. All I see is her face, peaceful and painless, the spark in her green eyes missing as she stares back at me. Still so beautiful despite being soulless, and for the first in a real long time, I'm shit scared, without her here I suddenly feel like the boy that first met her again.

I'm lost.

Maddy is exactly as I left her, arms suspended above her head, tied together around the low hanging water pipe, it's hot and humid in the basement and sweat has started to seep through the T-shirt she's wearing—my T-shirt. Hell knows why the fuck I'd put her in it.

Her risen arms stretch out her whole body and I pull that T-shirt up over her toned thighs, just high enough to give me a glimpse of her panties. My cock aches to be closer, to feel their black lace scrape against its tip and I have to quickly remind myself what I'm here for.

She'd looked almost hopeful when she first saw me, and it made my heart want to give up beating.

This is exactly the reason I wanted to keep Maddy distant. Why our paths should never have crossed. I'd known that if they did, that someday I'd have to make the choice I was making now. The choice between her and my club.

The club and my brothers are the only life I've ever known, Prez just made me his VP for fuck's sake. Loyalty to my club was never gonna be the loser here. But then, never in the worst of my fucked up thoughts did I ever expect it to come to this. Sweet, Maddy Summers, my very own guilty pleasure, the latest victim of my interrogation. The thought makes my guts wring themselves out, and my cock rock solid all at the same time.

My fingertips don't feel the usual sting of excitement they do when I have a victim in front of me, and I dread looking up in case I get a sick thrill out of the fear in her pretty blue eyes. Eventually, I manage to swallow back the fear. I grab the chair from the middle of the room and drag the legs across the concrete floor, leaving an irritating scrape in their trail, then settle it just inches away from her. Spinning it around, to straddle, I fold my arms over the backrest and lean forward.

My eyes sit level with her perfect round tits, and despite all the heat in the room her little nipples peep up through the fabric and make me even harder. She's distracting me, when I need to focus and I have to pull my shit together. Right now she's a club matter, and I need to concentrate on getting us the information we need from her.

"You ready to talk?" I ask, daring a look up into those eyes. It's wrong to find beauty in seeing her like this with long strands of blonde hair sticking to her face, and a trail of black mascara running down her cheek smudged with tears.

"I… Can't," she says through trembling lips, and I close my eyes because it isn't what I want to hear. I don't want to do what comes next, but she's leaving me with little choice.

"You know why they sent me down here, Maddy?" I tilt my head to see her from a different angle. She slowly shakes hers from side to side, her breathing uneven as she tries to hold back tears and show me a brave face.

"They sent me in here because I'm the best. I don't give up. I get what I need by any means, and I don't have a conscience about how I have to do it." That last part seems like a lie, because I'm pretty sure what I'm feeling right now is something that resembles a fucking conscience.

"I can't tell you, Jessie. I want to but I can't," she says through tears, confusing the fuck outta me. "Please don't hurt me," she begs, the quake in her voice humming all the way through my body, right down to my dick.

"I won't have to if you do as I say…" I tell her calmly, stroking some of the hair out of her face. Me getting angry is getting us nowhere fast, so I have to try a tactic I've never used before, something a little more… edgy.

Anyone can be broken, you just gotta find their fear. That's what Vex taught me.

"I gotta ask you some questions, and you need to answer them for me. Okay?" I pull the knife out of my belt, and the moonlight from the small window behind her reflects off the sharp blade when I twist the thick, black handle in my hand. Her eyes widen with terror, and my cock stretches tighter against my jeans, acting as a constant reminder why sick bastards like me don't belong with sinless innocents like her.

"You a virgin?" I ask, already knowing the answer. Hayley told me they'd talked about it. But I want to test if she has any intention of being honest with me, that, and the fact I want to hear the words come out of her pretty mouth myself.

"Yes," she whispers closing her eyes, her head falling forward like she's ashamed.

"Say it." Crushing her jaw in the arch of my hand, I force her to look back at me. Waiting to hear confirmation from her that she's untouched, while a sick idea of how to get her to talk roots itself in my head and makes it hard to stay focused.

"I'm a virgin," she manages to muffle against the strain of my fingers. Her lips look fucking delicious pushed together, and I have to try real fucking hard to stop myself wanting to taste them. Seeing her like this has any chance of backing out of what I'm planning, up and fucking off completely.

Maddy had told Hayley she was waiting for the right one. She had the perfect little package all wrapped up ready for some special guy to take. And it doesn't take a bright mind to figure that I was never gonna be that fucking guy.

I don't even know who the guy is, I don't think she's even met him, and already I want to hunt him down. The thought of another man touching her made me kill crazy. Whoever he is he doesn't deserve her, no one does. Least of all me.

I imagine how it would break her, to rip perfect away from her, to steal the innocence that she's been preserving for real love.

Love never had a place in the world I came from, but loyalty fucking ruled it, and if it comes to it... I'll have to take something precious from her, same as she's taken something precious from us.

I roll the T-shirt higher over her pert tits, leaving it to sit on top of them, my fingers ache to leave a soft trail across her flawless skin, and somehow I manage to hold them back.

"Has anyone ever touched you here?" I ask, my eyes dropping to her round tits, my knife blade pressing against one of her hard, pink nipples.

"No," she whispers, head shaking nervously. Her eyes tearing through to my cold, heartless soul and seriously fucking with my head.

"Here?" I slide the steel between her tits, all the way down to her cute as fuck bellybutton. Again, she shakes her head, painfully slowly.

"How about there?" I drop my eyes down to the perfect little v between her legs. I want to touch it, claim it, and ruin it for any fucker she deemed good enough to give it to.

She wets her lips with her tongue then shakes her head again. I press the knife tip against the bumpy lace of her panties, flush with her center, knowing that with the stuffy temperature in the room the cool bite of the blade will travel right up through her body. Maddy lets out a tiny gasp, her body shivering, and goose bumps forming under the skin on her thighs.

"Why did they take you and Hayley?" I whisper, my nose touching at her cheek, inhaling the scent of fear. It smells good on her.

"I don't know," she answers. It's a lie, one that leaves me with little choice. Sliding the knife across to her hip, my cock twitches, and I smirk when I notice the tiny wet patch that's soaked through the lace at the front of her panties. I slip the blade into the waistband and slice it through the flimsy fabric, causing her eyes to grow wider. Then slowly I trace the cold steel across her waist and repeating the same action on the other side. Her panties flitter to the floor, leaving her pussy exposed to me.

FUCK this is meant to be torture for her, not me.

"Do you know who those men were?" I can hear the strain in my voice. I try blocking all thoughts out, thoughts like the one telling me to drop down to my knees and find out how good that fucking pussy tastes riding against my face.

"I have never seen those men before," she tells me with a newfound confidence, the lie is written all over her face, almost daring me.

She thinks she's taunting me now, she's trying to convince herself that she has some kind of control over the situation she's in. It might have worked, if she hadn't tensed up and squeezed her legs together, giving me an indication of weakness that's enough to spur me on. She'll soon buckle when she figures this isn't just pussy play, and she's in some real trouble.

"Foot here," I order, tapping my thigh, and she surprises me when she not so reluctantly lifts her foot, placing it exactly where I tell her to. The new angle spreads her pussy a little wider, and I edge my knife closer, let it touch at the pink flesh between her slit. When a scared moan trembles from her mouth, I know I've won.

"What ain't ya telling me?" I pull my attention from between her legs, and flick my eyes up to hers, waiting on a reply.

"Please." The fear in her voice is almost too much to resist. "I can't," she breathes in, closing her eyes. I slide the knife away, letting it brush the inside of her risen thigh like a feather. Then with just enough pressure for the tip of the blade to pierce into her skin I slice it through her flesh. The mark I make is only small but it's deep enough for blood to trickle. Maddy rolls her head back, exposing her long neck to me and an instinct so strong I can't fight it off, forcing me to move.

My tongue slides from between my lips and catches the blood as it drips down the inside of her leg. I lick its trail, right through the freshly carved graze. Glancing up at her, my lips smile against her skin when I meet her eyes and watch them swell with shock. The tangy-coppery taste of her tingles my tongue, and I can almost feel her pussy throbbing as my tongue works its way towards it.

Forgetting all motives, I let my tongue rule my head, moving it slowly through her neat little folds. I taste her because I need to. I have to test how wet she is and prove I'm not imagining it. The sweet taste that spreads itself all over my tongue confirms it, she is wet, wet and ready for me. Even in the most fucked up of situations, her pussy can't tell lies like her mouth can, and when her slender hips begin to move against my mouth, I know she's completely fucked... not only is she gonna break for me, but she's about to receive the best interrogation I've ever fucking served.

When I pull my mouth away, she moans, and I snigger because as much as I enjoy the way her body responds to me, it's time I get what I came for. Answers, and something tells me she won't enjoy the part that comes next quite so much.

Standing up I kick the chair away and unbuckled my belt. Pulling my jeans open I release my cock, and let my hand squeeze around the top of her thigh at the same time. With her arms still tied above her head she has nowhere to go, and the force of my body pressing against hers smashes her back against the stone wall. She shivers against me, looking up with her pretty little face still attempting bravery, but she's failing, unable to mask the fear that she's trying so hard to keep from me.

My cock is painfully hard, so close to the spot it aches for now, and for the first time ever, I doubt my abilities. What if she doesn't talk? Would I really go that far? But then a slip of her

LOST SOUL

toes accidentally moves her hips forward, and the tip of my cock skims between her legs. Feeling how slick she is I grab at her other thigh before my newfound conscience wins and forces me to change my mind.

I lift her off the ground and push her body tight to the wall. It breaks my contact from her pussy and her tight virgin hole hovers above the thick head of my cock, coaxing me to push inside, willing me to stretch it open and make her my perfect fit.

To break her completely.

"What ain't ya telling me, darlin'?" I ask again, focusing on her mouth, watching her lips part and I don't know if I'm relieved or destroyed when instead of speaking, she shakes her head. Her ocean blue eyes brim over with tears, and the scared breaths her body fights to pull together are the only sound in a room full of tension. I reach up and I take her throat with the arch of my hand remembering her scared reaction to it earlier.

"I want you to think of the worst thing I could possibly do to you right now..." My eyes lower to where my cock holds firm against her unexplored entrance.

"Close your eyes Maddy and imagine it." I wet my lips as her eyes squint shut, squeezing more tears from them as they close.

"I will do it," I warn harshly but she remains silent. Her neck pulsing at my fingertips, she's scared, and now is not the time to be stubborn. "Don't doubt me, Maddy... You need to tell me," I whisper the warning one last time into her ear, my forehead pressed against her temple while I try to think about anything other than how good it would feel to be buried inside her. Finally, she realizes how serious I'm being, her eyes opening wide and her head shaking.

"Why would you do that to me?" her voice quivers as she speaks, and the hurt on her face weighs down my chest. It makes me question again, if I'll be able to see this through. "I thought you liked me," she sobs, pretty tears dripping down her cheek that I can't resist tasting. My mouth moves across her warm skin, catching one of them on my tongue. I regret it the moment I do it. I never let my guard slip down here, but then I've never had to put one up in the first place.

"Tell me!" I hiss through my teeth, my tip burning against her firm little opening. My restraint weakening as I wait. She isn't gonna talk, I know this because she is biting down hard on that damn lip.

I can't let her fuck with me anymore. Can't let guilt stop me from what I'm about to do next. I'd warned her that this was who I am. I'm doing it for my club. I pull back just enough to slam inside her. Instantly missing her softness against my solid cock.

The hate I develop for myself forces me to look her in the eyes, and to fucking own the shit I'm about to do.

"I'm a hacker!" she cries out before I can push my hips back into hers.

"I hack for him." Her breaths are desperate between her sobs, and I don't know if I'm disappointed that she broke before I could carry out my threat or relieved that I don't have to watch the hate on her face as I force myself inside her.

Sure, I'm a monster, but would I have really been capable of that?

Maddy just saved me from having to find that out. I need out of this room, right the fuck now. The thin string holding my restraint together is liable to snap any moment. I nod, letting her know that she's satisfied me with her answer… for now. Then unwrapping her legs from my waist, I place her shaky feet back on to the ground and pull away from her completely. Her lips quiver as I back away and her head shakes fearsomely, I can't tolerate the hurt in her eyes a second longer, so I turn away from them.

"No," her voice yells out, all weak and broken from behind me, but I ignore it.

"No, you can't," she screams. "You said if I told you…"

I stop moving, turn around, and look back at her perfect body stretched out, wrists tied above her head. There's a furious look on her bewitchingly beautiful face. I wonder how the hell I'd found the strength to stop.

"Yeah, and you told me," I remind her, my cock still hard as steel and my mind confused as fuck.

"So why are you leaving?" she asks, her voice soft and painfully innocent.

I leave, not quite sure if I've lost my head or my balls when I get myself the fuck out of that basement. Because leaving is the only way of stopping me becoming the victim of my own fucking interrogation.

CHAPTER 27
MADDY

He's stripped me of everything, my clothes, my dignity, and worst of all... my self-respect. He had been right about two things at least. He is good at what he does, *the best*. I have no reason to doubt his self-proclaimed title. And he'd definitely been right about the second, he didn't have a conscious bone in his body. Knowing all this should put me off him, but it almost makes me want him a little bit more.

I rub my legs together, trying to sustain the ache he's left between them, the ache that I'd been sure he was gonna make better if I told him the truth. I hadn't even been nervous when his cock was about to enter me. Desperate, and emptiness is all I'd felt, and the need for him to fill it became the only thing I could focus on. And now my selfishness could have cost my mom her life.

For his plan to work Jessie must have seen me coming for miles, he'd have read the way I acted around him. Noticed how much I liked him. Maybe he even guessed that I fantasized about him being my first, or maybe Hayley had told him. Either way, he'd used it to taunt me, found my weakness and then shattered me with it piece by piece.

I deserve everything I get for being stupid enough to believe a guy like Jessie would ever be into a girl like me. He never did take me out for that ride, and why would he? I'm boring and dull and don't have the experience like the club girls Hayley told me about. I don't have any experience at all.

Had I wanted him so badly, that I'd blanked out the sheer brutality of this whole fuck up?

My best friend is dead. I'm their prisoner, being kept in an overheated room, forced to stare at the blood stains of people who were no doubt kept down here before me. Jessie has licked, yes, licked blood from my raw flesh, blood that he spilled when he'd cut me with the blade of his knife. The same knife that the sadistic sex Satan had pressed against me, setting alight nerves up until now I never knew existed.

I should have been stronger, let him walk away when he threatened to leave me writhing for him. But I'd had no choice, my lady parts had already overtaken my head and my mouth.

Turns out I never had the choice in the first place. Despite telling him the only secret I have. The one that if the guy I work for knew I'd told another living soul, would no doubt fulfill his promise and kill me and my mom. And now we're both as good as dead.

It hurts that Jessie is the one punishing me, and now he's left me down here to wait, panicking over what will happen next. Nobody here is gonna help me, I'm responsible for the death of their president's daughter. Hayley died saving me. Maybe that's what this has been about all along for Jessie. Not an interrogation, but a punishment.

Well, it worked, because despite the worry of what Jessie is gonna do with his new information, I can't seem to distract myself from the frustration that lays heavy in the center of my body. Yes, Jessie's torture mission has been a success, he's left me pulsing with need. Desperately wanting anything he'll give me, even down here in this horrifying dirty room that I'm starting to believe will be the place I die.

The darkness turns heavier, and my arms ache heavily as darkness steals the last of the light from the room. The door to my prison is opened, and Skid steps inside followed in by a petite, dark-haired woman, her smile is so warm I know she has to be Carly. She makes straight for me and pulls the T-shirt back over my body. Then Skid unties me, and my arms fall at my sides like lead weights.

"Are you letting me go?" I ask with a tiny glimmer of hope…

"Not exactly, sweetie." The woman's voice is equally as kind as her smile. "Jessie spoke to Prez, and he's gonna let you sleep in one of the rooms upstairs."

"I just wanna go home." I start to cry, I can't carry on anymore. I feel so guilty for what's happened to Hayley, and for what is likely to happen to Mom. They can kill me if they want to, I just wish they would hurry up. The woman catches me when my knees give way.

"Come on, it's been a tragic day for everyone… You wanna get some sleep, don't ya?" She smiles. I manage to nod back, though I doubt I'll ever sleep again after today.

"So let us take you upstairs. Jessie just wants to ask you a few more questions, and then you can get some rest." She strokes my arm. "Maddy, answer the questions, sweetie. Even if you think it will get you in trouble with the people who killed Hayley, okay?" The seriousness in her tone has me completely defeated, and I find myself agreeing. Either way, I'm gonna get hurt, my mom is probably already dead. What's the worst that can possibly happen to me now?

Carly, followed by Skid, leads me out of the room, then up the stairs where the air is thinner. The club seems different to how it had been the night Hayley brought me here, there's an eerie silence filling the huge reception room as I follow Carly through it and then up another staircase. Climbing the steps one by one, I fear who waits for me on top of them. I'd known who Jessie was, and what he was a part of. But I never expected him to hurt me.

That blonde hair and heavenly smile had sure managed to fool me, because right now it feels like he's ripped out my heart and crushed it to ash in his fist. I understand he's hurting but, Hayley was my friend too. My only friend, and she's dead because of me, surely that was punishment enough.

We reach the top of the stairs and I walk along the narrow landing. It's a long way down to the reception when I look over the railings, and a part of me wants to throw myself over them just to make the pain stop.

Skid opens one of the doors, gesturing with his massive arm for me to step inside, and Jessie is already waiting for me. He sits in a chair in the corner of the room, bottle in one hand cigarette in the other, looking tortured. Despite everything he's just done to me I still want him to hold me so we can share our grief together.

"Sit down," he orders, tilting the neck of his bottle towards the single bed, I move towards it and sit on the mattress.

"You can leave," he tells Skid and Carly, his eyes not moving from mine.

"Remember what I said," Carly whispers, placing her hand over mine before she leaves with Skid. It's just me and Jessie in the room now, the air crackles like a spreading fire, but his intense stare causes a cool stream to slither through the heat in my spine.

"So, you work for them?" he says, his face looking far more hurt than angry.

"No…" I shake my head. "Well… maybe. I've done things for the man who was at the warehouse before you got there," I try to explain.

"What man?" he asks leaning forward, crossing his arms over his knees.

"Their boss... President thingy, whatever you guys call it. I never knew he was part of a club, he never had the waistcoat on when he came to me."

"Cut," Jessie corrects me sharply.

"Sorry, cut."

"What kinda work you do?" His voice is rough and intimidating, making me even more on edge.

"I told you, I hack."

"And what exactly did you hack, darlin'?" he questions sarcastically.

"I tracked cell phones, intercepted some emails, moved money from accounts, got a few warrants dropped, nothing too difficult." Jessie does a terrible job of hiding the shock from his face as he listens. "But I promise had no idea I was doing it for a club," I add, "Not until…"

"Until when?" He sits up straighter, his interest peaked.

"That night Hay…" Her name gets caught in my throat. "Hayley brought me here to that party, and I saw someone I recognized. I'd seen his face on some file I'd been told to lift."

"Someone from this club?" Jessie says, looking back at me with such anger it causes tears to sting the back of my eyes.

"Yes." I look down at my feet shamefully.

"So you used Hayley to get to us." His voice turns gravelly, and when his words sink in and I realize what he's thinking it devastates me that he would think I could do such a thing.

"No. Jessie, no, not at all. I had no idea it was you guys that I was getting the information on. What I was hacking were just words, figures, and locations on a computer screen. The messages you send are basic, details, times, and places I could never have known it was you. It wasn't until I saw that guy here that night that I suspected anything, and then when I put the two together, and who they were having me look into I got scared and started ignoring his calls. I guess that's why he came after me." I need so badly for him to believe me because the truth is all I have left to save me.

"I call bullshit… You must have known something," he says, tilting his head in suspicion.

"Honestly. You have to believe me, Jessie, I didn't. The man never wore his cut when he came to the house, but, even if I had known who he was, I would still have had to do what I did. I didn't have a choice." Jessie charges at me, his hand fisting the hair at the back of my head, pulling back and forcing me to look up at him.

"There's always a fuckin' choice," he tells me through clenched teeth, wild with rage. But I shake my head against his firm grip.

"Not when someone's threatening your family." His hold on my hair doesn't falter, but the hard look on his face does.

"Clunk threatened you?" he checks, instinct tells me his anger is no longer aimed at me.

"Yeah," I nod. "I promise you, Jessie, I would never have done anything to hurt Hayley, or you or your cl—" I'm shocked when he shuts me up with his mouth. His lips crushing mine, without any warning, and stopping me from finishing what I had to say. The grip he has at the back of my head pushes my face tighter on to his. Gripping my bottom lip between his teeth, he gently tugs it so my lips open for him. His tongue slides through them, exploring the inside of my mouth desperately, and I automatically join in on the action.

My head spins with confusion, too much has happened today for me to be enjoying this as much as I am. Yet my hands reach up around his neck and pull him closer, petrified that he'll pull away. He hisses into my mouth, and my pussy clenches when his fist in my hair tightens again. This is everything I never imagined my first kiss to be, not gentle and far from soft. Instead it's frenzied, desperate, and raw. I never want to be kissed in any other way or by anyone else as long as I live, and I almost cry out when he forces himself away from me and takes a step back.

"Fuck," he mutters, holding his hair back from his face and staring at me like he's suddenly become scared of me.

"You're gonna need to tell me everything, darlin', start to

fuckin' finish, everything you did. Okay?" His finger is gentle as it slides over my cheek, all traces of the monster from the basement now vanished.

"What, right now?" I ask, still trying to catch my breath.

"Yeah, then I got something needs takin' care of," he tells me, crouching in front of me and taking my hands in his.

"Something like what?" I ask, wondering how he can kiss me that way, and then get back to business as usual.

"Something like goin' downstairs and beggin' the Prez for your fuckin' life," he tells me, and I suddenly wish I hadn't asked, especially when I see real worry in his eyes.

So, I tell him everything. Even the parts I swore I would take with me to my grave. I tell him because, weird as it sounds, I trust him. And if by some miracle my mom is still alive, I believe there might be a chance that Jessie can save us both.

CHAPTER 28

JESSIE

So kissing her was a bad idea. A real fucked up bad idea. But I'd held back too long with her, as soon as I saw that truth in her pretty blue eyes and I'd felt that gut instinct to trust that she was telling the truth... The hurt in her voice and guilt on her face forced me to try and take all that pain away for her. Ironic, as I'm usually the one trying to inflict it.

It's a perfect example of the kinda of shit Maddy Summers does to me, she makes my world spin in a completely opposite direction.

She tells me everything, and it makes me want to find Clunk and take him the fuck out. Before any retaliation to this whole mess can be plotted, I have to talk Prez into letting Maddy live. It isn't gonna be easy, but I'm prepared to die tryin'. There ain't no way she's gonna be taken away from me too, she's my final light in a world of darkness, and I'll do anything I can to keep it shining.

I head down to the bar and find Grimm. He's filthy, covered head to foot in dirt and god only fucking knows what else. He hoovers up a long, thick line off the bar with his nostril, widens his eyes and breathes a sigh of relief when a rush accelerates. I ask him where Prez is, and he tip his head towards the door that leads into the lounge bar.

"Thanks. You get it done?" I ask, slapping his back and he

nods. Clean up was a big job on this one. Grimm would have had help, but he would have only used them as body shifters, maybe diggers judging by the state of his clothes. What I do know for sure is with Grimm taking care of shit, wherever the evil riddled bodies of the Bastards are, they wouldn't be being found anytime soon. He lifts his thumb and brushes over his nostril to check for any residue. Then offers to cut me a line. I refuse, ignoring the fact that after all the shit today I could really do with one; a clear head is needed for what I'm about to do.

I walk back through the foyer towards the lounge, a hand stops me before I can enter, curling around my bicep with a gentle squeeze, for a split second my heart leaps back to life.

Hayley.

Then it dies all over again when I turn around and see Carly.

"She talk?" she asks sounding hopeful.

"Yep. It ain't great, but I'm gonna talk to Prez, she could be of use," I say. I'm grateful for all Carly has done, it was her idea to use a different interrogation technique with Maddy. She had seen how on edge I'd been after I had damn nearly forced myself on the only girl, beside Hayley, that I've ever bothered to care about.

"I'll take her something up to eat and drink. Do your best, Jessie. He's bound to be hurting, we all are," she says, her eyes glassy with tears.

"No one's gonna hurt her," I promise Carly, meaning every fucking word. I never thought I'd ever consider going against my Prez, but that was before I got a taste of Maddy Summers sweet little mouth, among other things... Now that I have, hell as my judge I would protect her from anything, even my own club. Though I really hope I'm not gonna have to.

I find Prez sitting in darkness, the small bar room so full of smoke it even has me choking.

"She rat?" his voice croaks. I step closer, and he holds up the nearly empty bottle of Jack. "Grab another, son," he says tipping it up and drinking the dregs. Then he smashes it to pieces when he hurtles it against the wall. I lean over the small but well-stocked bar, and grab him a fresh one because he's gonna need it.

"She's been the one helping them. Fucking up our deals," I cut to the chase. There's no easy way of saying it, and Prez looks back at me like I'm making some kind of joke. "She's clever Prez, can't only track cells but she can fuckin' intercept them too. They saw all our messages to the Russians, knew what we were offering, that's how they guaranteed they went in with better." Prez doesn't react, just stares and waits to hear more.

"She traced regular cell phone signals to find out where our warehouse was. Took money from big corporate business accounts, and fed it straight into the Bastards' funds so they could sell for less and take us out of the industry." Prez roars with laughter, and I'm confused at what he finds so funny, guess it must be the effects of the alcohol.

"So what you're telling me, is that sweet lookin' little bitch could have been the end of this club?" He snatches the bottle out of my hand, screws off the lid and pours it straight into his mouth.

"That's what I'm tellin' ya," I confirm.

"Well, at least now we know what the problem is, we can eliminate it… Kill her," he tells me, without a single shred of emotion, and I'm pretty sure it would be less painful if he sliced open my back and ripped out my spine.

"She didn't know who she was working for. Clunk was blackmailing her, told her he was gonna kill her mom if she didn't do what he asked." I know how ashamed Maddy had been when she told me this next part.

"Her mom works for Clunk, Maddy's pretty sheltered she doesn't know exactly what it is she does for him, but I'm sure you can figure it out. My guess is her mom had been bragging around the club about how proud she was of her daughter, boasting about the things she could do with a computer and the

Bastards saw an opportunity. Maddy said Clunk had called in on her one day when her mom was out, he told her he'd hurt them both if she didn't do everything he asked her to," I retell what Maddy just told me.

"You know, Jessie, that's a real touching story. Maybe you could tell it at the bitch's funeral," Prez slurs knocking back another mouthful of Jack. He's boiling my blood hotter by the second, but I have to stay cool if I want to get him on board.

"She didn't know it was us she was screwing, she was just given cell numbers to trace. She only figured something was off when she recognized Chop. She was the one who got all his old warrants reissued," I explain, still shocked myself at all she's been capable of.

"Which is making me wonder why you ain't already slit her pretty little throat yet Jessie." Prez stares at me blankly and I'm starting to lose my patience.

"And you think that's what Hayley would want?" I ask. My blood burning now, spreading like wildfire beneath my skin and disturbing all the nerves that settle in the pit of my stomach.

"Hayley just died Jimmer," I remind him. "She died fuckin' saving that girl's life, and now you want me to put all that to waste and end her anyway?" I shock myself at the tone I speak to him in, and his hard face doesn't falter as he stares back at me.

"Come on, Prez, she's scared as fuck right now, she got the two biggest MC's in the state as her enemy. She ain't gonna rat on us. Hayley trusted her and… I trust her too." I watch anxiously for his reaction and he takes a while to think, too long.

"Fine, offer her life in return for her silence, but you let her know that if she ever fucks with us again, or thinks about going to the cops, we will find her, and the Bastards will be the least of her worries." I nod coolly, hoping he doesn't pick up on how relieved I am.

"Get her the fuck out of here, Jessie, before I change my

mind," he orders, his voice bitter as he flicks me away with his hands.

"They'll kill her and her mom the minute she steps off this compound, you know that. I'm gonna need to offer her a little more than that?"

"We don't gotta offer her fuck all," Prez fires up again. Looking at me as if I just grew an extra head.

"Hayley wanted her to live so badly that she threw herself in front of a bullet for her, we need to do this for Hayley. Come on, Prez." It's selfish of me to use the fact Hayley laid her life down, but it's all I have to keep Maddy safe. Tears reform in Prez's eyes and as much as it hurts to see, I take his weakness as a good sign.

"We need to help this girl, Hayley would have wanted us to," I add.

"How?" he asks, his voice low and defeated.

"Protection, Prez, club protection. She could be as useful to us as she was to them. Would be a shame to waste a talent like that," I suggest, clutching at just about anything I have that might keep her safe.

"You want this club to protect the person who's responsible for my daughter's death? Someone who has been feeding the Bastards our information for months?" He folds his arms over his chest. Okay, hearing it back makes it sound unlikely, but I'm not about to let Maddy leave here a walking target.

"I want this club to consider keeping safe the person whose life your daughter valued above her own." My tone is harsher than it's ever been when talking to my Prez, he's a man I've respected my entire life. "Girl had no clue what she was dealing with, you only have to look at her to know that."

Jimmer scratches his beard the way he always does when he's deep in thought, and I feel myself aging while I wait for his answer.

"And you think she's really as good as she says she is?" He narrows his swollen eyes.

"Well, she's been fucking things up pretty well for us over the past six months," I remind him.

"Fine," he utters, and I finally breathe. "She stays. Bunk her in with one of the girls over down at the sanctuary." He's in a rush to get me out of here. I can sense he wants to be alone.

"Prez she ain't that kinda girl, she was Hayley's best friend. Despite what she's capable of she's innocent to a place like this." Prez pauses for longer than I can handle. I'm not about to push him though, not while he's trying to find a shred of decency for the girl who's here in place of the daughter he's strived to protect since the day she was born.

"Okay, but she's your problem, Jessie. Your responsibility. And she better start showing her value, or she's fuckin' out, you got that?" he warns, and I nod while relief floods my body.

"And her mom? She's in danger too." I push for a little more, for all I know Maddy's mom is already worm food, but if she isn't we need to make her safe too.

"Sure, why the hell not. Bring her in too." Prez throws his arms up, the sarcasm all over his face masking his heartbreak for just a second.

"Soon as she's settled, I'll get Maddy straight onto burying Chop's warrant again," I assure him. "And Prez…" I step closer and take his hand in mine. Our club signet rings touch, only 12 of them exist. They were made for the original Dirty Dozen, the founders of the club. The one I wear had been my pa's, Prez gave it to me when I turned eighteen. It always reminded me that this club had been built for our future.

"We're gonna get through this. Losing Hayley is breaking me, same as it's breaking you. I loved that girl like a sister," I tell him, squeezing his hand beneath mine. "She'd want us to be there for each other, and I want you to know that I'm right here," my voice cracks as I speak. Prez stands up and stumbles towards me, gripping my cut to pull me in for a hug. His palm slapping hard at the leather on my back.

"Me too, son, me too." He releases me, and we nod to each other before I leave him alone. Carly and Skid are propped against the wall waiting outside, and both of them straighten up when I step out the door.

"So?" Carly speaks first, desperate to know what Prez said.

"She can stay, she's got club protection," I tell her on a sigh of relief that gives me away too much.

"That's great." Carly sounds almost as relieved as I am. "I'll make her up a guest cabin, best not send her down to the sanctuary," she adds awkwardly.

"She's staying with me,"

I choose to ignore the shock on both their faces as I move past them. I need to find Troj and tell him we're getting a house guest.

Troj is in the gym, no surprises there. It's late, and the club isn't lively like it usually is. Everyone is dealing with their shock in their own way, this is how Troj deals.

He's doing chin ups on the pull bar using hardly any effort, and when he sees me he drops off and thunders straight towards me, grabbing at my shoulder and pulling me in.

"You look like shit," he says, trying to reign in his emotions.

"I feel like it."

"Anything I can do, brother, it's done," he assures me.

"Thanks." I loosen myself from his grip.

"You get the girl to talk?" I nod back. "So, what's the deal?"

"She was working for them, tracking phones, hacking shit. She's the reason things have been fucking up around here lately."

"Shit. That pretty little thang causing all that trouble. Don't know if I wanna throttle it or fuck it." Troj rubs his hands together disturbing the gym chalk in his palms. "Wouldn't mind having a go at both." He winks then slaps me on the back. I try not to scowl at him, and the temptation to pick up a kettlebell and smash the fucker in the face with it takes all my energy to hold off. "Hell, I wouldn't wanna be her right now," he adds.

"She's got club protection," I tell him, and the reaction that follows is exactly what I expect. His mouth drops open, and his eyes search for sense.

"What the fuck? She's been screwin' us over. Hayley's dead because of her and now we're protecting her?"

"Yeah well, she had no idea who she was fuckin' with."

"Damn straight," he nods.

"No, I mean she had no idea it was us. Our texts are cryptic as fuck. She only had cell numbers to go on and only ever saw figures. She recognized Chop from a file she'd pulled and then she got scared, started avoiding their calls. That's why they picked her up."

"And you believe that?" he asks, one of his eyebrows lifting up higher than the other.

"Yeah, I do. Hayley saved her life. It's all got to mean something," I explain as best I can why I feel the instinct to trust Maddy, leaving out the part that I really want to. Troj raises his shoulders seeming to accept my answer. Troj is trusting of those he's loyal to. If it's good enough for you, then it's good enough for him not to question it.

"That's why I'm here," I continue. "I need to pick up the girl's Mom, she's involved with the Bastards somehow, they used her to keep Maddy doing what she did for them. I need someone to ride out with me to get her, bring her back here so we can find out how she's involved and protect her too."

"Gotcha." He's already grabbing his cut off the bench and pulling it over his shoulders, no questions asked.

"And there's another thing," I add. "I'm gonna need to keep an eye on Maddy, Prez ain't gonna trust her a hundred percent, he wants eyes on her 24-7. I thought maybe she could stay with us, just until all this shit blows over. You cool with that?"

"Ain't got no problem with her staying at ours, brother, but playing house with two bitches… Far too much drama for what I can handle. I'll move into one of the spare cabins while they're here. I'm sure Prez won't mind. It'll give you guys more space, her and her mom can share my room."

"Thanks man." I pull him back in. Troj is my most solid brother in this club, not once has he let me down when I need him.

"Let's go pick up this chick's mom and get back so we can get some sleep. I wanna write this fucking day off," he says, leading me out of the gym.

CHAPTER 29
MADDY

A gentle knock on the door disturbs me from a sleep I hadn't realized I'd fallen in to. I'm startled when I open my eyes and don't recognize my surroundings. It's a small room, dark and dingy but still better than the basement where I'd been kept before.

The basement.

The knife.

The kiss.

Jessie.

Hayley's dead!

When it all floods back to me I suddenly wish I was back asleep, where none of those things had happened. Except for the kiss. That part had been amazing.

The door knocks again reminding me what woke me in the first place, and I call out for whoever it is to come inside. The door opens slowly, and the friendly woman from earlier pokes her head around the door.

"Hey, you mind if I come in?" Carly asks with a half-smile on her face.

"Sure." I shift on the mattress to prop myself up.

"Here, this is for you," she holds out a neatly folded pile of clothes. "They might be a bit big, but I figured you'd want something a little more…" Her eyes look me over pitifully. "…Comfortable."

"Yes. Thank you so much." I take the items of clothing from her, and she turns her back while I change into the jeans and vest top, then throw the baggy hoodie over my head.

"Jessie and Troj have gone to get your mom. They'll bring her back here. Prez has promised you club protection, so you're safe," she tells me with a warm smile, a surge of relief that I'm not expecting seems to make my whole body relax.

"Jessie asked me to take you back to his and settle you in. You don't wanna be sleeping in here tonight." Her eyes wander around the room, and my head nods back in absolute agreement.

"What time is it?" I yawn.

"Just past eleven. You hungry?"

"Starving."

"Come with me, we can raid Jessie and Troj's cupboards, see if I can fix you something up." She reaches out offering me her hand, and I take it. She leads me out of the room, down the stairs, and into the foyer where Skid is waiting for us. He tips his chin at me, and I manage a smile in response.

"What's gonna happen to my mom?" I ask them both as we walk outside to the yard. I don't like the way the two of them look at each other.

"Jessie will bring her back here. Talk with her about her involvement with the Bastards, then you can see her in the morning," Skid assures me, climbing on to his bike and kissing Carly before she carries on moving us towards a white Mercedes.

"Jump in," she calls over the roof, opening her door and ducking inside.

"I didn't introduce myself earlier. I'm Carly, Skid's old lady." She sounds so full of pride as she introduces herself as Skid's.

"Old lady?" I almost laugh, Carly is far from old. Late twenties at most. Small and petit, her cute pixie-like features are complimented by a neat bob of black hair. She's a complete contradiction to Skid who is built like a three-story building.

"I figured. Hayley told me about you." I feel it again, that awful pain in my chest that comes whenever I speak her name. Carly places her hand on top of mine and squeezes, before she slides it away and uses it to shift in to drive. Pulling away from the yard, she drives us up a dirt track, with Skid following close behind on his bike.

"Few things you should know now you're gonna be sticking around," she starts. I'm gripping the handle of the door, because for someone so small and sweet looking, the woman drives like she belongs in the wacky races.

"First off, keep out of anything that involves the club. The likelihood is you're not gonna want to know. Second, avoid the clubhouse after dark, the girls that hang around there at night make themselves available, if you know what I mean." I don't, but I nod back at her all the same. "The last thing you want is the guys getting the wrong idea about why you're here." She gives me an awkward smile. "Thirdly, and most important, stay away from Squealer, he's merciless." She chuckles to herself.

"Squealer? I think I've met him before. The night of the party." Who could forget him? Solid body covered in tattoos, cheeky grin, and eyes full of mischief. I remember thinking he was kinda hot, but by then it was too late, Jessie had already ruined any other guy for me.

"Yeah, you'd have met him." She rolls her eyes, continuing to drive the track. Eventually she veers right into a clearing, and I see the cabins in front of us as we approach them. Most of them have bikes parked outside, some have cars or trucks too. She pulls up beside two bikes outside a cabin that has no lights on.

"Me and Skid are just there." Climbing out of the car, Carly points to a cabin three doors down. Their cabin looks different from all the others. Their porch light shines bright, showing the pretty hanging baskets and pots outside. Skid holds up his hand as he steps inside and I wave him goodnight, grateful for the kindness he's shown me today.

Carly steps on to the porch of the cabin that I assume belongs to Jessie, and I follow her to the door. She opens it up and stepping inside feels around the wall for the light switch.

"Here we are, home sweet ho…ly shit," she gasps looking around the room. "My god, they live like animals." Quickly she starts to pick the clothes up off the floor. Sniffing them and turning up her nose before she pushes them straight inside the washing machine.

"Sorry about this," she says, looking embarrassed as she gathers up all the empty beer bottles and tosses them into the trash. "Here, take a seat." She moves a damp towel off the sofa, clearing a space for me to sit down. "I'll go check the bathroom." She leaves me with a worried look on her face as she walks towards a room at the back. I take a look around the room. There's a TV on the wall, a sofa, and chair in the living area. In the open plan kitchen I can't see the surfaces because it's covered in dirty dishes and crap, and there's a table in the middle of the room complete with four chairs, although I doubt from all the food wrappers on the couch that it's ever used.

I walk to the back of the cabin and open the large French doors, an automatic light clicks to life, and illuminates the beautiful scene in front of me. The cabin has a decked balcony that overlooks a large lake, moonlight reflecting brightly on its surface, and I take it all in with shock. It's such a peaceful, hidden treasure, the last thing I would expect to find in the confines of an MC club compound. I look either side of the deck, the cabins horseshoe around the lake, all having the same decked area and splendid view. I spot Skid and Carly's right away. Lit up prettily with twinkling lights, and a swing chair sct in the center. Windchimes gently move in the evening breeze. Jessie has a rusty table, and two outdoor chairs, one with the seat torn through, and the small outdoor grill is filled with old cigarette ends. I turn around to go back inside to find Carly watching me from the door, a sad smile on her face.

"You're gonna be okay, hon." She holds out her arms, and I go to her because right now she's the only person I can go to. "They ain't all that bad you know, and if it gets too much, you can always come find me." She leans back. "I found a box of mac and cheese. Come inside, I'll rustle it up for you." She does her best to make boxed mac and cheese sound appealing, and my stomach growls like it would be grateful to receive anything.

I follow her inside, leaving the door open behind me, figuring some fresh air isn't gonna do this place any harm.

Carly sets to making the food, while I make a start on the massive stack of washing up. We work around each other, chatting as if my best friend hadn't been shot in front of me just hours ago. I'm grateful for that. I can't let myself go back there, I'm not ready to deal with that grief just yet.

I finish up the bowl of mac and cheese quickly, then set straight back to making the place habitable. Carly finds me a mop and bucket, and I clean the floors while she takes out the trash and throws some bleach around in the bathroom. We turn the cushions on the sofa, finding some questionable stains, and then flip them right back around again.

Carly has just suggested that we stop for a break when we both hear a truck pull up outside. The engine stops. Footsteps follow, crunching along the gravel at first and then patting across the wood on the porch. My heart beats fast as the front door opens, and Jessie walks in carrying a bag over his shoulders, I cross my fingers that Mom will burst in behind him. Instead, He's followed by the tall, long-haired guy who'd tried consoling him back at the warehouse.

"What the fuck happened in here? What's that smell?" Long-haired guy, who just so happens to be hot as hell, sniffs at the air.

"It's what clean smells like, Troj." Carly places her hands on her hips like a scolding mother. "Seriously guys, this place was a dump."

"Well ain't all of us as lucky as Skid, havin' a hot ass wifey takin' care of us." The guy gives her a killer smile, and I can tell by her eye roll that she couldn't stay mad at him even if she wanted to. "I'm just getting some gear then I'm heading off, gonna be staying in cabin 6 for a while."

"You get the keys off Prez?" she asks.

"Yeah," he says, fishing them from his pocket and dangling them out in front of him.

"Toss them here, I'll go make you up a bed and open it up. Last people to sleep in there were Sasquatch and Bricker. I'll bet it smells worse in there than this place did."

"You sure you ain't holding back a hot younger sister from me?" Troj teases her, his voice full of charm.

"Positive. Not that it would matter, even if I was, ain't no way in hell I'd let any of you lot near her." Carly walks towards me. "I'll leave you to get settled, you know where I am." She kisses my cheek. "Try and get some sleep." I notice how she stops and whispers something to Jessie on her way out. I'm desperate to ask Jessie where Mom is. I know he's been to my house, the bag he has with him is from my wardrobe.

"You okay?" He looks over to me when Carly closes the door behind her. I nod back, almost too scared to ask the question.

"Jessie. Where's my mom?" I blurt out, and it isn't a good sign that he looks disappointed as he steps closer to me.

"Your mom left town, darlin'."

My heart freezes when my head manages to recite his words.

"No... she can't have. She wouldn't leave me." He had to be lying, there's no way she would just up and leave me.

"It's okay, I saw her before she left. She was fine, she said it was too dangerous for you if she stayed. She's in a lot of trouble with the Bastards. She knew they were using you, it was to pay off her debt to them."

"What debt?" I ask, still struggling to believe him.

"Your tuition, mortgage repayments, she'd been borrowing from them faster than she could pay it back. You were her repayment plan, darlin'." My hand slams over my mouth, I'm trying to take in what he's telling me, and all I'm hearing is that this is all my fault. My tuition fees, our house. I would never have applied for college if she hadn't told me she could afford it.

"But she worked for the man who's in charge of them."

"She worked for the club Maddy... Well, she hung out at the club kinda like..."

I hold out my hand for him to stop.

"Please don't finish that sentence," I beg. I can't face hearing it. I've always suspected her job wasn't legal. She never spoke about work with me, and when the guy who'd threatened me had introduced himself as her boss, I knew I'd be ashamed of whatever it was she did.

"I promised your mom I'd take care of you. She packed you a bag," he changes the subject, placing the holdall on the table. "Nyx picked you both up a pre-pay." Taking a cell from his pocket he places it on the table next to the holdall. "Your mom's number is stored inside... Mine too," he adds that last part a little awkwardly. "I've told her to turn hers on at 3pm Sunday afternoon so you can talk."

"Where is she now?"

"Nyx is taking her to Utah, we got people there who will keep her safe for now. She's right, if the Bastards think she's skipped town they'll assume she's taken you with her. They'll stop looking for you for a while at least. Tommy took her car and headed in the opposite direction. He'll dump it somewhere and hope the news gets back to the Bastards, it'll throw them off the trail."

All this seems too much for me to take in at once. First, losing my friend, and now I'm not even sure when I'll get to see my mom again. Still, at least she's alive, and I'm safe, for that I have to be grateful.

Troj walks back in the room, flinging a holdall over his shoulder, his long hair now tied up roughly on top of his head.

"I'm outta here kids." He smiles at me and slaps Jessie on the back. "Don't do anything I wouldn't do." His eyes slowly roll over me and I feel myself blush as he walks out, closing the door, and leaving us alone.

"Follow me." Jessie grabs my bag and shows me into the room next to the one Troj just came out of. He turns on the light and throws my bag on the bed before starting to pick up more dirty clothes from the floor.

"This your room?" I ask.

"Yeah. I'll take Troj's room. At least I know this bed had fresh sheets yesterday. You should get some sleep it's been a crazy day. I'll be out there if you need anything." He doesn't give me a chance to say anything back, he just walks out and closes the door behind him.

I check inside my bag; there's clothes, a toothbrush, and underwear. My laptop too. Everything I'll need for my stay, however long that might be.

Slipping out of Carly's jeans, I fold them up and hang them over the end of the metal bed frame. I tuck myself in under the sheets, feeling pleased that Jessie chose to give up his room for me when his natural scent comforts me. My head touches the pillow, and I start to unwind. I quickly realize that no amount of comfort will take away my pain. Hayley is gone, forever, and there's nothing anyone can ever do or say to make that alright. Guilt plants itself in the pit of my stomach and embeds its thick heavy roots, ones that I know I'll carry with me forever.

CHAPTER 30
JESSIE

I take a bottle from the cupboard and head outside to my deck. Slumping myself on the good chair I look out on the lake that I'd promised Hayley we could swim in this summer. I'm watching the water gently rock when it hits me that we never will take that swim. It's just another promise I couldn't see through for her. Like the one to teach her how to ride a motorbike, and how to blow smoke circles. Even though she didn't smoke, and there was no chance of Prez letting her have a bike. What crippled me most is that I'd failed to keep the most important promise. The one I'd made to her the night her mom died when I told her I'd never let anybody hurt her.

It's my fault she become friends with Maddy in the first place, they'd been together today because of me. I'm the reason Hayley is dead, and I don't know if I can let Maddy carry that guilt around for another day.

Prez decided to make Hayley's death legit, he wants Hayley to have a grave we can visit. Grimm took Hayley and rested her somewhere she would easily be found. I called Roswell and explained the situation, and Tommy made the anonymous call from a Prepay to the station to report her body, which was conveniently on Bastard territory. Grimm would have done a thorough job of covering up any traces of moving her. Smart fucker even had the idea to claw her fingernails through one of the dead

Bastards wounds before he buried them. Hopefully, the Bastard he chose has previous, and his DNA is already in the system. Me and Prez hated the idea of Hayley's body being out there alone, but it's the only way that we could bury her with her mama. Being together is what Hayley would have wanted.

I take a long drag of my cigarette, holding in the smoke until it burns my lungs. I'm still furious at myself for losing it with Maddy earlier, what I nearly did makes me feel sick to my stomach. And yet after everything, she'd still let me kiss her… she'd even kissed me back. Now she's staying here with me, alone. The girl's a lot braver than I'd given her credit for.

Down in the basement, for a tiny second, I'd convinced myself that she actually wanted me to carry out my threat. That sliding my cock inside her and taking her for myself was what she needed. I'd even imagined hearing disappointment when I walked away and left her tied to the pipe. Like she thought not having me was her punishment, but then I couldn't blame my head for playing tricks on me, not today.

"So she's a hacker 'ay?" a voice comes from the deck next door, and Squealer hangs over the wooden rails that divide our balconies. I wasn't surprised that he already knew, word spreads around this club faster than Mel spreads her legs.

"Yep," I nod, taking a swig from the bottle then hold it out to him.

"Skid filled us all in, says she's under club protection now." He downs a mouthful before he hands it back over.

"She is, and she's off limits," I warn him straight off before he gets any ideas, and the fucker smirks back at me. "I fucking mean it Squeal."

The way he rolls his eyes tells me he's clear, though I'm sure there will be times when he'll require a reminder.

"Having her could be a real bonus for the club." He relights a joint, taking a toke before passing it over to me, and I take a long slow draw of it.

"That's why she's here," I tell him, tipping back my head and blowing out the smoke, giving it back.

"Whatever ya need to tell yourself, brother," he sniggers, then shakes his head and pushes himself off the railings. He disappears back into the cabin he shares with his twin, Screwy. I don't let the fact that he's called me out on my shit piss me off. This is Squealer, he's always pissing people off. Besides, he's only saying what everyone was probably thinking, Maddy would have been better off staying with Carly and Skid, they have a spare room. But I want her close to me. Something inside me seems to want to cling to her, and the way she'd kissed me back earlier gave me a stupid glimmer of hope that I might be able to actually have her.

I just have to be selfish enough to take her.

Today's events have proven that there's no tolerance for selfishness, I won't let Maddy become another victim of it. I can't have her, not the way I want her anyway. It's gonna be torture having her so close, but there is no way I'm gonna let her be looked after by anyone else. Hell no, Maddy Summers is mine to protect. Even if that means protecting her from her biggest threat of all.

Me.

I wake up with a sore head and an emptiness in my heart. I get out of bed and head to the kitchen, then search through the cupboards for aspirin and something to eat. We're never well stocked. I usually have breakfast up at the lodge with Hayley, and Troj gets fed at whatever cabin he ended up in down at the sanctuary.

I manage to find some cereals and some milk, which thankfully I check before pouring on top because it smells like rotten ass. I heave and chuck it straight in the trash. When the bathroom door opens I look up, Maddy steps out wearing just a towel tucked around her chest. Her hair still dripping wet as she rubs at it with a hand towel.

"Hi," she says shyly, tiptoeing back into her room with an awkward smile. I'm still trying to calm down my cock when my phone vibrates in my pocket.

"Church in a half an hour," Prez's voice cracks down the phone before he hangs up. I tuck my cell back inside my pocket and continue searching for something edible. When the door knocks, I could not be more relieved to see Carly standing on the doorstep with two steaming plates. "Bacon and eggs for two," she says, moving around me to step inside and lay the plates on the table. "So how was her first night?" she asks, rustling her way through the kitchen draws until she finds the one that contains knives and forks.

"Good, I think. She just got out of the shower."

"Cool, Skid just got the call from Prez, church is in half an hour. You send her round to me when you leave, she shouldn't be alone after all she's been through." I nod in agreement. "I'll leave you to it. See you later," she says making her way out the door.

"Hey," I call after her. "Thanks. For breakfast, and for everything else, she's gonna need a friend," I tell her when she turned back around.

"Everyone needs a friend, Jessie." Carly smiles sadly before she leaves. Minutes later my bedroom door opens and Maddy steps out wearing one of the summer dresses I'd packed from her wardrobe.

Okay, I'd lied, her mom never packed her stuff. I did. But I had promised her mom that I would never tell Maddy about the barely a fuckin' live state mc and Troj had found her in last night. She'd heard from the Bastards that a girl had been killed along with six other club members, and naturally she'd assumed it was Maddy. Marilyn Summers had downed a heavy dose of pills, then finished them off with a bottle of vodka. Lucky for her we found her and managed to get her to the hospital in time.

It was me who had told her to get fuck out of town as fast as possible. The Bastards were a threat, their numbers had built since we had thinned their herd a few years ago and their sister Charter was only a few days ride away.

I need for them to believe Maddy and her mom are long gone, so when retaliation comes for us, they won't be able to get it through her. Nyx had rung early hours this morning and told me she'd managed to discharge herself from hospital, they were on their way to our sister Charter in Cannonville.

Nyx would be shattered. Me and Troj had left him at the hospital to watch over her and give my instructions when she came round. Apparently, she'd been so relieved that her daughter was safe, she was prepared to do anything to keep it that way. A wise choice on her part because she didn't really have the choice anyway. I'd set her up with some cash, and Nyx would make sure she got safely to Utah. In time, I'd come up with a plan for the two of them to be together again safely.

"Morning." I gesture with my head for Maddy to sit opposite me, where the plate of eggs and bacon wait for her.

"Wow, this looks fantastic," she says, trying her best to be cheery as she shoves a fork full of eggs into her mouth.

"Wish I could take the cred, darlin'. Carly dropped them by. She wants you to call in when you're done," I tell her, and she nods eagerly, her mouth full of food.

"So what do you need me to do today?" she asks after she's swallowed. She seems eager for a distraction, I know how that feels.

"We're gonna need you to bury Chop's records again, I get that the damage has already been done, but anything you can do to slow the feds down will be appreciated."

"You mean Tobias Saunders." She winks at me playfully, making my cock jump to life.

"Call him what you want, darlin', you need to lose him back wherever you found him from. Your laptop should be in the bag. Getting Chop back will be a real start in getting Prez trusting you."

"And what about you? Do you trust me?" she asks biting into a crispy slice of bacon. Her eyes focusing on me the whole fucking time.

"Yeah, I do," I admit, staring right back at her, I want her to know that I mean exactly what I'm saying. Then, when the connection suddenly feels too intense, I move up from the table and put my plate in the sink.

"I got to be at church. So, I'll catch up with you later. Help yourself to anything…" I look around knowing the fridge and the cupboard are pretty much empty. Maddy's eyes widen, an irresistible smirk appearing on her lips.

"Yeah, alright point made. I'll head to the grocery store after church," I laugh a little, shocked that despite the dull ache of loss lingering in my chest, the girl sat in my kitchen still manages to make me laugh.

"Church?" She looks up at me, confused.

"Not that kinda church, darlin'." I smirk, lifting my cut from the back of the chair and making for the door. I struggle against the urge to kiss her again, only this time I'd want to do it the way Skid kisses Carly whenever he leaves her. Like he doesn't want to leave her. I don't want to leave Maddy, and the thought of her tongue back inside my mouth makes me solid, again.

"Jessie," her sweet little voice calls after me, the tiny hint of desperation in it makes me turn around. My arms automatically reach out and catch her when she runs into me. Her lips gently press against my mouth, holding them there for a few beats before she pulls them away.

"Thanks… For trusting me," she whispers, her cheeks brighten with a sudden flurry of embarrassment. I could grab her up right there, do all the things I ever imagined never being able to. But instead, I nod politely and walk out.

Screwy is already sat on his bike, no doubt waiting for Squealer. He lifts his chin at me like he usually does, only today there's a little emotion in his normally stone hard eyes. I guess it's his way of checking I'm okay.

"Yeah man. I'm good," I answer his unasked question, at the same time Squealer comes out of their cabin, still doing up his pants. Mel trails behind him, kissing his shoulder as he steps off the porch. When she looks over to me, she smirks and snakes her arms around his neck.

"Mornin' Jessie," she calls over, shrieking loudly when Squealer slaps her ass then makes his way over to his bike.

"Mornin' yourself," I hit back. I start up my bike and take off down the track to church. I wonder how the hell we're supposed to fix this fuck up of a situation, especially when there's nothing we can do to bring back what we've lost.

Prez is already waiting at the head of the table when we walk in. He looks like he hasn't slept all night, I think I managed about an hour myself. Too busy thinking of all the different ways I could make the Bastards pay for what they did to Hayley.

Everyone takes their usual places, Except for me, it feels weird sitting in the VP's Chair where Chop usually is, a fuckin' awesome kinda weird though. None of us really know what to say to Prez. He's just lost everything, and there's a blankness in his eyes that I doubt will ever leave them now that Hayley isn't here anymore. He breaks the silence by bringing everyone up to speed on the Maddy situation, he tells everyone she's to be treated as a friend of the club, although there's nothing friendly about the tone he uses when he says it. To him, Maddy will always be the girl who lives and breathes in the place of his daughter. He's keeping her safe because he knows she'll be useful to the club, and I like to think that maybe he's keeping her safe for Hayley too.

"So what we gonna do to make them pay?" Thorne asks, taking the words right off my tongue.

"Right now. We do nothing," Prez tells us, and everyone looks very confused.

"We took out six of the fuckers yesterday, and now we've got their secret weapon too. We're playing the long game this time. We're gonna close them down from the outside in, make them paranoid."

"Prez?" Squealer asks, looking as disappointed and shocked as the rest of us.

"I mean it, this time I want them finished. Done. The whole Charter wiped out and then I'll set to ruining every other fucking Charter until Bastard is just the name for a kid whose mama can't remember who knocked her up. "

"So we don't get to kill anyone?" Squealer checks.

"Not today," Prez shakes his head.

"Sorry, kid." Squealer slams his brother's rock-solid chest but doesn't get a response.

"We start small. Let them think we were satisfied with taking the six. Skid's got a list of names from Rogue, people she's heard are dealing around town. Jessie and Troj, you take on Nyx, start making your way through that list. I don't care how you do it, I'm sure you'll come up with something. Warn them enough never to deal again. Take their stash and take their money. It's business as usual."

"Sure thing Prez," I tell him leaning across the table to take the list from Skid, surprised when I see that there are at least fifteen names on it. This problem in town is bigger than I thought. Me and Troj can get real inventive with these shits, I'll bet Nyx'll get a kick out of learning from us too.

"Skid we need back in with the Russians, now that we don't have a certain little bitch tracing our every move, see what's about. If you don't get any luck try Shaun, the Irish are always shifting." Skid nods and Prez lets out a long, exhausted breath.

The kind that tells me he's been building himself up to this moment, and his eyes fill up before he speaks. "You've all heard what happened to Hayley, and can understand why I wanna be alone right now. You need anything, you speak to Jessie, He can make decisions on my behalf or come to me if he thinks it's important enough. I need a few days out." He hits the gavel down weakly then stands up and walks out. His actions leave us all speechless, Prez is always the last to leave. Always.

CHAPTER 31
MADDY

I've spent a whole week at the club, and as he never seems to come home, hardly any time with Jessie. Thankfully, Carly makes sure I'm never lonely, I join her and Skid for dinner most nights, we sit on her deck and drink wine while she fills me in on how everything works around here. I spend most of my days hanging out with her too. If I do see Jessie it's always brief, he only ever comes home to shower and to sleep. Every night he goes down to the club and he stays out until the sun rises the next morning. The only trace of him ever being here are restocked cupboards.

It's pathetic that I miss him, that I'm frustrated he hasn't kissed me again. All I can think about when I'm not grieving Hayley, are the things she told me about the women that hang around the club at night. Carly confirmed it. And secretly, I hate to think of Jessie spending time down there with them.

Today is different though, it's the day he's been dreading as much as I have. Today, we say our final goodbyes to Hayley. I dress in the black lace dress Carly loaned me, then head out into the living area. Jessie is sat at the table staring into a cup of coffee. While I've been dashing between my room and the bathroom, drying my hair and getting dressed, he's made breakfast, and I'm pleased to see that there's a plate set in front of him too.

"You should eat, today's gonna be hard." Eyes filled with

guilt stare me over, he's been looking at me that same way since he came home without Mom. I can't be sure if it's because he feels sorry for me, or if he's struggling to forgive me for what happened to Hayley. As much as it hurts to think that, I couldn't blame him if he did.

"You look real nice," he says, looking back down and taking a sip of his coffee. I step closer to the table, tugging down the bottom of the dress to stop it riding over my ass when I walk. It's much shorter than what I'm used to, not exactly what I would consider appropriate to wear to a funeral, but Carly insisted it looks good, and I don't exactly have a lot of other choices.

Gorgeous blue eyes peer over the rim of his cup as he drinks, a smirk lifting his cheeks. Obviously, he finds amusement in me walking in these ridiculous heels while trying to keep my modesty.

"The dress is Carly's," I explain, taking the seat opposite him and trying to hide the flush in my cheeks.

"It means a lot that you convinced Prez to let me come today," I say picking up my fork.

Jessie shakes his head like it's no big deal, but for me, it means everything that I get the chance to say goodbye to her properly.

"Do you think I'll be safe today… from the… you know?" I check, the thought of leaving the safety of the club makes me nervous.

"You think I'd let you come if I wasn't?" he snaps, then suddenly looks guilty again. "Look, they wouldn't dare show up today. We have brothers from every Charter riding in to pay their respects. You'll be safe, I prom…" Something stops him from finishing his sentence. Instead, he screws up his eyes and swallows his words. We eat the rest of our breakfast in silence, and he waits for me to finish before he stands up and clears the table.

"I'm heading down to the club, Carly said you could catch a ride down with her."

"And Mads…" He moves to stand in front me, shocking me when both his hands take hold of mine. Him touching me feels good, and I look down to where his thumbs rub over my skin. "I'm gonna need you to stay real close today."

I smile at the thought of being close to him for a whole day as he backs up and pulls his cut over his black shirt. He rolls his sleeves up to his elbows, and with the thin black tie around his neck, he looks delicious.

"I can do that," I assure him, and we spend the next few seconds staring at one another. Jessie relieves the awkwardness when he shakes his head and steps out.

Carly and I drive down to the club a little after Jessie leaves, and the scene that greets us punches all the air out of my lungs. The yard is bursting with chrome and leather, bikes are parked in rows, and there are swarms of people, way too many to count. Carly struggles to find anywhere to park so ends up dumping the car behind the garage and grabs my hand, leading me through the people congregating outside into the club.

The smoke-filled room is packed, the noise deafening as people greet old friends and glasses clatter on the bar. I take a few steps inside and all conversation stops. All eyes move to focus on me. The silence pinches at my ears and blood rushes to my cheeks, heating my face.

Carly tugs on my hand trying to move me forward, but I don't budge, the judgmental stares are anchoring my feet to the floor.

What had made me think it would be okay to come here today?

I didn't deserve forgiveness from these people, every single person here knows it would be me being buried today if it wasn't for Hayley's sacrifice.

They all wish it was me.

I manage to control my body enough to turn, preparing myself to run and retreat back to Jessie's cabin, but I'm blocked.

My eyes raise slowly over the tall, bulky body standing in my way until I reach eyes that resemble hers. It strikes me how different he looks, his crisp white hair combed neatly back off his face and his beard trimmed to perfection.

"Where you think your goin'?" Hayley's dad looks down his nose at me, his voice rough and so deep it vibrates in my chest. I don't need to turn my head to know that Jessie is beside me now, I can feel that flutter in the pit of my stomach that comes whenever he's close.

"I…" My words fail to come out. "I shouldn't be here. I'm so sorry." I attempt to step around him, but with a simple slide, he blocks me again.

"Why?" He folds his arms across his broad chest and waits for my answer like it might give him the pleasure he's been craving. So, I tell him exactly what he wants to hear. It's the truth after all.

"Because it should be me. I should be the one who's being mourned today. Not Hayley, not your daughter who was loved by all these people," I tell him, somehow managing to look him in his eyes.

"Sir, there aren't words that will ever tell you how sorry I am that it was her and not me, and I can't imagine the pain you must be feeling." I push through tears to finish what I have to say. "Every morning I wake up with the same heartbreak, feeling like I can't face another day being tormented by that guilt. But I make damn sure I do. Because of Hayley, and what she gave up for me. That may be little or no comfort to you at all Mr. Carson, but I wanted you to know it."

I've rambled but I'm still impressed that I managed to say everything without bursting into tears. Embarrassed, and more than ready to leave, I step around him again. This time he doesn't move, and I'm almost clear past him before his hand reaches out and grips the top of my arm. I feel Jessie tense, as his

Prez leans his head into my face, close enough so no one other than myself, Jessie, and Carly can hear him.

"You were my daughter's friend. She'd want you here, and today that's all that matters. Now turn the fuck around, hold up your head and come to say goodbye to her." Even the heat in his fiery eyes doesn't take the chill out of his voice, and I nod until he lets go of my arm. He walks on past me like our encounter never happened, and when I turn around Jessie is staring back at me equally as shocked. I don't know what to say to him, but the way he dips his head and gives me a trace of a smile lets me know I haven't imagined what just happened.

Jessie takes my hand, and leads me out the clubhouse and to his bike in the yard. It's parked in front of all the others, directly behind the hearse, and I guess the bike beside it belongs to Hayley's dad. Jessie lets go of my hand and slings his leg over its leather seat. Steading the bike between his thighs he grips the high handlebars with one hand, then holds out his other one to me.

"You want me to ride with you?" I ask in disbelief.

"Told you, I want you close," he reminds me. "You got a problem riding with me, darlin'?"

"No. Just Carly told me there were rules about girls riding on the back of bikes." I bite my lip, regretting the words as soon as they come out of my mouth. He'll probably make me ride in the truck now, and I really do want to ride with him.

"Carly's rarely wrong." He shrugs. "Now you gonna stand there gawking, or are you gonna get on?" He treats me to that sexy smirk that always triggers a reaction from me.

"My dress, it's real short, and I'm wearing these heels." I look down to the ridiculously high heels that Carly's convinced me to wear. Hardly bike riding get-up.

"I noticed," he said, looking me over like a predator sizing up its prey, his eyes creating a heat in their trail that forces me to squeeze my thighs together.

No Maddy not here, not today.

"What will everyone think?" I whisper glancing around us at all the people filling up the yard.

"I don't give a fuck what they think. I told you I wanted you close and that's exactly where you'll be." His hand wraps around my waist and with a not so gentle tug, he forces me closer. I give in, placing my hand on his shoulder to steady myself, then hitching my leg over the seat. My thighs press against the outside of his, and I fumble behind me trying to locate the bar to hold. Jessie reaches his arms right back around me, taking my wrists, and pulling them forward. He makes sure my hands slide over the warm leather of his cut before he settles them on his chest.

"Don't worry, it'll be a real slow ride. I promise to take you on a proper one next time." He looks over his shoulder at me and my chest hums at the promise of a next time. I smile, just before splinters dig into my heart and I remember him asking me to take a ride with him a few weeks ago. Back then I never imagined that the first ride we took together would be following the hearse that carried my best friend.

My smile fades when I focus forward. Beautiful white lilies surround the shiny black casket, and I let my eyes cry out. To know that no amount of tears I cry will ever bring her back is suffocating, and I have to keep reminding myself to breathe. Jessie's fingers loop through mine and squeeze my hand tight against his chest, and it's just enough to ground me again.

Prez appears from the crowd behind us and gets on his bike, starting his engine and causing a ripple of roars as everyone behind us follows his lead. Jessie releases my hand and starts his bike, the sound rumbles right through my body. I grip him a little tighter when all the noise becomes overwhelming. The hearse begins to creep forward, and we move behind it, taking the ride slowly just as Jessie promised. We follow Hayley along the windy mountain roads, through town, and all the way to the cemetery.

I manage to hold myself together as my friend is sunk lower into the ground, I fight against the sobs that ache the back of my throat, but fail to withhold the tears that fill my eyes and stream down my cheek. Jessie squeezes my hand like he can sense I need him, he hasn't let it go since we got off his bike, and it gives me a small comfort to think that maybe he might need me too.

We walk away, leaving Hayley in the grave she shares with her mama, I hope that both of them are at peace now, together. Safe, and free from a world that can be so cruel. Jessie leads me to where the bikes are lining both sides of the long, narrow cemetery road. Then straddling his, he reaches back to help me on behind him. This time I don't wait for him to tell me to hold him. I wrap my arms around him, resting my cheek on his back, and I don't let my grip loosen the whole way back to the club.

I expect him to drop me off at his cabin when we arrive back at the compound. But instead, he parks up and leads me inside the club, through the foyer, and into the large bar room. His palms press into my ass keeping me walking forward, and it sends tiny electric sparks all the way up to my neck. The room has transformed since we left just over an hour ago. A huge table now stretches along the back wall of the room that's crammed with food, and the large empty space soon becomes crowded, making the place look so much smaller.

Jessie places a drink in my hand, I have no idea what it is, but it looks like he's drinking the same. I take a sip, and it stings at my tongue and ignites my throat at the same time. But not wanting to be rude. I finish it anyway.

I feel a chill when music starts to play from the speakers set up on the stage, and I realize what's playing.

"Never saw you guys as Mac fans," I lean in and speak to Jessie over the noise. Fleetwood Mac are the only thing I have in common with my mom. When I was younger and she was home, we used to dance together in the kitchen to their album. Now, they remind me of Hayley. She was always telling me how lame they were, and that I needed to pull myself into the 21st century.

"Carly's idea, we found Hayley's iPod in her jeep when we recovered it from the gas station, figured she should have her own music played at her party. Carly's always coming up with thoughtful shit like that." He shrugs with a half-smile, then tips his empty glass up at the woman behind the bar. *Say you Love me* continues to fill the room full of bikers, and my eyes prickle with tears while my heart bursts open. Seems Hayley didn't hate my music after all, it was typical of her stubbornness, and if it's even possible it makes me miss her even more.

People spend all afternoon offering their condolences to Jessie and Hayley's dad. Every time I try to move away and give Jessie some space, he tugs me right back. He's taking this protection thing far too seriously, he told me himself no one here would hurt me, and now that we're back on the compound I know I'm safe. A guy I don't recognize pushes through all the people to get to Jessie, wrapping him in his arms and squeezing him so tight I fear a vein might pop out of his neck.

"You good, man?" he checks, his hard face baring something that resembles concern.

"No..." Jessie answers honestly, pulling away first. "This is Maddy," he introduces me, and the guy tips his head at me the same way all the guys around here do. "Maddy, this is Brax."

I look Brax over, he's attractive in a totally different way to Jessie, a rough kind of handsome with short, brown hair, and dark eyes that seem suspicious of everything. I don't know if the slit that runs through his eyebrow is a scar or if he shaves it in, but it adds to the harshness of his face. Hell, just looking at him feels dangerous.

"Pleased to meet you, Brax, where you from?" I've watched people talk to Jessie all afternoon, most of them wear a patch on their cut with the state of their Charter. Brax doesn't have one, and it makes me curious.

He smiles at Jessie before he answers. "Anywhere I wanna be, darlin'… I'm nomad."

Jessie helps me out when he notices my confusion.

"A nomad's a member of the club but doesn't belong to a Charter, they travel around, mostly go where they're needed," Jessie explains.

"And it looks like you guys could use me around here," Brax says turning the conversation serious.

"Hell yeah. You serious?" Jessie's eyes light up. "Speak to Prez, man. You know you're always welcome."

"I just might," Brax says tapping Jessie hard on the back then moving on to talk to Skid.

"Seems a nice guy," I say to Jessie when Brax is out of earshot.

"He's a good guy, would be handy to have around, but I wouldn't use the word nice to describe him." Jessie smirks at what has to be a private joke as we watch Brax talking with the guys. He seems to blend right in. The idea of someone choosing to be part of a club but not staying among friends seems odd to me, but then, a lot of things around here don't make sense.

"You seem to know him well."

"He prospected at my pa's old Charter, I've known him since I was a kid. We did some training with Vex together a few years ago after Mary-Ann died. He stuck around while we needed extra protection for the women and kids."

"Kids lived here?" I ask, not meaning to sound quite so mortified.

"This used to be a proper family club, look at the facilities we got here it's perfect. But after the Bastards killed Mary-Ann. Some brothers thought it was safer to move their families to quieter Charters. Prez never held it against them. It just meant we ended up with all the crazy motherfuckers who have nothing to lose." Jessie lights up a cigarette and makes sure to direct the smoke away from me.

"Having Brax back in town will be a real step forward for the club," he tells me looking over at Brax, who's now deep in conversation with Prez.

"He really that bad?" I ask, wondering how one person could make such an impact.

"He's clever, hard as rock, and he doesn't have anyone to give a fuck about. That makes him dangerous if you're his enemy."

"And what about you... Are you dangerous?" I ask, looking into his eyes so he can't avoid my question, alcohol must be making me a little braver than usual.

"Yeah, I am," he says without hesitating.

"Like Brax?" I push for more.

"Nothing like Brax. I have people I care about Maddy, and that makes me worse." He leans in closer to me. "I've lost, a whole lot. And I know enough about how that shit feels to make sure it never happens again," he tells me holding my eyes with his. With no escape from them, I pick up my glass and seeing that it's already been topped up, I tip my head back and swallow it down. Jessie watches me as the fireball settles in my stomach, then laughs before he's interrupted by another biker.

I get sensible and switch alcohol to water when the atmosphere in the club starts to change, things get rowdier after Prez leaves. I don't miss the look of concern on Jessie's face when he'd announced he was going. Not long after, Jessie takes my hand and pulls me towards the door.

"You want to leave?" I ask a little shocked when we get outside.

"I want to take you somewhere," he says, getting on his bike.

"Well then let's go." I hop on behind him without any hesitation because the more I do it, the more I realize how much I like it.

CHAPTER 32

JESSIE

Today was harder than I anticipated. I thought I'd done all my grieving, I've been taking my anger out on the list Rogue put together for us, spent every night since Hayley's death fucking over people who dealt for the Bastards. It never made me feel any better, but it did keep me away from Maddy, and all the temptation that came from being around her. Putting space between me and her was the right thing to do.

I've started to understand why Prez never wanted Hayley at the club, I don't want Maddy around it either. The guys may be my brothers, but that doesn't stop me wanting to kill every one of them that dares to eye fuck her. At least with Hayley everyone knew she was off limits, no one would have had the balls to look, let alone touch Prez's daughter. Today, after seeing Maddy on the back of my bike I hope I've sent a clear message to them all that she's off limits too. It's bullshit, but if I can't have her, I sure as hell ain't about to let any of those assholes.

Maddy trusts me. She's willing to get on my bike when I ask to take her somewhere without question. Her soft hands grip me as I ride us out to the main road, up through the mountains and to my spot. I've never brought anyone out here before, not even Hayley. But today I feel the need to share it with her. We ride all the way to the top of the mountain, the road tapering thinner and thinner until it fails to exist. My timing is perfect, the warm oranges starting to blend into rich purples and illuminating the sky in front of us. But tonight she's distracting me from all that.

"It's beautiful." Maddy smiles, her wide eyes watching the sun slip behind the mountains, causing black shadows to cast over the valley below us.

"I've been coming up here since I was a kid," I tell her. "You see that tree line over there? That's the start of the forest that edges the compound, and this side…"—I point into the valley — "That's the reservation."

"Reservation?" Her sweet voice sounds intrigued.

"Yeah, a Cheyanne tribe, pretty sure it's one of the only remaining ones around here." She looks back at me confused. "Ain't many tribes left now, not like these anyway. These guys still live the traditional way."

"That's crazy," she laughs, and hearing her excitement makes me smile, even after the day we've had.

"So no electric, no cars, no running water?" she asks, leaning forward to peer over the rock and get a better look.

"Nope, they do it the same way their ancestors did it for years and years before them. Everyone at the club and people in town thinks they're crazy, I think it's kinda cool," I confess. Come to think of it I've never admitted that to anyone. There's no love lost between the Cheyanne tribe and the club. We've been asking them for years for passage through their reservation. If our escape trail through the woods could be rerouted to come out on the edge of the reservation, we wouldn't have to risk going on any main roads at all. Every time we reach out to them their chief refuses us, and although it fucks us off, there's always been an unspoken respect between them and us.

Both our people live by our own rules. So I guess we're not so different.

I light up a smoke and watch her be enthralled by the tiny figures moving below us. Children dancing and playing with each other while men sit and smoke. The women chat while they clean up after whatever meal they've all just enjoyed together. A few women walk towards the tree line on the opposite side of the reservation, probably going to use the natural spring at the bottom of the hill to bathe. It's simple living, but I understand its benefits.

"It's like stepping back into history," Maddy says, and I notice how she shivers slightly, her skin's starting to turn a little paler, and goosepimples raise on her arm.

"You cold?" I ask.

"I'm okay. Really. Please let's just stay here a little while longer?" she pleads. She's crazy if she thinks I'm gonna say no to her. Especially when she's being so damn cute. Balancing my smoke between my lips, I let the stream of smoke sting my eyes as I shrug out of my cut and drape it over her shoulders. Her dainty fingers touch at it, pulling it tighter around her.

"Thanks." She looks up at me with those perfect eyes. "And not just for all this, for today too. Letting me out for the funeral, bringing me here. I really needed it."

"You're not a prisoner, Maddy," I remind her, feeling a sharp punch in the gut at the thought of her seeing it that way. "I'm not trying to punish you. I'm trying to keep you safe."

"I always feel safe when I'm with you," she whispers, avoiding my eye contact by pretending to be distracted by the scenery.

"Never let your guard down, Mads. Hayley felt safe around me too and look what happened to her." It's my turn to look away now, I've never admitted that out loud before either, and the words sting my tongue on their way out.

"Yeah, me. I happened to her," Maddy laughs, but not a happy one... a self-loathing one that I hate the sound of.

"Stop that. Stop blaming yourself for what happened to her. What Hayley did was her choice, you never asked her to jump in front of you and take that bullet."

"Okay, Jessie, if it's so easy then why don't you stop blaming yourself too?" she snaps back, turning her head she looks right at me, her eyes burning me for an answer.

"That's different." I shake my head knowing there's no way she'd ever understand.

"No, you blame yourself the same as I do. I can see it eating you up, and you need to let it go too." Silence hangs between us, neither of us really knowing what to say next. Maddy goes to say something, her lips parting slightly. But before her voice can come out I lean into her, and I take those lips with my own. I want to kiss away all the guilt and pain she feels, and it surprises me how the heavy weight of mine becomes a little lighter as I do.

Her hand weaves into my hair, and she holds me close like she's afraid I'll pull away. She doesn't have to worry though, I'd kiss her until my lips felt raw and I couldn't draw any breath. Or at least until I remember who I am and exactly what I'm trying to protect her from.

I force myself away when that eventually happens.

She smiles at me, in a way that's unintentionally seductive. Placing my hand on the back of her head I tuck her down into my chest then set a kiss on the top of her head, and hold her there. My lips press tightly against her soft, golden hair, just so I don't have to look into her eyes. Because if I do, any morals, and good intentions I possess, are likely to up and leave me.

"Come on, darlin', let's get you back." I nudge her after too long a silence, and I stand up from the smooth rock we've been sitting on. When I offer her my hand to help her up, she takes it and her fingers wrapping around mine puts a comfort in my chest that doesn't belong there.

The tighter she clings to my waist on the way back, the tighter I grip my bars. The entire way she rests the weight of her body against my back, her thighs pressing tightly against the outside of mine and I already know that after kissing her again, I'm gonna need an outlet tonight.

My head insists on fucking with me, making me want to do things to her that I've never done before. I don't want to fuck Maddy Summers. I want to lay her out and fucking worship her. I find these days that my impulse to do just that has become stronger than my urges to create pain and cause suffering. How the girl's managed to conflict my brutal mind with thoughts so beautiful baffles me and terrifies me all at the same time.

The party is still pretty loud when we get to the club, and I ride straight on past up to my cabin. Then resting up my bike I follow Maddy inside.

"You hungry? I could make you something?" she asks, making her way towards the kitchen. She sounds nervous, like she can sense how my mood has shifted.

"I'm good," I reply, aware of how cold I sound. But just being around her feels like I'm being strangled. My fingers twitch for her skin, and if I let them touch again I know they'll never stop reaching. She's a line that once I cross I'll never come back from. And I have to keep the promises I've made to myself.

My dirty soul will not bleed hers of its goodness, I can't give her what she needs. She deserves everything, or at the very least someone who knows how to love her.

"I got to head back out," I tell her, hating the look of disappointment that instantly falls over her face knowing that it's me who's caused it. I even consider going back down to the club, screwing the shit out of Mel or one of the others to rough-fuck Maddy right out of my head for the night. But I already know without trying that it wouldn't be enough.

Tonight, I need more. Tonight, I have to remind myself of the monster I'm protecting Maddy from. I'll prove to myself that the thoughts that have been twisting themselves in my head since the first day I saw her, don't belong there. Taking my cut from where she's neatly placed it on the back of the sofa, I check that what I need is still in the pocket, then slide it back on. Then I walk out of the door without saying goodbye.

I don't look back, the hurt staring back at me will haunt me for the rest of the night if I do. Sitting on my bike, I pull out the list. There are still eight names waiting to be crossed off it and Cameron Slater's is the name I pick out at random. I instantly feel sorry for the unlucky bastard.

CHAPTER 33

MADDY

I'm starting to think he enjoys the teasing. That giving me a glimpse inside, and then shutting down and snatching it all away again is a game to him.

Getting away from the compound with him tonight has been incredible, him kissing me again was everything else on top of that. It's different to the first time he kissed me. Less feral, gentler, almost like he's trying to tell me something. Then somewhere on the short journey back to the club, I lost him again.

I guess riding past the club reminded him what he was missing out on. The women down there are experienced, they'd know how to get him off. Why would he waste his time here with me?

Thinking about it's too painful, so I decide to distract myself. I make myself more comfortable by changing into a vest top and some boy shorts. It's been hot all day, so I take advantage of the cool evening air and set my laptop up out on the balcony.

Breaking into government files isn't all that tricky, it's the doing it without being detected that takes all the effort. People work 24/7 to keep people like me out, so I have to make sure I'm smarter than the people I'm up against. I've always loved computers, growing up I spent a lot of time on my own, but I never felt lonely. How could I when I had the whole universe under my fingertips.

I taught myself how to hack mainly out of curiosity. When I was fifteen I was desperate to find my father. Mom refused to talk about him, and all I had to go on was an uncashed cheque that I'd found when I was snooping in Mom's things. That uncashed cheque had provided information though. A name and account details at least.

I was well aware that a fifteen-year-old couldn't just walk into a bank and demand information on her suspected father. Luckily, I had a pretty vivid imagination. I'd seen what people could do on TV. When it came to the worldwide web nothing was impossible. Nothing is secure, and there is always a way in. I got on to some forums, learned the basics, and then I used those basic skills to further my knowledge. I practiced a whole lot because being unpopular meant I had nothing but time.

I found my father eventually, a happily married man who lived a few towns away. He had the perfect life and a beautiful family. A son a few years older than myself, twin girls a few months younger. I figured the generous cheque had been to keep Mom and me from jeopardizing all that.

It gave me a whole new respect for my mom. We had nothing, and I'm sure there would have been more than one occasion where she would have really needed to use that money, yet she never did. She was too proud and too strong. It made me grateful for everything she'd ever given me.

Over the years I decided to forget about that man and his family. He lived close enough, it would have been easy for him to find me, check in and see how I was doing. But he was weak. I was a mistake he'd made that he thought he could buy out of. I may not have many people in my life but there's no room for people like him. He could keep his fancy house and his respectable job, eat around the table with his perfect family and pretend to them and himself that he didn't have secrets, because like my mom I'd never need him for anything.

It doesn't take me long to find Tobias Saunders' file, and it would take even less time for me to delete him altogether. But when his mugshot fills up my screen and I take him in properly something about him makes all the hairs on the back of my neck prickle. His eyes were riddled with evil, looking fit to burst from the pressure of the secrets they hold. I try telling myself that mugshots aren't designed to get people's good angle, although that hadn't been the case with Jessie's.

Yeah, I've checked.

Jessie still looked wickedly beautiful in his, and his offenses had only been minor—well if you call GBH and carrying a firearm minor.

"So, you can really make him disappear with just a click of a button." I follow the voice up to the cabin deck on my right, it's been empty since I arrived. Brax moves to sit up on the railings that separate the decks, a cigarette hanging from the corner of his mouth.

"Brax... I didn't see you there. You made me jump," I laugh nervously, pulling my laptop screen down just a touch.

"You should read that file before you delete it," he tells me, holding in a breath that keeps his lungs filled with smoke, then his eyes crease together as the thick cloud releases from his mouth. "You don't know how long you're gonna be sticking around here, and you should ask yourself if that's the kind of man you wanna to be living in the company of." He points his head towards my screen.

"He's part of this club. I thought you all had some unbreakable bro code," I remind him, curious at his difference of opinion to the others.

"Tobias Saunders has been hiding out behind this club for years. No one here knows who he really is, not even his real brother. How many of them down there do you think have read those offenses?" He draws his teeth back over this thick bottom lip.

"They've asked for me to do this for them. I don't know if

you've heard, but I kinda owe them," I explain sarcastically, hoping the guy has a sense of humor as well as the ability to make fear tingle at the base of your spine.

"I'm just asking you to take some time out to read that file. If you're as good as they say you are, you can make that file disappear along with all the people he's hurt. You should know what you're burying, Maddy." Brax slides off the railings and steps back inside his cabin. It leaves me conflicted over what I should do next. If I read the file and find out what horrors truly do lie behind those eyes, will my conscience let me wipe his slate clean for him? If I don't, I'm putting myself at risk. Jessie tells me the club are protecting me and I'm too afraid to doubt him. Clunk made it clear he would kill me if I didn't do as he asks and that was before the Dirty Souls became involved. If I fail to do what they ask me, these men could turn on me too.

My head aches coming up with all the scenarios. I need time to think. So, without reading it, I leave the file where it is. For now at least. No one apart from Brax knows that I've already accessed the file and I get the impression he'll want to keep the conversation we've just had private.

Brax seems to know a lot about Tobias Saunders, and it makes me wonder if he's shared his concerns with the others. He's wrong about one thing though, even if I could bury the file again it will never vanish entirely, there will be a paper trail. Whoever made this disappear before had to have been working on the inside.

I shut everything down and decide to go to bed. I hope Jessie comes home tonight, and in a better mood than he left.

Getting into his bed, I snuggle myself into his sheets. Sleeping in his bed makes me feel close to him. He keeps me distanced but I like to pretend two people like us could be together, even in a world like his. It's with that beautiful delusion that my mind finally stops running circles and I drift off.

CHAPTER 34
JESSIE

Cameron never expected what I had for him, and I'm confident that after what he's just endured he'll never work for the Bastards again. I'd chosen well, he was the perfect target for what I needed tonight, he'd even put up a little fight to start with.

Adrenaline is still surging in my blood, I could easily have taken out another name on the list, but instead, I choose to go home to her. She'll be asleep by now, that makes it a little easier. It's crazy how sharing space with her can soothe me and fuck me up all at the same time. When she's sleeping, at least I can enjoy watching her without fucking anything up.

This time of night the club is quiet. Everyone's either passed out or fucking by now, leaving only the sounds of crickets and the breeze whistling around the trees. I pull up outside my cabin and open the door quietly so not to disturb her. I know I shouldn't care, I am who I am, but I don't want Maddy seeing me like this.

It's surprising how much, when hit in the right spot, a nose can bleed, and the top half of my body is pretty much covered from where Cameron's exploded all over it. My T-shirt is ripped from where he desperately clawed at me while I held him in a choke hold and warned him what would happen to him if he ever so much as looked at a Bastard ever again.

I could have left it at that, he had the message loud, but I didn't, it was about more than a list tonight. I was proving who I am, what I do. The more time I spend near Maddy, the more I seem to be forgetting. There'd been a time during the onslaught that I hadn't been sure If I was gonna stop. All the frustration that had been mounting up for so long became easier to handle when I'd been kicking him in his ribs and bending back his arms until they cracked.

I'd punched the son of a bitch until my hands were tacky with his blood, and luckily for Cameron, that's when she'd managed to make her way back inside my head. Her pretty, pleading eyes begging with me not to go too far, not to take someone's life just because I couldn't get a grip on my own emotions. It was Maddy who Cameron had to thank for his life tonight.

It's dark inside the cabin, and completely silent. I creep my way through to the kitchen and open the fridge searching for a bottle of bud or anything that might help me wind down enough to attempt some sleep. I'm all out, and as I move to swing the door shut, I feel a hand land on my shoulder. Spinning round quick I realize just in time that it's her and lower the fist I've risen.

Fuck, the girl crept up on me in the dark like a fucking panther. Her eyes grow wide and I know the light from the open refrigerator is illuminating the room enough for her to see me. I haven't seen the state of myself yet, but I know it'll be bad.

"Jessie, my god, are you okay?" Her hands lift to her mouth with concern when she sees the blood.

"Ain't mine," I tell her, watching relief I don't deserve calm the panic from her face.

What reason have I ever given her to give a shit about me?

Her hands move slowly reaching out towards me, but I can't let her touch me, not like this.

"Don't touch me," I warn, quickly shoving past her making a

gasp for air. She remains standing in the kitchen while I storm into the bathroom. Pulling my T-shirt over my head, I stare back at my reflection in the mirror that hangs above the sink. My face has a few splats of blood across it, and there's a scratch under my eye where Cameron had caught me while I was throttling him. It's nothing too major, but scary enough to someone like Maddy. Now in brighter light, I can see that my hands are a complete mess. I look down at my scratched up torso and when I look back up again her eyes met mine through the mirror.

"What are you doing?" I manage to soften my tone for her this time, none of this is her fault. Maddy shrugs her shoulders, unable to pull her eyes from the reflection of evil that's standing right in front of her.

"I just wanted to..." She looks down at her feet like she's ashamed. "I want to help you," she whispers. I turn around to face her, resting my ass against the sink and I let her see me, all of me. Raw and fucking uncensored. I want her to see what she should be running from, then turn and fucking sprint.

But she doesn't. She stays, keeping her pretty eyes connected to mine like helpless bait.

"Yeah well, I'm a lot past helping, Maddy. So you're wasting your time." I do a shit job of holding back the weakness in my voice. I need her to stop looking at me like that, to crush any hope she has of making something decent out of me.

"Why are you always so hard on yourself?" Her soft whisper has a bitter bite that twists my insides.

"Hard on myself? Maddy do you have any idea what I am? What I do?" She looks back to the floor. "You wanna know whose blood this is?" I hold up my bloody T-shirt in the small space between us before throwing it in to the laundry basket. "He was just a kid, some stupid kid who's been selling for the Bastards. Some poor fuckin' kid who wanted to make a few bucks and probably had no idea what he was getting involved in."

"Did you... Is he..." She's so pure she can't even say the fuckin' word.

"Did I kill him?" I say bluntly, watching her flinch. "No... Not him, tonight he got off with a real nasty warning." I hear the relieved breath leave her lips, but I'm not finished. She has to know the truth. She holds far too much hope for me, and it's what makes her so hard to resist

"Not all have been that lucky though. I have killed, and I will again. And what's fucked up, Mads, is that there's never been a time that I haven't really fucking enjoyed it..."

There, it's out there, there's no coming back from what I've admitted. But at the very least she will see me for what I am. She can move on from whatever she's been thinking might happen between us and hate me the way I deserve her to. I'm not surprised when she starts chewing on her lip, it's what she always does when she's nervous, and finding out you're living with a murderous psycho would have anyone on edge.

"So... You still reckon I'm this great guy who should forgive himself now? Huh, Maddy?" I push, unable to control the rise in my voice as all the anger I've been holding for myself builds higher and higher.

I feel like a cunt when she bites down even harder, her face resembling a child who's being scolded as her eyes fill with tears that I've caused. I feel no relief from telling her, not like I thought I would. Especially knowing what the consequences are. She's disgusted by me now, and hell if I can blame her for it.

"I didn't think so," I answer the question for her, unsurprised by her silence. Turning my back on her because I can't look at the devastation on her face for another second, I twist on the shower. Kick off my trainers, pull off my socks and loosen my belt. Then shuffling the dirty heap aside with my foot, I step under the water.

Warm streams hit my skin and heat my body, and the room fills up with steam. I rinse my face and hair, then turn to let the water slide over my shoulders and back. And when I open my eyes, the sight in front of me nearly knocks me on my ass.

Maddy Summers is standing, naked and flawless in front of me. Pert round breasts topped with beautiful pink nipples. My eyes slide down over her tight stomach and slightly rounded hips, all the way to the tiny well-kept patch of hair that covers her slit. I stand speechless, watching as she steps closer.

She seems oblivious to the fact that I'm covered in someone else's blood, and I watch her hands as they slowly reach out and spread across my chest. I draw in the longest breath when her soft fingertips make contact with my skin, and it feels like they were made for the sole purpose of touching me. I don't think I could stop them even if I wanted to.

Her face tilts as it moves up towards mine, her tongue trailing itself around her plump lips, it causes all my restraints to disintegrate. I go to her, taking her cheeks in my palms and letting my lips cover over her mouth. I turn our bodies and push her tight against the tiled wall, the warm spray of the shower rains down between us, soaking her unexplored body while she fills my mouth with her tongue. With my hands braced against the wall I kiss her like she belongs to me, her hand lifts up to my face willing me to keep my lips on hers. This, us, is better than any encounter I've ever had. Up until her I've never had the urge to kiss a woman, but since last week all I've thought about is kissing her again. I've held myself off for so long now my mouth can't get enough of her.

"Jessie," she whispers against my lips, and I pull back just enough to get a look at her. She looks incredible, blonde hair soaked, sticking to her face. Skin flushed and those wide expectant eyes begging me for more. She's impossible to resist.

"You want me to touch you?" I ask, my body shielding hers from the water. She nods her head back at me slowly. If I didn't know better I'd say she was being seductive. But Maddy is too innocent to know what she does to a man, let alone use it against him.

Rubbing my lips together I let my pointer finger trace the trail of the water droplets down her flat stomach. Her skin forms goosepimples at my touch and her nipples seem to shrink harder. And as I edge closer to her center she closes her eyes and sucks in a breath.

"You want me to touch you here?" I ask. My finger waiting for permission just above the tiny mound of hair covering her pussy.

"Yes." Her eyes speak to me so sincerely when she opens them, and slowly the tip of my finger slips inside that warm, enticing slit. Feeling her flesh on my finger makes me hungry to taste her again. This time feels so different to before. This isn't me interrogating her, this is her defeating me.

My fingertip circles her entrance, teasing and coaxing, and her pleasure coats my fingers. I watch for her reaction when I push one inside her, not too deep, just to the knuckle. Her sharp intake of breath and the way she steadies herself with her arms around my neck makes me fucking desperate to be inside her.

"How about my tongue, you wanna feel my tongue again, darlin'?" I ask, leaning my head forward to press kisses into her neck. Her pussy puckers around my finger giving me her answer.

"Please," she responds, her hands moving into my hair and grasping.

Moving down her body I leave kisses in my trail, and it's impossible to pass her tits without taking one in my hand. It looks fucking perfect in my grip, with her tight nub grazing at my palm. I lower my head hungry to taste her, sucking her into my mouth and letting my teeth graze over her nipple.

"Oh my god," she breathes, as my lips savor her skin and the finger I have between her legs strokes her from the inside. I break away and press kisses over her stomach. Maddy's body is wound up so tight that it's practically humming. All this is new to her, and knowing her skin hasn't been touched by anyone else makes it taste so much sweeter.

When I work my way down to her thighs, I notice she still has a tiny mark from where I cut her in the basement last week. I should feel guilty for it, but I can't help thinking how good my mark looks on her. When I touch my mouth to it she hums back at me, and when I look up at her she's watching me. Her bright eyes spilling with desire. She looks like she's been corrupted by the devil himself and I move my lips from her skin just for a second to smile at her. I hold her eyes, daring her to look away as I slide a slow antagonizing lick up through her pussy lips.

She tastes so sweet and fucking pure it's hard to believe that this girl nearly ruined my club with her secret talent, that she has the ability to bring a man like me to my knees. Yet she's oblivious to her power. "Jessie," she speaks my name again. Her fingers almost dragging the hair from my scalp now. I slip my finger from her pussy so I can take both her wrists in my hand and pin them against the tiles behind her. Then I eat at her pussy like a starved fucking animal.

Her hips thrash, rocking on my face when I find her clit with the tip of my tongue and give it my undivided attention. Her juices coat my mouth, making my cock stretch to the point of pain to feel the inside of her sacred little hole.

"Jessie, something's happening," she warns, her bright eyes stretching wide with something that looks a lot like panic. "Jessie, stop it feels like..."

I don't stop, and when she tries to rip her wrists from the hold I've got on them, I tighten my grip.

"Jessie," she pleads, and I smile wickedly at her with my eyes as one last flick of my tongue sends her over the edge.

Every muscle in her stomach clenches as her hot little snatch throbs for me. And I watch her come apart. She breaks the contact of our eyes when she squeezes hers closed. Her face creasing like she's in pain, but I know the only thing she's suffering from is pleasure. Pleasure that she received from my tongue. And I decide in this moment that it will only ever be me. I own that fucking look. I own this pussy, and my tongue will be the only one to taste any fucking orgasm that spills from it.

I don't give her time to come down, releasing her wrists and stalking my way back up her body. She struggles for oxygen, and I take even more away from her when I smash my lips over hers and let her learn for herself how good she tastes on me. She mewls her approval into my mouth.

"Final question, Maddy."

"You sure like to ask a lot of questions when you got me in a compromising position." There's no humor in her voice, just a hint of a smile when I pull back to look at her.

"Do you want me to take it?" I look down to where my cock is dangerously close to her opening. And Jesus, I want her to want to give it to me. Whether that be now or whenever she feels ready.

She nods her head, her eyes fixed on mine, and when her shaking hand reaches between us and wraps around me, I swear to god I almost shoot my load into it.

"I'm scared. I've heard it hurts." She's stroking me now. I can tell by her fumbling fingers that she's never held a cock before, and it makes me fucking weak at the knees. "I've never wanted something so much that I know will hurt," she adds, her teeth practically biting through her lip as she watches my cock pull through her fingers.

"I've never wanted to not hurt someone so much," I confess, hooking my finger and lifting her chin so I get a look at those eyes again. "Do you wanna feel me inside you now?" I ask her. It'll be painful but I can wait if that's what she wants.

"Yes," she whispers nervously, and my hands waste no more time reaching around her and grabbing her ass cheeks. I lift her off her feet, and when her legs wrap around my waist the tip of my cock bumps against her slick little hole. I should at least do the decent thing and wear protection but there's none to hand and I ain't breaking this moment. Maddy is an exception to all the fucking rules. I'm clean, I would never put her at risk, and I'll just have to be fast to the mark and pull out before I come inside her. Although the thought of that sends a rush of thrill shooting up my spine.

I press her back into the tiled wall behind her, feeling the water cascading over us while I tease her tight opening with the head of my cock. It physically hurts me how much I want to be inside her, and her pussy is pulsing to be filled. So I give into what we both need and slowly edge into her.

The inside of Maddy Summers has to be the closest to heaven a man like me will ever get. It holds me so fucking tight that I feel her throb around me, and it takes my breath away. Her nails dig into my shoulder and I try so hard to be gentle in breaking her.

"You okay, darlin'?" I check, my hand swiping some hair from her face to clear a path to her eyes. "Am I hurting you?" The thought of causing her pain cuts into my chest.

"A little, keep going though. I feel like I need it. I can't explain it."

"Okay," I whisper, reminding myself to take a breath. My eyes focus on hers as I sink a little deeper, and I hear my growl get drowned out by Maddy's screech as I fracture that barrier inside.

Words can't describe how it feels to be fully seated inside her, and I hold myself still for a moment. Not just so she can adjust, but because my head is spinning like I'm on a fucking trip. She makes a long sigh of relief and while one of my hands steadies us against the wall, I have to pinch at the skin on her waist in my other palm to check she's real.

She smiles at me, fucking smiles, and I feel that smile slip right into my soul. How can something so fucking good, be for me? I remember the priest at my pa's funeral had told me never to doubt God's will. Maybe that's what she is, God's gift to me for all he'd taken. A sacrifice made to cleanse me of all my wrongs. Or maybe the priest was talking shit and I'm just a selfish bastard. Either way I start to move, using the weight of my body to hold her to the wall while I roll my hips slowly into hers and explore every unexplored inch inside her.

She moans my name, and when I tuck my head into her neck she clings on to me like I'm the fucking world and she doesn't want to fall off.

As I continue to stretch her, it starts to feel a lot like Maddy Summers pussy was made solely for me. I feel release creeping up on me, she's too damn tight and feels too good for me to last. I'm tempted to let it spill inside her, to let those tight walls clench at me as I fill her, but I manage to tear myself out just in time. All I see is white behind my eyes as my heavy cock lands with a thud against her stomach. I look down between us and watch as it pumps hot jets of cum onto her skin. I'm fucking breathless, my head completely shot.

Maddy's watching it too and she must see the few blood streaks decorating my shaft, the final traces of her innocence.

"Thank you." She smiles up at me like she's fucking grateful, and I have to kiss her because it kinda hurts to look at her. What just happened is proof that I'm so much weaker than I ever thought I was. And it doesn't matter how hard I try to fight against it, I have to admit this bitch fuckin' got me. Heart, body, and fucked up soul.

CHAPTER 35 — MADDY

My stomach does a cartwheel when morning comes and I wake up next to Jessie. He's still fast asleep, and aside from the scratch under his left eye, there isn't a single line on his face. I can't remember a time when I've seen him look so peaceful. One of his arms is resting over me, and I can't resist stretching up and placing a kiss on his forehead. It makes him stir, and his grip tightens around my waist.

"Mornin', darlin'," he speaks without opening his eyes, curling his lip into a one-sided smile that makes me want to jump him.

"You want something for breakfast?" I ask, taking one of his blonde locks, and flicking it through my fingers.

"Mmmm, would love breakfast," he growls, as he rolls on top of me. His head nestles into my neck, and his lips tickle just behind my ear making me giggle like an excited child.

"You stay here. I'll get us some." He uses his arms either side of me to push himself off the bed, and I watch as he walks his fully naked ass out of the bedroom. Clattering and bangs come from the kitchen a few minutes later, and I decide to get up and take a shower. Picking up one of his T-shirts from the floor, I throw it over my head on my way to the bathroom.

I'm brushing my teeth when I hear a tap on the front door. I poke my head out of the bathroom and I lift my hand up when I see Carly. She almost drops the basket she's carrying when she notices Jessie naked at the stove.

"Jesus Christ," she shrieks, sheltering her eyes behind her fingers.

"You know you really shouldn't have that thing so close to a pan," she warns him, placing the basket on the table and looking over to me. I'm leaned against the bathroom doorframe, toothbrush dangling from my mouth, with a smile that I can't hold off as I take in the view for myself. Carly smiles at me with the tiniest hint of an eye roll.

"I guess I'd better leave you guys to it… Maddy, there are a few bathing suits in there. Thought they might come in handy for the party, and if you get a minute later, I could use a favor."

"Of course, thanks for the suits," I call out as she leaves, hoping she understood me through a mouthful of toothpaste.

After my shower, I change into one of the bikini's, and choose one of the summer dresses my mom packed me to wear over the top.

"So, what do I need the suit for?" I ask Jessie, as I walk out of the bedroom and sit at the table where he's set up two places.

"We're having a lake party today. Lift everyone up after yesterday," he explains, placing the loaded plates on the table.

"That sounds like a really nice idea."

"You wanna make a guess at whose idea it was?" He raises his eyebrow playfully.

"Carly."

We both say her name at the same time. Carly has to be the most caring person I've ever met, everyone at the club seems to adore her, and arranging something like this is just typical of her.

I'm nervous when we leave the cabin a few hours later. We walk past all the other cabins then into a stretch of woodland that leads towards the flat beach area, on the opposite side of the lake from the cabins. Carly and Skid walk just ahead of us hand in hand and it would feel like the most natural thing in the world to take Jessie's hand in mine too. I don't, mainly through fear of how he might react. With the exception of Carly, and maybe Skid, people around the club don't like me much. I'm certain Jessie wouldn't want his friends to know about what had happened between us last night.

Today isn't going to be the same as the funeral yesterday, I'm still not entirely convinced I should be going at all. I worry about how I'll feel if Jessie flirts with those girls who make themselves 'available', and I'm already fearing all the judgmental looks I'll get this afternoon. But I don't share my concerns with Jessie and stay silent as we walk towards the loud music, trying my best not to let my insecurities drive me crazy.

When we arrive at the lakeside, Jessie and Skid leave me and Carly and join up with the men around the grill. All the other women have set themselves up in line with the sun, tops off and tits out. Some of them venture into the lake to dunk their toes. But most of them hang around the men, not seeming to care when their most intimate parts are touched and groped at.

I lay out my towel beside Carly's, in our own spot away from the other girls. Lying on my back, I enjoy the heat from the sun warming my skin and lose myself in the memories of Jessie touching me last night. It was nothing like how the men are handling the women here. He'd been so gentle, and I wonder if he's like that with them too.

I try not being too obvious looking over at Jessie every once in a while, he's deep in conversation with Brax, but every time his eyes flick over to meet mine, he gives me a smile or a wink that reminds me that we share a special secret.

"You had sex, didn't you?" Carly interrupts my dreamy state, and I quickly tear my eyes off Jessie and focus them to her. She slides her sunglasses down her nose, peering over the top of them towards Jessie and all my blood rushes straight to my cheeks.

"Hey, it ain't nothing to be ashamed of, he's hot. And girl if I were you, I'd be making damn sure all of them..."—she moves her eyes to the topless attention seekers splashing around in the lake—"...know who he's coming home to every night."

"It isn't like that. Jessie wouldn't want anyone to know about us." Referring to Jessie and me as 'us' sounds ridiculous, but puts a warm feeling in my tummy. I look over at one of the girls rising out of the water, strutting like she's walking the runway. Her attention is set directly on Jessie and she makes straight for him, her perfect body glistening with water. When she reaches him, she places her hand on his shoulder and whispers something in his ear. I can't stand to watch on for his reaction. Pulling my summer dress off over my head, I make sure the bikini Carly lent me covers my modesty, then flip over on to my front and let the sun drench my back.

"Oh trust me, honey, he'll want them to know." Carly laughs to herself, fixing her glasses back in place before she lifts her head up towards the sun.

Beers flow, music blasts from the sound system set up in the back of one of the trucks, and the BBQ smells amazing. Feeling fried from all the sun, I decide to cool myself off in the lake. I go to check if Carly wants to come too but she's sleeping. I don't disturb her, and tiptoe over the bumpy pebbles to the now completely vacant lake. The smaller stones dig into the soles of my feet on the way down, and it makes me wonder how on earth that girl had made her journey from the water to Jessie look so graceful. My walk being far more wounded duck than graceful swan.

I dip my toes when I reach the water, pleasantly surprised at how warm the water feels against my skin. Gradually, I step forward, being cautious of the ground suddenly slopping. The water is so clear I can see the tiny fish swimming around my legs and tickling at my ankles.

I make it in almost to the top of my thighs before I take the plunge, bending my knees and sinking myself into the water all the way up to my neck. Dropping my head back, I soak my hair, then scoop a handful of water onto my face. Laying back in the water I take a look at the landscape surrounding the compound. The view is so breathtaking that l lose myself staring at it. It's the first time I've taken the time to really appreciate what's here. My eyes follow the tree line set behind the cabins on the other side of the lake, all the way around to the lodges that sit higher up on the hill and look over the lake.

I can just make out a single figure leaning over the balcony of the biggest lodge watching everyone below, and I know instantly that it's Hayley's Dad. Guilt strikes me like lightning, everyone down here is laughing, drinking, and enjoying each other's company. While he stands alone and watches, consumed by loss and grief. I pull myself out of the water before the heavy weight of guilt drowns me completely, taking my towel and drying myself enough to slide back into my dress.

Heading over to the food table, I grab a plate and serve up a bit of everything until the plate is towered high and crammed full.

"Hungry much?" a voice speaks into my ear, and just from the tingle it spreads across the back of my neck, I know it's Jessie.

"It's not for me, silly." I swat his hand off my ass, being cautious not to upset the plate in my other hand.

"I thought I'd take Hayley's dad some food up," I explain, managing to squeeze a spoonful of potato salad onto the last remaining available space on the plate.

"Mads, that's a real nice thought, but maybe I should take it up. I don't think…"

"Please let me do this?" I interrupt looking up at him through my lashes, I can tell from the way he frowns back at me that he thinks it's a bad idea.

"He just ain't in the best of places, darlin'."

"I know, and I won't impose, I'll just drop off the food and leave. I Promise. I just really wanna do something nice for him." The smile that twitches on Jessie's face is enough to know he isn't going to stop me.

"Thanks." I smile back, wishing l could reach up on my toes and kiss his cheek, I'm just too scared to embarrass him in front of everyone.

"Just drop it and then leave, okay?" he warns, and I agree. I leave him standing at the table as I start my walk up the rough track to the lodge on top of the hill.

It takes a little longer than I expected to get to the top. The plate seeming heavier and heavier in my hands, it isn't helped by the fact that the closer I get, the more they start to tremble.

Once I get there I knock on the door and wait, and then I wait some more. After a few minutes without an answer I notice a side gate that I figure leads out to the balcony, and I forge together enough courage to open it. When I step around the corner and see him, suddenly I lose my nerve. Prez has moved and is sitting on a chair just a few meters back from the balcony railings. His feet are propped up on the table in front of him. There's a lit cigarette hanging loosely from his mouth and a pile of empty bottles scattered around his feet.

"What do you want?" he growls, not taking his eyes off the lake below us. The noise from the party echoes up through the valley and is almost as loud up here as it is down there.

"I thought you might be hungry, so I brought you this." I fight against my nerves, trying to sound cheery as I move forward and set the plate down on the table in front of him. Then remembering my promise to Jessie, I turn around and start back towards the gate.

"Wait," his voice calls out, so coarsely that it makes my stomach turn over.

"Sit down." His order is followed by the sound of a metal chair scraping against wood when he kicks it out from under the table. I swallow down the massive lump that's wedged itself in my throat, taking the few steps back towards him and lowering myself on to the chair.

"You know I've spent more time up in this house this past week than I did the whole time my girl lived here," he speaks in a tone that rumbles. I don't know how to respond to that, so I'm thankful when he doesn't give me a chance to.

"I never gave her the attention she deserved." He shakes his head. "She never complained, but I always knew I could have given her more."

"She loved you, sir," I tell him, my voice shaky as it passes through my lips.

"I didn't deserve her love," he snaps, leaning forward and tipping the bottle of vodka on the table up to his lips. I'm shocked when he offers it over to me when he's done, his action seeming almost hospitable. Shaking my head politely, I hope he doesn't take offense at my refusal.

"Why do you think she did what she did?" he asks me, like I hold the cure to his suffering.

"I don't know, sir," I reply, tasting tears at the back of my throat. "I wish I knew," I add before silence falls, a long uncomfortable silence that feels like it might never end.

"I don't hate you." His words come out of nowhere, like he suddenly feels the need to reassure me.

"I appreciate you letting me be here, and keeping me safe. I know it must be hard to see me inste—" A grunt that comes right from his chest stops me mid-sentence.

"Crazy as it sounds, seeing you, is just about all that's keepin' me goin'," he interrupts. A small ironic laugh hidden behind his words. "You're a reminder that my daughter lived, that she had someone who cared about her. A friend who she loved enough to die for, same as I would for any of 'em down there." His head nods down towards the lake. "How can I hate someone for being my little girl's friend?" he says weakly.

"You ain't the reason she's dead, Maddy... I am," he adds, taking another swig from the bottle.

I feel like I might choke on tears when I try to talk.

"That's not true," I force out. "Those men, they took me. What happened to her was meant to happen to me. It should have been me."

Prez stands up on to his feet, then with a thud that rattles right through my bones he slams his fist on the table.

"Look how Hayley was raised, what she's seen since she was a child. Friends, brothers putting themselves on the line for the people they care about every day. Should I be surprised that she jumped in front of that bullet to save you? Should I be so angry that I can't stand to look at you? Blame you? Or should I be proud? Proud because if she had been born a son, I would have expected her to do that from the day she was born. Loyalty is what this whole club is built around." Tears slide down his face, as he shatters right in front of me, and I get the impression this is the first time he's said any of these words out loud.

"You know, I nearly lost her before, and I still didn't learn. Those men that tried to kill you tried to take her, the same night as they took her mama. Lucky Jessie was there to save her. Not me... Jessie, and you know why?"

He doesn't give me a chance to guess,

"Because I was balls deep in a fucking club slut..." His voice is full of anger, but only for himself.

"I failed her every day of her short life." His tone softens from anger to devastation. "You know what I see looking at you in front of me now, Maddy? I see a chance. An opportunity to do something for her. My little girl wanted you to live, and I'll raise hell if have to, to make sure that happens. Whoever you are, or however you came to be in my daughter's life doesn't matter. You did something that earned her loyalty, and for that reason, you got mine. This club's too." I take in all he's said and all I can do is stare back at him, speechless.

"This club will protect you from the people who tried to hurt you, and anyone else. This is your home now, and we'll be your family for as long as you need us. You can toss your laptop in that damn lake for all the fucks I give. You owe us nothing. All I'm asking is that you stop hating yourself. That you live that life she gave you. Let me take the burden. Let me fucking take it, turn it to hate, and use it to get vengeance on the people who took her from us." Prez slumps back down in his chair, running his hands through his white hair as if his outburst drained him completely.

I have no control over my body when it launches towards him, my arms wrapping around his neck. I swaddle him with gratefulness, and at first, he doesn't respond. He remains weightless between my arms then just when I'm about to pull away, his hand reaches around to my back, and he taps me with an unexpected softness.

"You need anything, feel free to help yourself to what's in her room. I'm sure she would have wanted you to have it." I can't begin to think how hard this must be for him, and I take a look up to the clear blue sky and hope Hayley is watching when I make a silent promise to her that I'm gonna take care of him too.

"You should get back down to the party," he says, his curt voice suddenly back, cuing for me to pull myself away before things turn awkward.

"Sure thing, Prez," I whisper, forcing a smile through my tears. He nods his head managing to drag out a little smile of his own from somewhere. And I know what I've just witnessed was really special, that it isn't often Jimmer Carson shows any sign of weakness.

CHAPTER 36

JESSIE

She's been gone ages, definitely long enough for me to start getting worried. I know Prez wouldn't hurt her, I'd never have let her go alone if I did. Prez is good to his word, I trust him above anyone else. But the longer she takes to come back the more anxious I become. He doesn't know what she means to me. He can't, not yet, not while he's still so angry at her. I'm hoping he appreciates her thoughtfulness. Sees what Hayley saw in her and understand a little why she'd wanted to save her.

"Hey Jess, where's blondie?" Troj asks, zipping up his jeans as he walks towards us. Squealer's been talking to me too, but I haven't been listening. When I see her at the top of the hill making her way back down the relief that passes through me makes me feel guilty. I should never have doubted my Prez, even if he isn't himself and no one really knows where his head's at.

"She just took Prez up something to eat," I answer Troj's question, curious to why it matters to him.

"You see her sun snatchin' in that bikini? That fuckin' body man. No wonder you're hoarding her in the cabin all for yourself. Maybe I should move back in," he threatens with a playful wink.

"Maybe you should shut your mouth before I fill it with my dick, asshole," I snap back.

"What's the deal anyway?" Squealer asks. "You fuckin' it?"

His head gestures over to where she bounces along the path towards us, wearing a smile that lights up her whole face.

"She's off limits." My eyes dart a warning between them all. Screwy too, he may not have much to say for himself, but that doesn't stop his cock walkin' the fuckin' walk.

"Says who? You ain't made no claim," Squealer reminds me, continuing to look her over as if she's just another club bitch.

"You waitin' on the Prez's approval?" Troj asks, sounding serious now.

"While he's waiting, I don't mind being the warm-up act." Squealer laughs and it takes all I have not to rip the fucking pick from his teeth and dig it through his eyeball, even Screw's lips raise up into a sneer. I'd seen the way every single one of my brothers watched her walk into the lake earlier, admiring how the sun sparkled against her wet skin and how she'd hopped from foot to foot over the pebbles, every curve on her body dancing as she moved.

She. Is. Mine. And I feel a crushing pressure to make sure everyone around me knows it. I ignore the fuckers, leaving them behind me to walk towards her. Completely driven by the need to make sure everyone gets my message loud and clear. I can't think about how it might fuck off Prez, even if it does, it won't stop me. The closer I get to her, the higher that smile reaches on her face. I'll speak with Prez, I'll tell him everything, and I'll take the fuckin' consequences.

"Hey," her sweet voice chirps, and I don't answer. Instead, I lean in, grab the back of her head, and pull her to my lips. She freezes at first, but it doesn't take long for her mouth to open for me, letting me in to taste that delicious tongue. This is nothing gentle, I'm rough, territorial, and by the time I'm satisfied I've made my point to our audience, we're both starved of breath.

I need to get us out of here before I pull up that pretty little sundress and fucking own her right the fuck here, to really hammer home my point. When I pull away, her eyes are distracted over my shoulder.

"Everyone's looking at us," she whispers, looking suddenly embarrassed.

"Good, let them fuckin' look, darlin'." Taking her hand, without looking back, I drag her through the woods towards my cabin.

"Jessie where we going?" she giggles, struggling to keep up with my pace.

"I'm taking you home, I need to be inside you again." I march us along the path that leads to home.

"Jessie." Her voice holds a doubt that stops me moving forward, causing her body to accidentally tumble into mine.

"What is it?" I turn around, praying she isn't gonna back out of this, not now. Not after I've had a taste of how good it is with her.

"I'm not on anything, I should have said something last night, but you kinda distracted me," she says, an awkward look on her face, as she fiddles with the seam of her dress.

So fucking cute.

"That ain't a problem, I'll speak to Doc tomorrow. Get that situ sorted ASAP," I assure, kissing her forehead with a relieved sigh before setting off again.

"Jessie." She stops me again, tugging my arm back. "I don't know what this is… but you need to know. I'm not one of them, I won't be passed around between you all. What happened last night, I did because it was with you, I don't want to be a club… whatever it is you call them. And I'm not asking anything of you, but…" her voice trembles as she speaks, and I never thought hearing the words she just said would bring someone like me satisfaction. I place a finger over her lips, forcing her to stop rambling, I've heard all I need to.

"Damn straight you're not one of them. You're mine. I won't be sharing." I move a strand of damp hair away from her freshly sun-kissed face. "I ain't ever done anything like this before, Mads, I can't change who I am, and I'm probably gonna fuck up at times. But I'll never intentionally hurt you. You reckon you can see past all that shit and give not being normal with me a try?" I lay it out for her because I have fuck all to lose and everything to gain.

Waiting for her response seems to take forever, but as a tiny smirk teases her lips, I dare to hope that she's in. She stretches up on to her tiptoes, her lips brushing lightly over my jaw before she whispers inside my ear.

"I'm yours. If you think you can take me." Her eyes glisten as they glance sideways, her words traveling directly to my cock and leaving me at a disadvantage when she runs. She skips over fallen branches and jumps rocks making the most of the head start she's got on me. I let her get far enough ahead to make it a good chase, then set off after her. Catching up in just a few seconds, she squeals when my hands grab at her waist and I pull her back into me.

"Oh, darlin', I'ma take you," I promise. "All the fuckin' way."

I throw her over my shoulder, slap my palm hard onto one of her ass cheeks, and carry the girl laughing all the way back to my cabin. It's silent with everyone down at the lake, and I'm gonna make my girl scream loud enough that they all hear that she's untouchable. Of limits. Mine.

When Skid's front door opens and Tommy steps outside, he seems shocked to see us together.

"Everything okay, Grunt?" I lift my head and call over to him.

"Yeah, just returning Uncle Skid's drill, had some shit to fix in one of the cabins down in Sluts sanctuary."

I nod back and leave him to it. Kicking open my cabin door and carrying Maddy inside, I sit her up on the kitchen counter. Standing between her legs, I kiss down her neck, crossing her collarbone, and pull her dress straps off her shoulders. I grab a fist at the front of her dress and rip it down, leaving it to rest underneath her tits. Taking them in each of my hands, I run my nose through the tight gap I leave between them, then reach around her back and pull on the strings that hold her bikini in place.

Maddy's head tips back, forcing her hot flesh closer to my mouth and I take it. My tongue rolling and my lips pulling at those perfect nipples until she's moaning that soft sound that makes my cock ache even harder to be inside her. I leave a trail of kisses all the way down her body, keeping her dress moving with me. When I stop at her hips, she reads my mind, lifting her ass up off the counter so I can rid her of it altogether. Then with a quick tug on the strings either side of her bikini bottoms, she's fully bare and mine to be taken.

I spread her legs open wide, and my tongue reacquaints with her center. Sliding up through her pussy lips and absorbing that sweet, unique taste that belongs to me now. Her nails scrape against my scalp, gripping a fist load of my hair and making me want to give her every pleasurable sensation imaginable.

The innocent little creature has somehow turned sex on its head for me. Changed it into something I don't recognize but can't get enough of. It isn't about rushing to get release anymore. Everything is for her, her pleasure is the trigger to mine, and we're both getting off as her delicious pussy trembles against my tongue.

Her hips wiggle, keeping tight to my face, needy and hungry for more. And more is exactly what I give her when I stand back up and without warning thrust two fingers inside her. I slam my mouth onto hers, and she moans into me. Breaking away so she can look between us, she watches intently as I finger fuck her tight little snatch until it erupts around my hand.

My other hand releases my cock, then grabs a hold of her ass as I drag us both down to the floor. I may not have had the patience to get us to the bedroom, but I do enter her slowly. Savoring her tightness as it strains around my cock, pushing deeper until she's taken every inch of me. She whimpers a little, probably still a little sore from last night, but when her eyes open back up and she smiles, I know she's okay.

I try to remind myself that this is all new to her as I stir my cock inside her. The last thing I want is to hurt her, but the urge to pound into her almost chokes me.

"You're mine now, Mads, you understand that?" I thrust a little harder. Her head bobs up and down in agreement, but it doesn't seem good enough.

"Say it out loud." My fingers press hard into her ass.

"Yours," she says without hesitating, the chill of her blue eyes burning like frostbite into mine.

"But…" she starts, and fuck, I don't think I can handle a but right now. That doesn't stop my hips, rotating into her as I wait for the words. Her hand grips my hair tighter, almost painfully.

"You… you're mine too. No more of them. I don't wanna share either." She holds me with her eyes, daring me to argue back… As if I fuckin' would.

"You got me, darlin'." It comes out sounding exactly like the warning it is, and I slide my hands all the way up her arms and take her wrists, pushing them up over her head and pinning her to the floor. I let her have it, all of me. My cock sliding easier in and out of her body every time it re-enters.

I'm close, so close that I feel the blood rushing to my head, but I need to hold out for her. I'm relieved when her legs start shaking against my hips, and I know she's almost with me.

I need to pull out of her, she's unprotected.

Maddy screams out, clawing at my T-shirt as her pussy clamps around me. Owning me, and the sensation keeps me trapped inside that magic little slit of hers. The thought of her draining everything out of me makes it even harder to stop.

"Jessie, fuckin' god, Jessie." Her nails dig through the fabric and scratch at my skin, and it takes every scrap of my willpower, but somehow I manage to pull out. My cock landing hard between us, and long beads of cum shooting all over her sun-bronzed stomach.

I grip her hands a little tighter and feel myself twitch against her warm skin.

"You have no idea what it took to fucking stop that firing inside you," I sigh, letting my head fall down and press against hers.

"Can I taste it?" she asks, and my head shoots up to check I've heard her right. She blushes as she looks down her body. I close my eyes and take a breath before I answer her. The girl is too much to fucking take.

Sliding through the warm sticky mess I've made on her, I soak my finger, then slowly outline her already open lips. I watch her tongue trail behind it to lick them, and then she takes my finger inside her mouth and sucks it clean, releasing it with a pop.

"Maddy Summers you fucking own me," I whisper into her ear before sagging on top of her, exhausted, not just physically, but mentally from all the things this girl's got me wanting.

CHAPTER 37

MADDY

Knowing where I stand with Jessie is a relief from a burden I didn't even know I was carrying. We don't go back to the party, everything we need is right here in his cabin. He promises he will speak to the doc tomorrow to sort out birth control, despite me telling him I'd be happy to eat him clean whenever he needs me to.

This morning we both smile pathetically at each other while we eat breakfast, and he gives me the sweetest, drawn-out kiss before he heads out the door. It's barely closed behind him when I realize he's left his phone on the table, so I pick it up and chase him out.

He's just about to mount his bike and looks back when I call his name, instantly turning my bones to jelly. I ignore the other guys, some on their porches, others waiting on their bikes, as I skip down the steps.

"You forgot this," I smile. Everyone around us fades into the background and out of existence when he takes the phone out my hand.

"Thanks, darlin'." He moves towards me, knocking me off guard when his hand slides round the back of my neck, drawing me to him. He kisses me. Hard. Not gentle or soft, but primal, and I want to drag him back into the cabin and make him fuck me all over again. With his fist still tangled in my hair, he takes a long breath through his nostrils before releasing me.

This is a snip of the Jessie I got down in that rotten basement, and as much as I love his kind side, I'd be lying if I said brutal Jessie didn't turn me on a little too.

God, I've already spent too long with these people.

The whoops and wails from around us soon bring me back down to earth, and Jessie smirks when he pulls away. There seems to be a happiness that I've never seen on his face before now, and it spreads warmth from my cheeks all the way down to my toes.

"Eyes off my bitch, Squealer," Jessie says without taking his eyes off me. I quickly look over my shoulder to Squealer, who's staring mouth open. His hands lift into the air as if he's being held at gunpoint. I suddenly remember that I'm only wearing one of Jessie's T-shirts.

"I better head back in," I whisper to Jessie, nearly drawing blood from my bottom lip when I bite at it.

Jessie's grin doesn't drop as he mounts his bike and starts it up, the ground beneath me rumbling as more bikes roar to life. I stretch the T-shirt down as far as I can and rush back inside for a shower.

It surprises me how quick the morning goes. I grab my laptop to have a look into Tobias Saunders a little more. Yeah, Prez said I didn't have to, but I still want to help the club out if I can. It's the least I can do after all the trouble I've unwittingly caused for them.

I start with an easy hack into the local county, search his name but come up short. So I search the compound address, and freeze when I read that a warrant to search the club has been issued by a state judge just this morning. I pick up the phone Jessie got for me to call and warn him. Imagining all the things lying around here that could get them into trouble.

There's no answer, and I keep trying as I slip on my sneakers and rush out of the cabin. My heart is thumping against my chest the whole way down to the club. I don't know what the feds will be searching for, but I'm certain that if I don't get a warning to Jessie they'll find it. And if they do, it could mean Jessie doing time.

I forget all my manners when I burst through the doors of the club and called out for Jessie in the foyer.

Silence. Nothing.

I take the left door into a small lounge-like bar but it's empty, so I dash into the right one swing the door open and knock straight into solid man muscle.

"Whoo, black betty." The guy with a bald head, who fucks women against trucks, holds on to both of my arms.

"I need... to speak to... Jessie," I fight the words out as my chest grasps at air.

"Calm down, I can take you to him," he tells me. I let him lead me out the club and towards the chapel at the bottom of a small cobbled path, and when we reach the double oak doors he taps his tattooed knuckles loudly against the wood.

A mumbled voice inside responds, and he opens it halfway.

"Jessie your bitch is here. Seems urgent." I hear scraping wood followed by hard footsteps. The door swings wider, and I manage to get a peek inside. It isn't a regular chapel, there are no pews, but instead there's a huge wooden table that Hayley's Dad sits at the head of. Other than him it's just Jessie in the room.

"You okay?" Jessie grabs at my shoulders and holds me out, examining me. As tempting as it is to melt into his arms, I need to get this out... and fast. They could already be on their way.

"There's a warrant," I stop to catch air. "Issued this morning, to search this place."

"Issued by who?" Jessie asks like he doesn't quite believe me.

"Judge Jackson. For the Feds... I was looking into Tobias,

thought I'd start with the county files, and when I glanced through most recent it flagged up."

"Jackson," Prez's voice comes from behind Jessie.

"Yeah, sir?" I watch him step around Jessie.

"Jess, Tac, get as much manpower down here as you can pull together, we'll clear the vestry and get Nyx and Skid on the fuckin' road as fast as possible."

"Sure thing boss." Jessie nods. "Good work." He leans in and kisses me on my cheek before he rushes off with his phone pressed to his ear. Prez nods his head at me to show his appreciation too.

"There anything I can do to help?" I ask.

"You've done enough. Head up home Maddy… and thanks," he adds the words thoughtfully. I half smile at him before I make my way back up to the cabins, then I go straight round to Carly's to explain over an iced tea what's happening.

"Mads, that's gonna go a hella long way with Prez." Carly places the iced tea on the table in front of me when I've finished telling her.

"So… you've saved the day… great. Now let's talk about the important shit like what happened down on the beach yesterday." She looks intrigued, and I fill her in, watching her shocked face as I reveal way more details then I intended.

"You know what this means don't ya?" she says, sitting back and crossing her arms. My head shakes in confusion. "You're Jessie's old lady," she tells me, hardly able to contain her excitement.

"Let's not run before we can walk." I smile trying not to match her enthusiasm, although crazy as it sounds… I like the thought of it. I've never had anyone care about me the way he does. Then suddenly I remember something else about yesterday.

"Hey, you asked me for a favor yesterday. I totally forgot." I feel awful after all the things Carly's done to help me since I've been here. How had I forgotten that she needed me for something?

"It's nothing really. It's just when the guys cleared out Chop's lodge they found this chest full of old paperwork and stuff, there were some cute photos of Chop and Skid when they were younger, and then I found this..." She disappears into her bedroom, coming back moments later with a wooden trunk that she places on the table. She opens it up, shifts through some papers, then pulls out a USB stick.

"I wondered if we could have a look at it on your laptop?"

I take it from her and inspect it carefully, the outer casing is a lot larger than the ones that are made these days. It's old, but would plug into my laptop the same way any modern one would.

"I was hoping there might be some more pictures on this stick thing," Carly says, closing the trunk back up and pushing it to the other end of the table.

"Yeah sure. Looks like the guys are gonna be busy today, this will keep us entertained."

"Cool, I'll make us a salad for lunch." Carly hops back up from the table, and I slip the USB into my pocket.

"I'll grab my laptop after we've eaten." I smile, Carly moves around the kitchen boiling eggs and slicing up ham, while I chop up lettuce and grate some carrots before we sit out on the deck and eat.

"So, what photos you looking for?" I ask.

"I just want some of Skid when he was younger, thought it would be nice to get some photos up around here," Carly says, placing down her fork.

"I can't imagine Skid ever being a child," I laugh. "He's so manly. I'll bet he was born with a beard and clutching a spanner," I tease, making Carly giggle.

"Let's hope not, or this little one's baby photos won't be winning any baby competitions." She strokes her hand across her stomach with a proud smile on her face.

"What?" I look down to her hand, my eyes growing wider, and my mouth forming a huge smile. "You mean..."

"Uh-huh," she nods. "I've been desperate to tell someone since I found out. You can't tell anyone, Skid doesn't know yet and I really wanna make it special."

"Oh wow." I reach over the table and squeeze her, Carly is gonna be a fantastic Mom, her natural instinct to care and love has shown since the day I arrived here.

"We've been trying a while, I was starting to worry, but turns out I had nothing to panic about," she beams.

"This is the best news, Carly, just what everyone needs. Have you told your family?"

"No, you're the only one who knows. I just can't keep it in any longer, and I need you to help me with a few things... I want to tell them in person but they're so far away, and I only visited a few weeks ago before I found out. Has your laptop got that Skype thing my mom keeps telling me I need to get?"

"Yes, I have." I clap with excitement. "I'll hook you up, show you how to use it."

"I want to see their faces rather than tell them over the phone."

"So when you gonna tell Skid?" I ask. "He's gonna be so happy."

"Well I did have this idea, I saw it in a movie and thought it was kinda cute," she tells me, suddenly looking embarrassed.

"Go on?" I urge, this was just the distraction I need.

"So this woman, cooks up her guy's favourite meal, gets his favourite movie, lights some candles, and when they sit down to watch it, she's replaced the DVD with a DVD of herself telling him he's gonna be a Daddy... it's ridiculous right?" She rolls her eyes. "But it made me cry."

"Carly that is the sweetest thing I've ever heard, and we can use my laptop to do it. There's a recording function."

"Really...? Then let's do it," she says, her voice full of excitement.

We finish lunch and I nip back to Jessie's cabin to grab my laptop. Carly makes more ice tea, and we set to work. I set her up a Skype account and show her how to use the movie maker app, before she drives into town to buy some recordable DVD's while I clear up the lunch plates. Carly already has all the ingredients out for the pot roast she's making for Skid, she'd even offered to make one for me and Jessie too. So, I figure I'll save her some time and start taking care of her for a change. I make two separate pots, then carry them both round to Jessie's and place them in his oven so I can keep an eye on them while I clear the kitchen up from breakfast.

I'm putting out the trash when Carly's car pulls up.

"You get what you need?" I call across the yard, and she hold up the bags smiling.

"I'll return your laptop soon as I'm done making the DVD," she says.

"Keep it for tonight, you can Skype your mom together after." I check around me to make sure no one is around to hear me. "I've made the pot roasts, I'll bring yours round when it's done," I tell her.

"Really?" Carly looks back at me stunned.

"Thought I'd save you the time. Get used to it, I'll be taking care of you from now on." I wink.

"You know, Maddy, I got this amazing feeling that you're gonna do wonderful things. Not just for Jessie but for the club too."

"You'd do the same for me." I shrug it off.

"Sure would, girl. It's nice having someone around." She smiles at me before heading inside her cabin.

The pot roasts are cooking nicely, and with no laptop to distract me I sit in front of the TV and watch some of the daytime crap that Hayley had gotten me into.

I don't know how long I've been out for, but the sound of tires skidding out of the yard disturbs me from my sleep. I leap up and rush to the oven to check the dinner. The smell when I open the door at least gives me hope that I haven't been out long enough to have ruined dinner for everyone. Thankfully it's still looking good.

My cell vibrates in my pocket, and like a thirteen-year-old girl my stomach flips when I see Jessie's name flash up on the screen. I swipe to answer it, pressing the phone between my ear and my shoulder while I place the pots back inside the oven.

"Hey, darlin'," Jessie's voice soothes through the speaker.

"Hey." I smile to myself, loving his voice when it's soft.

"Whatcha doin'?" he asks.

"Just made us something for later," I tell him, swinging the oven door shut with my foot.

"Mmmmm, you know I could get used to this," he tells me.

"How's it going down there?" I ask, hoping they've managed to get things clear.

"No sign of the feds but we're ready for them. Skid's just called, he's made the drop and he's on his way back."

"That's good." I'm relieved that they've managed to get everything done in time.

"I'm just sorting a few things out then I'll be home. Skid tried calling Carly, you mind popping your head around and telling her he'll be a little late tonight?"

"Sure, she's probably in the shower. I'll drop in and tell her now," I say, about to hang up.

"Hey…" he stops me before I do. "Anyone tell you today that you're amazing?" he asks, his voice sounding sexy as hell.

"No, but you can tell me when you get home as many times as you like," I try to sound sexy back, but, I'm pretty sure I fail at it.

"Sure thing baby, be seeing you in a little while."

"Get off the phone before you grow a fucking pussy," a voice shouts out from the background I already recognize as Squealer's.

"Bye Jess." I hang up the phone. Then, quickly jump in the shower, giving the pot roast the extra twenty minutes it needs before I take it to Carly.

I'm careful as I walk across the yard holding the handles of the boiling pot with a tea towel, and I have to use my elbow to push down the doorhandle when Carly doesn't answer the door. I figure I'm past the stage of knocking on Carly and Skid's door now, there's not a day since I've arrived that I haven't spent time in their cozy home.

"Only me," I call through the house, kicking the door shut behind me. I scan the room, but there's no sign of her. The heat of the pot is starting to burn through the towel, and I quickly head towards the kitchen table so I can place it down. My eyes catch something sticking out from the other side of the sofa, something that when my brain registers what it is makes me lose the function of my hands.

I ignore the loud crack the pot makes as it hits the floor and the boiling splatters that scold the bottom of my legs. The sight of Carly's arm lying awkwardly across the floor tells me something is very wrong, I rush towards her. My body prevents me from taking any more steps when I get close enough to see her face. Her skin is completely drained of color, lifeless eyes strained red and etched with terror.

I open my mouth to scream but nothing comes out, I'm choking, completely paralyzed by shock, sadness, and fear. This can't be happening, not again. I look away, unable to handle the sight for another second. That vacant look blazing deeper and settling into my memories with every passing second. Suddenly, like my feet have been released from the sinking grip holding them, they finally move, and I run…

I bang on every cabin door hoping someone will answer. This has to be the Bastards. Have they come for me? Are they still here? Part of me wishes they are and they would just take me. No pain can be worse than this. I would go with them freely if it meant they'd stop taking the people I care about.

Nobody answers as I continued to pound on the doors, my sobs and pleas for help getting fainter and fainter. I can't leave her all alone up here, but I need help. I rush back inside Jessie's cabin and grab my cell from the table, my hands fumbling as I try to scroll to my last caller. Hitting call, I wait as it rings once, twice.

"Hey," he answers with a beautiful ignorance to his tone. I try to speak, but all I can manage are muffles and sobs as I slide my back against one of the kitchen units and settle in a heap on the floor "Maddy!" Jessie's voice switches to worry.

"Maddy, you okay?" Still nothing comes out of my mouth. "Fuck, Mads, what is it? Speak to me... I'm coming up." The phone goes dead, and my hand automatically drops it to the floor. I wait for a sound, any sign that he's coming. I need him and that safety that always comes with him.

I can't close my eyes, if I do all I'll see is Carly's face, and I start to panic when already I can't remember how she looked when she had color in her cheeks, or when she smiled...

I'd been asleep.

I try shutting my eyes again, hoping to get her back how I want to remember her, but the deeper I look the worse it becomes because now, I see Hayley too. Her eyes still bright with color but an equal blankness in her expression.

I breathe slowly. In and out. Not wanting to open my eyes. Too petrified to keep them shut. I see his hands. Jessie's hands, soaked, dripping with dark red blood. They reach out for me, they touch but I jump back.

"Hey... hey relax it's me, it's just me." I open my eyes, and he's here, no blood. Just Jessie, his face wracked with worry as his arms wrap around my head and cradle me tight to his chest.

Just me and him. Safe.

"What's happened? Christ, Mads, you're shaking." The way he rocks me reminds me of how he held Hayley when she slipped away in his arms.

"Maddy. Fucking speak to me. You okay?" He checks me over, that look of worry on his face heartbreaking to see again.

"It's not me, I'm fine," I tell him, feeling his body sag as his chest lets out a long breath of relief.

"It's Carly," I whisper. The rocking suddenly stops, his body stiffens against mine again and I hear three words spoken in a weak voice that doesn't sound anything like his.

"Oh god, no."

CHAPTER 38
JESSIE

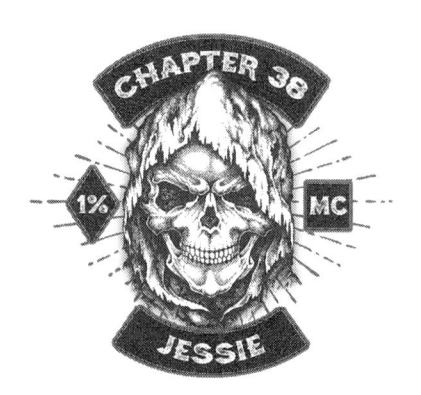

I swear my heart doesn't make a beat from the time I cut Maddy's call till I have her in my arms. Feeling her chest move, hearing her sobs is enough to let me know she's okay but something's happened. The ghostly whiteness of her skin, the fear in her eyes, all tells me that whatever it is freaked her the hell out.

She can't speak, and when she eventually manages to tell me it isn't her that's hurt, for the briefest of seconds I get relief. She's safe. My girl is safe. A little fucked up, but unharmed. Then my heart sinks again when I hear her say Carly's name.

Having to leave Maddy in the state she's in tears me apart. I want to comfort her, tell her whatever it is, it's gonna be okay, but I need to help Carly.

"Baby, where is she?" I lift Maddy up from the floor and carry her to the couch.

"Home," she whispers as I pull a blanket over her, hoping it'll stop her from shivering.

"Stay here. I'll be back. Okay?" Maddy doesn't answer, just stares right through me. "Mads, I'll be back, okay?" I tell her again, grabbing her face in my hands and holding her until she focuses.

"Okay." She nods, her hands pressing over mine, gripping me like she doesn't want me to leave.

"Okay." I kiss her forehead, then rush out of my cabin having no idea what the fuck I'm gonna find when I get to Skid's place. The sound of bikes come from the dirt track, alerting me that help's on the way. I'd been with Grimm when I got Maddy's call and left him in charge of assembling backup. I rush across the yard to find Skid's door wide open.

Soon as I step inside its clear there's been a struggle. Stepping over the broken crockpot on the floor, its contents still steaming and soaking into the wood floor. There's upturned chairs and a broken lampshade, and then there's her… Beautiful, not an evil bone inside of her, Carly.

Her distorted body bent awkwardly across the floor. I don't need to feel for a pulse to know I'm too late. The whiteness of her skin and the expression on her face gives that much away.

"What's going on? Grimm said there was… Oh Shit." I look up from Carly to Nyx, who's frozen in his tracks when he sees what I'm looking at.

"Is she?"

"Yeah," I nod unable to take my eyes off her. Carly is a massive part of this club, and she's gone. Hayley, now her, I can't make any sense out of it. "Go sit with Maddy, Nyx, she's on her own in my cabin. I need to know she's safe."

"But…"

"Go," I snap back, thankfully he knows what's good for him and doesn't argue. I back out of the cabin and onto the porch just as Grimm, Troj, Thorne, and Tac pull up in the yard.

"What is it?" Troj dismounts his bike and races towards me with a real worried look on his face.

"Carly," I manage hoarsely, rubbing my hand over my face. I steady myself to sit on the porch step because the world feels like it's spinning under my feet. Troj speaks into his phone, panicked words that I can't pay attention to. The only sound I hear is the hollow sound of Carly's wood chimes as the wind touches them. I've never noticed them before. It ain't long before the power of a flat-out shovelhead engine drowns them out.

Skid looks wild when he pulls up, and luckily Grimm is waiting to take hold of his bike, or I swear he'd let it drop. He storms towards his cabin, and I stand back onto my feet. Troj's shoulder presses against mine, forming a two-man wall to stop him from getting inside.

"Move out of my way…" Skid barges his body into ours. "Carly… Carly," he calls through the gap between our heads, fighting to get past us, the two of us only just manage to hold him back, at one point I think he'll scramble over the top of us.

"Man, you don't wanna go in there," Troj tells him, closing his eyes like he's seeing it all over again.

"Move, or I'll fucking kill the pair of you, brothers or not," Skid threatens. I take a breath and step aside.

"Let him through," I tell Troj, who's still struggling to hold Skid, looking at me like I've gone crazy. I nod solemnly and he backs down.

Skid races past us, and when Troj goes to follow him I block him with my arm and shake my head. The cabin won't be a safe place for anyone when Skid sees what's happened.

Pain stabs at my chest when I hear his cries, sad ones at first, that gradually build into angry roars. I've been there, felt it all when I lost Hayley, and I'm feeling every step of it over again alongside him. We all wait it out, no one outside speaking a word. Not even making a glance at each other. There's no concept of time. It wouldn't make any difference anyway, it could be minutes, hours, or days. We would all still be here for him when he walks back out that door.

Squealer and Screwy roll up, and Tac quietly fills them in, their identical eyes stretching open with both shock and sadness at the same time.

Tommy pulls up, and when he hears what's happened the kid's devastated. So much that he gets back on his bike and rides off. Guess the kid has feelings after all. I don't know how close he was to Carly, but she was his auntie, and probably the only female he's ever really known in a motherly way.

I feel terrible for him that he's lost her.

I feel terrible for all of us.

When Prez finally gets here he manages to talk Skid out of his cabin, and Tac uses Skid's truck to drive them down to the club. I need Maddy close and I'm torn between comforting her and being there for Skid. So, I come up with only one option. Maddy will just have to come to the club with me. I'd spoken to Prez about us this morning, before she warned us about the feds. She's a part of this fucked up little family too now, and now's the chance for her to see that at times like this, family sticks together.

I don't know what the fuck's gone down while we've been panicking about the feds, but Carly's death has proved that I'm gonna have to step up my game when it comes to protecting Maddy.

I relieve Nyx of his duties when I get back to my cabin, and drive Maddy down to the club in my truck still wrapped up in a blanket. She doesn't speak a word, but then neither do I. What is there to be said? There ain't no words for what's happened these last couple of weeks.

Everyone sits in shock in the lounge bar. Skid slouched in the armchair that's usually occupied by Prez, pale, and his eyes drained red raw. Prez seems to have kicked back into leader mode, pacing the room while speaking down the phone to Roswell. There's no discussion to be had over what will happen to Carly, she'll be treated the same as Hayley. Ain't no way she's gonna be hidden and lost all trace of.

But we still have to be smart about it.

Maddy sits curled in a ball on my lap while we wait for Roswell to get here, hoping it'll be before the feds do or we're fucked. She's still shaking, and I worry she might never pick herself back up from this. I've seen how close her and Carly have become in the short time she's been here. Losing two people so close together is going to shatter her.

"This is your fault," an angry voice snaps from across the room, and when I lift my head I see Skid's finger pointing directly at Maddy.

"We should have let the Bastards fuckin' take you. Then this wouldn't have... She'd still be..." his words become less and less understandable as he breaks down. Maddy crumples in my arms, and I hold her tight, trying to protect her from Skid's outbreak. At the same time wanting to strike him for even thinking this could be her fault.

"Hey come on, let's get you a drink." Prez takes Skid by his shoulder and drags him towards the bar. Skid's eyes still burn anger at Maddy, and if the guy hadn't just lost his wife I'd scoop them out with a spoon and force them down his fucking throat for daring to look at her like it.

Maddy hides her face in my chest and sobs. I feel helpless. There's nothing I can say to take her pain away. I still don't know what's happened. If she saw anything. All I do know, is that shit's about to get real fucking serious around here.

"Roswell's here," Thorne, who's been keeping a look out for the feds, pokes his head around the door. The tired looking cop enters the room not long after. I've noticed his wrinkles deepening lately, and I hope he ain't losing his sharpness 'coz he's a real handy person to have on side.

"What's happened now...?" He heads straight for the bar, then as soon as he sees the seriousness in all our faces, his expression changes.

"Bastards came onto the fucking compound. Killed Carly," Tac explains, and the look on Roswell's face catches up with the rest of the room.

"Fuck." He sinks his ass onto one of the barstools. "They came here?" he checks, in disbelief.

"I've just checked the CCTV, they didn't use the gate, doubt they'd know about our trail through the woods so they must have been on foot and come through the trees," Thorne informs us.

"But why? why would they risk coming here, especially on foot, it makes no sense." Roswell knocks back the shot that Nyx pours him, and I try to ignore the way Skid's eyes hatefully glare at Maddy before he empties the contents of his own glass down his throat, slamming it on the bar.

"Come on I'll take you up to the cabin," Troj says, prompting Roswell to stand up and follow him out with a sympathetic look to Skid as he leaves. I need to get Maddy out of here too. The atmosphere in the room must be unbearable for her. Gently I shift her off my lap, take her hand into mine, and head out after them.

"That's right, you take her the fuck out of here. Your new fuck toy's caused enough trouble for this club, Jessie." Skid's harsh voice hits on every one of my nerves. Releasing Maddy's hand, I launch across the room at him, and luckily for him Screwy is there, his humungous arm slamming across my chest and blocking me from getting to him, his brother comes next, wrapping himself around my shoulders.

"Skid, I get you're hurting man, but you speak about my bitch like that again, and I swear you'll be hurting a whole lot more," I growl through my teeth, my jaw too tight with rage to unwind.

"Just take her home, Jess." Prez pats my shoulder in an attempt to calm me down. I reconnect with her, my anger calming slightly when I feel her fingers slide between mine. She manages to hold off until we get outside to the yard before she falls to pieces. Loud sobs and wet tears hitting my chest as her hands grip my T-shirt, she clings at me like I'm all she has left.

It dawns on me that right now I probably am, and that makes me tense my arms and hold her tighter.

I drive us up to the cabins, and when we get there Roswell's cop car is parked outside Skid's. Troj is leaning against a pillar on the cabin porch, and I give him a nod as I pass him taking Maddy inside and straight to my bedroom.

I take off my cut and the rest of my clothes, and she watches me in a confused silence. Then I lift up her arms and strip her of hers too. Pulling back the covers, I slide in and tuck her in beside me. It's just me and her, skin against skin, away from all the evil outside. I got her wrapped up in a world where I can protect her, and I want to keep her there forever.

CHAPTER 39

MADDY

I haven't seen or spoken to anyone other than Jessie in three days. Grimm dropped my laptop off the night everything happened, but he hadn't said a word, and it still remains untouched on the kitchen table where he placed it.

Jessie makes sure Nyx is here to guard the door whenever he has to go down to the club, but he's never away from me for long. We still haven't spoken about what happened, we haven't really spoken at all. We watch TV, we eat when I could stomach to, but mainly we fuck. We fuck as if that alone is the cure to the pain. But it never takes very long for the pain to come back.

Today, Jessie is trying a new approach, the let's just pretend two innocent women never got killed because of you, kind of approach. When I get up, I take the blanket with me and head straight out onto the deck. Settling in a chair that overlooks the lake, I listen to birds chirp, watching the water on the lake rock and the sunlight dancing on its surface. Nature is still going about its business despite all that's wrong in the world. It has no choice but to carry on.

Jessie brings me out a coffee and places it on the table. Then bends down to kiss the top of my head.

"Mornin' darlin', what you want for breakfast?" he asks stretching his arms over his head. I know he's not getting much sleep at night because neither am I. Sleep is impossible when there's so much going on in your head.

"I'm not hungry," I answer, waiting for the lecture I know is sure to follow, the same one I've gotten from him every morning since Carly's been gone.

"Come on you haven't eaten properly in days, I could try and make pancakes," he offers.

"What did you do with her?" I ask, ignoring his last sentence. It's all I've been thinking about the past few days, and it's driving me crazy.

"Mads. I don't think…"

"Tell me," I interrupt. I need to hear it. Nothing can be worse than the image I have of her laid out on the floor when I'd found her.

"Okay." He shrugs, defeated. "We want her to have a funeral same as Hayley did. We couldn't have the body found here because it would bring too much heat on the club. So Grimm took her to a motel out of town and called it in, Roswell made sure he was the first officer on the scene. It'll go down as suicide."

I look up at him in shock. Carly had family, it would destroy them to think that's what happened. Surely Skid couldn't be okay with this.

"But…"

"We already have the feds on our backs, we had to think fast. Things would have been a damn sight worse when they showed up here yesterday if they were investigating a body too. Yeah, it's shit, but it's the only way we could guarantee a proper funeral," Jessie explains.

"You could have gone legit on this one, it's obvious who did it. That cop knows you, he would have explained. The people who did this need to be in prison," I argue, feeling my anger multiplying.

"The people who did this need to be dead," Jessie snaps back at me, instantly looking guilty for the sharpness in his tone. "Look, things don't work like that around here. If they get put away, Prez and Skid don't get their retaliation, and right now that's the only thing keeping them both going."

"And what about you? Is that what you want too? Retaliation?" I ask, hearing the harshness in my voice.

"Yeah, Mads, I do," he answers without any shame, a stark reminder of the guy he can be when he isn't trying to feed me and cradling me in his bed.

"Do her family know the truth?" I change the subject hoping that at least Carly's family are in on the cover-up.

"Yeah, Skid told them," Jessie assures me, and I nod, taking a small comfort at the same time as feeling devastated that there are now even more people on the planet that hate me.

I fix my eyes back onto the lake. I'd sat out here with Carly almost every day since I'd been here. We'd talk and laugh, having her with me was helping me deal with losing Hayley. Now I didn't have her, all that pain's back too.

"It should have been me… I wish it had been."

I must say my thoughts out loud because Jessie flips.

"Don't you fuckin' say that." He crouches down in front of me, the tone of his voice full of anger but the expression on his face hurt. "Don't you ever fuckin' say that. Hayley gave up her life for you. You can't think like that." He grabs my face in his palms and forces me to look into his ice-blue eyes.

"Listen to me, Mads. You got to fight those demons out your head, fight 'em away or you might as well be dead too, and that can't happen 'coz I fuckin' need you." He shakes me. "You hear me? I need you!" When he forces my head into his chest, I'm relieved that I don't have to see the worry on his face anymore. I feel his heartbeat thudding against my cheek while his hands stroke my hair.

"She was pregnant," the words tumble from my mouth and muffle against his skin. I don't know why I say them now, maybe

I want him to understand why I wish I could have taken Carly's place, or perhaps it's because the burden of being the only person who knew just how much Skid's really lost is dragging me into the ground.

"What?" Jessie pulls back, his face pleading me to tell him that he's heard me wrong.

"Carly was pregnant, she was gonna tell Skid that night, had this whole amazing idea planned out." Jessie's head falls as he listens. His head shaking slightly as he tries to absorb what I'm telling him.

"This is gonna finish him." He slumps onto his ass, his back resting against the railings, and his arms hanging over his knees.

"The autopsy will discover it, he'll know soon enough."

"Doc's got a connection down at the mortuary, we have the paperwork, but an autopsy was never done. It couldn't have been, or it would have been found that cause of death wasn't suicide," Jessie explains, scrubbing his face with his hand, like he's ashamed of what he's telling me.

"Someone's got to tell him," I whisper, Skid has to know, Carly would have wanted him to.

"How the hell am I supposed to do that?" Jessie stands up and turns his back to me, squeezing the ledge of the wooden rails in his fists and looking out on the lake as he thinks.

"How can I tell him he lost a fuckin' kid as well as a wife?" His boot slams hard into the wood.

"Fuckin' Bastards," he huffs, and then I remember something.

"Maybe Carly could tell him herself," I stand up, throwing the blanket off my shoulders and leaving Jessie confused. I rush to my laptop. Taking a seat at the table and powering it up.

Jessie follows me inside and watches over my shoulder as I click onto the cd drive and a file begins to load. I sit back on the chair and take hold of the hand Jessie's placed on my shoulder.

Pain digs like tiny shards of glass into my heart when Carly's face appears on the screen. Her perfectly structured cheekbones risen up by the widest smile.

"What is this?" Jessie asks, and I ssshh him, leaving it to Carly to explain.

"Suprissseee. It's not Scarface..." her sweet, excited voice comes out of the speakers. "But it's not like you don't know how that turns out." She rolls her eyes.

"You're probably looking at me now like I've completely lost it, and I'll be hiding behind a cushion, because, well... no one likes the sound of their own voice. So, I guess I should tell you what this is all about." Her eyes blink and she looks a little shy before she continues.

"Skid, the moment you first stepped inside that health hazard diner I used to work at, I knew you were who I wanted to spend the rest of my life with. It's a true story. I told Patsy when you left that I was gonna marry you.

Do you remember the first thing you ever said to me?

You asked me to smile.

I was having the shittiest day and didn't feel like smiling, 'come on,' you said, 'I'll bet that face is even prettier wearing a smile.'" Carly attempts to make her voice low like Skid's, and I can't help smiling at the screen.

"I gave in, and I smiled because who wouldn't? The totally hot biker who'd been coming in every day for two weeks straight, just called me pretty. When I gave you your check, you told me that if I were yours, you'd give me a reason to smile every day for the rest of my life.

I took that chance, and as it turns out, you were right.

You've made me smile every day since. You have the biggest heart Skid, so big and full of love that I feel kinda selfish taking it all for myself." Tears fill her eyes, as the smile on her face spreads even further.

"You're gonna be a Daddy." She laughs and cries at the same

time. Her hand covering her mouth as if she's hearing the news for the first time herself.

"And you're gonna be so great. Our kid is gonna be the luckiest kid in the world because you're gonna be there every day making us smile and..." Her speech is interrupted by a loud bang in the background that takes her attention away from the screen and towards the door.

"Oh... hey." Her bright smile quickly morphs to a fake one, and her voice feigns enthusiasm.

"Skid will be back soon," she tells whoever is standing just out of view of the camera, and I detect the sound of panic starting in her throat.

"Where is it?" a low rasp comes from behind the screen, and I feel Jessie's hand tighten on my shoulder. This voice belongs to the person that's killed her, and if the dreadful intuition I feel is accurate. The whole thing has been caught on camera.

Carly stands up from the chair, walking towards the voice and disappearing from the screen.

"Where's what?" I hear her ask the intruder.

"Don't play clueless fuckin' bitch with me. You know what I mean." The silence that follows seems to go on for ages, and fumbles and shuffles can be heard for a while until a loud sound cracks in the background and Carly stumbles back into view. She backs up against the living room wall holding her left cheek in her hand, and we both lean forward when the tall figure moves into view and looms over her.

"Fuck," Jessie whispers when the face of the man comes into full view. I know the face too. I've seen it before, and it doesn't belong to a Bastard. This man is a Dirty Soul. One of their own.

Tobias Saunders' face is full of evil as he wraps his hand around Carly's throat and pins her to the wall she cowers against. She tries to fight back, kicking her legs and clawing at his wrists, gasping for air against his grip.

"Skid always did land on his feet." Tobias laughs, watching

as she struggles and fights to unwrap his fingers from her neck. "The perfect fuckin' brother, the perfect fuckin' son, lucky cunt even found himself the perfect bitch to worship the fuckin' ground he walks on too." He pushes his face tight into hers, and with a grunt so loud even the laptop microphone picks it up, he slides his tongue over her cheek. "You ever wonder if you picked the wrong brother, sweet cheeks?"

"Please, Chop," Carly cries, as his free hand lifts her skirt above her hips, and he frees himself from his jeans. "No. please…" she sobs, her beautiful eyes drowning now with terror. "Skid will be back soon. He'll kill you. Don't Chop… please." Both her hands pull at his arm trying to free her neck, but he doesn't budge.

Tears prickle my eyes as I watch him roughly hook her panties over to one side. It's too much, I can't watch anymore. I turn and bury my head into Jessie's torso, listening to grunts and sobs combined, and Carly's cries become weaker and weaker until eventually, they vanish.

CHAPTER 40
JESSIE

Shock forces me to carry on watching what's happening on the screen. Chop, one of my old man's best friends forcing himself on his own brother's wife. Carly pinned helplessly against the wall, crying as he thrusts his cock inside her over and over again. She fights against him to start with, but the cocky grin on his face only indicates how much he fucking enjoys her resistance. It doesn't take long for her energy to give in to exhaustion and her fight fades to nothing.

With one hand firmly wrapped around her neck, Chop continues to rape Carly until her face turns blue. His grip becoming tighter and tighter as it slowly crushes the life from her body.

I hold Maddy closer, keeping her pressed against me so she can't change her mind and watch the horror for herself. I cover her ears with my hands to try and muffle out sounds that are all too familiar to me. Spluttering coughs and gags, desperate gulps for breath, and then for the briefest of moments, groans when the fight comes back.

Carly's hands push and scratch at Chop, and although I already know how this ends, I still pray that somehow she'll get away.

She fights, hard, but he responds by ramming himself into her harder.

"There, you like that," he speaks to her.

"See... I always knew there was a dirty girl hidden underneath that cute little smile. You just needed me to bring it out of ya."

Carly shakes her head, defeated by his strength, her arms flopping beside her signaling that she's reached that place. If the camera had been a few inches closer, I'd see it. Pleading eyes silently begging for death to hurry and come, followed by that flicker of relief as the lights dim from behind them.

Carly's body sags heavily, drained of any life, and the sick fuck continues to thrust inside her. When he releases her neck, and her head slumps forward, he pins it back to the wall pressing his forehead hard against hers.

"I gave you chance after chance, I told you one day I'd have you for myself. It didn't have to be like this. But you thought you were too good for me." He speaks to her as if she can still hear him.

"And look at you now, no more special than the others." His body spasms, and he moans as he finishes inside her. His heavy body propping up her lifeless one.

"You never even gave us a chance," he tells her. "Helen, Mary-Ann, I destroyed them all. I never wanted to break you too." An evil laugh escapes his mouth as he takes her body in his arms and lays her out on the floor beside the sofa, pulling her skirt back in to place and with a grunting laugh he looks down at her like she's nothing.

"Skid's perfect old lady," he says to himself. "Will you look who fuckin' owns you now, bitch." He steps over her body and disappears from the camera's view.

He doesn't leave straight away, shuffling around the cabin for a few minutes, before finally, I hear the door closing and tires screech off. Then there's nothing, just the sound of wind chimes.

I slam the laptop shut and kneel in front of Maddy.

"It's over now," I tell her, keeping her so tight to me I worry I might crush her. Her sobs don't stop, and all I can do is hold her, while pure anger builds in the pit of my stomach and spreads through my body.

Mary-Ann? I heard him say her name. Wondered if he meant Prez's old lady, Hayley's mom? I can't make any sense of it.

"He raped her," Maddy manages between snuffles. "She was his brother's wife, and he raped her and then…"

"Ssssh I know. We'll get him, he'll pay." Part of me wants to toss the footage, pretend I never saw it, but where would the justice in that be. I have no idea how I'm gonna tell Skid, one of the nicest guys I know, that his own brother just raped the love of his life. But he has to know so he can see Chop off on his journey to hell.

"I was right there Jessie. I was sleeping."

"You couldn't have done anything, Chop would have hurt you too and Christ, Mads, the fact he didn't is about the only thing that's keeping me together right now." I kiss her hair not daring to imagine what I'd be capable of doing if anyone tried hurting her like that.

"She was so happy. She was gonna tell Skid about the baby, and now her last memory was him… it's unbearable to think about, Jessie." My girl crumbles in my arms all over again, and there is nothing I can do or say to fix her.

I sniff at her hair hoping to feel that calm she usually brings me, but it doesn't come, and so I carry Maddy back to our room and tuck her into our bed. I place a kiss on her cheek, and let the taste of her tears touch my lips.

"I need to call Prez," I tell her, and her eyes don't pull away from the spot on the wall she's focusing on when she nods her head. "I'm gonna be in the next room. You need anything?" Her head shakes a no but her eyes still don't move, and I can feel her slipping further and further away from me.

"Mads. You know this means none of this was your fault. It wasn't the Bastards, they weren't looking for you. This was…"

Who am I kidding, I have fuck all clue what this is. "This ain't on you, Maddy." I untwine my hand from hers and leave her with her thoughts, waiting until I'm out of earshot before I pull out my cell and call Prez.

"What's up?" he answers.

"You need to come to my cabin. Alone…" I tell him and hang up before he can argue. Sure, he's dealing with the unimaginable himself, but after the shit I've just seen, we're gonna need him to be a fucking leader and pull us the right way out of this mess.

Prez gets to me in less than ten minutes, and I waste no time showing him why he's here. Sitting him at the table, I hit the play button and lean against my kitchen counter, intentionally making sure I'm the other side of the screen this time. I watch his face turn white, and his eyes flare with the same shock and anger as mine.

"Fuck." Prez rub's his hand through his beard when he's done, and I wait in silence, giving him the chance to take in for himself what he's just seen.

I hand him a beer from the fridge, and he takes a mouthful before looking up to ask if I got anything stronger.

"What we gonna do? This is gonna destroy Skid." I reach into the cupboard and take out a bottle of Bourbon, pulling out the cork with my teeth I place it in front of him.

"Why though? Why would he risk running into the feds to come back here?" Prez asks taking a long swig, then lights up a cigarette. I don't tell him that I've stopped smoking in the house since Maddy moved in, it'll make me sound like a fuckin' pussy.

"He sounded like he was looking for something when he first came in. He asked where *it* was. Maybe he came back for something important?" Second time around I'd paid more attention to his words.

"Yeah, but what?" Prez asks, then takes a long drag of his

smoke. And I wonder if he's missed the Mary-Ann mention through shock or if he's choosing to ignore it for now.

"We're gonna have to ask Skid. Chop didn't rush off, he was there for a while after, maybe he found whatever it was. Skid may be able to figure out what's missing." Prez points out.

"You realize once Skid finds out about this, Chop better hope the feds get to him before he does."

"Son, Chop took one of our own. Carly wasn't just Skid's wife, she was our family. As far as I'm concerned, he's a dead man running. We make sure we get to him before the feds do. Tear him apart piece by piece, and then Skid can shit down his throat."

I couldn't put it better myself.

"Send out word I want everyone around the table at three today, everyone needs to be there… no excuses."

"You got it." I take out my cell, bring up the group message and type out a text to everyone with Prez's orders.

"It's done. What do we do now?" I ask, though I already know what has to come next and I'm not looking forward to it one bit.

"Right now, we grab our fuckin' dicks and go tell Skid what happened to his wife." Prez stands up and takes a long swig of the bottle. "And I think we're gonna need a whole lot more of this shit," he says, slamming it back on the table.

When I check on Maddy she's sleeping, so I call Nyx to come wait at mine. Then together, me and Prez go to find Skid.

He isn't at home or at the club, so we check the garage. Rolling up the door and letting daylight into the dark space, we find him. He's propped up against a Snap-on toolbox, overalls on, and an empty bottle in his hand. He doesn't respond to our intrusion, not even raising his eyes off the ground when we both move and stand in front of him.

"You got some fuckin' balls getting in my space, Jessie. You shipped that fucking bitch of yours out of here yet?" he asks, raising his head and finding me with dark, hate-filled eyes. Prez takes hold of my wrist to prevent me lunging forward, with a look that reminds me what he's been through and what we're about to tell him. And it prevents me grabbing a spanner and lobbing his face with it.

"Skid. It wasn't the Bastards who killed Carly," Prez tells him, letting go of me steadily.

"Bull-fuckin'-shit. I always knew you were soft when it came to the kid, Jimmer. But to be standing up for his bitch now too? Come on. You're losing your touch, old man." Skid goes to stand, but Prez squats down to his level and pushes his shoulder back down.

"Stay there a second and listen to me," he tells him. "You heard from your brother?"

"No, and what the fuck's that got to do with the fact we're still protecting the hacking bitch?"

"There anything you think your brother would need or want that he might come back here for?" Prez asks.

"No, what the fuck's this about?" Skid looks confused, and Prez looks up at me like he's run out of words. The silence is deafening and running real thin as Skid's eyes roam between Prez and me. "Does someone wanna give me a clue into what the fuck is going on here? Have you heard from chop? Is he okay?" His sudden panic makes me feel sick, he's worried something has happened to his wife raping brother.

"Chop came back," I tell him swallowing the lump in my throat.

"Fucking idiot, he must have heard what happened... wants to be here for me. I got to tell him I'm fine, get him back on the road before the feds get a sniff that he's back." Prez stops him from getting to his feet for a second time. Leaving his hand rested on his shoulder as he speaks, his eyes closed, no doubt because he knows he won't want to see the look in Skid's eyes when he's finished saying what he has to say.

"Chop came back the night Carly was mur… taken." I watch as Skid's eyebrows draw together with confusion. "He was the one who took her, brother. I'm sorry." Prez's voice is raw with pain, and there's no going back now. The words have been said, they're out there whirling around us in the air just waiting to be taken in.

"Fuck," Skid laughs. "Does she mean that fucking much to you? You would protect that bitch over family? Come on, Prez, why you protecting her? It was the Bastards, they came for Maddy, and they took my Carly." He's up and on his feet, his finger pointing into Prez's face. "Chop's laid his ass on the line for this club for eighteen god damn years, me too since I've been old enough, and you'd put protecting her over us?" Prez takes Skid's anger without flinching, and I can tell he's lost for what to say next, so I step in.

"He's telling the truth, Skid. It was Chop. He killed her and he…"

"Jessie," Prez warns me, but he knows as well as I do that Skid has to know.

"And he raped her, and we know this because we just had to fucking watch the whole thing." A long silence falls after my words.

"It was all recorded on Maddy's laptop," I whisper, regretting my words instantly.

"No…" Skid shakes his head as he stumbles backwards and crashes into the toolbox. "You're lying. He would never… he loves her... he loves me. Sure, we fight, disagree a lot, but we're brothers. He wouldn't."

"Jessie's telling the truth," Prez tells him. "I've seen the video myself."

"You're trying to tell me that my brother, r-r-r…" he stutters, taking a breath, unable to get the words out past his lips. "Raped and then killed my wife?" his voice breaks through tears.

"I wish we weren't," Prez says.

Skid lifts his head and looks at me, eyes bulging with rage and nostrils flaring like they might flame.

"Show me."

"That's not a good idea, you don't want to see that, brother." I shake my head, recalling the sinister brutality of what Chop has done.

"You show me that fuckin' video." Skid's finger points between my eyes, and I'm about to argue back. I love Skid like a brother, and for that reason I can't let him watch that fucking video. But Prez's arm slaps at my chest.

"Jessie, go get the computer," he says keeping his eyes on Skid.

"But Prez…" I try to argue, Prez must have lost his fucking mind.

"He needs to see it for himself" he explains, defeated.

"Fine, but I'll warn you now, Skid, you can't unsee what's on that video," I warn, before I leave and ride up to my cabin. Nyx is sat on my couch drinking a beer and watching TV when I walk in and grab Maddy's laptop from the table. He tells me she's fine, but I check in on her anyway. Then making my way back down to the garage I prepare to ruin Skid's life beyond any possible repair.

Skid sits at the desk in the small office at the back of the garage, and I set up the laptop in front of him, still not entirely convinced that this is a good idea. As soon as I hit play, I move to the opposite side of the desk, noting how Prez moves to stand beside me too. Probably for the same reason.

Carly's sweet, excitable voice fills up the room, and Skid's face automatically brightens when he sees her face on the screen. A sad smile tugging on his lips when she talks him through the memory of the first time they met.

There are no smiles from me and Prez though, we know what's coming, and we also know it's gonna destroy him. Right now he thinks he's lost everything, in a few seconds he's gonna realize that he's lost a whole lot more. Watching his face is like watching the video for the first time all over again. She tells him he's gonna be a dad, and his fingers shake as they reach out and touch the screen. His eyes filling up with tears, like in that moment he's forgotten that she's gone.

When I hear Chop in the video, I have to give him one more chance to back out.

"Skid, man you sure?" I check, and when his eyes flick up to mine, I know there's no way he's not gonna watch on.

I try to focus on something else as the sounds comes out of the speaker. Prez moves and leans next to me on the glass windows that separates the office from the garage that the two brothers have kept together for years. We watch on as all Skid's pain turns to anger. The tears in his eyes dry, and after we hear the smug laugh that we know Chop lets out when he's standing over Carly's body followed by, "who fuckin' owns you now bitch?"

Skid snaps.

He pushes the table across the room as he stands up from the chair.

"Motherfucker," he roars, grabbing one of the filing cabinets and crashes it to the floor. Ripping open the door he storms into the garage, and like a tornado he destroys everything that stands in his path. He's lost his shit, and who can blame him after everything he ever cared about has been taken by his own blood.

How can anything ever be the same again?

CHAPTER 41

MADDY

When Jessie comes home I know he's told Skid, and the thought of him having to hear what had happened to Carly breaks my heart.

We only have a short time together before Jessie has to go again. Prez called church and I guess that's where everyone will find out about Chop's betrayal.

The emptiness I feel when Jessie isn't with me is unbearable, and it's even worse now I don't have Carly. Nyx is always close by, but he never really speaks to me. He's far too wrapped up in his own head.

I have no one except for Jessie, he's quickly become my everything and I feel myself needing him more and more as each day passes. It scares me that I'm losing myself, and I can't help thinking what Hayley would tell me to do if she was still here.

I can't let myself slip away. I need a purpose, a distraction from all the shit that's happened lately. Sure, I'm young and I don't have the life experience that the people around here do. But there is one thing I can do, something I'm not just good at, that I kick ass at.

Armed with a computer I can create just as much havoc as any Dirty Soul can. The Bastards killed my best friend, forced my mother to hiding. Tobias Saunders has taken another friend from me, and I'm going to make sure they all get nothing less than what they deserve.

Violence has always been something I've avoided at all costs. It scared me about Jessie at first, but I'm learning to deal with it. Whoever Jessie is when he was with them doesn't matter, because when he's with me he's my Jessie. The caring, loving Jessie with a soft heart who would do anything to keep me safe.

Jessie is right, the club needed to take care of this their way and despite me knowing that it means violence, I'm prepared to do whatever I can to help them. All Tobias Saunders and the Bastards can do now is sit tight and wait. Justice is coming for them and I have every reason to believe that it's gonna be brutal.

Jessie gets home from church just after five and I can tell straight away that although his mind is exhausted, his body needs release. I want so badly to give it to him, but he still sees me as fragile. He'll be gentle for me, but I don't want this to be for me. I want it to be for him.

Gentle isn't what he needs right now.

I'm not what he needs right now.

Jessie doesn't say a lot, he eats the meal I've prepared for him and then takes a shower. He looks shocked when he comes out of the bathroom and finds me waiting with the list of names I found in his jeans pocket a few days ago when I was doing laundry. I try not to be distracted by how hot he looks wearing just a towel when he comes straight at me and snatches it from between my fingers.

"Are these the people you hurt?" I ask him.

"That's club business, ain't for you to worry about, darlin'." Wet drips fall from his hair onto my chest when he dips his head to kiss my forehead.

"Maybe you should get out of here tonight, you could cross another name off that list," I shrug casually. I want him to understand that I accept him and the things he needs.

"You need me here." His head shakes, but I can see that he's tempted.

"And what do you need?" Scooping his hand up in mine, I bring it to my lips and press them against his knuckles and club ring. "I'm safe here, and I'll still be here when you get back. Go do whatever it is you need to do. Just come back to me after."

"What the fuck did I ever do to deserve you?" he asks me, opening up his hand and stroking it over my cheek. His touch is so delicate it's hard to imagine him leaving here and causing anyone any pain.

He grabs his phone from the table and sends a text, then heads into the bedroom. He returns minutes later fully dressed with his hair tied back. He moves over to one of the drawers and takes out a handgun and slips it inside his shoulder holster, then puts his cut on over the top. When he bends down to tie up his boots, I stand right in front of him, and his eyes crawl up my body as he stands back up. My whole body catches fire when he takes my face in his hands and kisses me hard on the mouth.

"Be careful," I whisper, and he smirks back at me as if he's invincible, then places another kiss on my lips before he heads out the door.

I wait until I hear his bike leave the yard before I gather myself together. I open up my laptop and get to work.

I find Tobias Saunders' file and pour myself a large glass of wine while I prepare myself to read it. He's wanted for murder. The murder of Helen Saunders, his own wife and Tommy's mother. I see the reports on what he'd done to her, the whole case was built and ready to go to trial but he'd skipped and vanished without a trace. I read the witness statements, friends of Helen's who said she'd been planning to leave him, that he scared her. I wonder how much Skid knew about all of this.

Also linked to his file are a list of unsolved cases that he's a suspect for. Another murder, this time a prostitute, and numerous rapes and assaults. All ironically taking place in the same town that Tobias Saunders had lived during the time they happened.

By the time I'm done reading I can understand why Brax had wanted me to bury the file. Chop needed a taste of real justice, and getting it from the authorities wouldn't be enough. Skid deserves to execute whatever punishment the club comes up with and I will do anything I can to help make sure that happens.

My hands shake as I bring up the video, and begin watching it again.

"Where is it?" He'd asked Carly that question as soon as he arrived.

Where was what? What had he been looking for? Whatever it was must have been important enough to bring him back to the club despite the risk of him being arrested.

"You don't have to play the clueless fuckin' bitch with me. You know what I mean." If Carly knew she would have told him, she wouldn't have put herself in danger especially knowing it wasn't just her he could hurt. Finding out what he wanted could be the key to finding out where he is.

I rush out of the door before thinking, dashing three doors down to Skid's cabin, and my hand is knocking at his door before my brain can tell me it's a bad idea. When the door swings open, Skid rocks in front of me with his broad, hairy chest exposed, and jeans undone, hanging loose around his waist. There's a half full bottle swinging in his hand, and judging by the way he's swaying with it I'd say he's drunk. The way his eyes are empty of emotion tells me that he's broken apart and can never be fixed.

"Can I come in?" I ask, surprised when he actually opens the door wider and stumbles back enough for me to enter. I follow him inside, and he slumps back into the arm chair and takes a swig from the bottle.

"Skid, I'm so sorry—"

"This ain't on you," he interrupts me with a low growl. "This is my fault."

"You can't blame yourself, nobody expected Chop to…" I can't finish the sentence.

"He was your brother, he was everyone's brother and he betrayed you. Surely you see that?"

"Why are you here, Maddy?" Skid asks me impatiently. "If you think you can make me feel better, save your time, it ain't gonna happen."

"I'm here because I want to help you, I want to help you all find Chop and make sure he gets what he deserves."

"And how do you figure you're gonna do that?" He huffs a laugh, looking at me like I'm a stupid child.

"When he came here, he was looking for something. Maybe if we can figure out what that something is, we can find him. Is there anything missing?" Skid shrugs his shoulders, unmotivated. "Come on, think. Is there any family he could go to? Where's that trunk, maybe there's something in there, an address, anything would be a start."

"What trunk?" Skid looks at me puzzled.

"There was a chest full of old photographs and paperwork. Carly was looking at pictures with me that day…" And suddenly it clicks. "That's what he wanted. The chest, that's what he came back for." Skid sits forward and scratches his head.

"So you're telling me my brother risked coming back here, then raped and murdered my wife, all to pick up some chest full of old pictures?"

"Well is the chest here?" I ask, not meaning to sound quite so sarcastic.

"I told you before. I don't know jack about any damn chest. Grimm cleared the place up after…" He pauses, taking in a painful breath. "Maybe you should ask him."

"And where might I find Grimm?"

"Same place you'll find everyone this time on a Friday night.

Down at the club, probably getting his dick polished." Skid laughs bitterly, taking another mouthful from the bottle. Before I turn away to leave, I reach down and wrap my arms around his wide shoulders.

"Carly wouldn't want you pushing people away, you need to let people help you through this," I tell him, feeling his body tense while I hold him for a little longer. I start making my way towards the door to go find Grimm.

"I'm sorry," Skid's voice comes from behind me, and I turn around. "I gave you a rough time when I thought it was the Bastards that took her."

Skid's apology is sincere, I know this because his eyes warm ever so slightly as he speaks it. I give him a grateful smile before I leave, closing the door behind me I head towards the club.

The music coming from the club is so loud I hear it right from the top of the track. Nerves root deep in my stomach as I walk closer and the music gets even louder. I know Jessie wouldn't want me to be down here without him, but I open the doors and walk through the foyer anyway. Following the noise through to the back room.

My heart thumps heavy as I step in among the chaos. The women dance for the attention of Jessie's friends while they sit at the bar drinking, some touching, others just watching. I catch Nyx in the corner of my eye, and decide he's my best bet. He may not be the friendliest, but I'm more familiar with him than anyone else around here. I head over and ask him where I might find Grimm. Despite him looking pissed at me, he tips his head to the corner of the room. Grimm sits on a stool with his back facing the room, looking like he's staring at the wall. I collect myself together and make my way over him.

He's wearing his cut with black jeans, his hair cropped tightly at the back and sides, but tonight the longer, almost black hair on top that usually flops over to one side is slicked right back. I get closer, and realize what it is he's so intrigued by and it stops my feet from moving forward.

There's a girl on the floor in front of him, maybe a little older than myself. Brown hair flows around her bare breasts, and her index finger hangs from her mouth while her other hand plays between her legs. She's completely naked except for her black heels, and her eyes are staring right into Grimm's.

I step to the side, watching how intensely he concentrates on her. Like he's desperate to touch her himself. He chews at his bottom lip the way I do on mine when I'm nervous, but this isn't the same. Grimm isn't nervous, he's holding himself back. Almost like the girl's a test and he's torturing himself by watching.

I realize that Grimm is his own unique kind of beautiful. His lips are naturally colored rose pink, and despite being thin have a natural pout. He wears a ring through his slender nose like Nyx does, and his dark eyes are rimmed by thick, even darker lashes. His skin is pale and would be flawless if it wasn't for the small tattoo under his left eye that looks like a cross.

A tilt of his head to the side and the slight tightening of his eyes is the only sign that he's turned on when the girl starts bucking against her fingers, his tongue slowly rolls over his lips as she comes. She scurries herself up the wall and starts to walk towards him when she's done. He warns her away by shaking his head and she takes his rejection like a pro, shrugging playfully and walking on past him.

Grimm stares at the wall for a while longer before spinning around on the stool, and just as he's about to stand up I step in front of him.

"Hey," I open with a friendly smile, and his face creases together suspiciously. "I'm Jessic's, um..." I suddenly don't know how to label it.

"I know who you are," he says sternly.

"I was wondering if you could help me with something." His

eyes look me over. I get the sense he's judging me, and it bugs me how much I want to know what his conclusion is.

"When you cleared up Skid's place, was there a brown chest on the table next to my laptop?" I continue. I've wracked my brain, and that's the last place I can remember seeing it. Grimm's eyes narrow as his brain works to remember.

"Yeah," he nods, and my heart sinks, if the chest had been what Chop wanted he would have taken it. I've fallen at a dead end.

"Where's the chest now?" I ask, not wanting to take up anymore of his time.

"Gave it to Prez." He pulls a cigarette from his cut and lights it. Drawing back on it he clicks his jaw from side to side to release three perfect smoke rings, each one larger than the one before.

"Thanks, Grimm," I smile. "Do you know where Prez is?"

"Probably up at home," he tells me, cutting the conversation by walking away.

I head straight for the doors that lead out of here. It's stuffy and the room smells too much of smoke and sex. I need fresh air to cleanse my lungs and my eyes. Before I can reach the door a hand grabs at my shoulder and makes me jump. When I roll my head around, I realize it's Nyx. I forgot how huge he is, especially for his age.

"Where ya heading?" he asks.

"I gotta speak to Prez."

"Jessie wouldn't want you wondering alone down here at night," he tells me.

"I'll be fine." I struggle out of his grip, and he surprises me when he smirks back at me. Seeing Nyx smile is rare.

"I never said you wouldn't be, but Jessie would still tie me in the basement if I didn't make sure you got home safe."

I roll my eyes at him and let him lead me outside to one of the trucks. I notice that a light is still on over at the garage, and I know it can't be Skid, especially not in the state he was in when I left him.

"Who's working this late?" I ask Nyx, curious.

"Rogue, she'll be making up the work in the garage for Skid."

"Who's Rogue?" I've never heard anyone mention her before, not even Hayley.

"Just some girl who helps out." Nyx shrugs, he's not a big talker so I don't know why I actually expected a decent answer out of him.

When Nyx takes a right at the fork, I figure he's taking me back to the cabin instead of Prez's lodge and when we pull up outside I thank him for the ride and head inside. It's late, and it's been a long, difficult day for everyone. At least I know where to start tomorrow.

I keep checking the clock, it's been hours since Jessie left and I can't help but worry if he's okay. Before I'd met Hayley, Mama had been the only person that mattered. Since then I've become so much weaker. I've lost people I really care about, people who just a few months ago weren't even in my life. I miss Mama, I know it's for both our safety, but I wish I had more than a weekly phone call.

And now there's Jessie. What I feel for him is different to anything I've ever felt before. It's as if he holds the control to my heart and keeps it beating. I know what he does is dangerous, that *he* is dangerous, but I've never felt safer than I do when I'm with him.

Hearing his bike when it pulls up sets off fireworks of in my belly. I count the seconds in my head until the door opens, then spring onto my feet to go to him before the door that keeps us apart has even opened. When it does and he's standing in front of me, nothing else seems to matter.

The dark red stains on his jeans, the crusted blood on his knuckles, are all irrelevant as I launch at him. He catches me and

I wrap my legs around his waist, pressing soft kisses all over his face. There's a metallic taste when I touch them over his lips, and when I pull back I realize it's because it's split. He doesn't give me the chance to check if he's okay. Fisting at my hair he forces me back onto his mouth. I hear him kick the door shut behind him then he turns our bodies so my back hits against it.

"Fuck, I've needed you," he tells me, burying his head into my neck. His lips deliver sparks with every touch they make against my skin, and my hands grip to him afraid he might let me go.

He is all I have left and all I ever want. I'm in love with him, there's no denying it. Every single part of him, even the savage side that he tries so hard to protect me from.

"Fuck me, Jessie," I whisper, causing his head to hold off its journey down to my chest.

"What you say?" he asks looking up at me, unsure.

"I said I want you to fuck me," I repeat. "The way you were going to when I was tied up in that basement." His face suddenly drops, so does my stomach when I realize how angry he looks.

"Mads, what went on down there should never have happened, at the time I was really fucked up."

"Then maybe I'm a little fucked up too, because I wanted it then, and it's what I want now." I bite my lip, and not because I'm nervous this time, but because I love the way his jaw tightens up whenever he notices me do it. I love affecting him no matter how small the reaction is. The pulsing between my legs is becoming unbearable, and the way his hips press me into the door is doing nothing to make it stop. I can feel him, hard through his jeans, and all I want is him inside me.

"I don't have to be that person, not with you," he tells me, gently tucking some of my hair behind my ear then uses his thumb to rub my cheek.

"No, not all the time. But maybe now… For me," I dare him,

taking his bottom lip between my teeth and giving it a gentle tug that makes him exhale heavily.

"You're pushing my limits, darlin'," he growls a warning into my lips.

"I went down to the club by myself," I taunt, trying my best to provoke an angry reaction out of him. His nose slides up my cheek and his warm breath sends shivers down to my spine as it covers my ear.

"I know ya did," he whispers, taking my lobe between his teeth and clamping it tight, forcing that shiver to travel straight to my center.

Fucking Nyx, I knew he'd rat me out.

My hips start to rub against him.

"Please, Jessie," I purr like a needy kitten. I'm rewarded when his hips crush me tighter to the door and frees both his hands to grip at my vest, pushing it up over my body. He lifts it over my head and tosses it aside, then slides his hands behind my back, pressing me tighter against him. My exposed nipples brush against the tough leather of his cut and I wriggle my hips against him some more, desperate for him to fill the emptiness between my legs. He snatches at my ass, his fingers indenting my skin so hard I'll bruise as they line me up with his rock solid cock.

Wedged between the door and his body, I feel like I'll explode from frustration, and I moan when his hand moves between us delving into the front of my shorts. His middle finger skims through my pussy lips, making every single nerve in my body tense as he teases my entrance with the tip of his finger.

"Fuck it," he commands, and I look at him puzzled.

"Sit your pussy on my finger and fuck it," he tells me again.

I don't hesitate. With my shoulders rested against the wooden door and my legs wrapped around him, I push my hips forward and let his finger slowly slip inside me. I ride his finger while his thumb circles my clit. His eyes stay fixed on mine, watching my reaction while my hips thrust against his hand, trying to stretch out the pleasure as I drench his finger.

I scream out his name, when an orgasm rips through me like a hurricane. Then just as I prepare to crawl back down to earth, the air whooshes around me and I'm back on my feet. Shaky legs barely hold me up as Jessie forces me forward, leaning the front of my body over the back of the couch.

He tugs at my shorts ripping them down to my ankles, then drops onto his knees, crushing my ass cheeks in his fists as he spreads them apart. I jolt when he nips at my flesh, his nose sliding right through me as he licks me from front to back. His tongue flicks over my tender flesh, teasing my pussy until I shatter and come all over again. I flush when he licks a trail through my ass cheeks, then up my spine until he's standing up behind me. His belt clinks, and his firm fingers pressing into my hip bones are the only warning I get before he pushes his whole length inside me.

I cry out his name again and he fucks me so hard that my head goes numb. All painful memories of losing Hayley and Carly disappear along with the worry of never seeing Mama again. All that exists is us.

Him and me.

Here and now.

Jessie's hand reaches around me, his palm crushing one of my tits before it slides up to wrap around my throat. The fingers of his other hand strums my clit, working me even higher. How he's capable of doing so much to me at once scares me a little, but I don't want him to stop. I never want him to stop, because I'm addicted to him.

He uses his grip on my neck to force my up body taut against his chest and his mouth finds my ear again.

"You're mine, Maddy," he rasps, his grip snatching all of the breath from my body. "Say it loud so I can hear it," he orders.

"Yours," I manage to choke, nodding my head against his forceful hold.

"Don't you fuckin' forget it." His teeth bite down on my shoulder and my pussy tightens, flooding his cock at the same time.

His deep groans muffle into my skin as his cock jutters inside me, filling me with warm threads of cum. I topple forwards and his hand presses against my back, I feel the tension in his fingers as he grasps at my skin and we both catch our breath. Without any warning he pulls out of me and spins me around to face him, roughly taking my face in his hands.

"I was so mad back then. I'd just lost Hayley. I needed to know what you knew so I didn't lose you too. That was the only thing I could think of to scare you enough to tell me. But I would never have hurt you. You know that, right?"

I nod back because even when I was there, locked down in that basement, I trusted that he wouldn't harm me. Jessie must believe me because his chest sags with relief and his hold on me softens.

"Come on, let's get you to bed. You probably need your brain bleaching after being down at the club by yourself." Taking my hand, he walks me to the bathroom with him. He pulls down the toilet seat, then gestures for me to sit. I sit watching as he steps in the shower and cleans himself, then hand him a towel when he's done.

"I could get used to having you around." He smiles at me as he wraps it around his waist then pulls my naked body against his dripping wet one. I let my arms wrap around his neck and my fingers slide through his damp hair. He smells like pine trees and fresh air.

"I should shower too." I look down between my legs, where I can feel him starting to leak out of me. But he shakes his head.

"I like you like this," he says, kissing my forehead as he moves us through the cabin and into his room. He dries himself off and then climbs into bed leaving the covers open for me to get in beside him. So I do, and I absorb the comfort in his arm wrapping around my waist and tucking me into him.

"Night, Mads." He kisses the top of my head.

"Night, Jessie," I manage before tiredness takes over and my heavy eyelids close. I'm with him, I'm safe, and as long as I have him, I'm gonna get through everything that's happened.

CHAPTER 42
JESSIE

Before my eyes even open, my instinct is to reach out for her. And when all I feel is empty space, I panic.

Jumping out of bed, I chuck on some pants before I race to find her. There's no sign of her, just a note propped against a glass of orange juice that reads.

Gone to see Prez.

It's written in her perfect handwriting, and I relax. I'd been speaking with him about Maddy and me when she'd interrupted to tell us about the feds coming, and he made it clear where she stood with him when he gave me a lecture about hurting her.

Maddy has shown him her loyalty even more since then, and I'm hella relieved that I have his support. I know he told her she could help herself to some of Hayley's stuff so I guess that's what she must be doing.

I decide to go check in on Skid while she's gone. When I let myself into his cabin, he's asleep in the chair, his fingers still clinging to the empty bottle of Jack that dangles over the armrest.

I think about how pissed Carly would be if she saw the state of the place and start to pick up some of the crap. Then taking some bacon out of the fridge I set to making him something to eat. Who knows when the last time he ate something was?

I hear him stirring as I plate up the food, and he doesn't seem at all surprised to see me when he staggers into the kitchen rubbing at his temples.

"Mornin'," I nod at him, sliding a perfectly fried egg onto the plate beside the bacon. "Thought I'd cook you up some breakfast."

"Nah, I'm good. Got all I need right here." He reaches up past me into the cupboard and takes out another bottle of vodka. I snatch it out of his hands before he breaks the cap.

"C'mon man. You don't need that."

Skid looks like he's gonna swing for me, but in the state he's in, he'd be lucky to get a hit.

"Last I checked, your bitch sleeps beside you every night, so what the fuck would you know?" he says taking the bottle back, he unscrews the cap and tosses it over his shoulder.

"You don't wanna be turning up at church later in a worse state than you're already in," I remind him that Prez has called a meeting for later.

"Yeah well unless the discussions about how we're gonna find Chop and take turns pissing down his throat, I won't be going." He sits down at the table, taking a mouthful of food and chewing it roughly.

"We're working on it, you know he ain't gonna get away with what he did. Come on eat up, shower. I got a few more names on Rogue's list if you wanna hammer someone's head in?" I smile to try and lighten the mood, but he doesn't respond.

"Garage's been busy, Rogue's been doing her best to keep up. I've been helping out too where I can, but she needs you. Maybe a focus would do you some good."

"I have a focus… Killing my cunt of a bitch brother," he says washing down a mouthful of bacon with a swig of vodka.

"Rogue's worried about you, at least call in down there see how she's doin'." Everyone knows how Skid loves the crazy assed bitch, he sees her as family. If she can't get him out this cabin there isn't much hope for the rest of us.

"She knows where I am," he shrugs.

"You know she's never been one for coming up here," I remind him, Rogue ain't the family kind. Carly was always inviting her to dinner, we try to include her in club events, but she won't have any of it. She just likes to work engines.

"We could do with shaping up around here too," I say looking around the room, there are doors ripped off hinges and busted up furniture.

"Tell me where you keep your tools and drill, and I'll set to fixing this place out," I offer. Grimm had cleaned up after Carly's attack, so all this mess has to be Skid's handy work.

"I don't own a fucking drill, that's what fucking prospects are for ain't it?" He stares at me blankly as he knocks back the bottle again. I could have sworn Tommy returned a drill he borrowed from Skid the day of the lake party, maybe I'd misheard, or maybe Skid's head wasn't thinking straight. It reminds me though that no one has checked in on Tommy since he fucked off that day.

Everyone assumed after he'd gone AWOL, that maybe he'd gotten word that his dad was responsible for what happened to Carly and he was too scared to come back. No one could blame him for that.

But with Tommy, there would always be doubt in my mind. I've never liked the kid. But I push those thoughts to the back of my head, right now trying to pull Skid out of the hole that's swallowing him up is more important.

"Let's head down and see what's happening, who knows one of those crazy fucks might have had an idea on how to find him," I suggest.

I'm surprised when he gets out of the chair and heads towards the bathroom, and I wait for him, staring at the spot where I'd found Carly lying until he reappears. He smells better and has fresh clothes on. I nod him a smile that isn't reciprocated, but I can live with that because he puts on his cut and we head down to the club on our bikes together.

We pull up outside, and are just about to walk in when he looks over to the garage. The door is already up, meaning that Rogue is in. She'd still been there when I got back last night. Maybe she hadn't even left.

"I'll be right behind you," he tells me, heading in the direction of the garage. I knew he'd have to check in on Rogue, he's been watching out for her since he caught her trying to steal parts from the garage when she was just a little girl. She's had him wrapped around her little finger ever since.

She's turned out to be useful for the club over the years, keeps her ear to the ground outside of the compound and is majorly underestimated by the people she meets outside of the club. If she'd been born with a dick, she'd have been wearing a prospect jacket years ago.

It feels like I've accomplished something by getting Skid down here, now all I can do is hope that someone has a plan that will find him that vengeance he fucking needs.

Maddy

I knock on the door but no one answers, and I somehow build up enough courage to let myself in. Hayley's dad's kitchen is brighter than I imagined. With a blue gingham tablecloth hung over the table, and whitewashed kitchen cabinets, it's almost pretty. The fridge is decorated with photographs, mainly ones of Hayley and Jessie pulling silly faces. Jessie looks so happy and unburdened, it makes me wish even more that I could have known them together for longer. There are a few more pictures of Hayley and her dad, but the one that breaks my heart most is the one of her and Carly. It must have been taken at Christmas because there is a huge tree in the background decorated to perfection in the living room I recognize to be Carly and Skid's.

"You want something?" a rough voice startles me, and I spin around like a caught out school girl, hands behind my back and rocking on my heels.

"I'm sorry, sir, the door was open and I just…"

"I've been expecting you." Hayley's dad smiles at me sadly. "I've already taken what I want to keep. Help yourself to whatever you want, the rest can be boxed up for now. Maybe you can take it to charity or summit." He grabs his keys from the worktop and starts to head for the door.

"Grimm said he brought up the chest from Carly and Skid's and gave it to you. I was thinking maybe whatever Tobias… Chop had come back for might be in there." I hope he doesn't think I'm poking my nose in, but I really want to see if I can find something to help track him down.

"Yeah, I thought that too, nothing in there stood out. Take a look if you want it's in the spare room on the bed." He shrugs before he leaves.

I breathe a sigh of relief when I hear his bike pull away. The man is intimidating, even when he's being what I guess is his version of friendly. I move through the house in search of the spare room and immediately know which one of them belongs to Hayley because it still smells like her. I pass it for now, not sure if I'm ready to go through her things just yet, and it doesn't take me long to find the room I'm looking for. The chest is on the bed just like Prez said it would be, and I carefully go through its contents. There are lots of photos and some old paperwork, but nothing significant enough to bring him back here and commit murder. I did find a business card for a lawyer in Utah, which I tuck into my shorts pocket to look into later. Aside from that my search results in nothing.

I give in to temptation and stop by Hayley's room on the way out. I smile to myself at how messy and disorganized her dresser is. I run my fingers through the shimmery particles of brown eyeshadow that are settled on its surface. The same one that she always wore on the edge of her eyelids. There are more photos of her and Jessie stuck around her mirror, and I feel guilty for the pang of jealousy I get seeing how close they'd been.

I open her wardrobe and touch her clothes. All of them seem too good to give away, they belonged to her. It just doesn't seem right. I half expect her to burst through the door and yell at me for even thinking of taking her clothes to charity.

But she doesn't, and the room remains silent and lonely.

Tears prickle at my eyes at the thought of all the things I'll never get to know about her, and when I see the corner of a box stuck out from under the bed, I wonder if it contains more photographs. Maybe I could take some back for Jessie to put up around the cabin, it might help us both feel closer to her. I slide the box out from under the bed then sit on the floor and open the lid. It's crammed full of envelopes, all of them written to Jessie. I skim through them all, digging to the bottom of the box and the writing varies from childlike to adult.

I'm confused why Hayley has so many letters for Jessie, and I'm almost tempted to rip one open and see what's inside. That wouldn't be right, but I do place the lid back on the box and take it with me, leaving everything else behind.

Hopefully whatever's inside these envelopes will bring Jessie some peace, he doesn't sleep at night, I know he blames himself for what happened to her. He's insistent that it was him who kept on at Prez to loosen her reins and let her do more by herself.

When I arrive back the cabin is empty, and there's a new note left in replacement to the one I'd left for Jessie this morning.

Gone down to club, back soon.
Miss you x

I giggle at how cute he can be and I place the box on the table ready for when he gets home. Then I set to making us something nice for dinner.

He gets home a few hours later, and I can tell straight away that things haven't gone well. I consider hiding the box for another time, but even when he sits in front of it, he's too tense to notice it. Running his hands through his hair he releases a frustrated breath, and I flick the lid on a beer and place it in front of him. His firm hands wrap around my waist and prevent me from walking away, and he pulls me back to him his head pressing against my stomach.

"Bad day?" I ask, stroking my hand through his hair.

"Shit," he answers.

"You wanna talk about it?"

And when he shakes his head, I decide not to push him any further.

"I made your favourite," I say, pulling away and making my way over to the oven. "Enchiladas," I try my best to sound enthusiastic.

"They wanna use you to find Chop," he blurts out as if the words have been burning in his throat.

"Sure, I've been looking into some stuff—"

"It's too dangerous," his voice cuts me off, and I take a step back, confused. This is what they wanted me to do, Jessie had told me that himself.

"What?"

"Suppose Chop finds out you're the one we're using to find him and he comes for you. What if I'm not here? I let Hayley down, promised I'd keep her safe and I couldn't. I ain't doing a thing to risk losing you too," he tells me, his fist clenching tight.

"Do you think Dirty Souls are dangerous?" I fold my arms.

"For anyone stupid enough to fuck with us yeah… which is exactly my point, Chop—"

"I fucked with you," I interrupt him this time. "I screwed you up for six months, and you didn't have a clue who I was. You couldn't trace me. You couldn't stop me, and you couldn't get to me because you never even knew I existed." Jessie looks back at me and I can tell he's speechless.

"Don't underestimate me, Jessie, let me do this. I want to help." I need to do this, to have a purpose. With the Bastards still after me, I can't leave the compound, and trying to fix this is the perfect distraction.

"Hey I wouldn't ever..." He stands up, and takes hold of my face the way he always does when he's serious. "I couldn't handle anything happening to you, and now we've seen what Chop's capable of..."

"Yeah, we have, which is exactly why he needs to be stopped before he can hurt anyone else. I'm good... trust me." I hang my head a little sideways knowing he can't say no to me when I try being cute. "And anyway, I got this kickass biker dude that's kinda protective of me, so I'm not worried," I add, and when Jessie kisses me I know he's gonna let me help.

"Could I stop you even if I wanted too?" he asks with a sigh.

"Probably not," I tell him honestly.

"Okay, then. The first thing you can do is find that file and fucking bury it back wherever the fuck you dug up from," he says. "If Chop goes into a federal prison, Skid's never gonna get the chance to make him pay. He'll sit safely behind prison bars, and now that we know that his loyalty level is a solid zero, I'm a hundred percent certain that he would rat and take us all down for the promise of an easy sentence."

It makes perfect sense. So, I grab my laptop and set to work, but not before saving the files to my computer first. What he's done to those other women shouldn't be forgotten about, and I'll make sure justice is served for them too.

It doesn't take me long to make the files disappear, once I'm in it's just a matter of wiping him from their system. I put in a request to close down the warrant for arrest using the name of a judge from Utah, and cross my fingers that might work. Now all that's left to do is to find him.

"I could do with getting information from the guys, anything small could help," I tell Jessie, as he tucks into his enchiladas.

"Sure," Jessie nods. "We can head down when you've eaten, most of the guys are around today."

"I know he probably won't feel like talking, but Tommy would be a good person to talk to, he knows Chop better than anyone. He could have childhood memories of places that might help." Tommy hasn't been around much lately, and who can blame him after what had happened.

"Yeah well good luck with that, he's been missing since the day Carly got killed." Jessie sounds frustrated.

"You can't blame him for that, Jessie. I know better than anyone what it's like to be ashamed of something your parent does."

"Your mama was doin' what she thought was right, she was providing for you. She didn't kill anyone."

I smile at his attempt to make me feel better before getting back to work.

"Mads. You remember the day of the lake party?" There's a curiosity in his voice that tells me something more was coming.

"Yeah." I glance up, trying to hide my smirk. I remember him kissing me in front of everyone around the lake and how we fucked on the kitchen floor, while I wait for him to explain what I should be remembering.

"You remember seeing Tommy coming outta Skid's place?" he questions.

"Yeah... He'd borrowed his drills or something, right?"

"See, that's the funny thing. I tried helping Skid out earlier, and he said he didn't own a drill."

"Skid's a mechanic," I laugh.

"Different kinda drills, Mads." Jessie smirks. "Tommy said he'd been fixing up something in one of the cabins down in Slu

—" he stops himself from finishing that sentence. "Tommy lied to me."

"Tommy must have been looking for whatever it was Chop wanted… It was the perfect opportunity with everyone down at the lake. He obviously didn't find it, and that's why Chop had to come back himself." Jessie nods as he takes in what I've said.

"You know what, darlin'? I got a real bad feeling you might be right."

We ride down to the club on his bike, and Jessie parks up and takes my hand before leading me inside. I don't know how the brothers will take to having a girl hanging around the club who isn't 'available'. Carly would hang around here sometimes, but she was Skid's old lady. I'm… well, I don't really know what I am, which makes things awkward.

"Hey girl," Squealer tips his head up at me as he walks past, and Jessie puts a possessive kiss just behind my ear. I can't help but like Squealer. The guy has a sense of humor. I wait for some kind of sexual slander, but it doesn't come, and I put that down to the stare he's getting from Jessie.

"You good, Mads?" Troj calls over from the doorframe he's leaning against, he winks before stepping out of the way so Jessie can take me through to the smaller bar room.

The blonde woman behind the bar greets me with a scowl that I choose to ignore, and I continue to feel her eyes burning through me when Jessie sits me down at a table.

"You're gonna be fine, darlin', just do your best." He brushes away some hair from my face and plants another kiss on my temple that I really hope she sees.

One by one the brothers come in and give me any information they think might be useful. I listen to stories Chop has told them, take details of people they know that live in the towns where he's got offenses. I circle keywords I might use in a search to find him. I get the license plate number from the car that he left the club in when the feds came, and the prepay number he had used to contact Skid a few days after he'd gone.

Hours later, I still have no leads and my head is really starting to ache.

"You look tired, we can try again tomorrow," Jessie says, moving over to me from the bar.

"I'm fine," I assure him. "My head just hurts when I strain my eyes. I have glasses up at the cabin, I'll go grab them."

"I'll go. You're fine here." His eyes flick back over to the bar. "Mel, make her a coffee or summit," he orders the feisty blonde. I hear the tut she throws over her shoulder as she makes her way over to the cafeteria and pours me out a coffee. Stomping around the bar, she slams the mug in front of me, sloshing black coffee all over the table as it lands.

"Could I trouble you for some sugar?" I ask her in the most irritatingly sweet voice I can manage. And she actually growls under her breath as she storms back to the bar, grabs two sugar sachets and flings them on to my table.

"Thanks ever so." I smile sarcastically and watch Jessie's face crease into a smile.

"Looks like you have things handled here," he smirks. "I'll be back in a sec." He leans down to kiss me, and I grab at his cut and pull him closer. Devouring his lips with my mine, I force my tongue into his mouth so I can lap him up from inside. I don't pull away until I'm sure I've made my point. I give the shocked-faced blonde a smile as I trail my thumb across Jessie's bottom lip and swipe away the remnants of my lip gloss.

"See you in a bit, darlin'." Jessie laughs to himself as he backs out the bar room, he knew what I was doing, and I'm not ashamed at all. I drink my coffee and continue to work despite the thumping between my eyes, because Chop's still out there, and I'm determined to find him.

CHAPTER 43

JESSIE

The girl gets my dick constantly hard, and these days the only place I ever want to be is inside her. Day and fucking night. The way she just made a point and claimed me in front of Mel was hot as fuck, and I can't wait to get her all to myself.

I reach the cabins within minutes. It's eerily quiet up here, everyone being at the club on Prez's orders so they can tell Maddy whatever information they have. Even Skid's managed to haul himself out his cabin and is down at the garage helping out Rogue.

I look around for Maddy's glasses. They aren't beside the bed where they usually were, nor next to the lamp in the living room where she sits and reads sometimes. Then after searching around the kitchen, I find them on the table perched on the top of some box. I've never seen it before and something about it makes me curious enough to open it. The inside is full of envelopes, and even stranger, all of them are addressed to me.

I tip the box out on to the table, some of the ones at the bottom have different handwriting, like a child's written them. I take one and rip it open, and when I realize who they're from my heart turns to pulp.

Hayley's letters change everything I ever thought I knew, starting right from the day I met her to just a few weeks ago before she died.

Our life, written in words that read so unfamiliar.

Words stand out from the letter she wrote on the day of her mama's funeral...

Who knows, one day if Daddy could see how happy you make me rules could change. Until then I'll just be yours without you knowing.

Painful truths from the day I told her about Maddy...

You asked me to talk to her. I may not know her, but I can tell already she's not for you. She's nothing like the women that hang around the club. She's too innocent, too guarded for the person you've become.

You need to see what I would do for you, how far I would go to see you happy, and if getting you a new plaything is a way to prove how much you mean to me then the game is on.

More words from the night I took her to that party...

You took off your cut. For her. You always said you would never hide who you were, but there's something about Maddy Summers that has you going against everything you believe in. I can't decide if she's bad or good for you. But I know she's bad for me, for us. Very bad.

And from when she brought Maddy here to the club and I got so mad at her...

Okay, it was a mistake to bring her here, although I probably won't apologize to you for it. Maybe the fact that you cracked a piece of my heart tonight without even knowing it may bring you comfort, but I will forgive you. I will always forgive you because that's what you do when you love someone.

I read them one by one, losing all sense of time. My tears splash on the pages as I read through them. Torn up between heartache and anger at myself for not seeing the way she'd been hurting for all those years.

I think back to her lying in my arms, her blood coating my hands and the words that she'd fought so hard to say. "It would always have been you." It had made no sense back then, I thought she was talking nonsense, but now it sliced at my heart like a jagged knife, and I tortured myself by opening another letter and continuing to read.

I know if I stand any chance, I'm gonna have to tell you how I feel soon or lose you forever. Then, I suppose I could lose out to worse people than Maddy Summers, at least she's not Melissa, who by the way is a dog-rough whore... Just hold on a little longer before you let go of me completely, Jessie, I just need a little longer to find the courage to tell you.

The door opening pulls me away from her words, and I quickly wipe away any tears to save face.

"Hey," Maddy says cheerily as she steps inside.

"You were gone ages I got worried." She closes the door and hangs up her jacket. "Nyx brought me up. I was done for the day. Managed a few leads but nothing solid…" I hear her, but I don't take a single word in. My eyes are still fixed hard on Hayley's letters.

"Jessie… you okay?"

"She loved me." Those are the only words my mouth seems able to form, and I hear how hoarse and weak they sound as they come out.

"Hayley loved me," I repeat still in shock.

"Of course she loved you. You were like her big brother. She thought the world of you." Maddy twists my hair around her fingers as she speaks.

"No," I shake my head. "No. She loved me. Not like a brother. More than that. These are all letters from her. She wanted me and her to be together, for all that time. I used her," I admit suddenly feeling sick. "I fucking used her to get what I wanted…To get you." I don't mean for it to sound so bitter but that's how it comes out. "I broke her heart and I never even realized, 'coz I was too fucking selfish to see it."

Maddy's fingers stop moving and she looks down at me confused.

"She never said anything to me, and we talked about everything." She sounds betrayed.

"It's here in black and fuckin' white." I push the table away as I jump to my feet. Grabbing a handful of letters, I slam them against her chest. "Every word, every feeling since she was ten years old."

Maddy scoops up the letters, and as she starts to read her face grows sadder.

"What does she mean, you asked her to speak to me?" she asks, sounding hurt. "A new plaything? Jessie what is this?" Her eyes glass over, and I take in a deep breath before I tell her something I know will shatter her.

"I asked Hayley to start speaking to you," I admit. "I'd noticed you months before, and had no clue how to talk to you myself. I wanted to know more about you, so I asked Hay to find out about you." Maddy chokes on her tears as she hears my confession, and when I reach out to comfort her she smacks my arm away.

"So you're telling me that my friendship with Hayley. The only friendship I've ever had, was something you fabricated so you could fuck me."

As well as all the sadness there's so much anger in her beautiful eyes, anger I've never seen before. It doesn't belong there and turns me inside out.

"No, it was nothing like that. Hayley had the idea to become your friend, said she could find out more that way. But in the end it was real, look read on she says how much she likes you." I scramble through the letters trying to find the one I had read earlier about her starting to like Maddy. But she's already starting to back away from me.

"Is that what I am? A plaything, Jessie."

"Fuck no, nothing like that. Mads, you fucking mean everything to me. That's why I wanted her to talk to you. I had to know more about you, and yeah, Maddy, I let her become your friend when I shouldn't have. But I ain't sorry for it, 'coz I got you now."

"You've got me?" She fakes a laugh that tells me I chose my words all wrong. "So that makes it okay that you used someone to become my fake friend. Had me believe I finally had someone who cared about me…" I get a horrible sense that she's gonna run and that's exactly what she does. She slams the door behind her so hard that it shakes the whole cabin.

I want to chase after her, to make all this better. But she needs her space, and being honest, right now, I need mine too.

Hayley must have been hurting so bad. I'd spent all this time thinking she wanted me and Mads to be together. Hoping she'd be looking down at us, proud of me for getting it together. Or is that just what I'd wanted to believe. Reality is, I'd spent the final months of her life breaking her heart and being insensitive.

I clear away the letters, placing the lid back on the box. There are still so many unread, but I can't face any more guilt. Not today.

This really is all on me, Hayley would still be here if I hadn't asked her to speak to Maddy. Maddy would still be hacking for the Bastards, she'd be safe from them and still have a life beyond the confines of this club.

I was bad news for both of them, and hell's fucked if I'm gonna let Maddy end up the same way Hayley has.

Best place for her is as far away from me as she can get.

I don't give myself chance to talk myself out of doing what I have to. Pulling out my cell I make the call. The call I should have made the day we brought Maddy back here, but had been too damn selfish to.

Yeah, it's gonna kill me, but it has to be done. I owe it to Maddy to make the right decision for her this time, and I owe it to Hayley to keep the girl who had become her best friend protected.

Chapter 44

MADDY

I must have walked the entire perimeter of the compound twice, and to say I never thought about running out of it would be a lie.

I stick to the perimeter and walk until my feet ache as much as my heart, and even then I still don't stop. Darkness creeps in, and the noises that come from inside the woods sound scary, but not nearly as much as the thought of going home and facing Jessie.

I've been stupid, how did I not notice that Hayley had loved him herself. I thought we'd been so close, that she told me everything, but everything had just been an act.

If I'd have known how she felt about Jessie, I'd never have spoken about him to her the way I did. She must have hated me for it. And if I'd any clue this was all part of a well thought out plan, I would have avoided them both. I wouldn't be feeling like my heart had been ripped out of my chest due to the loss of so many people.

Everything that is left for me to live for is all based on lies.

The evening pulls in fast and the chill in the air plummets, forcing me to make my way back to the cabin and face my problem. When I get back, the place is empty, There's no sign of Jessie, or Hayley's letters.

Just empty space and silence.

The hollowness I've been feeling in the pit of my stomach spreads further without him here. Confirming how much I've grown to need him.

Regardless of how I'd come to know him, I've fallen in love with Jessie. Never have I felt more safe or protected than I do with him. Somewhere on my way back here, I've decided I want to hear him out and give him the chance to explain. I don't have the strength to lose someone else who I love.

I just hope Jessie feels the same way, that he meant what he said and that I wasn't a plaything to him.

I try to distract myself by reading while I wait for him to come home. I don't think this cabin had ever seen a book before I came here, but as soon as I told Jessie that reading was something I enjoyed it's seemed like I have an endless supply of them.

When it passes midnight and he still doesn't come home. I give in to my heavy eyes and pull a blanket over myself. Hoping that when he does come back, he'll wake me and we can sort this mess out.

It isn't Jessie that disturbs me, it's the rays of sun that creeps through the curtains and warms the skin on my face. Standing up from the sofa and taking a glance around the room there's no sign of him. Nothing to even suggest he's been home.

Trying not to think about the reasons why, I busy myself by tidying up the cabin, then I take a shower. I'm making myself a coffee when the door opens, and Jessie stumbles through it.

His feet move faster than his body can keep up with, knocking over the kitchen chair as he stumbles towards me. The closer he gets to me, the heavier the stench of alcohol becomes.

"You want some coffee?" I ask. Instead of an answer, he walks straight past me, slamming the door to his room after him. A loud thud follows which I assume is him landing in a heap on the bed.

My mind goes into overdrive inventing all the possible

reasons he didn't come home, what he could have done while he was in such a mess, and the more I think, the sicker I feel.

I picture him letting the blonde bitch from down at the bar touch him, imagine him touching her back, and it's all too much.

What I need is a distraction. Jessie will be out of it for a good few hours, and instead of feeling sorry for myself I could make good use of the time and use some of the information I'd gotten yesterday to chase up some leads on Chop.

I start up my laptop then delve through my purse, my head is still thumping so I'll need my glasses, and while I'm searching for them my fingers stumble across something I wasn't expecting, and I pull it out for a closer look.

Staring at the USB stick in the palm of my hand triggers a memory, one that makes my chest heavy as it plays out in my head.

Carly smiling, asking if she could use my laptop to see what was on the drive. Her handing over the USB. The USB that she'd had found in Chop's trunk.

Shit.

This could be what Chop had come back for, and I could have had it all along.

Wasting no more time, I connect it to the USB port in my laptop and open the file. It's an audio, and despite being petrified of what I might hear. I turn up the volume and hit play regardless.

At first, all that can be heard is background noise, clinking glasses, and muffled voices. But then a voice comes in over the sound.

"Whatcha here for, Chop?" a man asks in a rough, unwelcoming tone.

"I needed to know everything's cool between us," the voice that I assume belongs to Chop replies, which picks up my full attention.

"It will be as soon as you've told Jimmer you been fucking

his old lady," the first voice threatens. Shocked, I sit back in my chair and wait to hear more.

"You know it ain't that easy. I got a kid to think about. You know how it is, if anything happened to me, he has no one."

"Your brother seems a good kid, he'd step up if he needed to," the cold voice responds.

"Yeah, well let's hope it doesn't come to that." Hearing the snigger in Chop's voice makes me hate him even more, if that's even possible. The guy is pure evil.

"Every day you don't tell him puts me in danger too. Just knowing this shit could get me buried right alongside you… You know club rules, Chop. What the fuck were you thinking?"

"Yeah well, I wasn't thinkin' with my head, was I?" is Chop's cocky response.

"I'm giving you a week, one week to tell him yourself or I'm gonna have to. I'm heading up to your Charter on business next Friday, I ain't gonna lie to his face. Jimmer's the closest thing I got to a real brother, and it's only 'coz I know how much you mean to him that I'm giving you a chance to tell him this shit yourself."

"It ain't that easy, brother."

"I never said it would be, but then that ain't my problem. I ain't the one who's put my dick over the club."

"I guess that's all there is to say," Chop's tone softens and what sounds like the scraping of a chair signals the end of the conversation. The audio ends a few minutes later.

Whoever the other voice belongs to must have been a member of this club. No one mentioned to me yesterday that Chop had slept with Prez's wife. Seems it wasn't just Skid who Chop has betrayed. And I'm beginning to wonder how many more secrets the man is hiding.

Unable to just sit on what I've heard I decide to go speak to Prez myself. This could be the missing link to help us find Chop. So, armed with the USB and my laptop I head down to the club.

The track down seems longer than usual, especially with my feet still sore from last night, and when I eventually make it to the yard I find it empty. Clinking sounds come from the garage, and I figure it will be Skid working the skin off his hands in attempt to shut all the hurt out of his head.

I walk on past, it's best I don't tell Skid about the new information just yet. Instead, I need to find Prez before the USB stick I'm carrying burns a hole through my hand.

"You reckon you can be ready for midday, Utah's a fucker of a drive," a voice calls from behind me, and when I spin around I see it belongs to Nyx.

"Midday?" Looking around the yard, I check that he's actually talking to me.

"Yeah, I wanna get going as soon as. Sooner we leave sooner I can get back."

"Are you taking me to Cannonville?" I ask excited, this is just what I need, the Utah Charter is where my mom is hiding out, and I'm really starting to miss her. "You sure it's safe enough for me to visit," I check.

"Take it you haven't spoken to Jessie?" Nyx scratches at the back of his head looking suddenly awkward.

"No."

"It's a one-way trip, I'm just dropping ya off," he tells me, almost sounding like he feels sorry for me. Nyx is the kinda guy who doesn't seem to feel anything.

Unable to shake off my panic, I rush past him and into the club. I search all the bars, but there's no sign of Prez anywhere. I'm even brave enough to knock on the doors of the bedrooms upstairs, and I'm still unable to find him.

It's becoming harder and harder to breathe, the temperature of my body rising and making me feel giddy as I search, trying to focus on what I'd come down here for, when really all I can think about is what Nyx has told me.

I need to speak to Jessie, ask him about this impromptu trip.

It takes priority over talking to Prez about this new information. I know I won't be able to focus on anything else until I've spoken to Jessie about Utah, so I head back up to his cabin in hope of some answers.

There's no sign of him in the lounge or the kitchen when I burst through the door, and so I storm straight through to the bedroom. Jessie doesn't stir, his body laid out flat on the bed, still clothed. Suddenly furious at him for being so selfish, I grab the closest thing to hand and launch it at him. He hardly moves when the tub of moisturizer lands hard on his back.

"Get up," I scream, tugging at his leg. "Get the fuck up, Jessie"

"Fuck, darlin', calm your clit." Jessie rolls over, rubbing his eyes as he sits up.

"So. You're done with me now then? Packing me off to Utah without so much as a goodbye. That's a low fucking blow even by your standards." I pull my holdall from under the bed and start filling it with my stuff. Scrubbing his hand over his face, Jessie rises up on his feet.

"It's for your own good," he croaks, stumbling past me and heading for the bathroom. I carry on tossing my things in the holdall, trying my hardest not to let the tears filling my eyes leak.

I'm almost done packing every trace of me from his room when Jessie returns, dripping wet with a towel tucked around his waist. His blonde hair hangs wet around his face, and I watch his fingers run through the strands pushing them back over his head.

"Look, Mads, I'm doing this for you, the Charter in Utah will take care of you. Cannonville's a nice place, there are families there and you can be with your mom." He steps closer and reaches his hands out to mine. "I ain't no good for ya, and you got nothing for you here but a shit ton of painful memories." He speaks so softly that it breaks my heart and terrifies me at the same time.

"Jessie, we had a fight." I hate that he isn't making eye contact with me, it makes me feel so distant from him.

"A stupid fight, and now you want me to leave?" I find it harder and harder to contain my emotions, and when his head slowly nods back at me. The tears finally spill from my eyes.

"What about Chop? You need me to find Chop," I tell him. I can't leave, the club need me here, and I need to be here, with him.

"You have all the information. You can do whatever it is you do from Utah. You're safer there." He shrugs.

"How can I be safe without you protecting me?" I ask. "Please don't shut me out again, Jessie don't do this to me." I'm begging now, because I have nothing else.

Jessie closes the space between us, his wet body pressing into my T-shirt, and sucking it to his skin. Strong hands lift to my hair and when his lips contact with mine, I lose myself.

He kisses me long, hard, and heartbreakingly slowly. He kisses me goodbye.

"I'm doing this for you, darlin'," he speaks against my lips. Lowering my head, and marking my forehead with another kiss. Then he pulls away and slides into jeans and a plain white tee.

"Nyx will be here in a few minutes," he tells me quietly.

"He said I had until midday." I cling desperately to some hope that a few more hours might change the outcome of this mess.

"I text him and told him you were ready now, he's eager to get goin'." Leaning forward Jessie grabs my holdall off the bed and stops right in front of me. He curls a lock of my hair around his fingers, and when he finally dares to look in to my eyes, I see it. The same sadness I'm feeling, the same pain. I just can't understand why he's doing it to us.

"I'm so sorry, Maddy." He closes his eyes to hide that pain away from me again.

"You should be with your mama. You're safer there, I've been selfish to keep you here."

"Then be selfish again, keep me here," I yell, just as the door opens and Nyx walks in.

"I can't do that, darlin'," Jessie whispers, and just like that my world collapses around me. My chest feels too tight for my lungs to stretch for air. I need him. I don't want to go to Cannonville, not even if it means I get to see Mama. I want to stay here where I belong.

Jessie leaves me standing in the door to the bedroom, walking past me to hand my holdall over to Nyx.

"Don't, Jessie, please." My tears leave a cool trail against my hot cheeks, and I wipe them away with the back of my hand and chase after him.

"You need to go, Maddy," Jessie whispers like he has no patience left in him.

"Jessie, come on," I plead, refusing to budge. I'm not leaving with Nyx, I'm not going to Utah, I'm taking charge of my own life for once.

"You want me to say it? Keep on pushing. But don't blame me when you're hurting like hell," he warns.

"What? Say what Jessie?" I yell at him.

"Jessie, you don't want me to leave, you said you couldn't lose me," I remind him, clawing at anything to stop him sending me away. "You promised you'd never hurt me."

"And you should never have trusted me. I gave you enough warning," he tells me. "Hayley was right, you were just a plaything. I was fed up of club whores kneeling and sucking whenever I told them to. You were a challenge, something different, and I got what I wanted. Now I want you to leave." The way he speaks so emotionlessly drives a stake into my heart.

"You don't mean that." I shake my head, and he answers me with silence. I choke on my own breaths while I wait for him to tell me he's sorry. But he doesn't and I lose it.

"You selfish bastard." My hand raises and my palm stings like hell when it impacts his cheek. Jessie doesn't react, just takes my assault with his eyes fixed on the floor. I gasp in shock, ashamed by my own actions, and when he looks up at me, instead of the anger I'm expecting his expression is blank.

"Yeah well, I never claimed to be anything else." Jessie shrugs.

"You promised me you'd never hurt me," I remind him through sobs.

"I told you what you wanted to hear." Jessie nods at Nyx over my shoulder.

"Don't say that, Jessie, you don't mean it. You take that back." I feel an arm on my shoulder tugging me away, and I fight it off the best I can, but it's too strong, and it drags me further and further away from Jessie. I'm not sure what I would do if I did manage to get to him. Hug him or attack him?

Jessie's crystal blue eyes turn stormy as Nyx manhandles me out of the cabin and into the truck outside. I don't care about the small crowd of people that have gathered outside and are watching me fight against Nyx, screaming my demands at him to take me back inside.

My life isn't in Cannonville. It's here with Jessie and this fucked up brotherhood that he calls a family. But he doesn't even follow me out, nor does he watch as I give up my fight and stay seated in the seat that Nyx practically throws me into. Troj offers me an apologetic smile as Nyx pulls away and speeds off down the dirt track.

Even Nyx looks a little sad for me as he pulls out onto the main road heading in the direction of the freeway.

"You'll feel better when you see your mom, and you'll like Utah there are more families around." Nyx sounds friendly for the first time ever, and I'm sure if I didn't feel as though I'd been stabbed repeatedly in the chest I would appreciate his attempt of comfort. Though I don't answer him, just press my forehead against the cool glass window and close my eyes. I try to focus on the fact that I will see Mama in a few hours. But it only reminds me that I won't be with Jessie.

I can't let myself believe the last words he said to me. There was more to us, I'd felt it. Or, had I just wanted it so badly that I imagined it? None of that matters now anyway, not as I get further and further away from him.

CHAPTER 45

JESSIE

I let her go.

It was the right thing to do. For once in my life I'd done the decent thing, and if this is being moral, moral fucking sucks.

Surely doing a good thing wasn't supposed to hurt so fucking much but seeing the hurt on her face when I lied to her, told her all she was to me was a challenge, had stung like a thousand needles. It burned me inside that I had to make her leave. But she belonged with her mom. I should never have kept them apart. It was just another selfish scheme I'd concocted, telling myself at the time that it was the best for Maddy's safety.

Me and Maddy were based on lies, all selfish decisions I'd made to make myself feel better.

I liked the thought of having Maddy to myself too much, I knew her mama being around could have made things difficult. Besides I wasn't sure if I could trust a woman who whored for the Bastards.

My head pounds, and when I look in the cupboard there's nothing left in the bottle of scotch. I throw it against the wall and let it smash to pieces.

Why did I have to be so spiteful to her? Her last memory of me would be all the cruel things I'd said to her before she left. Surely there was an easier way.

There's only one way to make the pain stop, one way to void my mind of her, and that's to hurt.

I search around for my list of the Bastards' errand boys. My personal directory of wrath. It's a bad idea in the mood I'm in, and I already doubt I'll be able to stop at just a warning, but I have to do something, anything to remind me of who I am. To stop any doubt that I was wrong to let her go.

I search through the pile of clothes Maddy had neatly folded on the table, looking for my jeans and hoping the list hadn't been in the pocket when Maddy washed them. Something falls to the floor, but it isn't my list. It's a letter with my name boldly written in Hayley's handwriting.

Another reminder of what a cunt I am. All those years she'd loved me, and I'd been too wrapped up in myself to even notice. I'd used her to get Maddy, and she'd been so desperate to please me she'd made herself miserable.

None of this would have happened if I hadn't have asked her to find out about Maddy for me.

Hayley's words are so painful, just the thought of reading them make my guts clench, but it's no less than I deserve.

I could easily take out a few names on that list, causing actual pain to the people who are on it. But what's the point when the person who deserves to hurt the most is me. I try to imagine how she must have felt when I was talking to her about Maddy, how mean I was to her the night she brought Maddy to the club. I was too busy giving a shit about myself and this club to even notice she had those types of feelings for me.

My fingers tear open the letter before I can talk myself out of it, and I slide down to the floor, resting my back against the refrigerator. I start to read.

Jessie,

I don't know where to even start this time. These letters have been my way of outing all my feelings for so long it seems strange to think this will be my last one.

You know, I had every intention of giving you the first one I wrote to you. I was ten years old and thought I could make such a difference to your life with a few stupid words. Over time I've realized that I've been writing these letters for myself.

I've never really had anyone I could talk to, no one who would really understand me. And no that's not a dig. I know how much you care about me. I could hardly talk to you about this, could I?

Today I admitted something to myself that I've been denying for way too long. I finally accepted that no matter how deep I look, or how hard I wish, I'm never gonna find that look in your eyes. The one you've saved up your whole life to give to Maddy. It's a look I was worried you'd never be capable of giving to anyone. Jessie, all the years I've known you I've been so scared that you wouldn't fall in love with me that I got distracted from what I'd feared most.

That first day I met you, the coldness in your eyes made me worry you'd never be able to love anyone again. I didn't want that for you, but now I know from the way you look at Maddy, the way you hide yourself to protect her.

You love her.

Now, I'm not about to pretend that I'm not pissed that it's not me you fell for, I've never been one to sugarcoat, but if a girl's gonna lose out to anyone, Maddy Summers is the girl she'd want to lose to. She is perfect... Fucking perfect. I've tried hating her, believe me I've tried so damn hard, but the fact is she's impossible not to love. She's caring, smart, and the most beautiful girl I've ever seen in real life. But what I love about her the most is the way she sees you. She sees My Jessie. She looks far enough past your cut and the people you hang around with to know who you are and what you're capable of. Her eyes are open to the Jessie that I've been crazy about since I was ten years old, and if you give her a chance to, I know she'll love you right back.

For god's sake, Jessie, give her your heart and let her keep it safe for you.

I talked to Skid today, he's onto me. He knows how I feel. I'm guessing he has for a while. He's worried, reminded me of all the reasons why me loving you is a bad and dangerous idea, and he's right of course. When isn't he?

He got me thinking about what was really important too.

I'm never gonna stop loving you, not ever, and I won't apologize either. This shit is sloppy enough without me turning in to a do-gooder. But the thing that really matters is that you are loved by someone. Someone who can love you freely, and who you can love back.

So as much as it breaks my heart that this will be the last letter you never read. I can't torture myself by writing any more.

We can be happy.

You and Maddy together, the most beautiful couple that ever existed, and me knowing that I did the right thing. I'm gonna speak to you next time I see you, tell you to stop being a dick and have some faith in yourself. You need to know that you're good enough for a girl like Maddy Summers. I'll even help you make sure you don't screw this shit up. I'll remind you of all the amazing things that you are, things that you so easily forget. Like the passion you put into everything you do, and the way you care about the people close to you.

Most of all, I'm going to make sure you know how special you are, that hidden underneath the surface is a really good guy who you let out for the people who matter to you. I'm so privileged to be one of those people Jessie.

I told myself for so long that you couldn't give yourself to anyone, that you belonged to the club. But I was wrong, Maddy makes you want things you never knew you were missing out on. She makes you want to be a better person, and she made you lose the god damn cut. You should give her all that shit and more.

Belong to her.

I'll be okay, I can love you through silence and without pain, because you found love, and that for me will always be enough.

Be happy.

Your Best Friend always,

Hayley

xxx

I hold the letter to my chest. Everything clear now. Why that day at the warehouse Hayley valued Maddy's life over her own. She saved Maddy for me. She wanted me to be happy. She took a fucking bullet for me to be with the person I loved, the same girl I've just forced out of my life.

"I fucking love you right back, pretty girl," I speak out loud as if she's sat right in front of me. I don't know if it's my hangover or my imagination gone wild, but I swear I feel a warm touch at my shoulder. It makes my body shiver and urges me to stand up off my sorry ass.

The door to my cabin nearly flies off the hinges at the same time, and a huge figure blocks the sunlight from entering behind him.

"What the fuck you playing at?" Skid's voice bellows as he marches towards me, pushing me hard in the shoulder so my body slams back against the refrigerator.

"The fuck, man?" I shout.

"Tell me Nyx did not just leave the compound with your bitch." Skid squares me with his eyes and when I go to answer, he cuts me off before I can speak.

"Jessie. She loves you and don't even try telling me that you don't feel the same. Hayley fucking gave up her life for you to be with her, there I said it… Hayley loved you, and I'm done pussy footin' around your sorry ass. She knew she couldn't be with you, but she still wanted you to be happy and that's why she took a fucking Bastard bullet. So you'd have a chance to be loved. And you repay all that by packing that chance the fuck off to Utah."

"Skid I—"

"Save your shit, man, stop feeling sorry for yourself. I didn't give my chance up, it was fucking taken, stolen from my fucking hands, so you won't get sympathy from me. Now pull up your big boy pants and get the fuck out there and get her back."

"If you'd let me finish, I'd tell ya that's exactly what I'm about to do." I shrug him off and straighten myself out.

"Well, then what you hanging around staring at me for?" Skid grabs my cut off the chair and forces it into my chest. "Go get your bitch and bring her home where she belongs." For the first time in a week my friend smiles, and I grab him by the shoulders and bring him in, slapping his back. I grab my keys and head straight out to my bike. "I'll call Nyx, tell him to turn back," he calls after me.

"Don't bother he won't answer. I told him if he took a call while he was driving with my girl in his truck I'd slice open his stomach and strangle him with his own intestine."

"Got it," Skid says, nodding at my point and placing his phone back in his pocket. He follows me out and stands on the porch, watching me as I hop onto my bike.

"Hey, Skid," I shout over the engine. "You're gonna be alright. Yeah?" I check, still amazed at how the man could be thinking of anyone other than himself right now.

"Never again," he shakes his head. "But luckily I got you assholes to keep livin' for." He nods, and as much as his answer cuts like a knife it's good enough for now. I let my wheels kick up the dusty earth and I speed off to get my girl. Praying that I haven't pushed her too far to get her back.

CHAPTER 46
MADDY

As travel buddies go, Nyx is up there with the worst of them. He could tell I was distraught, and he was making, what I guess for him, an effort. He'd asked me some questions about my mom, and I gave him back one-word answers because I wasn't in the mood for a conversation. I doubt it hurt his feelings though, like he would care about my mother anyway.

As we get further out of town and further away from Jessie, I can feel panic starting to overtake rationality. I force myself to take slow, deep breaths, and try not to let the fact I don't think I could ever go back to not having Jessie in my life again consume me.

My chest is a dead weight, struggling to lift high enough to take in my next breath as the truck continues on the freeway. I start to imagine things. At first, it's the sound of Jessie's bike—yes, I can tell his apart from any other bike because it's a sound I listen out for whenever he isn't with me. Then I swear I see his sandy blonde hair, blowing wildly as he passes Nyx's window and cuts in front of us.

"What the fuck?" Nyx says leaning forward over the steering wheel to get a closer look. It gives me a little hope that I'm not hallucinating.

"Is that...?" I ask leaning forward myself.

"Yeah it's Jessie, crazy son of a bitch," Nyx confirms, and I suddenly feel the weight lift, my body calming and hope begins to spark.

We follow Jessie for a few kilometers until he sticks his left arm out and points at the next junction. "He wants me to pull off," Nyx says, following him off the freeway and up the slip road. Jessie leads us to a rest stop and I watch him get off his bike then run towards the truck, and he rips open my door. I barely have chance to absorb what's happening when he lifts me out of the seat, then without any explanation, he grabs my face between his hands and kisses me until I become dizzy from lack of oxygen. Despite all my confusion, I let him. It's everything I've been thinking about since I left Manitou Springs.

"I'm sorry," he pulls away to tell me, pressing his lips straight back onto mine, like he doesn't want to break away even to speak.

"So."

Kiss.

"Sorry."

Kiss.

"I don't understand?" I manage to get out in between breaks of his lips.

"I noticed you the first day I dropped Hayley off at college," he starts.

"You were sat on the steps all by yourself, totally unaffected by all the chaos that surrounded you. Freshmen not knowing where to go, everyone trying so hard to impress and make friends on the first day. You were eating an apple, and your hair was tied up on top of your head. You had those sexy as fucking sin glasses on and looked so beautiful. Everything stopped for me. Everything. I hadn't even spoken to you, and I doubted everything I was." His hands on my face are trembling as he speaks. "Hayley got out of the truck and I drove home, and I couldn't get you out of my head, not even for a second. I wanted to know everything about you. Every little fucking thing, like what it felt like to touch your skin, and how your hair would smell up close."

"Jesus Christ," I hear Nyx huff.

I try to tone down my goofy smile by biting down on my lip.

"I wanted to talk to you myself, to ask you what your deal was but I was fucking petrified. So for the next few months, I just watched you. You went to Bernie's every Friday the same as us, and every single Friday while I was driving to pick Hayley up I'd try and convince myself to talk to you, but then as soon as I saw you again, I'd back out."

"But why? Why couldn't you just be normal, come over and ask me my name? Why all the deceit and fake friend crap?"

"'Coz fucking look at you, Mads, you're just about everything that's fucking right about the world, and I'm just about everything wrong with it. A blind man could see that you were as pure as fuckin' air. That you were too innocent for me even to be looking at.

And, because I've never cared before, never wanted anyone the way I want you, I didn't know how to fuckin' deal with it. You put things in my head that I didn't even know I was capable of thinking. Even then, that first time I saw you, I'd figured by the time I'd gotten home that I liked you enough to stay away from you. I've spent every day since then trying, trying so hard to do what I thought was fuckin' decent, but failing.

People try telling me I'm a good person, but when I'm with you, the feelings you give me actually make me believe that maybe I could be..." I see how sincere he is, and feel the tears form in my eyes as I listen.

"Mads, I fuckin' love you, and for that reason, I can't give you up." His forehead rests on mine, and he breathes as though the heaviness of the whole world has just risen from his shoulders.

I wish I had words for him, but I'm speechless. I've never

had anyone say things like that about me before, and I realize I only ever want it to be him who does.

"Fuckin' says something, Mads." He swipes his hands through his hair, then bangs his fist on the door of the truck like he's being tortured.

"I love you too." The words come out by themselves, sounding as though I've been saying them my whole life. I know by the way his eyes check me over that he's trying to catch me in a lie, but he won't. I mean every word.

"Come home with me?" he asks, tipping his head to one side and making my heart leap. I let him think that I have to contemplate the idea, leaving a heavy silence in the air before I speak.

"One condition," I tell him, crossing my arms like a bratty child.

"Name it," he snaps back, shaking his head as if there's nothing I could say that he wouldn't make happen.

"You stop making assumptions over what you think I want. Why do you think I went to Bernie's every Friday after class? I could have sat alone in my room and done my homework like I did every other night."

"What you trying to say?" He looks back at me with a hint of a smirk.

"I'm trying to tell you that Maddy goody-two-shoes had the hots for the sexy biker who hung out in Bernie's every Friday," I tell him, a little embarrassed. I'd noticed him months before Hayley became my friend. Used to watch him and wonder what it would be like to be with a guy like him. I'd known Jessie was part of the club before I'd asked him because I'd seen him in his cut so many times. I never really understood why he kept it from me.

"So stop assuming. Jessie, you've given me so much. You care for me in a way I've never been cared about before. I love everything about you, even all the wrong things, you don't have to hide yourself from me. I want you, all of you."

"You're gonna regret saying that, darlin'," he tells me, just before his lips press back onto mine and he lifts me up off my feet, I feel the smile on his lips as I straddle his hips and let him carry me across to his bike.

"Hey, does this mean we don't have to go to Utah?" Nyx calls out from the truck behind us, and Jessie drags his lips off mine to speak.

"It means we ain't going to Utah... But you still are."

"The fuck?" Nyx moans. "What for?"

"I need you to pick something up for me." Jessie looks for my reaction as he speaks. "I need you to go get Mad's mama and bring her back to the club." My breath catches in my throat as I replay his words in my head.

"Really?" I check I heard him right.

"Yeah, I'll speak to Prez, we can get her a job in the bar." Sitting me on his bike seat he must have noticed the horrified look on my face and he quickly corrects himself. "Not that kinda job." He rolls his eyes and climbs on in front of me. "We have free cabins, she can make herself a home, and she'll be safe on the compound, I promise."

"See, just when I don't think I can fall any deeper, you go prove me wrong." I reach my hand around him and flick his nose playfully with my finger.

"Keep on falling, darlin', I'll catch you at the bottom." He winks over his shoulder.

Nyx looks unimpressed as we turn around and pass him on the way out and I hold on tightly to Jessie as he rides us home. It's the longest journey I've taken on the back of his bike, and it feels amazing. Wind wraps around my hair and tightens my skin and if it weren't for the purring and vibration of the engine beneath me, I would feel like I was floating.

We make it back to the entrance of the compound without me even realizing, and Jessie cuts the engine and twists his body around. The sad look on his face makes me panic that he's changed his mind again.

"Mads, you know this is all I can ever offer you, right? You sure it's what you want?" He waits nervously for my answer, but he should know by now that this is all I want.

"I want you, this club is where you belong, and they're your family. So I belong here too," I tell him. "Besides, the guys are kinda growing on me," I giggle.

"I know it's shit right now, you being trapped here because of the Bastards, but I promise I'm gonna find a way for you to feel safe again," he assures me.

"I know you will," I say without any doubt.

"So no turning back?" he checks one last time.

"Never," I shake my head then lean forward and cuddle into his back.

"You must be fucking crazy," he shakes his head and laughs as he restarts the engine and takes off up the dirt track that leads to the club. We pass the clubhouse and the garage where Skid lifts his head from the hood of a car he's working on and nods to us. I cling a little tighter as Jessie takes us further up the track and all the way back to his cabin.

Our cabin.

Our home.

I dare anything left out there to be thrown at us to come and try. I know we will always make it through fighting. Because Jessie and I were two lost souls, and now we've found each other, we're indestructible.

EPILOGUE

I've never been a religious man. Yet this place has been my sanctuary for the past ten years. Somewhere I could always come to clear my head and think straight.

Before I lost Hayley, I used to admire the beautiful windows. I had an appreciation for whoever put the time and effort into achieving such intricate detail. The people in the scenes weren't just figures on display, each one of them were characters telling a story. But just lately, as the sun bursts through the glass and illuminates the stunning artistry, I'd felt their eyes burning into me. Judging me, and it was becoming suffocating.

Fuck. If Mary-Ann had been right about nothing else it was that Hayley hadn't asked to be born into this life, and she certainly hadn't deserved to be taken from it.

Being a woman in our world was never going to be easy.

I tried for her, and I failed. Thinking about it now it made the decision I'd regretted since the day I'd made it eighteen years ago all the more justifiable. Which has me wondering why the hell I couldn't just let that shit lie in peace, and why I'd asked Jessie's old lady to dig up a past I swore I'd laid to rest.

I look away from the windows unable to bare the scrutinous eyes any longer. I know I can trust Maddy with my secret. She's trusted me with hers. The USB stick Maddy had given me not long after Jessie hauled her back here was still sitting in my safe.

I'd known as soon as I'd heard what was on it that it was what Chop had been looking for the day he came and killed Carly. I should have shared the information by now, told the brothers what I knew, but I couldn't have my new VP losing his head at a time like this, not when I need him more than ever.

The voices on that recording belonged to men I considered to be my best friends, one already dead, the other about to be dead. What the girl hadn't realized when handing the device over to me was that the information she was giving me wasn't all new to me, just a confirmation of what I'd thought I heard. Chop had mentioned Mary-Ann in the video before he killed Carly, it had weighed on my mind ever since. Not saying Mary-Ann hadn't gotten what she had deserved, she'd been screwing me over since the day she got knocked up with Hayley. She was never supposed to be my old lady. But learning that Chop had deceived me had been a sledgehammer to the fucking balls. He'd gone behind my back, and I know now that he'd killed my wife and almost killed Hayley in the process.

I've acted like a leader, chosen not to react, and ignored the blood that boils beneath my skin when I heard him mention Mary-Ann's name. You don't become in charge of the biggest club in the state by losing your shit on a whim.

Maddy's recording had given me an explanation to why Chop had killed Mary-Ann, and proven that there wasn't shit wrong with my hearing. In my eyes though, Chop's death still belongs to Skid. He'd taken away the person he loved.

There was something else Maddy hadn't realized when she handed over her latest evidence against Chop. In doing so, she had brought something else to light. Another action Chop would pay for when we found him. She couldn't have known who the other voice in the recording belonged to, and she'd promised me no one else had heard it. So the secret remained at my hand for now. Only I know that the man who was giving Chop the ultimatum in the recording never made it to Manitou Springs to take care of business that week. That he was found two days later dead in a motel room, and his kid had been unlucky enough to have to witness the whole thing. The hairs on the back of my neck had stood up when I'd first heard the voice, coming at me from the fucking grave. Brian Donavon. Jessie's dad. It's best for now that this stay hidden. I'm weak, and there's so much anger within the club I need Jessie focusing on club business, not vengeance.

The knock on the chapel door echoes loudly pulling me out of thought and back on to the reason I came here. I call out for Nyx to enter, and he marches in with his usual bad attitude, his baggy jeans hanging over his bright white trainers. It still surprises me how a lad his age can be so tall and broad.

"You asked to see me." He nods, keeping his shit together as always, though he couldn't help his eyes skating around the room. Prospects are all the same when they have a chance to enter church, no matter how guarded they are. Being in here is a reminder of why they put up with all the shit we throw at them. I'm well aware that a few of the brothers don't like his attitude, reckon him to be too big for his boots. Some go as far as to say disrespectful, but I disagree. Nyx reminds me of myself when I was his age, intolerable to other people's bullshit. Kid has spent his whole childhood in foster care, who could blame him for wanting to prove to the people around him that he has no weakness.

But I know differently. I may not have figured out what his was just yet, but everyone has a weakness, even me. The kid's about to find out exactly what mine is.

"Yeah." I gesture for him to sit in the space that's usually occupied by Troj, and he makes himself comfortable slouching back in the chair. His elbow hangs lazily on the arm rest and his hand rests on his mouth. He's a cocky shit alright.

"You never finished high school. Am I right?" I question him.

"School weren't for me. I dropped in 10th," he replies. I shrug, not many of us here could say we made it through to the end.

"You know a few people around here don't think you're ever gonna patch in. Think you don't have enough respect." His facial expression may not change, but I notice how his fists clench.

"You've been a prospect a few years now. You gotta be eager to make the cut kid?"

"Wouldn't be here if I wasn't," he responds, and it gets a laugh out of me. I can't help admire his integrity.

"See, I think you're misjudged, Nyx. Reckon you think you have a point to prove. That the day you left your foster home you promised yourself that you would never be walked over again, am I right?" His face remains stone, but the way his eyes swell with recollection and his jaw clenches tell me I'm getting somewhere.

"I'm gonna give you a chance to prove yourself once and for all," I tell him. Nyx's posture suddenly changes, and I can see he's intrigued when he sits up and leans forward. I've fed his hunger.

"I'm about to share a secret with you, something very personal, and I'm expecting your discretion." I push the file that sits in front of me across the table towards him. He's hesitant to open it but when he does, and his eyes fall onto the photograph that sits on top of all the information, I don't miss the way they flair.

Seeing the picture again chisels away another piece from my heart, and I watch as he studies her for a moment, his pupils widening as he takes her in. The hazel colored hair that falls on her shoulders and frame her perfect oval face, and how it matches perfectly with her brown eyes. He thinks she's beautiful, I can tell, and I'll bet there isn't a single man in this world who wouldn't agree with him.

"She's something, ain't she," I speak, but he doesn't look up, still fixated on her, and it makes me doubt for a moment that this is a good idea. The kid isn't stupid though, he knows the fucking rules, he just doesn't realize that she's protected by them yet.

"Who is she?" he asks still staring, his finger spontaneously reaching out and touching at her hair as if he can feel it's silkiness.

"She's someone I need you to keep an eye on for a while. I need information, more than what's in that folder, personal stuff. I need to know if she needs anything, if she's happy."

He nods seeming to understand what I've said.

"Tac tells me you got the brains, just weren't one for discipline. You're gonna have to work on that."

Nyx tears his eyes off the picture and looks up at me in confusion.

"If you can do this. You're in," I tell him.

"You mean…"

"Yeah, you pull this off you get your patch kid. No more prospect crap."

"Okay, I'm in," he says without hesitation, then closes the file and tucks it under his arm.

"I'm glad. Enjoy senior year kid. You're going back to high school."

"You're fucking with me. Right?" He twitches his lips together with an unimpressed smile.

"I don't fuck around when it comes to something important, and this is fucking important. You can't fuck this up," I warn.

"I was shit at school. How am I ever gonna get back in? It's been years, and I never finished tenth grade. I'm pretty sure you can't rock up whenever you want."

"You can when you're Nicholas Anderson," I tell him.

"Nic the fucking who?" he asks blankly.

"Jessie's old lady hooked you up. Got you enrolled, you're even in some of Ella's classes."

"Ella, that's her name?" he asks as if it's the answer to a question he'd been desperate to ask, and I brush off his all too eager reaction.

"Yeah, that's her name. So you're straight on what to do?" I check.

"Sure, make nice with Ella, make sure she's okay. Report back to you. Sounds pretty straightforward."

I laugh at the hint of enthusiasm in his voice, a trait no one would usually associate with the kid.

"Can I ask a question?"

I nod permitting for him to ask.

"What's so special about the girl?" His eyebrows draw together curiously.

"She's all I got left," I tell him, my voice sounding a lot weaker than I'd intended, and causing him to look even more confused. Then I let the realization of my final words settle in, his face falling flat with disappointment.

"And because Ella Jackson's my daughter."

The End

ACKNOWLEDGMENTS

Firstly, I'd like to thank you, the reader for coming this far. Not everyone will agree with the outcome of Jessie's story. Whether you loved it or hated it, I appreciate every single one of you for reading on.

Sharon, I don't even know where to start. You were the first person I ever spoke to about this idea I had. You've been there for every stage of the journey. I don't think anyone understands more than you do, what these guys mean to me. Thanks for being such a huge part of their development.

To my Beautiful beta's Angela, Karen, Julie, Andrea, Corrine, Aliana, and Sarah. Your input and encouragement have meant the world to me. I am eternally grateful for your support. And to Apryle for loving Jessie as much as I do.

I need to give a whole heap of credit to Sarah at Sassi's Editing Service for her patience. Working with you has been a pleasure, I can't wait too (see what I did there,) drive you wild with my punctuation all over again really soon.

Kerry at Rebel Ink Co for doing such another fabulous job on my cover and formatting.

And to Linda MILWBIM for reading something completely out of your comfort zone just because I wrote it.

Finally, I need to thank my own little tribe, Rob, Mikey, Ben, Max, and Layla Lou you are my happily ever after.

ALSO BY EMMA CREED

His Captive

🖤 His Captive is a Dirty Dark Romance 🖤

US: https://amzn.to/35GxYDf

UK: https://amzn.to/3klppSc

CA: https://amzn.to/33CXPJr

ABOUT THE AUTHOR

Come find/stalk me on the following social media platforms.

Printed in Great Britain
by Amazon